These Are

THE GEORGIANS:

ANGUS DUNLIE, THE PATRIARCH: Only by breaking his solemn vow to the Colony's Founder could he save his clan and his two beautiful daughters from ruin.

ORDE BARSTOW, THE ROGUE: He grew rich flouting the laws of God and the Colony—Dunlie possessed the one thing he could not live without.

ZONAH, THE MULATTO MISTRESS: Her most unselfish act—and her greatest sin—set Dunlies against Barstows in a blood-feud that would rage through three generations.

JACK BARSTOW, THE HEALER: He could never cure the wound of a secret love denied.

FAYETTE DUNLIE, THE ROMANTIC: She gave up too much for a passion that couldn't survive one fatal moment of temptation.

CATTIE DUNLIE, BELLE OF SAVANNAH: She gave herself to the son for love, to the father for money—to the others for the devil of it.

JAMES DUNLIE, THE ROYALIST: Unknowing, he pursued a fierce vengeance against his own flesh-and-blood.

MICAH STONE, THE OUTSIDER: Cuckolded by a runaway slave, driven to the edge of madness, he became a deadly agent of Fate.

IRA, THE BUILDER: Rejected almost-white son of Barstow, his genius was to restore the family fortunes.

THE
GEORGIANS

Cynthia Van Hazinga

A DELL/JAMES A. BRYANS BOOK

To Jim, editor and friend.

Published by
Dell Publishing Co. Inc.
1 Dag Hammarskjold Plaza
New York, New York 10017

Dell ® TM 681510, Dell Publishing Co. Inc.

ISBN: 0-440-04271-2

Printed in the United States of America

First printing—June 1978

GEORGIA . . .

"Whatever shall be said upon the Subject here . . .
it is the most amiable Country of the Universe . . . .
Nature has not bless'd the World with any Tract, which
can be preferable to it, that Paradise with all her Virgin
Beauties, may be modestly suppos'd at most but equal
to its Native Excellencies."

—SIR ROBERT MONTGOMERY, 1717

THE
GEORGIANS

Prologue

Saint Simons Island, Georgia, 1757

The woman held the squalling, squirming new-born boy gratefully and panted. A wave of the relief from extreme pain that so closely resembles ecstasy washed over her, and she cried tears of happiness. Instinctively, she held the infant between her breasts, its heart next to hers and fondled it, examining its tiny, perfect arms and legs.

"Blessed child, what will become of you?" she whispered. "I can only assign you to God's protection . . ."

The woman blinked and looked up. Someone had entered the room. It was not the midwife, but in the semi-gloom, she did not know who it was. Then, as he moved closer, she could smell an outdoor man's odor, the odor of skins and sweat and fresh air and wood smoke.

She gave a little cry of surprise. The looming figure moved closer to her, and she gasped.

"Husband!"

It was he, the woman realized, but he had gone wild. His hair was dirty and tangled and as long as a trapper's. His hunting shirt, a kind of loose homespun frock that reached halfway down his thighs, was torn and soiled and belted at the waist with a rawhide thong that carried a fringed pocket and his hunting knife.

The woman was struck with fear. He looked possessed. His eyes glinted with anger and evil and his dirty hands reached out for her. She sat up and shrank back, clutching the baby to her bosom, too frightened to scream.

"Don't come nearer, husband," she warned. "Don't touch me, or him. In God's name, I tell you—stop!"

The man spat on the floor. "Whore!" he shouted, "Worthless cheating bitch! Vagrant fleecer! Slattern!"

"Go away!" the woman begged, trembling with fear. "Call me any name you choose, but leave me alone. I can't help what happened. It's all over now and you just have to . . ."

"Harlot! Damned strumpet! Give me that child!"

"No! No, you shan't touch him! By God, you are mad!"

The man reached out and with a merciless strength ripped the naked new-born baby from his mother's arms. He held it up by its feet with his left hand and let it swing back and forth. The baby screamed and the woman struggled to rise.

"Help!" she screamed, "Help! Oh, come at once! Oh, someone, please help!"

There was a strange silence outside the room, only a momentary silence. The midwife had lingered in the kitchen for a bite to eat with the other women. They were all out of earshot.

The man laughed horribly. The woman, on her knees, crawled across the room and grabbed his legs, but he drove her back towards the bed with a powerful kick.

Still the baby screamed as the man swung it back and forth. Then he carefully removed his hunting knife from the loop on his belt. The woman choked on her screams and she fought to regain her feet, but she was stunned and weak and she swayed, blackness nibbling on the edges of her vision. Everything seemed to lose definition in the gloom; all she saw clearly was the glint of the knife.

Carefully, as calmly as skinning a rabbit, the man touched the tip of the knife to the baby's throat and slit its chest from neck to navel. Then he worked the knife around in the tiny cavity and cut out the baby's heart. He replaced the knife in his belt and tugged at the twin lobes of the heart wih his fingers, loosening them, pulling them free and then hurling them into the woman's face.

Chapter One

Savannah, 1740

Jack Barstow rode east into town along the narrow river road from the military encampment on Yamacraw Bluff. It was the first day of May, a fine day, and the sun's strong rays burned his shoulders and neck. Jack yanked at the knot of sandy-colored hair at the back of his head, then carelessly tucked it up under his three-cornered black hat.

Jack was tired and stiff and longed for a swim. The clear, sweet waters of the Savannah River below the bluff tempted him. Although it was still morning, he had ridden for hours, ridden since first light beside the General at the head of the small scouting patrol recruiting Indians upriver.

The General, or course, was General James Edward Oglethorpe, His Majesty's highest-ranking officer in the Colony of Georgia. The General was a great man: Jack had known him for all of his life that counted, ever since they had crossed the ocean together and come to settle the new colony. Jack's respect for the General was tempered with familiarity—they had ridden together, eaten together, walked together, prayed together and faced death together on the sea and on land—and together they had laid out the streets and squares of the town of Savannah, sleeping in tents like Indians, fishing for giant sturgeon in the river, seeing and hearing and smelling this new land and everything in it for the first time.

Not that, at the time, Jack had been able to think about it so philosophically. He'd been only sixteen, and everything he saw and did then was an adventure. If I'd known then what I know now, Jack thought . . . but he could go no further. He'd seen so much in seven years in America: seen the General make a treaty with fifty Creek Indian leaders under the four tall pines on the riverbank, seen Jews and Englishmen and German-speaking Salzburgers sail up the river to join the colony, seen Savannah take shape and grow. He'd seen men march off to fight the Spanish in Florida and not return. He'd seen yellow fever and starvation, seen Negro slaves sold at auction, seen grog shops open up and heard John Wesley preach salvation.

And now he was a soldier, a volunteer for the defense of the colony, pledged to fight with Oglethorpe against Spain. The thought made him straighten his shoulders and throw back his head. He had enjoyed this first patrol, just ended, the recruitment drive to Coweta with the General. They had seen splendid sights in the interior: huge herds of buffalo, high waterfalls, shining swift rivers, and they had gone into Chickasaw and Cherokee villages, giving gifts and asking for aid against the Spanish.

Coming home to Savannah now, Jack could see many changes. He slowed his mare just west of the first farmlands. The quiet of the pine forest was broken by the ringing of hammers and the shout of a child. More than one hundred and fifty houses now stood in Savannah, and according to the provisions of Georgia's absentee governors, the London Trustees, the colonists had their farmlands outside the palisades.

Jack saw a man he knew from the regiment, Thomas Earle, bent with a hoe in a field of Indian corn. Earle was a good man and had a good wife. Jack called out to him and he waved. Beyond Earle's land and the stand of sweet-gum trees lay the Barstow holdings, land Jack knew well. That land, most of it rich and fertile, amounted to five hundred acres, all in title to Orde Barstow, Jack's stepfather.

Jack knew he owed everything he had to his stepfather, and yet, sometimes he hated him as much as he loved him. They had quarreled bitterly on the day Jack had left Savannah to ride upriver, and he was dreading their reunion this morning. Orde Barstow was a hard man, and a contradictory man. He was an old friend of the General's, Jack knew. They had been like-minded when they had set sail on the *Anne* in 1732. Unlike most of the settlers, who had come here on the charity of the Trustees, granted fifty acres and tools, seed and sustenance until they should become self-supporting, Orde Barstow was a gentleman colonist. He had paid his own passage, brought servants, and taken advantage of the larger land holdings he could afford.

Orde Barstow had prospered here, and yet he was discontented with the few strictures the Trustees had put on the colonists.

More than discontented, he was openly rebellious. Jack's mother had died in England, and Orde had not remarried. Instead, he lived with a Negro woman he had bought at the slave market in Charleston, lived with her openly and raised their children in his house.

Although this situation was preposterously unconventional, Jack admitted that Zonah was a good woman; she had been almost like a mother to him, too, when he was still young enough to need mothering.

But owning slaves was against the colony's law, and Orde owned more than Zonah. Hard spirits were prohibited, too, and Orde imported rum and sold it. He had built himself a fine house, the grandest in Savannah, and he used his illegal slaves to clear and till his land.

Anger stirred in Jack at the thought of it. He was torn between the two men he loved and respected most in the world. And somehow, he had to find his own way. He wanted, not this year—this year he would ride with the General—but soon, to have his own wife and family and his own land. He had some fine ideas for planting, ideas for new crops to raise in this rich soil. Georgia was a great opportunity for a young man willing to work hard, and Jack was ready.

Jack slowed his mare to a halt and jumped off. He tied the reins over a low branch of a young cypress and crossed the bluff to look down the river at Savannah. A single ship was anchored in the river, sails furled. He'd already heard she was the *Pretty Maria*, just in from Gravesend with needed supplies and a score of new settlers. The four tall pines where the General had pitched the tents their first night in Georgia stood at the edge of the river bluff, and stairs had been built down the steep slope to the water.

Jack could see a dozen canoes and small boats crossing the river, and beyond them the thick woods on Hutchinson's Island, toward South Carolina. Last year the first wooden wharf had been built, and crates and boxes now covered it, some of the *Pretty Maria's* cargo already making its way up the bluff on a crane built just west of the four pines.

A wave of unbidden nostalgia swept over Jack as he surveyed the new buildings, the new wharf, the new colonists milling about on the Strand. Savannah was far from being an urban metropolis, like London or Charleston, but it had already begun to resemble an English village. In a way, Jack missed the old days, the first frontier days, but of course he could have all the wilderness he craved, one day's ride west or south.

He untied his mare, remounted, and rode slowly into town. He knew he was putting off the inevitable: facing Orde Barstow, but he postponed it a bit longer, riding along Bay Street to Bull Street, the main north-south thoroughfare. The public draw-well was in the middle of Bull Street and he saw a crowd of women before it, gossiping as they filled their buckets. Nearby was the public bake-house and the lot set aside for Christ Church.

Jack rode aimlessly through Johnson Square and along Bull Street to Percival Square. Here the remains of the great and ancient Yamacraw chief Tomochichi had been buried last October. Jack remembered the day well: there had been a large crowd for the state funeral, and the General had served as a pall bearer for his friend. In a hushed moment he had given the signal for the militia to fire off three volleys in salute. The assembled Indians had been very impressed, and afterward, Jack remembered, he had singled out Fayette Dunlie, the elder of Angus Dunlie's comely daughters, and together they had walked along the river-bank, talking of many things.

Fayette Dunlie was, Jack thought, the most-fine-minded and cultured girl in Savannah. She was well read and spoke easily of religion. She was musical, possessed a sweet clear voice, and knew many songs. It was for religious reasons, primarily, she had explained to Jack, that she was so opposed to the institution of slavery. Her position, Jack knew, was in agreement with her father's, as well as the General's, and Jack himself agreed with them, even in opposition to his own stepfather.

One of the women at the well reminded Jack of Fayette, and he let his mind drift to the pleasant prosect of seeing her again, perhaps today. He had thought of her often on the expedition into Indian lands. Jack was a healthy young man, handsome in a lean, rangy way, and he had been lonely. Many of the men considered women of the Creek and Cherokee nations pretty enough, and took them to wife, but lank-haired, musky-skinned women did not appeal to Jack at all. Thinking of Fayette's modest, English-style prettiness stirred lust in his body; of course, his intentions toward her were purely honorable—they had to be, for he knew her father well, but guilt mixed with his lust when he remembered that he should by rights speak to Angus Dunlie before he took any more steps toward courting his daughter.

Well, Jack thought, time enough for that when I've seen my stepfather. He turned his mare toward King Street and rode close by the jailhouse, a flat-roofed log building with tiny slitted windows. Before it stood a wooden whipping post and two sets of stocks.

Jack thought he heard a cry from the jailhouse. He bent to peer in one window. Flies buzzed around the window, and there was a nasty, rotten stench. A mosquito whined in his ear and he slapped it. The air here was thick and fetid; the breeze from the river didn't reach far inland.

"Who's there?" Jack called out. He hesitated.

"Water . . ." a thin voice begged.

Jack dismounted and approached the jailhouse. "Jailor!" he called. Where was the man? No prisoner would be left alone, would he? Surely, no prisoner would be left without water, no matter how wretched.

"Water, kind sir, for the love of God, kind sir . . ." the voice croaked.

Jack looked around Percival Square. It was strangely quiet. A dog trotted past carrying a bone, and a man on horseback rode along the far side of the square without looking in Jack's direction. Jack felt it was his Christian duty to give the poor jailed man some water. He walked around to the front of the jail and saw a wooden bucket with a dipper. There were a few inches of water in the bottom of the bucket. He knelt and scooped up a dipperful and carried it back to the window.

The man inside pushed his grizzled face up to the wooden bars and grinned toothlessly. "Ah, kind sir," he wheedled, "Ben Sykes thanks ye, and God will bless ye."

"Here," Jack said flatly as he passed the dipper carefully through the bars. Ben Sykes? The name sounded familiar.

Sykes grabbed the dipper and aimed it at his open mouth. With his other hand, heavy with a metal chain, he reached out and grabbed Jack's wrist. He gulped, choked, and some of the water ran out of his mouth down his stubbled chin.

"Good sir," Sykes gasped, "I can see you're a military man. I used to be one myself. Can you find it in yer heart to . . ."

The man's smell was raw and repugnant. Jack pulled away, but Skyes had a grip like an iron cuff. "Unhand me, Skyes!"

"Take heart, take heart," Sykes whined.

"Let go at once!" Jack ordered. Sykes's grip was desperate, and his breath smelled of disease. Jack's other hand reached for his knife and jerked it out of its leather loop. If need be, he would cut the man's fingers off. He remembered now what he'd heard of Benjamin Sykes. The ruffian had been suspected of being a Spanish spy and had been whipped and drummed out of the regiment. Some months later he had been involved in a plot to kill the General and had succeeded in slitting the throat of one of Oglethorpe's own servants.

"God have mercy . . ." Sykes sobbed.

"Pray, you devil!" Jack advised as he jerked his hand free and walked away. "Pray to God, for no decent man will pity you!"

Jack was shaking with anger as he remounted and rode out of Percival Square. The burning blue sky and the endless green forests that stretched beyond the wooden palisade seemed a mockery of the human evil that had already taken root inside. Man seemed so small and poor compared with God's works, Jack thought, but if he could enlarge his spirit and grow into a more noble sort of being, where had he a better chance than here? Where a better chance than in Georgia?

Chapter Two

The Dunlies at Home—Oglethorpe Visits—Passion Flares

All members of the Dunlie family were at home on Abercorn Street on the May morning when Jack Barstow rode into town. There were only four Dunlies lying abed as the sun rose that day, but it was to be a significant day in each of their lives, a day they would all remember, and not only because it was the day the great hand-hewn pine rafters were lifted into place on the new third story of their house, not only because Angus Dunlie expected and received a visit from the General, nor only that the *Pretty Maria* carried disastrous news of London financial ventures Angus Dunlie had hoped would bolster his sagging fortunes.

The day would be best remembered, and Catherine Dunlie, Angus's faithful wife, would have been gratified to know it while the sun was still high, as the birthday of the Dunlies' first son and heir. For Catherine Dunlie was in the throes of labor. Her pains had started on Friday. It was now Monday morning. At first they had come about one hour apart, at first an ecstatic sensation that filled her with joy almost unmixed with fear. But now the paroxysms were so close together that Catherine had no time between them to recover her strength, or even her breath.

Catherine Dunlie was confined in a small rear bedroom on the second floor of the house. None of her family was with her. She had forbidden her young daughters to be present, partly out of modesty, partly out of her conviction that if Fayette or Cattie were to witness her agonies they would refuse to marry and become mothers themselves. Catherine was a small, wiry, resilient woman with a deceptively fragile appearance which had been inherited by her namesake daughter, but she had reason to dread the rigors of this labor. In the sixteen years since she had been safely delivered of her younger daughter, she had miscarried six times and given birth to two stillborn infants.

Catherine was attended in childbed by a half-breed Creek woman named Joan. Joan had served as midwife to most of the women in Savannah since the departure four years ago of Elizabeth Stanley, a midwife who had delivered 128 native Georgians but then returned to England to lie in herself.

For three days, Joan had squatted in a corner of Catherine's room, her eyes half shut, silent, listening to Catherine shift position and cry out, watching her occasional lapses into sleep, and eating the meals the Dunlies' servants brought to her. Sometimes, while Catherine dozed, she had slipped out of the room and gone—somewhere—but as far as Catherine was concerned, Joan was just there, waiting for the time when she would be needed to do her work.

Catherine's trust in Joan, such as it was, was founded on her recent success. All but two of the babies she had delivered last winter had survived till spring, and that was a remarkable record. One of them, a fine healthy boy, had been born to Catherine's good friend Sarah Whitman, and Sarah had recommended Joan to Catherine. Sarah herself had come to visit Catherine in her confinement, twice on Sunday, but at her last visit, Catherine had asked her not to return until the baby was ready to be born.

"I need all my strength," she'd told Sarah. "Seeing anyone takes from my strength. Except Joan."

Whenever she felt like groaning, shouting, or praying aloud, Catherine did. Joan paid no heed to anything; Catherine was sure the half-breed woman understood little English. Having her there was just like being alone, and feeling as she did, it was the best way.

During the long four days of intermittent pain, of watching day turn to night and night change to dawn, of hazy states of sleep and waking, Catherine had been visited by many strange thoughts. This was her first confinement in the five years since the Dunlies had come to Georgia, and she'd relived those years as she lay abed, thinking also of the home she'd left behind in England.

Sometimes I think we've made a terrible mistake, Catherine thought, in coming so far away from home and civilization. She thought back to the sad parting with her sister in Dorset, of the little graveyard near the church where she had left two tiny children, and fears about her family's future gripped her strongly.

She feared, too, for her own life. Thirty-five was old for childbearing, though she knew that many women were safely delivered well into their forties. Somehow, she feared less for the life of this child. This baby seemed so healthy, so large, that she had a strong and growing conviction that it was going to be born alive.

Catherine ran a reddened, swollen hand over the

dome of her belly. She could feel the baby kick as she did so. For months it had been kicking vigorously, pounding at her, thrashing about with a fierce will that both amazed and delighted her. She had gained so much weight that in the last month she had felt sluggish, sometimes even stupid as she'd moved slowly about her daily tasks. Angus had been concerned for her; although he had many concerns and worries, she knew that foremost among them was his desire for a male heir.

Well, Angus would be pleased, then, Catherine thought, for she was sure with a woman's instinctive conviction that this robust baby inside her was a boy. She wasn't nearly as sure that she would live to bring him up.

"What day is it?" Catherine demanded suddenly. "Joan, what day is it?"

Joan looked up and blinked. Her expression was unreadable. Instead of answering, she stretched, rose, and left the room. Catherine permitted herself a long, sharp-edged groan. The pains were getting very bad. When one gripped her she could no longer think. Her mind went clear and silvery blank—blind, cold and empty. She panted noisily after the pain subsided and before the next began. It was less than a minute, or seemed so. Now where had Joan gone? Catherine had forgotten asking her a question, forgotten seeing her leave the room. It was as if the Indian woman had disappeared. The last time Catherine had looked over into her corner, Joan had been crouched there as usual, but now the room was empty.

"Joan!" Catherine screamed.

Almost at once the door opened and Joan stepped inside, followed by the servant girl. Rose was carrying a mug of steaming tea.

"Here, missus, she says to give you this. She says to

tell you what day it be. It's the first of May, ma'am. It's Monday, ma'am." Rose's voice shook with fear at the sight of Catherine. Catherine was drenched with sweat from her labor. Her blonde hair was damp and matted, her face was bright red and tightened into a mask of wrinkled agony. Her fists gripped the two poles Joan had laid next to her in bed, and her knuckles showed white.

"Get out!" Catherine groaned at Rose, hating to see the shock and fear on her face.

"Yes, ma'am. Only, please drink this," Rose said. She held the mug out toward Catherine, but Catherine had turned away. Joan took it and Rose fled. Downstairs she ran into Thomas, one of the carpenter's assistants who was sweet on her, and she replied to his usual pinch with a fast slap. Outside in the kitchen shed, she burst into tears and told Annie, the cook, that the missus was surely going to die.

Catherine sipped at the bitter herbal tea Joan held at her lips. It was frightening to think that these rhythmic pains were totally beyond her control. It reminded her that all life was uncontrollable. She must rest in God's hands. She felt a wave of nausea rising and tried to push the mug away, but Joan looked at her sternly and shook her head.

"Drink," Joan ordered, and Catherine knew that she must try. This tea was some awful Indian thing that Joan had brewed, but if she thought it necessary . . .

In another upstairs bedroom, Fayette Dunlie was seated on the floor, resting her arms on a low wooden chest where she had arranged an inkwell, two quill pens, and her private, secret journal. Fayette had received the journal as a parting gift from her tutor in England, five years ago. Her tutor, a thin tubercular Oxford student, had advised her to record the events

of her life in the new world, as well as her highest
spiritual thoughts and her secret aspirations. You will
no doubt have many adventures, he had told her, and
see any number of strange and marvelous things. Perhaps your journal will be of interest, some day, to
your children, or even to you when you are old.

Fayette had smiled, then, her green eyes amused at
the notion that she would ever be old, and she had
blushed at the idea of having children. Now things
were a bit different. She was nineteen, and she had
indeed witnessed many strange things since she had
come to Georgia. One of them was the sound of her
mother crying and screaming in the back bedroom.
Fayette was deeply disturbed by it. She wondered how
long it could possibly go on. Fayette was a sensitive,
thoughtful young woman, more like her father than
her mother in that she had an introspective, idealistic
turn of mind; but although she and her mother had
many differences, she felt a strong, even agonizing,
kinship with her mother's womanly ordeal.

"May, the first, *anno domini* 1740," she wrote at the
head of a fresh page in her diary. Fayette was slim and
graceful, yet taller than average and full-breasted, and
her handwriting was as clear and strong and bold as
her physique.

> My mother lies abed, with child, this day, and I pray to
> God to deliver her from her travail. It is hard for me to
> think that such agony as hers is natural and good. I
> fear for her mind and spirit, even if the child survives
> and she, too, recovers to succor and raise it. But I re-
> mind myself, we all rest in God's hands . . .

Fayette set down her pen and rose to look out the
window. Her mother's cries had ceased, at least for the
time being. Out her window she could see that it was a

beautiful day. She heard the ringing of hammers and the sound of chopping in the side yard, where the laborers had gathered whom her father had hired to enlarge the house. They had been working at the Dunlies' for nearly two weeks, and her father had said that he hoped the new roof would go up today.

Fayette had taken an interest in the building. She had looked at the plans with her father and the master carpenter, Mr. Libby. She had seen the men bring in the huge pine logs, seen them planed and shaped into long beams and boards. As she watched, she had become increasingly aware of one of the workmen, a tanned, brawny, blond Englishman named Micah Stone. Stone, she'd learned, had come to Georgia as an indentured servant, but he had recently worked off his four-year contract, and he was now hiring himself out to Mr. Libby as a day-worker.

Micah Stone was as much on Fayette's mind today as her mother's labor. She looked toward the path he usually came along on his way to work, but she saw no sign of him. Her longing to see him was a physical pain, and Fayette permitted herself a soft sigh to ease it. She was half-ashamed of herself, but it was a natural state, and Fayette was not self-conscious. She had heard about love all her life, wondered if and when she would feel it and what it was like, and now that she was feeling it, she was ready to enjoy it.

The last time I wrote here I wondered if I was falling in love with him. Well, now I am sure of it. He seems to me the kindest, most honest, most handsome man I have ever met. My heart begins to pound faster when I see him coming along the road, and yesterday, when I tried to speak to him, I felt my tongue as great as a log in my mouth, and I had to wait, swallowing, a whole minute before I had the strength to speak. I do not know how he feels for me, but I must somehow find out and soon. For I am gripped by love's fever, and I burn.

Fayette set down her pen and actually wiped her brow with the sleeve of her blue striped cotton gown. She sighed again. Her hair, which was fine in texture and of a beautiful dark, rich brown, was extremely curly and tendrils of it escaped the lady-like upsweep she had constructed earlier. Her eyes, unlike those blue ones she admired in Micah Stone, were a lively gold-flected green, and like her father's, were deep set.

A silence fell over the house and she heard a bird call. Fayette cocked her head and listened. Another bird answered the first, and then the two sang together, a pair of mockingbirds in a love duet. Fayette felt her heart fill with a wonderful, curious feeling. She seized her pen again.

Even the singing birds remind me of him. Last night I dreamed of him, that he lay beside me in my bed. I know that my love for him is strong, so strong that if fate wills that he cannot love me, if God has other plans for us, I will never marry another. I must have him. No other man will do.

As she finished writing, Fayette heard her mother cry out again. A workman shouted for Mr. Libby and drew Fayette to her window again. She looked out just in time to see her younger sister, Cattie, dressed in her best pink bodice and gown, disappearing down the path toward town. Cattie was skipping along; Fayette could see by the spring of her step that her sister was feeling as gay and full of promise as the day itself, but she had no way of guessing that Cattie was on her way to meet Micah Stone.

The friendship between James Oglethorpe and Angus Dunlie was a bond between equals. Both men sprang from landed Tory families and combined, in their personal philosophies, conservatism and near-radicalism. Both men were humanitarians but self-righteous ones. Both had slipped, as early as biology permitted, into the role of patriarch, although Oglethorpe was in fact a bachelor.

Happiness flooded Angus Dunlie when the maid came to the door of his study to announce that General Oglethorpe was approaching on horseback.

"He's alone, sir, but for his ensign, and he's lookin' so tired, sir," she reported.

Dunlie set down his correspondence with relief and hurried to the front door to welcome his friend. He was more than glad to postpone writing letters to his London agents and to stop worrying, for a moment at least, about dear Catherine's confinement.

The front door of the Dunlie house stood open, and Angus Dunlie saw that the General was just dismounting. His ensign took the reins and led his horse across the grassy yard toward the stable.

"Good day, my friend! God bless your safe return!" Dunlie said.

"Thank you for your kind words."

James Oglethorpe was an impressive but not a handsome man. He possessed a long face and a high forehead, a big Roman nose, slightly protruding eyes, and a definite double chin. Everything about him suggested self-confidence and an inexhaustible supply of energy. He was also vain and belligerent, quick-tempered, demanding, bold and reckless. By the age of twenty-six, he had served as a lieutenant in the British infantry, attended Oxford University, fought in Eastern Europe with Prince Eugene of Savoy, inherited his family's estates in England, sat in Parliament, and killed a man in a drunken brawl.

Shortly thereafter, Oglethorpe happened to visit his friend Robert Castell, an architect who was in Fleet Street Prison for debt. Oglethorpe was appalled by prison conditions and the injustice of imprisonment for no real crime. Characteristically, he was moved to action. He procured a parliamentary investigation and then a statute freeing thousands of debtors. It had opened his eyes to the concept of a worthy poor, and eventually he and the other Trustees of the Colony selected a shipload of such folk to be transported at the Crown's expense and to become the founding fathers of Georgia. Oglethorpe had sailed with them, and with others who, like Dunlie and Barstow, were not "on the charity." Oglethorpe was the only one of the Trustees ever to set foot in Georgia.

"A long journey?" Dunlie asked, as he led his friend inside.

"Long enough, but as ever, Angus, I feel I've come home when I come to you and Catherine."

"Catherine is close to giving birth," Dunlie said as he led the General into the large, airy room on the first floor that he used as his office and refuge. Here he kept his records and accounts, his personal library, his violin, and the tiny spinet he had taught Fayette to play. A shuttered door opened off the room onto the piazza, which ran along the east side of the house. Here also, on a sideboard, stood a bottle of fine claret, just off the *Pretty Maria*, and he set about pouring a glass for his friend.

"Ah, thank you," Oglethorpe intoned, "an excellent color. How is Catherine doing?"

"I am worried. It has already been a long labor."

"She has a midwife with her?"

"Yes, of course, though I wish she would permit Dr. Jones . . ."

"Jones! I suspect the man! Someone told me he was among those who wrote to the King that Savannah is in a despicable condition. They will do whatever they can to ruin our colony. Angus, our enemies are within!"

"I doubt that Dr. Jones can be counted among the malcontents."

"Perhaps not. Perhaps I am misled. At any rate, Angus, we have much to discuss." Oglethorpe swept off his stiff black hat and began to unbutton his scarlet, gold-trimmed coat. "Would it be too much, my friend, to ask you for a bath?"

"A bath?"

"Yes, only that. Bathing is one of my odd habits, and as far as I know, you have the only decent tub in town."

Angus Dunlie laughed. "Why not? Dispatch your ensign for fresh linen, and I'll call Rose for the tub. But really, James, you should see about building a house here in Savannah."

"I have a house in Frederica . . ." Oglethorpe mumbled as he put his head out the front window to call his ensign. He began removing the rest of his travel-soiled clothes. When Rose returned with Angus Dunlie, he was wearing only a shirt, seated in a straight chair at the mahogany card table, and his wine glass was empty.

Rose giggled and set the small wooden tub on the hearth. She ran out of the room to fetch water.

"Luckily, the women are keeping water hot for Catherine," Dunlie said. He poured himself a glass of wine although it was not his custom to drink in the morning. Unless I help myself at once, he thought, I won't have even a taste of this new claret.

When Rose had filled the tub half-way, Oglethorpe removed his white linen shirt and lowered himself into the water. His body was long and well muscled. "Ahhhh," he sighed, "what a pleasure! Why do they speak ill of bathing? What a good idea!"

Angus Dunlie tugged his favorite chair, a high-backed cherry armchair with brass nails, to a spot where it caught the breeze from the piazza. Dunlie was a tall, lean man with large, handsome features and the freckled-and-sandy coloring typical of Scots. He also had a good deal of their characteristic reserve. His eyes were deep-set—a clear hazel—and inspired confidence, despite his somewhat stiff bearing.

"What luck did you have with the Chickasaws?" he asked.

"At first their chief was incensed," Oglethorpe reported as he splashed water over his chest. Although his chest-hairs were tinged with gray, the General was in splendid condition for a man of forty-four years. Of course, he had led a rigorous military life.

"He said that British scouts and traders have brought smallpox and rum up the river to his people and that nearly one thousand have died. We had no choice but to offer tribute and reparations. The Spanish promise them one hundred pieces of eight for every English prisoner and fifty for an English scalp. I had to offer him equal bounties. Only then could I ask for volunteers to fight against Spain."

"No good can come from hard liquor," Dunlie said.

"No good at all. Too often, I have seen its degrading effect on the Indians—and the same on the working-men of our own race. Fah! The climate is too hot for strong drink! It's unhealthy! That's why the Trustees have prohibited it."

"Yet boats carrying rum cross the river from South Carolina every night, James. There are grogshops on every other corner. Some of our fellow settlers are criminals, born and bred."

"I know." Oglethorpe's knees poked out of the tub. "Sometimes I think we are a whole colony of rascals. And do you know what is their favorite toast?"

"No, I don't." Dunlie moved his chair back a few inches to avoid being splashed.

"They congregate in taverns and shout, 'To the one thing needful!'" Oglethorpe said, his voice lower.

"Aye. I have heard that," Dunlie admitted.

"But I will do all I can to stop it," the General vowed. "This constant agitation to bring in Negro slaves disturbs me deeply. It would destroy the fundamental structure of our colony."

"I assure you, I have not changed my own position."

"First and foremost, Georgia is to be a colony of small farmers. Importing slaves will discourage the small farmer, as well as weaken our defense. If the ne'er-do-wells can't understand that, let them remember the slave revolt in South Carolina only two years ago!"

"I dare say they do remember, but it won't stop them. While you were out of town, there were again Negroes sold publicly on the edge of the market."

"God damn it! Let them leave Georgia—the weaklings and the malcontents! Let them go north!"

"Many have, James. Many houses stand empty in the western part of town. We are fewer here now than we have ever been."

Oglethorpe sank down in the tub, letting the now-tepid water rise nearly to his shoulders. "God help us," he moaned. "But let us speak of other things. What of your own planting? And I see that Mr. Libby and his men have added to your house."

"Aye, they have. And I am making some progress— the crops of corn and peas and potatoes are set out.

But this won't be the year I get to my land on Saint Simons Island, I fear. Pray God, this will be the year my son is born!"

"No doubt of that, Angus. And perhaps your daughters married as well. I saw the younger one on my way in. She looks ready for a wedding."

"Cattie? Yes, and Fayette, though I shall hate to part with her. I was thinking of Jack Barstow for Cattie. You always speak well of him."

"That I do. He was with me only this morning. He's an honest, law-abiding man, though I can't say the same for his stepfather."

"Few have good words for Orde Barstow, but it doesn't seem to trouble him." Angus rose and poured the last of the claret into heir glasses.

Oglethorpe drank and then stood up next to the tiny tub. Water streamed off his body, splashing onto the bricks and the bare pine floor. "Ah. I feel worlds better, Angus. Once again, you've restored me, body and soul. It means a lot to have a good friend."

Dunlie passed him a thin, handwoven towel, then another. "You'll stay to dinner?"

"Thank you, I will. But I must be on my way soon after. Some of these mewling malingering malcontents seem to have forgotten that we are at war with the Spanish Empire. I have a new lot of dispatches to look over. We could be attacked from the south any day. The Armada is in St. Augustine, only five days away!"

"Pray God," Dunlie said as he admitted the ensign carrying fresh linen, "they don't attack until we've dined."

I am not who everyone thinks I am, Cattie Dunlie thought, hurrying out of Abercorn Street into the less-traveled path that led toward the river. Everyone thinks I am quite a child, but I am not. I am a full-grown woman and I know my own mind.

The sun felt hot, so Cattie snatched her linen cap off her head and swung it by a gathering thread. Her golden hair glinted. It was straight, but as thick as Fayette's, and she was pleased with the new way she'd learned of looping it up behind both ears so it tumbled freely over her shoulders.

Cattie was in splendid form, so integrated with her own young body that she felt every muscle working easily as she broke into a run, felt the cool breeze from the forest, felt her skin tingle with the sun's heat, even felt, without thinking of it, the coursing of her blood in her veins.

Cattie had been eleven years old when she had crossed the ocean with her family. She remembered England only dimly, for she never chose to think of it, and, in fact, in an unconscious rejection of her old life, she never read or wrote, and had nearly forgotten how. Her sister, Fayette, was so diligent and scholarly that Cattie left all that to her; Cattie never perfected her needlework, never learned to play the spinet or violin, although she liked the sound of music—it made her want to dance.

Instead of developing the skills and habits proper for an English girl of her age and breeding, Cattie had spent most of her time out of doors. Everyone had been too busy in the colony's first days to pay her any mind, and she had, as her mother ruefully admitted, "run wild." She had learned to swim and ride and hunt rabbits and birds with a sling-shot. She loved to climb trees and could plait a basket like a Yamacraw. She had learned to row a boat, paddle a canoe, kindle a fire, and she loved to walk alone in the woods.

She had also developed an independence of mind atypical of other well-bred young ladies.

"Aren't you scared?" Fayette had asked her once, after one of her long, solitary rambles. "Not at all," Cattie had vowed. "I know I can always find my way. I just stop and look and listen very hard. The forest speaks to me."

But there were things that scared Cattie. The ocean was one of them. It seemed she had never forgotten the horrors of crossing from England. Even now, sometimes, she woke crying, dreaming that she was back in that small and smelly ship, confined with so many others, strangers with squalling babies, soiled, damp, crumpled clothing, and awful diseases. She still dreamed she heard the endless rushing, heaving sea battering at her ears and her brain until she was ready to scream for silence. She remembered it all: the poor, dull food, the cramped quarters, the blank skies of day, and the lonely stars at night.

Never again, she vowed. No more sea voyages for me. Here I am and here I'll stay. Life's not so bad, but, oh, what a morning!

Cattie had spent the morning working with Annie the cook and Rose, washing sheets and counterpanes in the wooden tubs they set up outside the kitchen shed. Housework was another aspect of life Cattie detested, and there were endless numbers of boring, arduous tasks involved in running the Dunlie household. Catherine took charge, but Cattie could not easily avoid helping, especially now that her mother was with child. But she had escaped, for today, and she was so glad to be free that she could almost fly.

She did give a hop and a skipping leap, then passed out Trustees' Gate to the east common, open land where cattle ran free. Her thoughts turned to the meeting that lay ahead and her heart beat faster.

Some of the excitement of her liaison with Micah Stone was in its secrecy. No one knew of their clandestine meetings. She had first noticed him, like Fayette, when he was working at their house. Then she had encountered him one misty twilight when she was walking alone on the Strand, and they had really seen each other for the first time. Cattie had felt the magic of their meeting. She had felt as if she were perched very precariously on the edge of an abyss and that his touch might topple her.

She sighed, remembering. Micah was so broad-shouldered, so manly. Although he was only twenty, he seemed far older, more worldly than any other man she knew—a man aware of all his physical powers. When he put his arm around her, it was firm and controlling. His voice was deep and thrilled her in an awful-wonderful way. She feared that whatever he asked, she would have to yield to him, and last time they had met, he had kissed her as no one had ever kissed her before.

Last time had been only last night. Cattie shivered. She had slipped out of her family's house at his whistle, they had walked together for a few minutes, then she had promised to meet him again, today when the sun was high, on the edge of the Trustees' garden.

And in parting, they had kissed. I think I'm falling in love, Cattie thought. Oh, dear, suppose I do and . . . She felt changed by that kiss, so long and hard. It had left her dizzy and longing for more.

It had left Micah Stone longing for more, too, though Micah wasn't nearly as innocent as Cattie Dunlie. Thinking of her small, pleasingly round body, he sped along the river path from the woodland where he had worked all morning, taking down trees that would provide shingles for the roof of the Dunlie house. He whistled as he hurried through a stand of yellow pine. Just beyond was the Trustees' Garden, a ten-acre experimental plantation of exotic plants and medicinal herbs the utopian-minded Trustees hoped to cultivate in far-off Georgia.

It was here that she had promised to meet him. He stopped, heard a wood thrush call to warn her children of an invasion.

Cattie had heard him whistling. Playfully, she crawled into the bower formed by some fallen pines and brush. She waited, holding her breath, listening to the thumping of her excited heart. It was as deafening as the sound of the sea. She heard nothing else, no more whistling. Where was he?

"Caught! You're caught!" Micah shouted, leaping over a fallen log and pinning Cattie to the ground. She yelped in surprise and blushed.

"Mercy!" she gasped. "You scared me witless!"

"My poor darlin'," he soothed her, stroking her bare pink arms, her shoulders, her straight, shiny blonde hair. "Why, you tremble! I didn't know you were so easy to scare."

"I'm not! Only you took me by surprise." She lowered her eyes. He was on his knees on the soft carpet of pine needles, and she half-reclined on her back. They had never been so close together before. Her breath was coming in deep gasps, and her heart felt as if it would beat its way out of her skin. "You mustn't . . ." she whispered.

"Mustn't what? Mustn't kiss you, Cattie? A saint couldn't resist. King George himself couldn't stop me!" His mouth settled on hers and teased it open, then his lips brushed over her face, over her closed eyelids, her ears, down her neck. Her bosom heaved under the pink calico, and his fingers touched her breasts through the cloth.

Cattie was thrilled and delighted and afraid and ashamed. It felt so marvelous and it was happening so fast! She squirmed. It excited him even more. She opened one eye and saw that he had unbuttoned his trousers and lifted one knee to straddle her. He jerked up her petticoat with one hand while the other plunged into her bodice.

She closed her eyes. She had never known that love was so hot. She felt on fire, she longed to be naked, to be with Micah in a cool meadow, or swimming in the cool shallows of the river. She was slick with perspiration, and his fingers slid over her breasts, slipped easily up her silky-soft thighs.

"Oh, Cattie, my sweet, my beauty," Micah moaned. He thrust her legs apart.

"Hush! Hush, darling! Who's that?"

He had heard it, too, and could well guess who it might be. Damnation! Why hadn't he taken her farther off the main path? He was sure it was the rest of the work gang, heading right for them on their way back to Libby's house for their dinners.

"Quick!" he ordered, pulling back, buttoning his pants.

Tears welled up in Cattie's eyes as she settled her petticoat and straightened her bodice. Micah took her hand and hauled her back into the woods. Hand in hand they ran a dozen yards, their steps hushed by the fallen pine needles. They crouched near a leafy bush and heard the workmen pass. Cattie's heart was still thumping, but for her the moment was gone, the mood spoiled.

She wanted to go, then, at once. When she told him so, he did not protest.

"Tonight, my sweet? Can we meet tonight?" he asked.

"Perhaps."

"Don't be angry, my darlin'. I'll try to borrow a canoe. Couldn't you fancy a ride on the cool river?"

"I don't know if I can get away. Come by my house and wait for me. Whistle like the whip-poor-will when it is just dark. Will you, Micah?"

"I will. With all my heart."

Chapter Three

*A Quarrel—A Love Match—And a
Fist Fight*

Orde Barstow was a man with two life-long passions:
women and money. Since his arrival in Georgia, seven
years ago, the latter passion had occupied him rather
to the exclusion of the former, but as he admitted to
his stepson, Jack, "Females have gotten me in enough
damn trouble already!"

It was, in fact, because of a woman that Orde Barstow found himself in Savannah in 1740, replete after
a meal of fried perch, fried catfish, and cold roast
pork washed down with a bottle of the liquor he
called punch. Orde was a man even his enemies called
handsome. His eyes, bright and blue, were at the same
time shrewd and quixotic. His hair was dark and
curly, his color high, his face wide and full featured,
his physique robust and stocky. So strong were Orde's
charms that only his enemies were quick to point out
that he was also vain, stingy, greedy, and unscrupu-

lous. And there were some, mainly women, who never noticed Orde's failings at all.

Eight years ago, Orde, who was married at the time to Eliza Ferguson, Jack's mother, had taken a powerful fancy to a Lady Belinda Milledgeville. Lady Belinda was a true coquette and a fashionable flirt in the best London tradition, and she had led Orde a merry chase in and out of theatres and balls, clubs and carriages and caroches, until the disastrous day when Orde learned that he had been trifling with a woman beloved by his King.

Twin bailiffs arrived at his door with the news. They offered Orde a fortnight to leave town forever, and his ardor promptly cooled. Through the intervention of the clergy, the fortnight was extended to three months, during which Orde buried his wife, sold his house in Hanover Square and most of its contents, and arranged a passage to Georgia with his old friend James Oglethorpe.

It was never clear that the death of Eliza Ferguson was a direct result of her husband's conspicuous infidelity, but certainly her relatives thought so. Even as the *Anne* was weighing anchor at Deptford, Eliza's brother was pacing the wharves of that town, waving a warrant for Barstow's arrest.

Doubtless it was true, as Barstow insisted, that the man had "no damn grounds" for his charges, but it had made for a chilling departure from Old England. Orde had taken Eliza's tow-headed son, Jack, with him as a matter of course. Jack had lived with Barstow since his infancy and had taken his name; Orde scarcely remembered who the boy's father had been, except that the villain had ruined Eliza. In the ten years of their marriage she had never born him a living child, and she had died of natural causes—of a flux that had troubled her long before he had even glimpsed the Lady Belinda.

So Orde and Jack Barstow had settled in Savannah with the very first colonists. Their life was made considerably easier and more comfortable than that of their neighbors by Orde's private means. He had built himself a fine three-story house in St. James Square, modest by London standards, but solid and roomy. And Orde had taken care to acquire good fertile land outside of town, land that was well-watered and had access to the river.

But owning good land and turning a profit on it were far different things, and it was the profit that interested Orde. He was a sophisticated man. He traveled to Charleston, saw the pleasant, prosperous lives of the South Carolina planters, and compared the back-breaking struggles of his idealistic fellow colonists. The difference was labor; the key was to get someone else to bend and lift and plow and hoe. The difference was owning Negro slaves, and if Oglethorpe and the rest of the Trustees couldn't see it, that was their own damn fault.

On his first journey to Charleston, Orde Barstow bought six Africans. Five of them were men. They were very black and wild and spoke no English. The other was a slim, intelligent Ibo woman of about sixteen who had been raised on a sugar plantation outside Kingston on the island of Jamaica. Because she spoke fluent English, he had paid a premium price for her, but even before he had smuggled her into his house in Savannah, the woman had proved her worth. She called herself Zonah. With an effort Orde never appreciated, she served as an interpreter between him and the other Negroes. And she turned out to be an artful and passionate bedmate.

Both Zonah and Orde were driven by need. Orde

had not had a woman since Lady Belinda—and no two females on earth could have been less alike. But the sight of Zonah's supple, brown-skinned body, even the first time he saw her, barebreasted on the auction block, rekindled his lust. He felt like a young man again. She stirred his carnal longings with her smooth dark skin, her huge and inscrutable dark eyes, the soft curves of her body. She awakened in him desires and powers of endurance that he had never before experienced.

In fact, he fell passionately in love.

From Orde's point of view, it was the perfect love. Zonah was young and strong and fertile. In the past six years she had borne him a son and a daughter, both healthy and handsome. She was hard working. She ran his home and provided him and Jack with good meals and a clean orderly household. She was clever; she sewed and mended and spun for herself and her children and the other Africans. She was astonishingly bright and quick to learn. Jack managed to teach her to read and count and figure. By day, she was the perfect servant.

And by night, the perfect "wife." She was accommodating and passionate. And there was no question of jealousy, no question of courtship or delicacy or propriety or shame. He owned Zonah. She was his slave.

"Zonah!" Orde Barstow shouted, pushing aside his plate, empty except for a fatty rind of pork. "Zonah! Come here!"

A figure appeared in the doorway, but it was not Zonah. It was his stepson, Jack.

"Hello, father," Jack said, stepping into the dining room.

"Well! Here you are!" Orde said. He smiled tentatively. How long had the boy been gone now? He couldn't remember exactly. He had tried not to think of him, to avoid remembering the harsh words they'd exchanged at Jack's departure. Remembering only riled him up. "Had enough of soldiering this time, Jack?"

"Enough for today, that's sure." He crossed the small room in two strides and picked up a fried catfish in his fingers. He ate it appreciatively and took another. Then he ate a square of the flat white cornbread Zonah made so well.

"Not too good to eat my food, eh?" Orde asked contentiously.

"Shall we start right in again, father?"

"I reckon that's up to you. I haven't changed my opinions any."

"No, I see that. I came through the barnyard. You've acquired a new African?"

"So I have. He's called Moses." Orde smiled, his blue eyes satisfied. "Fine-looking man, isn't he?"

"Damn it, sir! Don't you see that owning slaves is against God's law? You know it's against the laws of the Trustees—in violation of our colony's principles!"

"I see that you're a young fool. God has no laws on slavery."

"You'll go to court, sir. You'll be called before the authorities and lose them all—even Zonah."

"Leave Zonah out of this, my boy."

"When did you buy that African?"

"I didn't buy him, Jack. I hired the man from my friend Henry Patterson, across the river in South Carolina, for a hundred years." Orde grinned. "In case of any trouble he goes back to Patterson."

"So you've found a way around the law?" Jack sneered—at the man he had idolized all his youth.

"It's only practical. I've invested in a lot of land here, and I'll be damned if I'll knuckle under to London's laws . . ."

"Sir, it's just not right!" Jack interrupted.

"Right! You've been riding too long with the General. You've sopped up his foolish dreams. And what do you intend to do with your own life?"

Until very recently, Jack had never considered this question. He had always assumed that his life would continue to be connected with his stepfather's—that he would work with Orde Barstow as he grew older and one day inherit his estate. But in the last year, their differences of opinion had hardened into bitterness.

"You can't live with me forever," Orde taunted. "You know that?"

"Of course I do!"

"And I won't set you up in splendor." Orde was only half-serious. At this point he still intended to help Jack get started, and Jack was his only heir, but he was angry now and enjoyed teasing Jack.

"I expect I'll ask the Trustees for a grant," Jack said. "And I want to marry . . . soon."

"Do you?" This development caught Orde's attention. "And have you a young lady in mind?"

"I think I could love . . . Fayette Dunlie."

"Dunlie! You'll not have my blessings on that match, Jack! You know Dunlie is a fool and a cheat."

"You only say that because of that boundry dispute on Saint Simons. Neither of you works that land. I don't see why . . ."

"Dunlie will fail on his own, doesn't matter what I say about him . He's a damn fool about working Negroes, just like you. I expect his daughter resembles him. Is that why you fancy her?"

"Fayette is a good woman, and . . . comely."

Orde Barstow threw back his head and laughed. "Perhaps you *have* learned a thing or two in my household. Is she passionate, Jack?"

"Don't talk about Fayette that way! She's . . . modest and innocent."

"Just like you, I'm afraid. Lord, you seem young for your years. Makes me feel old." Orde shoved back his chair and walked to the sideboard. He poured himself a glass of punch without offering any to Jack. "Well, never mind that. So you plan to take any fifty acres they give you—like as not some damn pine barren—and work it yourself with the aid of your good wife?"

"Just so."

"Fah! You'll be dead of exhaustion by the time you're thirty. This climate wasn't made for working white men."

"I'll never own slaves, that I vow."

"Before God! You anger me, boy, with your holiness!"

Jack gulped, but he could not keep down his own rage. "And you disgust me with your cruel presumption that one man can own another!"

"Disgust, is it? Towards the man who raised you? Who put bread in your mouth since you had teeth? For damn sure you are ungrateful!"

Jack stood before his stepfather and put out his hand. "I know, sir, that my debt to you is great. I am grateful, sir, but you are wrong on this matter. I believe it with all my heart. And time will prove me right."

"Right or wrong, I'm fed up with you! I won't be preached at in my own house."

"Search your conscience, sir." Jack still held out his hand.

Orde slapped it down with a ferocity that surprised both of them. They had not touched each other in many years. As a boy, Jack had often suffered Orde's disciplining, but in his manhood he stood taller than Orde and outweighed him by twenty pounds.

"I search it, and I find that I can still say this: get out. Get out of my house! Get off my land. You'll not see a penny of my money or an acre of my land. God damn you, goodbye, and good riddance!"

Jack's eyes widened. He stepped back, stumbled. "But father . . ." he began in a low, shocked voice.

"I am not your damn father! Your father, poor miserable bastard, is dead. As you will be to me from this day on. I mean it, Jack. Go at once, or I'll call for Beene to whip you like the niggers you love so much!"

Jack turned and ran without another word. He was hot with anger, trembling and felt sick to his stomach.

Orde Barstow felt the weight of his forty-two years as he staggered back to his chair. The veins on his temples bulged, and perspiration drenched his neck. When he had regained his breath, he began to shout for Zonah again, but at once she slipped into the room, seeming to materialize out of nowhere.

"Damn it, woman!" Orde thundered. "Where did you come from?" He knew well that she had heard the quarrel, or most of it. It didn't matter, he had absolutely no secrets from Zonah.

"Here I am, sir," Zonah said.

"I see that. Well, did you hear?"

"Yes, sir."

"To hell with him!" Orde paused. Zonah was very dear to him, but he had never allowed himself to wonder what she thought about slavery. After all, she had never known any other way of life. She was far too loyal, he assumed, to long for any other way of life. The woman was very happy; she was lucky and knew it. She loved him. What difference did it make if she was married to him or was his slave? It amounted to the same thing.

Silently, Zonah stood very still next to Orde's chair. With her small, long-fingered hands, she stroked his brow and smoothed his hair. Her hands were as cool as water, her touch as gentle as a bird's wing. He felt himself being charmed, relaxed.

"I know you like Jack," Orde said. Zonah had been good to Jack, and he had seen Jack help her with her work, particularly when she was with child.

"Yes, I do, sir," she said without slowing the motion of her hands. It hadn't changed its character, but now it seemed sensuous to Orde, almost seductive.

"But you know, he's not my real son."

"I know."

"Damn it, Zonah! I need to have a son, an heir!"

"I know. Perhaps . . ." And then her mouth moved onto the back of his neck where her hands had been, and she kissed him as softly as a child, but it excited him. Damn, it set him on fire! Zonah was a fine woman. She really knew how to please him, knew what he needed before he did himself!

Without speaking, Orde reached around and lifted her onto his lap. She kissed his Adam's apple and her fingers touched his chest. He began to unbutton his trousers as he pressed one of her soft, dark-skinned breasts to his mouth.

Jack had run out into the back yard looking for Zonah. He saw her two children, Ira and Mary, fast asleep cuddled together at the foot of a live oak trailing silvery Spanish moss. Jack admired them for a minute, then ran down the path to the barnyard, still hot with anger.

As soon as he reached the stables, Jack came face to face with a scene that exceeded his most extreme apprehensions. His stepfather's right-hand man, an ignorant London guttersnipe named Harley Beene, had tied the new Negro to two uprights of a hay wagon and was lashing the man's back with a leather thong.

"Beene!" Jack shouted. "Stop that at once!"

Caught by surprise, Beene stopped. "Why, Mr. Jack! I didn't know you'd come home."

"How dare you do that? Give me that whip, you bastard!"

Beene stepped back but hung onto the whip. "Who are you to call me a bastard? From what I've heard . . ."

"Shut up!" Jack said in a hollow tone. He shoved past Beene and examined the black man. His eyes were intelligent and terrified, and the man was nearly a giant. He was surprised Beene had dared whip him.

Beene's eyes narrowed. He had never liked Barstow's stepson, nor did Jack like him. The two men were the same age, but the difference in their social class was obvious.

"I'm just doin' my job, Mr. Jack," Beene said. He dodged around Jack and landed another blow on the Negro's bare back. The man shuddered.

"Leave that poor creature alone, and let's have a fair fight!" Jack shouted recklessly, for Beene was tough as a keg of nails and known as a fighter.

In answer, Beene raised his arm and tried to strike Jack with the leather whip. Jack side-stepped and swung a tight fist at Beene. He missed. Beene laughed and Jack started swinging in real anger. He launched himself at Beene, kicking and punching and swearing. His fist connected with Beene's jaw just as he took a punch to the stomach, but the blow to Beene's face snapped his jaw shut with a jolt that cracked two of Beene's yellow teeth.

Beene yowled in pain and spit blood. He swung hard and caught Jack's ear. Jack gasped and slammed Beene squarely in the chest so hard his hand hurt.

Both men were panting and had forgotten the Nergo, slumped forward now against the hay wagon. Beene danced around Jack, then pulled his right arm back for a roundhouse, but Jack darted through the middle of Beene's arms and pounded him squarely in the nose. Beene's eyes glazed. He saw the sun go black, then blood-red. He swayed, then crumpled.

Jack gasped for air. He hoped Beene was dead but didn't wait to see. Without hesitation, he strode to the hay wagon and untied the Negro.

"Come with me," he coaxed. "Do you understand?" Moses understood and nodded.

"Come along with me," Jack said and led him out of the barnyard. A plan was forming in his mind as he headed east.

Chapter Four

Catherine Gives Birth—Zonah Takes Action—Moses Is Saved

Late afternoon sun glinted through an open window into the room where Catherine Dunlie still lay. The sun made the room hotter than ever. Catherine Dunlie was swathed in a long, high-necked linen nightgown, but the midwife, Joan, had removed her own brown cotton gown and sat by the window in her petticoat and bodice.

Joan could see that the time was near. Her herbal anesthetic had taken effect, and Catherine seemed more relaxed between contractions, even slipping into unconsciousness from time to time.

But now she was awake and aware. "Dear God!" she gasped. "I feel like I'm bursting! Oh . . . I'm so tired, Joan! How long now?"

"Soon," Joan said flatly.

Catherine groaned. She couldn't remember her other deliveries being so agonizing. Of course, she had been younger then. Please God, this child would be healthy and be her last. She grimaced. There was little hope of that. She'd heard of a woman in Charleston who'd just given birth at the age of fifty-six.

But never before had she labored so long. Never before had the child seemed so heavy, so huge. Perhaps it hadn't really been so long. She had lost track again. This pain was timeless, beyond dimension.

Joan rose and washed her hands and face in the jug of tepid water that stood on a small chest near the window. She was watching Catherine closely.

Catherine was slipping into unconsciousness again. Her thoughts were hazy. This pain was everywhere, it was all: it was her back, her legs, her arms.

Joan knelt at the end of Catherine's low bed, little more than a pallet. "Push . . . push . . . push . . ." she coached.

Catherine obeyed without hearing. She had been pushing forever already, for hours, for days. She had to rid her body of this baby. Her pulse raced; sweat trickled down her face, into her eyes and ears, drenched the heavy linen gown.

Joan tugged the gown up over Catherine's waist. Modesty forbade Catherine to appear naked before any other human being, even a half-breed midwife. It was for reasons of modesty that she had refused to have a male doctor or her husband be present at this birth.

Catherine's fingers were wrapped tightly around the poles Joan had set next to her. Her teeth clenched and her mouth was set in a grin of pain. Her eyes were shut. They fluttered open. She saw Joan and for a moment she had no idea who the dark-skinned woman was.

Catherine's knees were drawn up and her legs were spread wide, but she was far too tired to hold them steady. They trembled; the long muscles in her legs jumped and cramped. Joan helped her to ease the cramps by straightening and flexing her legs.

Catherine panted with an open mouth. Her eyes were shut tight again. There was nothing to see; she was alone in this process which would have its own end, even if the end were death.

Catherine gasped with the sharp, new pain. Darkness nibbled at the edges of her consciousness, she felt a blackness, a void of feeling tempting her to give in to it, to slip away from the agony of her body.

Joan could see the baby's head emerging. "Push, push, push," she chanted in a low, steady voice, but Catherine did not hear. Catherine was screaming.

Angus Dunlie heard his wife scream and he frowned deeply. Fayette heard the screaming and burst into tears. Cattie did not hear, for she had run off to town on a secret errand of her own.

"Father! What should we do?" Fayette demanded. She wiped her eyes on a lace-edged handkerchief, embarrassed to cry before her father.

"First let us see about this man," Angus Dunlie said. The Dunlies stood with Jack Barstow and the Negro called Moses under the willow tree by the creek.

"Don't cry, Fayette," Jack Barstow said. He was dirty and disheveled from his fight with Harley Beene. A cut below his ear had bled into his collar and his shirt was torn, but he felt a certain powerful euphoria. "God's will be done," he philosophized, "woman is made to bear children. If it were not so . . ."

Fayette shuddered. So much pain horrified her. The Negro had dropped onto his haunches and his eyes were shut as he waited for his fate to be decided. Fayette could still smell the blood.

When Jack had led the Negro away from his stepfather's barnyard, his first thought had been of the Dunlies. He had come to their house at once, stopped under Fayette's window and called her. She had agreed to help, but insisted that her father be consulted.

"The man is intelligent and healthy," Jack said, "He understands English, he is strong and tractable."

"We could send him back to South Carolina," Dunlie said, "but there he will always live in chains."

"No! Don't do that, father!" Fayette begged.

"I don't want to get him punished again," Dunlie said. "But the situation is complicated. It is wrong to keep him anywhere in the colony."

"Couldn't you send him to your land on Saint Simons island?" Jack suggested, looking at Fayette. "No one will know he's there."

This young man is sound, Dunlie thought. He obviously cared for Fayette, but she didn't seem to value him as much as she might have. "Perhaps I could," Dunlie said. "Not now, but soon. For now, saddle up two horses and take him to the small shed in the fields."

"Yes, father," Fayette said. "I knew you would save him!"

"Hide him there and come right back," Dunlie directed. "Take the sheltered route, past the Indian burying ground, and be careful not to be seen. Alas, I have a feeling this unfortunate business is not finished yet."

A sudden breeze soothed Joan's bare back and neck like a cool hand as she bent over her task. The baby's head was showing clearly now, a small round dome covered with fine hairs and a thick coat of blood-specked mucus.

Catherine was as good as unconscious. Only a faint light of being flickered in her mind, but her body was still thrusting toward new life. With the next contraction, the baby's head burst through her vulval tissues, and its forehead, then its eyes, its nose, its mouth, its chin appeared successively. Joan hummed approval.

As soon as its head was free, the baby turned so that it was facing to the side. Joan nodded. All was as it should be. At this angle, the baby's shoulders and the rest of its body could slip along the birth canal easily. Joan took out the knife she had tucked under her petticoat. She weighed the long, sharp knife in one hand, hefting it, waiting and watching.

Catherine had slipped into concave darkness. She dreamed she was a girl in Gloucestershire, playing in a neat, stonewalled field as her spaniel Tommy chased rabbits. Tommy yelped and growled and she ran and ran. The field was speckled with daisies and yellow primroses. She was so free, so young, so light of foot that she could feel herself floating over tufts of grass, feel her skirts billowing behind. She was flying . . .

Joan was pleased as she witnessed the baby's birth. She took the tiny boy into her hands as soon as he had cleared his mother's legs. She raised him to her mouth and sucked the mucus from his nose and throat. Then she held him at some length from Catherine and watched as the umbilical cord ceased beating, and then she took the knife and severed it with one swift snap.

The baby cried out. Joan smiled. Catherine sighed in unconsciousness, then groaned weakly. Her travail was not over yet. Far from it. As Joan wrapped the tiny boy in a linen handkerchief and then in a small huckabuck towel, Catherine drew her knees up again in an instinctive gesture. A mighty contraction had seized her. Once again, she held her breath, then released it in a panting gasp.

Joan turned, cuddling the baby, and ran from the room. Annie and the rest of the servants were gathered in the front parlor with Angus Dunlie, praying for Catherine's safe delivery. Joan was swift and sure-footed as she crept down the narrow corkscrew of the back stairs.

Inside the stairwell at the bottom, Zonah was waiting.

Joan passed her the bundle without a word and ran back up the stairs. Catherine whimpered as she entered the room, and the crown of the other twin's head appeared in the dilated opening.

As Zonah fled with the firstborn twin, Angus Dunlie decided to take matters into his own hands. Annie beside him, he mounted the front stairs. He marched down the hallway to the room forbidden him for the past four days, and he arrived outside his wife's door in time to hear the birth cry of his second son.

"Praise God!" Annie exclaimed. She fell to her knees on the spot.

"Joan!" Dunlie called. "Catherine! Joan!" There was no answer. The door stood ajar three inches. He put his nose to the crack and peered inside.

He was shocked by what he saw. Poor Catherine was lying on her back with her head pointing toward him, her yellow hair matted and tangled, her knees in the air. Her gown was all bunched up and spattered with blood. Dunlie saw Joan cutting something with a huge, shining knife. At first he thought Joan was killing the baby, but then she dropped the knife and held the newborn high, catching Dunlie's eye.

Dunlie saw that the infant was male. He heard it scream and his face split in a grin. Clapping his hands together, he thrust open the door and ran into the room.

"Good . . . good," Joan muttered.

"Hallelujah! Praise the Lord! Catherine, how are you, my dear?" Dunlie demanded. He dropped to his knees beside Catherine's pallet and lifted her shoulders so that she could see the baby. Catherine took in a deep breath and blinked into awareness. She had eyes only for the baby and reached out for it. Joan passed it to her. Her arms trembled but she smiled faintly, relaxed against her husband's strength and fell asleep.

The baby was wide awake. Drawing air into his tiny lungs, he emptied them just as fast with a long, surprisingly powerful cry. He waved his hands. He kicked his legs and feet.

"Now just look at the spirit of that little 'un!" Annie said from the doorway. "Look at the way he's carrying on already!"

Zonah cradled the firstborn twin against her breast. Her feelings were strong. She was excited by the danger and success of her conspiracy with Joan. She was elated by the strength and vigor of the infant, even now kicking in her arms, squirming against the bonds of his swaddling.

Half way from the Dunlie's home to Orde Barstow's, Zonah stopped and spread the swaddling out beneath a holly bush to have a closer look at the infant. He was perfect: straight-limbed, round-headed, his skin smooth and only slightly mottled, though of course it was the flushed, yellow-tinged ruddy color typical of his race. She opened his fists and counted his tiny well-shaped fingers. Perfect. His light gray eyes were unfocused as he looked up—at Zonah, at the blue sky, and beyond, and the eerie blankness of their expression troubled her.

For as well as excitement and elation, Zonah felt apprehension and fear. She had always believed the birth of twins to be bad luck, a clear sign of the disfavor of the spirits, a punishment—often of adultery. Among the Ibo who had raised her, the birth of twins was a startling, unwelcome, mystical event. A diviner was consulted to determine which spirit or ancestor had been offended and a sacrifice was offered to appease the gods' wrath.

It was the Dunlies, Zonah figured, who had somehow offended a spirit, but she was wary of the bad luck which might cling to this child. Before she offered him to her white man, she would take care to exorcise any evil. For sure she would prepare a sacrifice—perhaps tonight.

But meanwhile, she would take the baby to Saraby. Saraby was a teenaged Negro woman who also belonged to Orde Barstow. She had a son of her own who was more than a year old but still suckling at his mother's breasts. She would take this little baby to her and let her nurse him until his belly was full.

Zonah wrapped the baby carefully and set off along the shaded path to the Barstow homestead. She hummed as she walked along.

Chapter Five

A Visit to the Dunlies'—Ben Sykes Is
Hanged—Zonah Goes to the River

At noon the next day, Orde Barstow rode his high-stepping black stallion, Lucifer, into the front yard of the Dunlies' town house. Orde had spent the morning making inquiries, and everything he had learned had confirmed his original suspicions that Jack had taken Moses to Angus Dunlie for hiding.

In the New World, just as the Old, a few pounds spent wisely in a waterfront tavern could buy a man any information he needed. Orde had started with the grogshop at the easternmost end of the Strand, and by the time he walked into Mickey Martin's place at the corner of Barnard Street, two unsavory river rats were waiting for him, eager to talk.

"Dunlie!" Orde shouted. He slipped off Lucifer and tied the reins around the hitching post. He'd probably come back to find Lucifer gone, he thought suspiciously.

Barstow made a fine figure as he strode across the

small grassy plot to Angus Dunlie's front door. His coat and waistcoat were sky blue; his boots and breeches were black, and he held his dark curly head high, although his lips were set in a sneer and the expression of his face was indignant.

"Good morning, sir." It was Rose, opening the door and curtseying, her white cap trembling on her cropped red curls.

"Mr. Barstow to see Mr. Dunlie, if you please."

"Yes, sir, and could you wait in the parlor?" Rose was excited to see this important visitor. She thought Mr. Barstow very handsome, though stirred up about something. A mood of general merry-making had prevailed at the Dunlies' ever since the dear child had arrived, and Rose herself had spent the night very pleasantly in the hayloft getting to know Thomas, the carpenter's assistant.

"I'm not planning to wait long," Barstow called after Rose. He looked around the parlor, noting with satisfaction that it was far less splendid than his own. Hardly worth being called a parlor, he thought, as it was furnished with only a fireplace screen, two tables, two wooden chairs, a mirror, and a couch with bolster. The windows were shut and the room was close and stuffy.

"Mr. Barstow!" Angus Dunlie began, standing in the parlor doorway. "What brings you to my house this morning?"

"I think you know, Dunlie," Barstow snarled. The sight of Dunlie immediately touched off his anger. "I've come to take back my damn slave!" Barstow's wide face was flushed, and he felt a trifle dizzy. Some of the rum he'd drunk in those river-front taverns must have been bad. He knew it was cheap rum, for he'd sold it to the tavern keepers himself.

"Let's discuss this like gentlemen," Dunlie said, thinking Barstow looked wild-eyed.

"Can a thief talk like a gentleman?" Barstow asked.

Dunlie stepped into the room, wary now. "Are you calling me a thief, Barstow?"

"Some man stole my African. Some man is keeping him. I heard it was you."

"In order to lose something, you have to own it, and owning slaves is not legal in Georgia."

"Legal? Some damn fool laws passed to please the preachers! They don't affect me. I ask you, sir. Do you know the whereabouts of my stepson, Jack? Is it true that that ingrate fool came sniveling to you? But never mind, I'll settle with Jack directly. I've come to you to take back my property." Barstow dug for a handkerchief to mop his brow. It was damn hot in this narrow room.

"I won't lie to you. I have the man called Moses."

"Where is he?"

"He was badly beaten by your overseer."

"Unfortunate. But have you never whipped a servant, or had him whipped? Would you not punish an unruly child? Would you then expect your neighbor to steal the child or servant from his home?"

"I would never beat another human being cruelly. And I will never own another human being or condone another's owning him."

"Hell's fire! You are so proud! You sound like Jack. How then, do you intend to live? We are not in England any more, Dunlie. This is a new land, a land open to enterprise, and I for one intend to prosper here."

"God willing, I shall prosper, too—but within the law."

"White men cannot work in this climate, 'tis already proved. Most of the men here don't do an honest day's

work anyway. This town is full of whores and thieves
and ne'er-do-wells already breeding more whores and
thieves demanding the rights of Englishmen. Why half
the men who call themselves Georgians are straight
from the cellars of Newgate! Lazy paupers! Common
villains! By your stubbornness you betray your own
class. As gentlemen, we have certain rights and responsibilities . . . Surely, you see that I am right?"

"I see that you are shrewd and justify your own
crime."

"Crime? No crime, it's business. I paid twenty-five
pounds for that black man."

"Money ill spent. You'll lose that much, and more,
to the magistrates, if you look any longer for him."

"Are ye saying you'd drag another gentleman to
court?"

"To court and back to London in leg irons before I
return that man to you."

"Angus Dunlie, you're a stubborn fool!"

"Then surely you won't linger in my house."

"Indeed I won't. I'll be gone at once."

Both men headed for the door and brushed shoulders getting through it as neither would step back for
the other to go first. Dunlie stiffened as he smelled
rum on Barstow; Barstow fought back an urge to
punch Dunlie in his narrow, determined face.

In the small hallway, they heard a door upstairs
swing open and the thin wail of the newborn baby.

"My son," Dunlie said simply. His voice was proud.

It angered Barstow even more. He'd heard Dunlie's
wife was with child. "I'll not forget this," he vowed,
turning on the threshold. "Never. I swear I'll have my
revenge against you . . . and your family . . . your
children . . . and their children. As God is my witness, this day will come back to remind you of my
vow, Dunlie."

Dunlie winced. Perhaps Barstow was drunk, but he could ill afford such a bitter, powerful enemy. "Watch your tongue. . ." he cautioned.

"I've no need of your advice," Barstow said, turning his stocky frame on the doorstep. "I've no need of you at all. But the day will come when you'll regret this. Mark my words, Dunlie."

Angus Dunlie watched Orde Batstow ride away from his house with a troubled heart. He was sorry for the quarrel and made distinctly uneasy by Barstow's heady words of revenge, but nothing could completely dampen his happiness on the day after the birth of his fine, healthy son.

Still, his unwitting acquisition of a Negro field hand created more problems for him. What would he do with Moses? He hardly knew. Of course he would consider him free and pay him for his labor. Though keeping servants of the Negro race was also forbidden in the colony, it was sometimes done, and likely his own infringement of the law would be overlooked considering his status. He hoped Moses turned out to be a good worker; many of the things Barstow had said about the workingmen of the colony were quite true. The bulk of them were indentured servants, commonly bound for seven years but sometimes for as long as fourteen, and they were an ignorant, untrained lot. Cases of disrespectful servants robbing their masters and running off were common; even the best of them ate a lot and fell sick whenever they had a mind to.

Dunlie's household already included a half dozen such servants. All the expenses of their board and clothing rested on him for the term they were bound to him, and though he tried to be a good master and had so far had no trouble with stealing, he knew that some of his neighbors had fared less well. Dr. Jones, he knew, had put one of his servants in irons for setting fire to a cornfield. Another man had been attacked by his servant with a sword. James Habersham, another gentleman and neighbor, maintained that less than half of his servants' expenses could be recovered from their labor.

A good number of men and women were indentured directly to the Trust which governed the colony. They worked farming for the Trustees, tending their cattle, working in the Trustees' Store, and building roads and bridges for the common good. It was the Trustees' intention that these bond servants would work out their time, even buy their own freedom before their contracts had expired, and then stay in Georgia to become reliable freeholders.

Some did, but many others fled. Unlike the Negroes, inconspicuous, they could change their names and claim a new identity in another colony. Pursuit of them was difficult if not impossible. From Savannah, it was an easy matter to find passage across the river to South Carolina, and from there post roads led clear to Portsmouth, New Hampshire.

Still, it seemed to Dunlie that the saddest, meanest, most useless servants never did run off. Oh, no, they stayed to make trouble. There was no denying it, men were not equal, in fact, and they proved that axiom every day of the year.

A cannon shot was fired from the Government House in St. James Square to announce the hour of the public execution of Benjamin Sykes, the man whom Jack Barstow had seen in his wretched cell.

Jack had made plans to be present at the man's hanging. So had at least half the population of Savannah: men, women, and children; soldiers, servants, and their masters; half-breeds and Indians—all had turned

out for the event, cramming Percival Square for an
hour before the shot was fired. Old friends met and
were separated in the crowd. A group of men crouched
at one edge of the square, bent over a game of chance
played with peas and shells. Corn cakes, fried fish,
beer and punch were for sale at little stalls. A pair of
lovers embraced openly, drunkenly, under a tree. One
old woman, her face drawn to a pucker by the pox,
taught two others a new knitting pattern, and whores
appeared among the crowd, then disappeared, only to
return to offer themselves again.

A pickpocket hung back, faceless, waiting until the
moment when all eyes would be on the gallows. He
knew the crowd's mood—it was restless, expectant. He
saw a fight breaking out between two soldiers and
crossed the square to avoid them.

There was no public executioner in Savannah,
though there was nearly enough work for one, so the
custom was to give the job to another convicted criminal. In return, he got a remission of his own sentence,
a small allowance, and, an important perquisite, the
clothes off the hanged man's back.

Benjamin Sykes had been tried by a jury of Magistrates. In general, the people had little respect for the
Magistrates. Some of them could neither read nor
write, and two years ago, one of them had been found
guilty of stealing several thousand pounds and had
been sent home. In an attempt to lend dignity to the
bench, the Trustees had sent from London some
splendid purple robes trimmed with fur—one for each
of the three bailiffs. They had also sent a copper-gilt
mace and an engraved seal, which together cost five
times as much as the log house in which the court met.

But the conviction and sentencing of Benjamin
Sykes had stirred no controversy. Despite discontent
with the absentee Trustees, General Oglethorpe was

still popular among the people, and Sykes had been convicted of plotting to murder him. The man he had succeeded in murdering had relatives in the crowd.

Sykes would be executed by hanging. A wooden scaffold stood next to the log jailhouse. Sykes was still inside, prey to the torments of bad boys who poked at him through the bars with sticks and taunted him. One boy threw a snake into Sykes's cell, and a rumor went through the crowd that it was a rattlesnake, but it was not—a harmless black snake slithered out under the door.

A few minutes after the shot, Savannah's famous preacher George Whitefield entered the square to speak to Sykes of repentance. Whitefield, though still a pale, round-faced young man, had stirred souls all up and down the Atlantic Coast, had moved even skeptical Benjamin Franklin to empty his pocket for his proposed orphan house. Whitefield had come to Georgia as the pastor for Christ Church, as yet unbuilt, but planned since the first day of the colony's settlement, and he made short work of getting a confession from Sykes.

Sykes came out of the jailhouse with tears streaming down his dirty, stubbled cheeks, calling out, "God has forgiven me! I am not afraid to die!"

"Die you will!" a drunken ranger shouted, lunging at Sykes, but he was hauled back by the crowd.

The stand-in hangman led Sykes to the gallows and set his feet on the first rungs of the wooden ladder. "Repent, ye sinners!" Sykes called out.

All eyes were on him. The crowd, no longer noisy or unruly, was hushed. There was an uneasy energy in the crowd, a tension tinged with defiance. There were so many crimes to hang a man for. Most of those present had seen this happen many times before—here and in England—and always to a poor man, never to a rich one.

Jack Barstow put his hand over his heart. He was moved, he shivered with terror and a perverse fascination.

"Live Christian lives!" Sykes called, prompted by Whitefield. Slowly, he climbed the ladder. He was trembling, his face pale and terrified. George Whitefield made a mental note of the occasion for his journal. The pickpocket glided among the crowd, lightening the load of coins in more than a few pockets.

Ben Sykes was to die without a blindfold. The hangman put the noose around his neck and spun him off the ladder. In an instant, he was dead. It was over. Still, the crowd was silent, and Sykes hung, nodding in eternal sleep, swaying at the rope's end, his toes pointed toward the dusty earth.

After their dinner that night, Zonah gave Orde Barstow a sleeping draught in his tea. Barstow attributed his drowsiness to the unseasonable heat and retired early. As usual, Zonah followed him to his bed chamber, but he was too drowsy for love-making, and when she saw that he was sleeping soundly, she slipped out of his bed and made her way down to the tiny one-room huts where Saraby and the other Africans lived.

Zonah smiled when she saw that the moon was new. A new phase of the moon was a good omen. Nodding, she offered a prayer of thanksgiving to the gods of the sky and air. The stars shone brightly in the clear night sky. For this, too, she was grateful.

Saraby was waiting for Zonah in her cabin. Her own son whimpered restlessly when Zonah entered, but Saraby laughed at him. "He misses me," she told Zonah, in the simple, improvised language they shared, "but it is time he learned to eat rice."

Privately, both women were far from confident that the new baby would live many more days. His color had improved, but he seemed to have lost weight; although he was regularly offered Saraby's milk, sometimes he turned his head and cried. His cries were thin and weak, and he did not kick as vigorously as on the day of his birth.

Zonah feared that the baby was still suffering from the evil his mother had stirred up. Had she broken a taboo? Had some enemy put a curse on her? There was no way to guess.

As she carried the baby away from Saraby's cabin, Zonah pondered the meaning of twin births. Sometimes, she had heard, both babies were put to death immediately and the mother purified. Usually they were drowned, but sometimes left to die in the forest.

"Small boy, what are your secrets?" Zonah asked the baby.

The Indian woman Joan had told Zonah days earlier that the white woman would bear twins. Zonah had been surprised that she knew. In Africa, if the midwife noticed in time that a second baby was coming from the mother, she tried to run away. Before running, she would break an egg on the floor to disassociate herself from the crime and ward off punishment.

But Joan had been unafraid. Zonah was impressed with her skill and amazed that both babies had been born healthy, both males.

Because both had lived, Zonah had thought hard about what to do for this one. She wanted to exorcise the evil that still clung to him. She had thought, had prayed for guidance, and tried hard to remember what she had heard as a girl. Because both babies were living, Zonah figured, the evil spirits had nowhere to go. Perhaps she should find the other twin and kill it.

But then she had remembered another method of dispelling evil. She had found a piece of smooth, forked wood, a length of the upper branch of a nut tree, and she had carved it with a sharp knife into a crude likeness of the baby. Like the baby, the wooden figure had thin arms, tiny fingers and toes, a tiny penis, and a distended belly. Zonah had soaked it in several waters and boiled it in tea, and now it was ready.

Near the edge of the river there was a clearing, far below the overhanging bluff. Here Zonah knew of a natural bower formed by the tangle of lush, thick-leaved fox grape vines and laurels. There was a narrow sand beach here, and clear shallows before the water dropped off. Zonah took the baby to the beach, and carefully spread out a cloth. On it she placed the baby and knelt.

Only a faint starlight penetrated the dense leaves over her head. It was all dark; the blackness of the night absorbed sky, air, river, and there were no sounds but the river's own sounds—a soft murmuring and the occasional splashing of fish or frogs or alligators—and the rustling, sighing sounds the wind made.

Kneeling, Zonah began to sing. She sang softly and the child ceased its crying and seemed to listen. She explained to God what she wanted to do—rid the baby of evil—and about the figurine she had made to accept that evil. She flattered God's powers a little, calling him "he who rewards prayer with good" and "all-powerful guardian and protector."

When she had finished singing and praying, Zonah picked up both the baby and the figurine. She leaned out over the water, holding each at the end of one arm, and then she dropped the wooden image into the water.

"Away, away, be gone, be gone," she chanted, drawing the baby back to her and holding it fast against her breasts. The wooden figure floated out of sight.

"Now, my little man, now you will grow fat!" she promised. She wrapped the crying infant in the cloth and carried him back to Saraby.

Chapter Six

*Orde Barstow Gets a Surprise—Jack a
Job—Cattie Changes Her Mind*

Early in the morning, Zonah had washed the baby
boy with milk and dressed him in an embroidered
white batiste christening gown, long-sleeved and
tucked, only a little yellowed with age. She had found
the baby's gown among the linens Orde Barstow's
London housekeeper had packed into a cedar chest
for shipment to America. Why the housekeeper had
included this garment, no one ever knew; in fact, it
had been Jack's, and his mother had saved it out of
sentiment.

The tiny baby was nearly lost in the billowing
width of the gown, but Zonah tucked it under him
and around him. The baby was drowsy, having just
suckled at Saraby's breasts, and his eyes were shut tight
when Zonah carried him into Orde Barstow's bed
chamber.

Ten minutes earlier, Zonah had brought Orde his
breakfast: tea with molasses, hot corn cakes, and cold

roast beef. He had consumed the food and now sat at his side table, drinking more tea and reading a letter from his agent in London as his mind relived the quarrel with that damn Dunlie.

"What's that?" he asked as Zonah entered the room with the white-wrapped bundle. His blue eyes widened in surprise. It looked to him like a baby, for God's sake.

Convincingly, the infant gurgled and pursed its tiny mouth like a pale fish gasping for air. Barstow shoved back his chair and took a closer look. It was a white-skinned infant, clearly no child of Zonah's, not that she'd been in the family way of late . . .

"Where did you get it?" he demanded.

Zonah spoke up in a low, steady voice. She had planned everything she might say, but she intended to say as little as possible. "He was just born . . . in the House for Strangers," she said. "His mother died. She was a bound girl. From the ship." Zonah handed the baby to Orde and his eyes blinked open.

"An orphan, eh? An English orphan! Was she English, the mother?"

"I don't know, sir."

"No mind. Here!" He handed the child back to Zonah. It was so tiny he felt afraid he would crush it in his hands. "So you thought to bring him to me, eh?"

"Yes, sir." Zonah held her tongue and waited for Orde to work it out.

He sat down in his chair, astonished. He was afraid he'd caused this. Women were so . . . literal, almost stupid sometimes. He'd said to Zonah that he needed an heir and damned if she hadn't brought him one. Poor orphan. The baby was helpless, needed someone to mother it or it would die. He watched Zonah cradle the infant adeptly, smoothing out the preposterous white gown she had it wrapped in. He smiled. Why not keep the baby? It was unconventional, but so was a lot of his life. Trust Zonah to look out for him and his needs . . .

"It's a male child, you say?"

"Yes, sir." Zonah started untying the cords at the bottom of the gown in order to show off the baby's sex, but Barstow stopped her with a gesture.

"I believe you," he said. Why not? he asked himself. Why not keep the baby? He peered over at him, asleep in Zonah's arms, his eyes closed, his dark lashes absurdly long on his pale cheeks. "Is he healthy?"

"Small but healthy," Zonah testified. She had noticed an improvement in the baby's spirits today, since the ceremony at the river. He was eating well today, and already his belly seemed hard with milk. "Saraby will feed him."

Why not? Barstow thought. Zonah had it all worked out. The baby might yet die, far too many did, but with Zonah looking out for him, he had a good chance. If the infant did live and was raised right here in his house, he would be almost as much his son as if he'd sired him. As much his son as Jack had been . . . and surely he would turn out better than that rascal Jack.

Barstow began to be comfortable with the idea. Fate had presented him with a son just when he needed one. This infant could save him the trouble of marrying again, of taking a strange Englishwoman into his house with all the demands and nonsense women involved. He was perfectly happy with Zonah, after all. Damn! She was a fine woman!

"Saraby can feed him?" he asked.

"Yes, sir."

Barstow grinned. He looked over at Zonah. She caught his mood at once, and her dark face shone with a sudden smile. Barstow broke into an amused, triumphant laugh. He clapped his hands, and Zonah—still holding the tiny baby in its elegant christening gown—whirled around the room in a triumphant dance.

Colonel Alexander Vanderdussen, commander of the South Carolina forces assigned to aid Oglethorpe in his planned invasion of Florida, stood at attention before his commanding officer. Oglethorpe was receiving Colonel Vanderdussen in the small tent that was his home and headquarters while the troops were gathering in Savannah.

Vanderdussen's provincial regiment included about five hundred men—ill-clad but well-disciplined. The Colonel himself was arrayed in all the splendor of a British officer: his coat was scarlet laced with gold, his waistcoat buff edged with silver, his sash crimson silk. In short, he was as gorgeously turned out as Oglethorpe himself, and he wore the same expression.

Both men were frowning.

"So we march south," Vanderdussen asked in a Dutch accent, "in two days' time?"

"In three days' time, or four. Perhaps five," Oglethorpe answered.

"My men are ready to march," Vanderdussen said impatiently.

"Without artillary?" Oglethorpe asked snidely. The General, self-confident as ever, was smarting over the stinginess of the South Carolina Assembly. Although that colony was also charged by the King with the defense of the southern frontier, although he was commander-in-chief of the forces in South Carolina as well as Georgia, the Assembly had sent him only two companies, no money, and laughably little hardware.

Vanderdussen shrugged. He would do what he could. Everyone told him that Oglethorpe's planned invasion was doomed to fail. The city of St. Augustine

was well defended and situated in the most miserable
of unhealthy swamplands. Oglethorpe had delayed so
long already that it was nearly high summer, the season of mosquitoes, sand flies, and malaria. The season
for dying. And he was not impressed by what he saw of
Oglethorpe's regiment. His men looked ragged and exhausted, weakened by fevers and dysentery and made
rebellious by the lack of opportunity for either dis-
charge or promotion.

"The men must have arms and horses, of course,"
Vanderdussen said, ignoring the General's irony. He
studied the General's long, aristocratic face in profile
as the tall, rigid Englishman strode back and forth in
front of his tent.

"They must have howitzers, twelve-pounders, coe-
horns, artillery wagons, and horses to draw them," Oglethorpe chanted. "The balance of my men are quartered at Frederica. And I expect the support of nearly a
thousand Indians."

"Creek?"

"Mostly Cherokee."

"They're no damn good. They'll never face fire."

Oglethorpe was well aware of the unreliability of
Indians, but he hated to be opposed. "See that your
own regiment does, and I shall marshal my Indians!"

"Yes, sir," Vanderdussen agreed. Oglethrope had the
feeling he was being mocked. Didn't the Dutchman
know he had destroyed both Fort Piccolata and Fort
St. Francis on New Year's Day, with only his Highlanders and the Indians? It had been a glorious victory.
True, the forts had been lightly manned, but so was
St. Augustine. His scouts and spies reported that little
more than six hundred fighting men were quartered
in all of the Spanish frontier outposts, and his easy
victories in January had instilled him with contempt
for the Spaniards' courage.

In fact, Oglethorpe was so certain of a quick summer victory that he had already written to Parliament suggesting that his next target be Havana, Cuba. Of course, to take Cuba, he would need a couple thousand regular British soldiers.

"As soon as it is possible, I want you to move your troops double time," Oglethorpe said. "The Highlanders will march with you. I will take my men south by water, and we shall meet at the encampment at the mouth of the St. John's River." He unrolled a map to trace the route for Vanderdussen.

Vanderdussen, a tall, stocky man, bent slightly to study the map. Was Oglethorpe a military genius or a fanatic, he wondered. Vanderdussen had been employed by the Spaniards in the Phillipines and South America before settling in Charleston and he had no illusions about their lack of courage. He was distressed by the sight of the troops in Savannah—they were dirty, disspirited, and diseased——and by Savannah itself—a squalid, primitive frontier post, even compared to Charleston. What, he wondered, was life like in Frederica?

But Oglethorpe was in command. "Yes, sir," he replied to the rest of the General's instructions. When Oglethorpe dismissed him, he headed directly for the public house on Broughton Street.

Almost as soon as Vanderdussen had left, Jack Barstow appeared at Oglethorpe's tent. The General, still discomforted over his interview with the Dutchman, was relieved that he had gone and—as usual—pleased to see Jack.

"Good morning, sir," Jack said, saluting.

"Good morning to you. Seen your family, then? Settled that?"

Jack nodded. "Yes, sir. And ready to ride with you, sir, whenever you say."

"Excellent. I want you to ride with the Highlanders, Jack, once we get south. And I have a special assignment for you. I want you to assist the surgeon, William McDavid, on this campaign."

"Yes, sir," Jack agreed. "I'd be proud, sir."

"Just so. Well, the South Carolina regiment is here. Commodore Pearce commands the fleet. With the Chickasaws, the Choctaws, and the Lower Creeks fighting by our side, God willing, we shall drive out the Spanish this time!"

"I know we will, sir!" Jack grinned. To him, Oglethorpe would always be a hero. He felt his heart beat faster at the thought of riding out with the General again. Perhaps he would never settle down to family life and farming. Perhaps, after all, the military life was the life for him.

In the past few days, Cattie Dunlie's love affair with the handsome blond carpenter had progressed from playful passion to a marriage proposal. Micah had taken Cattie out for a moonlit ride in an eggshell-thin birchbark canoe that rode on the river like a weightless leaf. Micah knew something of astronomy, and he showed Cattie the bear and the hunters, and then he had kissed her until she was breathless.

It was Cattie who had done the proposing. "Shall we be married soon?" she asked Micah when she opened her eyes and found herself lying on the bottom of the canoe.

"You know I love you," Micah said.

Cattie had no trouble at all believing that it was true. She was not yet a vain woman, but she had been led by the observations of others to think herself pretty, and she was alight with first love. Everything, since Micah, was wonderful; everything was shining and sparkling and sunny and true.

But her lover was wiser, at twenty, already far better acquainted with life's inequities. "Still, I haven't had your advantages," he said.

"What of it?" Cattie demanded.

"You are far more accomplished than I."

"Don't you love me?"

"With all my heart," he vowed, "but I haven't a fortune, you know. I'm just getting started. I have only my chest of tools. And now that my service is over, I will get fifty acres from the Trust."

"Don't trouble about money," Cattie said innocently.

"I was born in Berkshire, near Reading," Micah started to explain, not for the first time, "to honest parents, but my mother soon died and my dad took to drink. I went to school for a year, but then I was apprenticed to Mr. Williams, a carpenter in town. When my time with my first master was not yet up, he was killed one night, murdered by an Irishman for the few coins he carried. I didn't know what I'd do, but I'd heard talk of men working for passage to Virginia. I'd heard it was the land of opportunity where a man without land could get some. But instead of Virginia, I was offered a berth on a ship sailing for Georgia, my passage paid for a short term—four years. So here I am."

"And here I am," Cattie said, "and England is far behind us. We shall never see it again, I'm happy to say."

"Your father is a gentleman," Micah said.

"Aye. That's true."

"He will want to see you wed to a far better man than I," Micah said.

Cattie stared at him. Better? Micah's handsome features: his bold, straight nose, his clear blue eyes, his wide, red-lipped mouth, his blond hair pulled back and knotted with a black cord—all seemed to her the embodiment of masculine perfection. He wore the same suit of clothes every day, but to Cattie, it flattered his strong and muscular frame.

"Don't say such things," she insisted. "I'll tell him in the morning."

And accordingly, shortly after breakfast the next day, Cattie went to her father in his sitting room. It was an ill-chosen moment. Angus Dunlie was confronting his account books, and he was not in a cheerful mood.

"Papa," Cattie began confidently, "I have something to tell you that I think will please you."

"You do, my dear? Are you sure it's not something that will please you, as well? A new ribbon? A length of embroidered damask at a wondrously low price?"

"Not at all, Papa. I am not as young and silly as you think."

Angus Dunlie paused and took a good look at his sixteen-year-old daughter. She did look womanly: full-breasted, slim and narrow-waisted, ripely pretty. He knew well that she was nearly mature. He noticed that her yellow hair, so like her mother's, had been pinned up on her head in a grown-up fashion. And today she was flushed and looked very eager and intense.

"Ah, Cattie . . ." her father sighed. How fast she had grown up. Fayette had always been his favorite; she was more like him, and though Cattie was bright and pretty and chattered the way young girls do, he had never taken much interest in what she had to say.

"Papa, I want to be married," she said, interrupting his study.

Despite himself, Dunlie was startled. "You do?" he asked, not unkindly, turning his head to make sure he'd heard rightly.

"Yes, Papa. To Micah Stone."

"And who is Micah Stone?"

Was it then possible, Cattie asked herself, that not everyone on earth had seen him and taken notice of her love? She paused, thinking of how to explain this to her father. How aged and isolated her father must be not to have seen and admired Micah.

"He . . . works with Mr. Libby," Cattie said.

"You mean the joiner? The carpenter's assistant?" Dunlie asked, without hiding the distress in his voice. How far, he wondered, had this gone? Was there no end to his troubles? What nonsense! His daughter talking of marrying a common laborer, an uneducated man without a penny of his own. He had begun to worry about finding decent dowries for his daughters, and for sure he was eager to see Cattie suitably wed, but how could she be so ignorant as to favor a common workingman?

Cattie flushed deeper. "Yes, Papa, he's a carpenter. He's a good man . . . and I love him. Yes, I do!"

Dunlie paled. "How far has this gone?"

"What do you mean? We love each other, and we wish to marry. Oh, please Papa, I have never wanted anything so much before! Never!"

Perhaps, Dunlie thought, perhaps it is not yet too late. Love was all very well, but marriage was more than that. There should be a fitness of spiritual and material estate. Marriage should be governed by certain prudent considerations. Cattie was so young. She was not a bad girl, it was just that she was not capable of any of these considerations. An idea had come into his head, and he began to form a plan for dealing with this absurd problem.

"I take it, my dear, that your beloved has no family."

"His parents are dead. He was bound to Mr. Libby, but now he is free."

"I see. Just so. I suppose he is living with Mr. Libby. That is, when he is not engaged with hammering over our heads. Well, my dear daughter, let us go together to meet this young man and discuss it with him. I think that is no less than is due your father."

"Go, together?"

"Yes, let us seek him out—in his own world."

Cattie was wide-eyed. Her father wanted to go with her to see Micah? She had thought . . . well, that he would next come here, to her home, to ask her father for permission to court her, after she had . . . arranged it with him.

"Yes . . . I suppose that is all right," she said doubtfully, still confused.

"Very well, let us go at once," Dunlie said.

"At once? This morning?"

"Why not?" Dunlie asked, shutting his account book and standing up. "I'll be ready as soon as I put on my wig."

The neighborhood where the house of Thomas Libby stood was characterized by dilapidation. Nearly all of the houses in Savannah were modest frame buildings, built of the local soft pine and set upon wooden piers sunk into the earth to provide nourishment for termites.

"Can you show me the way to Mr. Libby's house?" Angus Dunlie demanded of a man wearing a brimmed hat and loitering near the courthouse. The courthouse itself was built on logs and listed so severely that its front door hung open.

"Why right down the lane," the man said, pointing, "down there. Everybody knows . . ."

"Thank you, kind sir," Dunlie said and Cattie shuddered. The man was horribly pock-marked and stunk and trembled as if he had only just recovered from the ravages of the disease. Cattie had seen pock-marked people all her life, but she never ceased to fear contagion, and rightly, for the fever could strike anywhere and was usually fatal.

"Next door to the Widow Singer's!" the man called after the Dunlies.

"I had heard the Widow Singer runs a shop," Dunlie told his daughter. "What else can a decent widow do when she's too ugly to marry again and has little children to feed?"

The lane the Dunlies followed was narrow and crowded. Chickens picked at the few blades of grass and the insects that scurried under the scattered hay and rushes. Two bony dogs rolled around in the middle of the path, locked in a desperate fight for the hind leg of a deer. The Dunlies' approach began to attract attention.

"Lookeee!" an old woman in a tattered brown dress called from the front stoop of her one-room house, a structure of round poles and split, unpainted boards.

Cattie looked at her. The woman was dark-skinned, probably part Indian, wrinkled, barefoot, and toothless. Her bodice was unbuttoned and a dark-skinned baby clung to her breast. Cattie stared, and realized with shock that the woman was not actually older than thirty.

Cattie looked away. The open sewer gave off an unbearable stench, and pigs and dogs both rooted in it, fighting for odd bits of edible garbage. Flies were thick on the carcass of a dead cat.

"Watch your step, dear," Angus Dunlie cautioned Cattie, but she had already hoisted her petticoat and was watching it very closely, trying to avoid garbage

and find the few dry spots to put down her daintily
shod feet.

Two drunken trappers, their feet together and their
heads resting on heaps of bloody pelts, lay asleep under a majestic live oak in the middle of a square. Deliberately, Angus Dunlie led Cattie close enough to the
men so that she could smell the raw, musky odor of
the animals mixed with the smell of rum that had put
the men under.

"Ugh!" Cattie commented.

"Look there," Dunlie said. He pointed to a crowd
of men in a side yard. When the crowd broke apart
Cattie saw that they were watching a cockfight. A
huge black rooster attacked a scrawny yellow bird, filling the air with feathers. Squawking, the yellow rooster fastened itself on the black rooster's neck and hung
on. The bigger bird flew straight up into the air. Still
the yellow bird hung on. The black bird danced crazily in a circle, spinning the yellow bird as he moved,
then slowed, bowed his long neck, shrieked, and fell
back dead. The yellow rooster staggered away, and the
crowd shouted and clapped.

"That yaller 'un is brought in from Charleston," a
young voice said.

Cattie looked down. A small boy wearing a pair of
torn trousers and no shirt stood at her elbow. "He's a
killer!"

"Where is the house of Thomas Libby?" Cattie
asked him, wrinkling her nose.

"Go ahead, down there, see?" the boy said. "Aw,
com' on, I'll show you the way."

"We have our own market day here, see?" he said,
leading the Dunlies around a stagnant pool of mud.

Down the next lane, some market stalls had been set
up. A poulterer plucking a limp-necked goose filled
the air with a cloud of white feathers. A fishmonger

had set out a basket of small fish and hawked "fresh oy-sters." Near him a hind quarter of beef, black with flies, hung from a pole. A cow, swollen with calf, was tied to the same pole, and lowered her neck to stretch for a handful of moldy hay.

"Mr. Libby's house is there," the boy told them. Angus Dunlie gave the boy a penny. Cattie looked ahead for Micah. She did not see him. Instead, she saw a poor frame building exactly like all the others on the street, a one-story structure with an attic about as wide as a good-sized wagon and twice as deep.

"Thank ye, sir!" the boy said, astonished. He looked at Dunlie's silver buckles, at his fine white wig, and sprinted off to alert his friends.

A woman came out of the house. She was young and looked tired. Her hair straggled out of a dirty white cap. Her dress was simple, and two small children clung to her skirt. "Good day, sir," she said to Dunlie with an air of exhausted astonishment.

"Good day, madam. We are looking for a joiner named Micah Stone."

"Dear me! What, is he in trouble, then? That man is bound to my husband."

"No longer," Cattie whispered to her father. "*Was* bound. He is no longer bound, Papa."

"Are you the mistress of this house?" Dunlie asked.

"Yes, I am, sir." A baby's thin wail came out of the house and the woman turned. "The men were working out back earlier, but now they're off to Mr. Dunlie's house . . ."

"I am Angus Dunlie, madam."

"Oh! What's wrong?" Her voice shook with fear. She dropped to a curtsey.

"Nothing's wrong, Mistress Libby. May we trouble you . . . for a moment's rest in your house, if Stone isn't here?"

"Yes, of course, sir. Please come in. I can offer you a drop of beer."

"No, no thank you. Come along, Cattie," Angus said. In a lower voice he added, "Remember, it's in a house like this that you'll be living when you're wed to . . ."

Cattie stepped ahead of her father into the dark, smoky interior of the small tenement. A wooden cradle stood near the hearth, where a pot was boiling on a short, wrought-iron crane. Another baby played near the spinning wheel, sprawled out on the dirt floor. A rough wooden table and chairs and a straw mattress on a bed frame were the only furniture. Behind this room there was another, and a ladder led up to a hole in the ceiling and a room under the eaves.

Cattie stopped, choked by the closeness of the room. It was hotter inside than out. The air was stale and buzzed with flies. The smell of green corn boiling and unwashed bodies filled the room and the baby's wailing was continual.

"What's wrong with the baby?" she asked. Libby's wife had found a mug and dipped it into an open jar of beer.

"Oh, dear, I think it's throat distemper," she said sadly. "We lost our William to it last year."

"I'm sorry . . ." Cattie murmured.

"God's will be done," the woman replied. Every line of her thin body drooped. Her scrawny shoulders trembled as she bent over the cradle and gave the baby a drink of beer. "Mary, come rock your brother," she called to one of the little girls who was hiding in a corner. "Four living, of ten born."

"Cattie, I think we'd better be going," Dunlie said. Cattie headed for the open door at once. As her eyes had become adjusted to the dingy light, she had seen that the corners of the room were alive with vermin.

"I thank you, sir, for the honor of your visit," Mistress Libby called after them. "Try the ale house on the square as you go by, in case they've not left it for your house yet."

"Poor, poor woman," Cattie said. "She should have help . . ."

"Let's find the tavern," Dunlie said. "She is one of the lucky ones. Do you think you would do better, under the same circumstances?"

"But I could never be like her," Cattie protested, "I should always be myself."

"You will be very much yourself, if you decide to marry this workingman."

"What do you mean, Papa?"

"I mean just that. I shall not forbid you to marry him, but if you do, I shall not give you a dowry, or assist you in any way. I dare say this will be a grave disappointment to Mr. Stone, but that is the way it will be."

"Do you think Micah loves me for your money, Papa?"

"If he doesn't think of it, he's more of a fool that I suspect he is, but here we are—let's see if . . ."

Before Cattie could say more, they had reached the small tavern run in the house of Tim Pitkin, one of the many unlicensed gathering places that had sprung up in Savannah. Angus Dunlie took its measure as soon as he approached the rum-and-urine-scented front steps. Taking Cattie's hand, he led her into the public room.

A hush fell. The smoky, windowless room was filled with soldiers in uniform and half-naked Indians lounging on rough benches. A few men in workers' clothes stood together at a rum key, raising mugs. As strong as the smells of beer and rum and human beings was the stench of vomit.

Dunlie stepped coolly over a man lying just inside the front door. He was almost enjoying this. In fact, he'd never been in this particular tavern, but it did not surprise him; the better taverns were little different except perhaps for their clientele. Rum itself was illegal, but of course it was as common as Indian corn.

Cattie struggled to escape her father's grasp. She was speechless with shock and fear.

"Can I he'p you, gov'nor?" a burly man in a leather apron asked Dunlie. He stood six and a half feet tall and wore a full black beard.

"Perhaps," Dunlie said in a clear voice. He lifted a hand to pat his white wig. All eyes were on him and Cattie. "We are looking for a man called Micah Stone."

But Cattie had already spotted him. "Micah!" she gasped.

"Cattie!" Micah lurched forward from the cluster of men near the rum keg. His shirt and vest were dirty and wrinkled, and his eyes were clouded with drink. Cattie winced and pulled back, as far as her father's grasp would allow.

"I think we have something to discuss," Dunlie began. "My daughter tells me . . ."

"No!" Cattie shrieked. Her voice was angry and determined. "Please, Papa, let's go!"

"But Cattie . . ." Dunlie said.

"No! Nothing! Go!" she begged, sobbing. A drunken Indian had crept close to her and reached out to touch her arm. Jerking out of her father's control, she whirled and fled the room. A roar of laughter followed her, and it made her stamp her foot with fury as her father caught up with her.

Micah Stone was right behind Dunlie, and Cattie turned to him first.

"How disgusting you look!" she shouted. "I hate you! Get away from me!"

"But Cattie . . ." Micah protested, swaying, "we were just . . ."

Cattie stepped back. The smell of his breath sickened her. "Get away! I never want to see you again!"

A pained, confused look crossed Micah's face, and as the Dunlies hastened down the street, he sat down heavily on the steps of the ale house.

Cattie and her father walked home without exchanging another word. Cattie was choking back her sobs. When they had reached their own home, he said simply, "I think you have learned a lesson, Cattie. We need never speak of him again."

Cattie stalked off to her room without answering, but time was to prove Angus Dunlie wrong, very wrong.

Chapter Seven

A Christening—A Lust Sated— A Watery Farewell

The christening was over. General Oglethorpe, who served as godfather to his tiny namesake, James Oglethorpe Dunlie, was the first to propose a toast.

"God bless this child, a welcome gift to a fine family! May he grow and prosper along with the Colony of Georgia! Long live the King!"

"Long live the King!" echoed Jack Barstow, for whom the christening ceremony had been a torment. He had stood as near Fayette Dunlie as he dared, but she seemed blind to him. She had never looked prettier or seemed more inaccessible.

"God bless James Dunlie!" Fayette called out, then blushed at the fervor of her voice. She had been lost in daydreams of having her own sweet baby, Micah Stone to be its father, of course. Last night she had dreamed of Micah, dreamed of him carrying her away on horseback, away to some far-off place of their own.

Cattie Dunlie tapped her foot restlessly. After a

bout of crying, she had slept very well in the bed next to Fayette's. Already she considered her brief passion for Micah Stone to have been a childish episode. She had been wrong, silly even, to have considered him her equal, but that was all past. Still, feelings stirred by sexual awakening were not easily put by, and she had begun to look at other men, including Jack Barstow, with new interest.

Most of the Dunlies' friends and neighbors had been invited to the christening, and Angus Dunlie had taken care to include Philip Minis, the first white male child born in Savannah. Dunlie hoped his presence would be good luck. Now seven years old, the dark-eyed, dark-haired boy stood solemnly between his parents, Abraham and Abigail Minis, who had been among the forty Jews who had arrived in the first year of the colony and founded the congregation Mikvah Israel.

"Fayette! Cattie! Call Rose or Annie to bring more beer and more cakes," Catherine Dunlie ordered. Catherine was still weak, but she was pleased with the baby's progress. He was small and fretful, but he seemed possessed of a wiry strength that promised survival. For her son's christening, Catherine wore her best gown, a blue and white embroidered damask hoop-petticoat with cherry-colored stays, a lace-edged cap and a soft fichu draped over her shoulders. The stays, according to the fashion when Catherine had last seen London, were very tight and forced her milk-laden breasts uncomfortably high at the same time they poked into her still-swollen belly. Catherine was hot and wretched and longed to escape to her room as soon as her duties as hostess were discharged.

"Will you take some coffee?" she asked George Whitefield, the eloquent clergyman who had just rescued her baby son from heathenism and welcomed him into the church.

"Thank you, madam," Whitefield said. He was a slender, cherubic-looking man in his twenties, newly ordained, just back from England, and on fire with his plans for building an orphanage outside Savannah. Whitefield's mild physical appearance belied his evangelistic authority. As a preacher, he stirred souls and moved men and women to change their lives, exhorting them ten and twenty thousand at a time to experience "new birth" and battle the wrath of heaven. In England, Whitefield had lambasted the Anglican hierarchy as unconverted heathens and hypocrites and, as church doors closed against him, had perfected the art of preaching out of doors. In the colonies he used this skill to good advantage, attracting large crowds in New England and the middle colonies and electrifying them with his preaching.

In spite of his youth, Catherine Dunlie thought, the Reverend Mr. Whitefield was dutiful and seemed firm in his belief. In this he differed from the Anglican ministers who had preceded him in serving the Savannah congregation. Everyone had been outraged by the Reverend William Norris, who had held Whitefield's charge while he was recently in England. Norris had played at cards and worse instead of doing his duty.

"Where is the Reverend Mr. Norris now?" Catherine asked Whitefield curiously.

"Ah, madam, I believe he is preaching in Frederica," Whitefield replied. He was wondering how soon to ask Dunlie for a contribution to his Orphan House. The man clearly had some money to spare: his new house was spacious if simply furnished, and the silver plate in the dining room could . . . could better serve the Lord. "But likely General Oglethorpe can give us news of Norris . . ." Whitefield said, thinking of his orphans.

"Norris! What? The man is not well liked," Oglethorpe said gruffly. In fact, Norris had gotten his German maid with child and was denounced by his congregation in Frederica as a fornicator. His predecessor there had died of drink. Men were free to worship as they chose in Georgia; no faith was outlawed except Papism, but to date, the clergy had not distinguished themselves by living good lives.

"How sad," commented Catherine.

"Sad also that we could not celebrate this sacrament in the new Christ Church," Whitefield said, "but God willing, we will lay the cornerstone for it next month."

Next month . . . Oglethorpe thought, his mind drifting to the Florida campaign. More than ever on occasions like this one he felt the great gulf between himself, the military man, and these civilians. After all, Savannah was naught but a frontier community in a buffer colony engaged in a world-wide imperial struggle. They could build twenty churches if they liked, but what good would they be if the Spanish marched up the Georgia coast?

"How soon do you move the regiment south?" Angus Dunlie asked. Dunlie had seen his son baptized with a quiet and profound pleasure. It was a turning point, he hoped, in the realization of all his personal dreams. Cattie seemed to have put her foolishness behind her. She had been mollified by his gift of a gold locket, a trinket he'd inherited from his own mother and saved for Fayette's wedding day . . . but there were times when a man had to change his plans, and Fayette was content with a copy of *The Whole Duty of Man*.

"We sail tomorrow," Oglethorpe answered.

Dunlie nodded. He would miss his friend. A man

with the reserve characteristic of Scots, he did not make friends easily, and he was pleased that the General had been present for this occasion.

"And you know, young Barstow sails with me," Oglethorpe said. "He is among thirty men from town." Oglethorpe was paying the wages of the Georgia provincials from his own pocket, but he was confident that Parliament would soon reimburse him.

"My hopes go with you . . ." Dunlie said.

"And my blessings," Whitefield added.

"Thank you, my friends," Oglethorpe said. "Angus, I have a gift for my godson . . ."

Eyes turned toward the General—erect, proud, and resplendent in his lobster-red coat shining with gold braid. Catherine took a deep breath and shifted her weight, easing the pressure of her stays on her soft flesh. Dear God, she thought, I hope it's gold.

"At my own christening," Oglethorpe began, lowering his voice now that he was the center of attention, "which took place, I am told, in the church of St. Martin-in-the-Fields in London, and was performed by the Archbishop of Canterbury, I was given a fine gift by my own godfather—a parcel of land in Kent amounting to sixty acres. Today, then, I would like to make a similar gift to this young Georgian. I shall give him a gift of land, also—six hundred acres of fine farmland, with the wish that he and his children and his children's children shall plow it and plant it and prosper."

"Most generous," commented George Whitefield. He had gotten only five hundred for his Orphan House.

"On behalf of my son, I thank you," Dunlie said, unwillingly remembering that other invocation of his progeny, called down in wrath by Orde Barstow.

"Land . . ." sighed Catherine. There was so much

land here in America. The baby, lying in state in his butternut bassinet, squalled and she hastened to his side. He was hungry. This was the excuse she needed to get upstairs and out of these stays.

But the party had just begun. Angus Dunlie had set out a huge silver punchbowl, full of a spiced wine punch that was making its cheerful effect known to the assembled guests. Out of consideration to the ladies, some of the gentlemen strolled out to the piazza to smoke their pipes and talk about planting; Fayette was persuaded to play on the spinet in the room her father called his office. The General followed her into that pleasant, airy room and sat in her father's favorite high-backed chair to listen and admire Fayette.

"Isn't it a shame there's no dancing?" Cattie asked Jack Barstow.

Jack was reeling from a conversation with Fayette. She had snubbed him, there was no other way to understand it. He had asked her if she would care to take a stroll out into the fresh air. She had replied, "No, thank you. I think it would be better if we were not seen walking or talking alone together, and besides, I cannot encourage you, for I am in love with another."

"Dancing?" Jack asked Cattie. He could hear the tinkling music from the room across the hall. It hurt him because Fayette was playing it. He was stunned, plain stunned, at the abrupt collapse of all his dreams.

"Shall I set out supper now, ma'am?" Rose asked Cattie, and Jack fancied that Rose winked at him. He stared at the maid, at the pink glow of her cheeks, at the way her white breasts curved over the top of her tight-laced bodice. His senses stirred, as yet unfocused, still partly trained on Fayette.

"Ask my mother," Cattie shrugged.

"She's gone up with the baby," Rose replied. "I guess I'll start, then."

"Why not?" Cattie said, tapping her foot and swaying slightly. Rose, who had known Cattie all of her life and was her closest friend, giggled as she left the room. Cattie was in a reckless mood, she saw that.

"Is your sister betrothed?" Jack asked Cattie, the words scraping his throat.

"Fayette? Why, of course not! Fayette is not interested in love, only in reading and music and writing in her journal book and . . . in talking to Papa. Whatever gave you that idea?"

"Just something she said."

"Fayette is too serious. And I declare, you have a long face, too, Jack, though why you shouldn't dance with me on the day before you go off to war, I can't say!"

Even Jack could tell that he had been issued an invitation, and from an extremely attractive young woman. Cattie was radiant in a floral-printed tabby silk dress of Prussian blue, laced very tight over stays and cut very low over her pale pink breasts. Her hair was shiny and pale as corn silk, her blue eyes opened wide. She smiled as she put out her hands, and Jack, who had never danced a step in his life, took them in his.

"You have two beautiful daughters," Catherine's friend Sarah Whitman commented to Angus Dunlie, who had strolled into the room to watch Jack and Cattie dance. Sarah and her husband, Robert, were the Dunlies' closest neighbors.

"Aye, I am a lucky man," Dunlie said dryly. Cattie's blatantly ripe beauty disturbed him. Thank God, he thought, I have one daughter who is both modest and obedient.

"Excuse me, Mr. Dunlie," George Whitefield said. "I must go soon."

"Before supper?" Sarah Whitman asked. "The servants are setting up the tables already. Do stay."

"Thank you, but I must hear the prayers of the orphans before they go to bed," Whitefield said. He paused, then began again. "My usual fee for a baptism is ten shillings."

"A fair price for God's blessing," Dunlie answered, "Come with me into my office."

The Whitmans followed Dunlie and Whitefield, leaving Jack and Cattie alone.

"La! Such fun!" Cattie exulted as she spun around in a graceful improvisation. The gold locket bounced on her flushed bosom. "Don't you like dancing?" she asked.

"I like it very much," Jack vowed. His eyes were fixed on Cattie. Was it possible that he had loved the wrong sister? "But I am hot! Shall we stroll together down to the creek?"

"I can think of nothing I'd like more," Cattie replied, and Jack, his ego much soothed, offered her his arm.

Orde Barstow had gone out to his harness shed to have a conversation with his overseer. Beene was occupied in repairing tackle, but he set the work aside willingly when Barstow entered the low-ceilinged shed.

"Damn niggers break everything," Beene complained.

"Untrained," Barstow said. "We need more trained servants."

"I'm willing to teach them, but they can't even talk English," Beene said.

"They'll learn. I wanted to ask you, Beene, about something new. I talked with a trader who's lived in St. Vincent for ten years. They have a sort of cotton down there that grows perennial, a hardy, high-quality type. What do you think of experimenting with cotton?"

"I don't know, sir. You need a lot of labor. Where?"

"Maybe on the Island. I want to find out more about it."

"Trouble with the Island, sir, it's liable to be run over with Spanish any day now."

"Where'd you hear that, Beene?"

"Oh, that's the common talk. The regiment sails tomorrow to fight in Florida, you know."

"I heard."

"And I hear your stepson is going with them."

"Damn fool. He'll end up cannon fodder."

"Could be, sir, that's what I heard."

"Did you hear where the young rascal is sleeping these days? Has he accepted the King's guinea?"

"I hear he's not a regular soldier, sir, so likely not. He's some special aide to the General. Heard he's spending time at the Dunlies' place, sir, that's one thing I heard for sure."

"You are remarkably well informed," Barstow commented.

Absent-mindedly, he switched the sides of his boots with his riding crop as he crossed the barnyard back to the house. A taste of real battle would toughen Jack up, show him the easy slide from life to death. Not that he wished the boy dead. Barstow was beginning to feel lonely, and his real hope was that Jack would return, beg his pardon, and come to him for advice on how to live his life.

"You know, I sail with the regiment in the morning," Jack said to Cattie. They were seated very close together on the lowest branch of the willow tree at the far edge of the Dunlies' south pasture. Both of them had removed their shoes and their feet dangled into the creek below.

"I know. Are you excited?"

"Sure I am. I am to be the surgeon's assistant. Perhaps after this I'll have a career in the Army."

"I'll come out tomorrow to wave good-bye, Jack."

"Will you kiss me good-bye, as well?"

"I guess so." Cattie laughed, wrinkling up her blue eyes. She had never drunk so much wine punch before, never danced so fast, never felt quite so careless and grown-up. It was the experience with Micah Stone, she reckoned. It had matured her. And to think, she marveled, that I thought myself full grown before. Why then I was just a child.

"Well, Cattie," Jack wheedled, "if you'll be giving me a kiss in the morning, why won't you give me one now?"

"Oh! Just because," Cattie laughed, and she started to pull a bit away from him, but Jack's hand covered hers and stopped her. His hand looked so big and tanned on top of her small, white one.

"Want to hear a secret?" Jack asked.

"A secret! What's your secret?"

"It's about you."

"Then for sure I want to hear it."

"What will you pay me to hear it?"

"Pay! What's it worth? A penny!"

"Any secret about you is worth a pistole at least."

Cattie laughed. "Watch out! Take care! You might fall into the creek!" She bounced with all her weight on the willow branch, catching Jack off-guard. He swayed back, then righted himself, and took the opportunity to wrap his arms around Cattie.

"You saved me!" he gasped, affecting fright. "For that, I'll tell you my secret."

"It seems I shall hear it no matter what I do."

Jack took a deep breath. His maleness was aroused almost beyond endurance, and the nearness of her made him ache for relief. "I think . . . I think I've been . . . I think I am falling in love with you."

Cattie sighed. Love. Love was in the air. She was pleased and flattered and yet . . . she ached for something else. It was still early evening, not yet dusk, but the songs of a thousand restless insects filled the air. The creek below their feet made soft, seductive sounds, the wind rustled the willow's drooping leaves, and in the distance, she could hear voices inside her family's home. She knew herself to be a part of it all, and yet she felt apart. She felt the same soft currents in herself as in the water and the willow, and yet she felt oddly frustrated, as if some important connection with her feelings was still to be made.

"Are you angry?" Jack asked.

"Noooo . . ." Cattie admitted. The way she felt was too hard to explain, all the harder that she didn't understand it herself.

"Damn! I've spoiled everything!" Jack said, confused by her silence. "You said Fayette was too serious. Why are you being so serious yourself, Cattie?"

"I don't know . . . I guess I'd rather not talk so much. Couldn't you just kiss me?"

Jack could and did willingly. Her lips were soft and trembled under his. He sensed the fear that hid under her boldness and it excited him. He kissed her harder, drinking deep, one hand firm around her waist, the other drawn to her half-exposed breasts, the sight of which had maddened him for hours. Cattie shuddered when his rough fingers found her nipples. She half-wanted to pull away, for his fingers were awkward, yet his touch, as it disturbed her, also pleased her. She swallowed hard, feeling something come alive inside her. The games she had played with Micah had not led to intercourse, but they had provoked her desire for it; she was awakened, bodily at least, she was prepared, capable of feeling passion.

"My sweet," Jack whispered, lifting his mouth from hers. He looked at her clear, innocent face. Her cheeks were flushed, her lips parted and rosy. "So pretty, so pretty . . ."

Cattie opened her eyes and they filled with an expression of fright. When she looked, she felt she oughtn't . . . but if she didn't look, if she let go and just let herself feel . . . why, she couldn't think at all.

Jack was not a virgin, but his experience had been limited to a few hasty sessions—one night with the half-breed daughter of an Indian trader and a few tumbles with loose-moraled servant girls in town. He had never seduced a woman of his own kind, but he had thought of it, fantasized about dark-haired Fayette for hours on end during the last long patrol. But all his fantasies were weak and pale compared to the reality of Cattie Dunlie. She was so warm, so real, so near! He was overwhelmed and his member strained, hard as a bone.

"Jack?" Cattie whispered hesitantly, doubtfully.

"Oh, my sweet beauty," he groaned. With a graceful leap he dropped off the willow to the soft ground beneath and put up his arms to catch her. "Come . . ." he wheedled, "come down and rest awhile with me."

Cattie fell into his arms with a whoosh of skirts, and he took a deep breath of her skin's scent. Taking advantage of the moment, Jack ripped off his shirt and spread it on the ground. For a moment Cattie hesitated, then she sat down daintily, hugging her knees with her bare feet between them. Jack grasped them with his hands, then ran his fingers up her calves, soothing her as he would a nervous colt, stroking her incredibly soft white skin, cupping her knees in his hands, parting them slightly, then pushing aside her petticoat and underskirt.

She sighed, keeping her eyes closed, and her free hands fluttered to muss his hair. How thick it is, she thought, and so like a creature's pelt. Her fingers touched his ears, slid along the hard cords of his neck onto his bare shoulders.

Holding her knees, Jack leaned over Cattie's body and kissed a path from her throat down to her breasts. She wriggled, thrusting her head back, rolling her head from side to side, feeling a surge of heat in her loins, feeling wet there, as she had when she had touched herself sometimes.

Jack fumbled, trying to get past the silky stuff that barred him from burying his face in her skin. He encountered resistance: laces, stays, something that cinched her dress tight around her waist, the bodice mysteriously fastened . . . His stroking, his touch through the thin fabric, aroused Cattie even more. She lay back, lifting her hands above her head so that her breasts strained upward, nearly out of the bodice.

The sight unleashed a determination in Jack, akin to a ferocity. With one gesture, he ripped the bodice down off Cattie's shoulders and freed her breasts. They were beautifully formed and stood out distinctly from her chest, hand-sized, pure white with dark pink nipples. Taking a deep breath, Jack sucked one into his mouth and Cattie gasped.

Very quickly, Jack unfastened her petticoat and skirt and pushed them off her body. The rush of cool damp air on her naked skin was as shocking as being plunged into cool water. She heard the creek murmur, heard her own ragged, excited breathing, and the slapping, sucking sounds of him kissing her, licking and tonguing and nibbling at her breasts. Wildness, instinct possessed her now; she thrust her loins up at him unthinkingly, encountered his erect member, now free of his breeches. It was so hot, so hard.

Jack was beyond stopping, beyond speaking or hearing. He had never felt such passion. All his energy was focused on this unexpected, unhoped for, unearthly pleasure. He panted, making low, fierce sounds that alarmed Cattie so that she wriggled and twisted under his long body.

His hands shook now as he stroked her, gentling her again, sensing her fright, but unable to take his mouth off her. The texture of her skin was so fine, so satin-smooth. He rolled his tongue around each breast, then nibbled at them, taking up the skin in tiny love bites. He nibbled, he sucked at her nipples, he lunged upward to catch the lobes of her ears, her top lip, her bottom lip.

Cattie whimpered, intensely aroused. Her eyes opened. Jack's pale, muscular body was shadowed and shone a greenish silver in the faint light that filtered through the willow. He looked strange to her, he *was* strange, a powerful and controlling stranger. As she watched, stunned, his head dove between her thighs, and again he was biting her. She hated it, it hurt, and yet it jolted her nerves and changed her. She felt now that whatever happened, had to happen. Whatever he did and made her do, had to be. She was completely open and completely stilled—not passive, for she felt slippery and subtle and strong, but submissive in spirit.

Her attention, emboldened, fixed on his member. It thrust at her, outstretched, reaching as she looked down her own naked body. She held it in her hand and felt its life. Jack's fingers pinched her sex and she stiffened. He was less gentle, but she was less afraid now. Then he bit her—there—and she screamed and closed her eyes.

His hands were reaching, taking. His fingers bore into her sides and her buttocks as he lifted her onto his member, thrusting it inside her. Cattie winced in surprise, writhed in momentary pain, then forgot pain as he held her so tightly to him that she felt their hearts beat together, and he moved her with him in a pulsing, rocking motion. She felt his tension grow, felt the muscles of his long legs, his strong back, felt herself helpless but cared for in his fierce grasp.

Then wonderfully, in his passion, she found her own place, her own rhythm, her own pleasure—more amazing than she could have dreamed—and she cried out in wordless joy as she took her own ecstasy as he took his.

When Jack left Savannah the next morning at dawn's light, Cattie was still at home in bed.

Colonel Vanderdussen and the South Carolina volunteers had gone on ahead by foot and wagon, taking the old Indian trail that led south. Oglethorpe and the Savannah men were to travel by boat, carrying supplies and artillery, including some badly needed pieces of siege artillery from South Carolina, large mortars and some eighteen-pound cannons.

Savannah was quiet and peaceful. The Union Jack flew on the Strand and from the mast of the small sloop anchored in the river. Yamacraw Indians, catching the mood of excitement, were crossing and recrossing in canoes the river they called Blue Water. As the mist lifted, it promised to be a clear day, and the sun glinted off the swift-flowing water.

Oglethorpe had ordered his men and the goods packed into fourteen sturdy piraguas—long, flat-bottomed boats built from large cypress or cedar logs, larger than canoes, their nearest relatives. Each had two gaff-rigged masts, oars, and a small stern cabin. Each could carry from twenty to thirty-five tons.

Jack Barstow was assigned to the first piragua. He felt stiff, exhausted, and very sorry to leave town. All his thoughts—at first—were of Cattie, most wondrous of women, and he scanned the shore for a glimpse of her. When, if ever, would he see her again, and how did she feel about him? He longed to know. Before boarding, some of the men had passed a bottle of rum, and Jack took a long draught, along with a handful of dry corn cake, for his breakfast. The rum hurt his stomach, but it cleared his head. He began to feel a bit better and less guilty about leaving Cattie. The excitement of departure—all the men in some semblance of uniform, the General exalted with important last-minute arrangements, the shots fired in farewell—everything diverted him and lifted his spirits, and he felt as only a young man can, the thrill of being part of a regiment, a man among men going off to war.

Angus Dunlie had ridden down to the Strand to see the regiment off, but Jack did not see him. Dunlie caught Oglethorpe's eye, and the General was pleased to see him. A good man, Oglethorpe thought . . . it's for his kind that we must rid this land of the Spanish menace.

"Farewell! God bless you!" Dunlie called out, waving.

"Ahoy! Ahoy!" one of the men called out as the last boat caught the river's current and headed for sea. The General settled down among his men, as was his custom. He was worried about this campaign, and he had good reason to be, but on one account, at least, he had planned very well.

To keep the convoy together on the rough, hot voyage south Oglethorpe had put all the beer in the lead piragua. He was confident that no matter how far apart the boats would drift each day, they would meet each night for a rendezvous.

Chapter Eight

*Fayette in Love—Cattie in Trouble—Jack
Barstow on the Southern Front*

During the next two months, the Dunlie sisters drifted
apart. Although they had always shared a bedroom,
each respected the other's privacy, and each girl had
always had her own thoughts and pursuits. But in the
weeks following the christening, each sister moved
further away from the family and became increasingly
concerned with projects and problems of her own.

Cattie had told Fayette about her first feelings for
Micah Stone and the horrifying tour their father had
taken her on, and the confession had plunged Fayette
into a chaos of confusion and despair. How blind she
had been! She had never suspected that her sister was
carrying on with Micah all the while she had been sa-
voring an innocent, unrequited love for him. She had
never dreamed of being as bold as Cattie had been—to
sneak off and meet him in secret—alone—and to make
him fall in love with her.

"Did you really love him?" Fayette asked her sister in a voice that trembled and quavered. Her green eyes could not meet her sister's.

"Fah! Of course I didn't! I was silly. How could I love a man so—so common?"

"Don't you think, though, that he's a fine, well-made and honest man?" Fayette asked, easing the pain in her heart by voicing her own opinion.

"Handsome he is, but a man of that class has nothing to offer me," Cattie did not tell her sister about Jack Barstow, but Fayette noticed that Cattie was changed after the christening. Cattie had spent the whole day in bed, but she refused to admit that she was sick or troubled about anything particular. "Just tired out," she told Fayette, and Fayette had to be satisfied.

Cattie bore that night's aftermath and consequences alone, although she was not aware of all of them until some time had passed. She knew, though, that she would never be the same again. She knew that Jack Barstow was gone, gone leaving her bruised and altered. Cattie counted ten tiny bruises on her body when she swam alone in the creek the next afternoon. Some of them were on her arms, some on her calves, and others on the inside of her thighs—those marks too clearly the traces of strong fingers gripping in passion. Cattie frowned when she examined her body, but she never knew that her neck and shoulders were also bruised, for she had no looking glass.

Cattie's emotions were jangled, too, in the first days after the regiment had sailed south. When she thought back to the time with Jack it seemed incredible—all like a dream, and she felt so different that she thought at first she had to hide, thought everyone must see it, but no one except Fayette seemed to notice at all. Her mother was very busy with the baby, Jemmie. Her fa-

ther, as usual, occupied himself with supervision of the
fields and his accounts; and Fayette was more aloof
and self-obsessed than ever.

As she pondered her life, Cattie thought that perhaps what she wanted was to marry at once. Probably
she could marry Jack, when he came home, but if not
Jack, then another man who could offer her security
and affection. In her own way—erratically and impulsively—she set about reviewing the few possibilities.
Every eligible bachelor in Savannah must be considered, and, she remembered, there were new ones arriving from England every few months.

Although he might have been distressed on other accounts, Angus Dunlie would have been pleased to see
how cool-headed and practical Cattie was in approaching the problem of her marriage. In fact, he was still
suspicious that she favored Micah Stone and watched
her with a sharp eye. His suspicions were misplaced.

For it was Fayette who had set out on a path not
calculated to please her fond father or any other member of her family.

Fayette, after much prayer and reflection, after
long, despairing epistles committed to her journal-
book, had decided to woo and win Micah Stone herself. As she wrote in that diary, on the evening in late
May when she commenced her campaign:

> Because my feeling for him has not diminished with
> knowledge of his dalliance with my sister, but has in-
> deed deepened, I have determined to make my feelings
> known to him. I still know not how he feels for me.
> Doubtless, he has never noticed me at all, for I am too
> shy and plain, not pretty like Cattie, but I know that
> I have many qualities that recommend me for wifehood,
> and I cannot be so dishonest as to deny my heart much
> longer.

In truth, Fayette was far from plain, but lovely in her modest, dark-haired way. Her avowed intention made her lovelier than ever. There was a new lilt to her step, a new purpose in the set of her slim shoulders, a new glow to her clear complexion.

Micah Stone's work on the Dunlie house had been completed just before the christening party, and he was now hired out by the colony's Trustees to work on the building of Christ Church in Johnson Square. The long-postponed construction of the church was an activity of great interest in Savannah, and Fayette, who was known to be devout, had no need to lie when she told her father she wanted to walk down to the square to observe the building of the church.

And so she did, dressed neatly and becomingly in a brown-sprigged fustian gown with a simple trim of narrow lace along the short sleeves and with her dark, curly hair piled up on her head. She walked down to Johnson Square and stood patiently beside the frame structure of the church, watching the men at work. There were a few other spectators.

One of them, the Dunlies' neighbor, Robert Whitman, spoke to Fayette. "A well-designed structure," he commented. "The pine was cut by the settlers at Ebenezer."

Fayette only nodded politely and Whitman bid her good day.

Micah Stone noticed Fayette, of course. He remembered her well from her father's house, but he was understandably wary about any further social entanglements with the Dunlies. His public quarrel with Cattie had been his last meeting with her, for Micah was proud. He would not beg, he would not force unwelcome attentions on a woman, and he was aware, and had been all along, of differences in station that had come to America from the old land.

Just seeing Micah and watching him at work filled Fayette with a quiet joy. At first, watching him was enough, but after a few trips to Johnson Square, this joy no longer sufficed. She longed to speak to him, so she timed her next visit to be at the end of his working day.

The story of the Dunlies' visit to the tavern had made the rounds of the neighborhood, and some of Micah's fellow laborers had been present. None of them failed to tease Micah about his new "sweetheart." Micah ignored them, but he suffered—both from the teasing and the incident with Cattie—and his mood was not amiable on the day when Fayette approached him as he was leaving the church.

"Hello, Micah Stone," she said simply.

"What do you want with me, Miss Dunlie? Why do you come so often to watch us building the church?"

Fayette was so nervous it was hard for her to speak, but she had decided that she must be as bold as Cattie had been, and as honest and straightforward as she wished him to be with her.

"The first thing I want is to become friends with you."

"Friends? Why should we be friends? Did your sister send you to tease me?"

"I cannot bear to have you speak to me so." Her voice trembled and Micah felt her sincerity, but he did not melt.

"Why? What relationship do you imagine could be between us?"

"Only let us walk together, Micah, and talk."

Micah was glad enough to lead Fayette away from the amused eyes of his mates, and they both heard laughter as they turned down Bull Street and headed for the Strand.

Fayette was unsteady on her feet as she walked with

her head turned toward Micah. She noticed everything: he was sweaty from working, and sawdust had settled on his yellow hair. His sleeves were rolled up, showing his tanned, well-muscled arms. He frowned.

"Where are you leading me, Miss Dunlie? I am tired and thirsty."

"Oh, please don't call me Miss Dunlie. You must call me Fayette."

"Must I?" Suddenly he laughed. It was amusing to see similarities between this girl and her sister. Their accents were so alike, and their innocence.

"And you mustn't think that I have come because of Cattie . . . or my father. They do not know. My wanting to know you has nothing at all to do with them."

"Hasn't it?"

"And I am sorry to tire you. Only walk with me a few moments. I have something I long to discuss with you." Fayette was astonished at her own boldness, yet pleased. She had hidden her feelings inside for so long, it was far easier to speak than she had imagined and gave immediate relief.

Micah was intrigued. He was still too wary to be flattered, but despite his knock-about life, he was relatively inexperienced with women. That this lovely, well-bred girl would take such an interest in him was, at the least, curious. Perhaps her behavior was motivated by some upper-class custom he knew nothing about.

"Something to discuss? What is it?" His voice had a country lilt and delighted Fayette.

"For some time I have been aware that my feelings . . . for you . . . are different from my feelings for anyone else," she said solemnly.

Micah stopped stock-still. "But . . ."

"No, please, let me speak. It's not easy for me, but I

must. You see, I have never been in love before, but I love you. I have thought about it, Micah, and prayed for guidance, and I have observed you as well and often as I can. But I need to know, soon—not today—if there is any chance you could ever return my affections."

"We have hardly spoken a word to each other!" Micah protested.

"I know, nor did it seem likely unless I made bold enough to insist upon it."

"I do not know you at all! Besides . . ." his voice dropped.

"I know that you thought you . . . cared for my sister, and that my father did not approve. I have thought about that, Micah, and it gives me both pain and hope. Cattie and I are very different. . . you don't know that yet, but I hope you will come to see it. And yet, your caring for her may mean that you are, as am I, in that stage of life when a man or woman must leave his parents and cleave unto . . ."

"Wait! You go too fast! Let's walk along the Strand, down to the end where it is more breezy," Micah suggested. They turned past a row of shops. The scent of fresh-baked bread was tantalizing as they passed George Parker's bakery, and a line of housewives and serving maids at the public well stared at them curiously.

"I guess you think I'm immodest," Fayette said. "I guess you think I'm o'er bold."

"Well . . . I never knew anyone who put things as you do."

"I will always be honest with you, as long as we both shall live." Her voice was charmingly serious.

Micah was attracted to Fayette, far more than he could admit, but he was confused. He had had a strong feeling that this could not be true. Perhaps she was teasing him, leading him into foolishness as her sister had. There was nothing on earth as strong as the power of money, he feared. Suppose she and he did love—just suppose—what would it matter if her family held her back? He could never offer her the pleasures she was accustomed to having.

"Don't you know that there are stronger . . . differences between people than sex or sense, Fayette? No matter what your feelings for me might become, it cannot change that I have been bound as a servant, that I have been a mechanic by trade, and will soon be a plain farmer."

"I have thought about that. I am not like Cattie. I am very sure of my mind and my heart. And I have decided that if you cannot love me, I will not marry at all."

"Oh, Fayette! You are so innocent! What do you know of real life?"

"Everything I have been able to learn, so far."

Micah laughed. "That is fair enough!"

His smile, his laugh, sent a bolt of good feeling through Fayette, and she lowered her head modestly for a minute. Her eyes were swimming with tears. Not looking, she stumbled over a root on the path, and Micah caught her.

"Oh, dear!" She laughed with him. "I shall be tumbling into the river, next thing! I am blinded with love."

"You don't see me?" Micah teased, turning Fayette so that she could look straight into his face.

She looked, and their eyes caught and held. "Oh! Yes, I see you!"

"And does seeing me, even this first time, does it still please you?" he asked as he held both her arms in his strong hands.

"So much."

Micah's blue eyes were serious. "Well, then, I think we should agree to ponder it, and to meet again."

"Tomorrow!"

"Tomorrow, if you will."

"Thank you, Micah."

"Let us meet here, then, far from prying eyes, but if you choose not to come, Fayette, I will not be angry . . . or surprised."

"Only death could keep me."

"You sure make Mistah Barstow a happy man," Saraby said to Zonah.

"Why sure I do. I try to. And I love that man."

"Where'd you get that baby, Zonah?"

"I found him, Saraby, yes I did."

"That was a lucky day when you found this baby."

The two women sat knee to knee on the side piazza of the Barstow house. Orde Barstow had gone with Harley Beene to inspect some land a few hours' ride off, and Zonah and Saraby were carding wool in the cool breeze. Byron Barstow, the baby under discussion, lay happily in a basket at their feet.

Carding wool was a painstaking operation. The rough wool was greased with precious pork grease and then combed between two thin boards set with bent wire teeth.

Saraby took a card in her left hand and rested it on her knee. Then she drew a tuft of wool across it several times, letting some of it catch on the teeth. She then passed the second card over the first until all the fibers were brushed parallel. With a deft and catchy motion, she rolled the wool off into small fleecy balls that were ready for spinning.

Zonah had taught Saraby how to card, and now Saraby was as agile as she was. While they worked, they talked, about the same subjects over and over again, the subjects that pleased them: life's struggle, the journeys each had taken, the meals they would cook next, and now the baby.

"That sure is a good baby," Saraby said. "What do you call him?"

"Byron. He calls him Byron Barstow."

Saraby laughed. "What a name!"

Zonah laughed, too. "That's what he calls him!"

"He's growing fast, that baby."

"Yes. He's bigger."

"Bigger every day, that baby!"

"All the little babies growing up," Zonah commented. Her own belly was swelling again with Orde Barstow's own child. "Mmmmmmhmmmmm," she hummed. It was a hot day. The sound of the heat was the singing of a million locusts, the smell of it was a blend of flowers and grasses and wood smoke and the pork grease they had worked into the wool.

"What d'you say happened to Mistah Jack?" Saraby asked.

"He's gone a long way. With the soldiers."

"Sure hope God brings him back safe," Saraby said. She sighed.

Only two hundred Indians, of the thousands he had expected, showed up to assist Oglethorpe in his campaign against St. Augustine. More than half of them were Cherokee. The General had counted on the Lower Creeks, banked on the enthusiastic reception they had given him when he visited their villages, but he was disappointed. Although the Creeks loved to fight, they 'fell back on their traditional neutrality when it came to this war between Europeans.

The Indian auxiliary troops had white officers, but most of the Indians were too independent and proud to obey commands from white men, so their officers served mainly as interpreters. The Indians only intermittently obeyed their own leaders; it made them an unpredictable element in the face of fire.

Oglethorpe's crack troops were the regiments of Scottish Highlanders, mostly from Darien, a settlement south of Savannah. The Highlanders were under the command of Big John Mackintosh, and they dressed in the traditional Highland fashion, in wool tartans about ten yards long, gathered and belted around their waists into knee-length kilts. The tartans were incongruous in Georgia's heat, but at night they served as blankets.

The Highlanders were organized into ranger units of fifty men each and armed with traditional Scottish claymores, dirks, and pistols. The British rangers wore English checked shirts and carried swords and hatchets. There were not enough horses to go around; the lieutenant sent to buy them had been robbed in a Savannah inn.

As recently as ten years ago, these troops had fought each other in the mountains between England and Scotland. Now they fought side by side in unfamiliar semitropical marshes and swamps, united against Spain.

The principal defense of St. Augustine was Castillo di San Marcos, a massive, well-built stone fort just outside of the town. Two miles north was little Fort Mosa, built out of earthworks to protect a settlement of slaves who had run away from South Carolina. Sixteen miles north of that was Fort Diego, a private plantation fortified by its owner. In charge of these scattered fortresses was Governor Manuel de Montiano. Oglethorpe knew little about the Spanish governor, but he hoped he was in awe of the British Army and that he would fight by the rules.

Unfortunately, Oglethorpe had blown his blockade

of the harbor at St. Augustine before he got his troops out of their tents at Frederica. The *Tartar,* a twenty-gun British warship, had been sent to cover the approach to the fort. The governor of Cuba had sent a convoy of two sloops and six half-galleys with more than two hundred men and a large supply of provisions. The *Tartar* was supposed to intercept the convoys, but three days before her sister ship, the *Squirrel,* arrived to relieve the *Tartar,* her captain gave up and sailed north. The Spanish slipped in, and when the poor *Squirrel* unsuspectingly arrived, the Spanish half-galleys charged out of the harbor and routed her.

Oglethorpe was justifiably shaken when he heard this news, but it was too late to turn back. All his troops—Highlanders, regulars, provincials from South Carolina and Georgia, and Indians—were assembled and waiting. The British Empire was waiting and watching, too; this war had been given a name. It was called the war of Jenkins's Ear, after the sad case of an English smuggler who had lost his ears to the Spanish and taken them in a jar to Parliament the year before.

Impatient to fight, Oglethorpe marched his troops south from Frederica at a fast pace. He never did anything slowly and only pushed his men as hard as he pushed himself. They made the long march through deep sand under a murderous sun. Jack Barstow saw two men die of sunstroke, trying to keep up; the Indians and some of the independent-minded Highlanders dropped behind.

Finally, the soldiers and their support troops arrived at the Saint Johns River, pitched tents, and set up camp. On the way they had captured Fort Diego, an easy victory, for the fortified plantation was held by only fifty men, including members of Diego Spinosa's household. But Oglethorpe was pleased by this small triumph, and though many of the men were exhausted, he decided to set out that night with a detachment of regulars and the Highland Company, to go back to Fort Diego and resupply.

Jack Barstow rode with the rangers who escorted the General. They set out after a light supper, taking advantage of the relative cool of the evening. They had seventeen miles to cover and pulled the supply carts behind them.

The moon was full but there was a high wind blowing heavy clouds past it, creating sudden deep, dark stretches that made the night heat seem denser and more oppressive. Jack's bones ached as he rode behind the General, and he had plenty of time to think about the dangers of the trip. Next to Jack rode a German from Savannah, young Gabriel Baugh, a ranger with thick blond hair and a fair skin burned red by the sun.

"Ach! It is so hot!" Baugh complained.

"That it is," Jack agreed. The heavy dew had drenched his feet and legs as they rode through thick marsh grasses, and now the blowing sand was sticking to his clothes and skin. He was as miserable as the rest of the men, as uncomfortable as Oglethorpe himself, whom Jack knew was suffering from dozens of insect bites.

"I have a feeling that the woods all around are full of Indians," Baugh told Jack.

"They may be," Jack said. Indians were just one of his fears. He worried about the wisdom of this maneuver . . . he'd heard complaints about the General, and not just the usual grumblers among the regulars. Vanderdussen's troops had been openly critical about this tactic and had warned the General not to waste energy on this midnight march.

But Oglethorpe had insisted. His personal energy

seemed unlimited; he would march all night and his men must keep up with him.

Every hour they had a brief rest stop, and three times they stopped to drink the warm beer they carried with them. Most of the men marched and drank in glum silence, but Gabriel Baugh was in a talkative mood.

"I'm thinking of planting indigo when I get home," he told Jack, "I've got land right on the river. That's if I get home."

"Of course you will," Jack said. He trusted the General, and the regular soldiers, above all—the regulars were hardened fighters. They would reach Fort Diego and then go on to take St. Augustine.

When dawn broke, Fort Diego was in sight. Aching with exhaustion, the men pulled the supply carts the last quarter mile.

Jack looked up with relief. Then he thought he saw a shadow move behind a line of palmettos. "General!" he called out, but his voice was lost in the whoops of ambushing Indians. He heard a man scream, heard horses whinny in terror. Jack jumped off his mount and saw the General dive behind a supply cart. He looked up to see Gabriel Baugh stagger and fall; it looked like he had taken a bullet through his heart. Jack ran to Baugh's side and saw his life's blood bubble out of his chest. The weary soldiers were firing back at the Indians, and they were falling back, but Oglethorpe commanded:

"Attack! Advance and attack!"

The Indians swarmed around, but began to retreat under fire. One leaned down off his horse and seized Baugh's limp body. With a single motion, he cut off his head and fastened it to his stirrups by the long yellow hair.

"Advance! To horse!" Oglethorpe yelled, and remounted to lead his rangers in pursuit of the Indians. They were Yamassee, allied with the Spanish. Most of the troops fell behind, but Jack followed the General and the rangers. They rode hard, whooping, for half a mile. As they raced their horses up a grassy dune, Jack saw the Indians drop Baugh's head. It rolled like a cannon ball down the sand dune, coming to rest at his feet.

Horribly, Baugh's blue eyes were wide open, and his sun-burned face still looked ruddy with health. Nausea choked Jack. He couldn't stand to see the head trampled. He turned his horse and rode back to pick up Baugh's head. At first he couldn't touch it; his eyes were blinded by tears. Gasping in horror, he grabbed the head and stuffed it into his saddlebag.

Jack remounted in time to see the General at the top of the next rise, flying spread-eagled in the air as his horse was shot from under him.

Oglethorpe pitched forward, his pistol blasting. Bullets pinged into the dune.

"General! Wait!" Jack shouted. The great man was down. Two rangers had caught up to him, and for a moment Jack lost heart, then he saw the General duck his head and roll away from the horse's kicking, thrashing legs.

"Ride on!" Oglethorpe shouted. His head was bare and Jack saw a powder burn on his red coat, but he struggled forward and climbed to his knees. "Ride on!" he shouted again.

But the Yamassee were nearly out of sight, and the rangers walked slowly back to Fort Diego with the General. In the early morning light, they buried the remains of Gabriel Baugh beside the Fort, and that day they rested.

If Cattie Dunlie was never far from Jack's thoughts, she had even more pressing reason to think of him. More than two months had passed since the christening, and Cattie had not been visited by her regular menses. She suspected she was with child and the fear and confusion of her suspicions made her symptoms worse. She felt swollen up; she felt sick when she awoke each morning, and she felt angry enough to do something desperate.

The immediate target of her anger was the baby—wretched unborn thing—who now threatened to completely ruin her life. She tried to remember all the ways she had heard of women ridding themselves of babies—what were they? Certain herbal draughts were sometimes effective, but which herbs? Cold baths and rum and hard riding . . . she'd heard of them, and so she tried them, secretly, hopefully, but without luck.

Cattie felt terribly alone. She was afraid to tell her parents, for they would be so angry and upset—her father might think of a solution, but she was afraid her mother would beat her to death. Fayette? What could she do, and anyway, Fayette was always off somewhere these days. Where on earth did she find to go?

Cattie cried and cried, for hour after hour, and felt so sick and weak from crying that she thought maybe her problem had gone away, but nothing had changed. One day she got up feeling less ill than usual and knew that the time had come to act. She determined to do something, no matter what; she felt oddly restless and energetic, and she had to talk to someone, so she confided in Rose.

Rose was shocked, but she was sympathetic and she had a suggestion. "Oh, poor Cattie! The same thing happened to Susannah, over at the Bullards', and here's what she did! She went to Joan the midwife, and Joan gave her an elixir she brewed herself and it cost her very dear but it worked for sure, though Susannah was very ill, as if to die. . . ."

"Can you go to Joan for me?"

"Oh, yes, Cattie! Of course I will! But why not, can't you . . . mightn't you marry him, Cattie?"

"No, I won't. I can't. Don't speak of him again, Rose, for there is no *him*. It's only me, don't you see?"

" 'It's only me,' she said. 'There is no *him*,' " she said Rose reported to her sweetheart, Thomas, that night. "So you see, Tom, that's why I will not lie with you . . . that way . . . until we're wed."

Cattie sent Rose with her gold locket to the man everyone said was a money-lender. His name was Isaac Ward, and he ran a small shop near Ellis Square that sold imported clocks and watches and repaired them. With Rose, Cattie sent a note that read:

> Do not try to cheat this girl for I know this locket is gold and worth at least £3.

When Rose returned with a single pound, Cattie was satisfied. She put most of the money in a leather purse hidden under her extra nightgown, and sent Rose to Joan with six shillings to pay for the recommended elixir.

Rose had begun to enjoy her part in the intrigues that surrounded Cattie's shame. There was a severe thunderstorm on the night she took the money and crossed town to get the purgative. Joan lived in a part of town Rose knew well—it was not far from the house where her Tom lived with his master.

Joan lived in a hut of poles lashed together with clapboard sides and a bark roof. She had no fireplace or chimney and the smoke from her cooking fire escaped through a hole in the roof. Just as Rose approached the hut, the sky brightened with lightning and the wind snapped off a branch of a huge live oak that stood beside the hut. The wind was as wild as a hurricane, and the rain soaked poor Rose through to her skin.

Dear Lord, what am I doing here? Rose asked herself, but she was too frightened to go back. "Joan! Joan, are you there?" she called, hesitating in front of the open door, a dark hole belching smoke that was blown back down into the house by the force of the storm.

When Joan came to the door, a man was behind her. Rose could see they were both bewildered with rum. Joan laughed when Rose explained her errand, staring at the huge, bearded man. He looked more Negro than Indian, though he was draped in skins and his broad chest was hairless, and Rose noticed with awe that he wore a gold ring in one ear.

"Medicine, sure I got that medicine," Joan mumbled, staggering around in the smoky room. Rose cowered in the doorway. Joan had no furniture at all, but she dug into a leather chest for the potion.

"Eight shillings," Joan demanded when she had produced a dirty-looking vial and sniffed its contents.

Rose burst into tears. "Eight? I only have six!"

"Six, then," Joan agreed, snatching the money from Rose's hand.

Rose fled home through the storm.

Cattie was afraid to drink the black stuff in the vial. It smelled like comfrey, which it was, in part, but laced with wormseed, wild senna, wild indigo, and rue. Holding Rose's hand, she drank it. Joan had brewed well; it was a powerful emetic, and an hour after downing the stuff, Cattie doubled over with violent stomach cramps.

"Oh, Rosie, help!" she sobbed. "Oh, dear God, I am going to die!"

But Cattie was not to die before she became a mother.

Ignorant of her sister's plight and suffering, Fayette Dunlie had chosen that same stormy night to elope with Micah Stone. Fayette was too wise to invite her father's intervention; she had learned from Cattie's experience and knew that Micah would never be accepted by her father. She had resigned herself to parting with her family forever, and the elopement had been her idea.

Micah was waiting for her on horseback when she slipped out of the darkened house. She had packed all she could into two leather bags: her best clothes, some of the sheets and towels she had brought from England as her trousseau, some sewing implements, a few knives and spoons, and her journal-book. Fayette had tears in her eyes as she left her parents' house. "Goodbye, good-bye, dear parents, dear Jemmie, dear sister," she whispered. It was entirely possible that she would never see the house or any of them again, she thought, but she hid her tears from Micah.

"Are you sure, my darlin'?" he asked her, holding her tight when they met by the sycamore tree. Thunder crashed nearby as she answered.

"Perfectly sure."

"Do you have everything you'll need?"

"I think so . . ." Fayette whispered. She thought about living with Micah, far away from other people. She thought of building a house and clearing land for a farm, about winter coming and long, dark nights. "Perhaps one more thing . . . " she said hesitantly.

"What?"

"Wait."

Her heart was thumping as she ran back into the house and crept into her father's office. It wasn't really stealing. Somehow she knew her father would understand and forgive her.

When she returned she was carrying her father's violin, wrapped in a tablecloth. Micah smiled. "So! We shall have music!" he said and lifted his love onto the back of her horse.

Micah had traded some of the valuable carpenter's tools he had brought from England for two horses. He had also his freedom dues: a suit of clothes, a few agricultural tools, and fifty acres of land. His land lay northwest of Savannah, beyond the trading post at Augusta. He had never seen the land, but hoped they could break ground at once and put up some sort of a house that would shelter them during the coming winter.

"We'll be married just as soon as we can," Micah promised. "But for now, we must make haste. We'll be far away by morning. Do you trust me, Fayette?"

"Of course," Fayette said serenely. "Just as soon as we can." She was very happy.

Outside of St. Augustine, Oglethorpe was still marching his troops back and forth. His plan was to lay siege to Fort San Marcos—by land and by sea—but to the frustration of all and the disgust of the South Carolina volunteers, he hesitated. Oglethorpe believed that any frontal attack on the fort would sacrifice too many lives, and so he refused.

Commodore Pearce warned the General that the eight ships of the Royal Navy would be available to him for only one more month. The hurricane season was nearly upon them.

Oglethorpe moved some of his men to Anastasia Island, a flat unoccupied island that overlooked the fort where the Spanish were confined and nervously waited. There he set up a battery, mounted the eighteen-pound cannons the South Carolinians had brought along. He now had about fifteen hundred men surrounding St. Augustine, but they were getting short on provisions as well as strength and time.

The General sent another portion of his troops, about one hundred and forty men, including Highlanders, Indians, and near-mutinous South Carolina volunteers, to camp out and harass the Spanish fort from the land. The men were low on morale and split by the open dissension between their leaders, who talked openly about disaster and speculated if Oglethorpe had sent them there to die.

Instead of camping outside Fort Mosa as they had been ordered, the men settled into the destroyed, deserted stone fort and set up temporary barracks of thatched palmetto. It was there that the Spanish ambushed them, early one Sunday morning, killing about seventy sleepy men before they could pull their trousers on. Others they took prisoner, not a desirable fate, for the Spanish were notorious jailors. Two prisoners who were too badly wounded to walk were killed and their heads and genitals cut off.

The defeat at little Fort Mosa was a turning point in the siege which was never a siege. When the remaining troops heard the news, they were plunged into despair. More than fifty of them were sick with dysentery. Surgeon McDavid died of it. It was high summer and the heat by day and the mosquitoes and sand ticks by night put the bored, restless troops through an ordeal of suffering.

Many of the Indians got fed up with waiting and disappeared into the countryside. Still the officers quarreled.

Commodore Pearce was determined to get his navy out of the harbor before a hurricane hit. When a freak storm began spitting up sand and snapping masts, he moved his ships out to sea to prevent their being beached, and seven Cuban supply boats slipped in to Fort San Marcos with badly needed provisions for the Spanish.

Despite his personal pessimism, Colonel Vanderdussen behaved professionally to the end. He busied himself on Anastasia Island with the battery facing the fort, but the cannons had to be set on sand dunes and every time one was fired, the recoil buried the barrel in sand. Besides that, only two of Vanderdussen's officers had experience as gunners.

Oglethorpe decided to take some men in a landing on the mainland. Jack Barstow, now the only medical man among the troops, was among them. They marched north, expecting ambush at any minute, and reached the battlefield at Fort Mosa to find the remains of the British who had died there weeks before: still unburied, headless and butchered by the Spanish, half-eaten by scavenging turkey buzzards.

Jack had changed. He had become silent and withdrawn, tormented by the sights he had seen—scenes of death and suffering, of jealousy and cruelty and dissension among the troops and officers. All of the patriotism and enthusiasm he had felt leaving Savannah was gone. He had not thought of Cattie Dunlie in weeks. He was tired and depressed: tired of the sight and smell and emptiness of war and depressed and afraid that it might all yet be in vain.

The corpses of the massacred men were bloated and crawled with maggots. Their stench was putrid. Seeing them, Jack forsook reason and raised his musket. He focused his anger and despair on the awesome and insulting sight of hundreds of wheeling, croaking buzzards, fat with blood, sated with human flesh and drawing near for more.

"God damn you!" he screamed. He shot one buzzard

with his long rifle, then another. The sky was full of them rising and falling without seeming to move their long, black wings, floating on air with an easy swimming motion. Three fell, then another. With one shot he brought down two.

"I'll kill you all!" he screamed. Dropping his musket and snatching another from the ranger next to him, he continued to shoot. When he had finished, more than a score of the huge black birds lay crumpled on top of the fetid corpses, and a look of stunned madness had settled into Jack's eyes.

Chapter Nine

Angus Dunlie Meets a Businessman—
Cattie Shells Peas—A Disappointment

Angus Dunlie rode very slowly into Savannah from his fields outside of town. It was a hot day—June was here again—and no weather for unnecessary exertion. Dunlie's discomfort had to do with more than the weather. His right hand went involuntarily into his coat pocket and fingered a crumpled sheet of paper—a letter from his agent in London. His creditors were growing impatient; they could not wait beyond this season for results . . .

Thus, Dunlie found himself reluctantly riding to see a man named Davis E. Strider, a trader from Charleston who was in town to accept investments from Savannah businessmen for his next voyages. Strider was said to give an extraordinarily high return on investments, though Dunlie hadn't heard exactly what his ventures were. Perhaps, he thought, by investing a few hundred pounds here, he could raise enough cash to appease these damned creditors until his farmstead began to turn a profit.

The past two years had changed Angus Dunlie. For him, as for many Georgians, they had been hungry years. Unlike some of the settlers, he hadn't starved, but neither had he prospered. The costs of labor and equipment were high, and the raw land was stubborn in resisting cultivation.

Dunlie sympathized with the charity settlers, many of whom had come full of hope only to find that their allotted fifty acres were not lush, dark soil, but infertile pine barrens. Many of these people had left, bankrupt and despairing, for an easier life in the other colonies or had taken passage back to England and the grim prospect of a return to debtor's prison.

And, Dunlie reflected, the Trustees had taken this time to withdraw the bulk of their financial support, judging from their perspective of two thousand miles that the fledgling colony was now ready to make its own way.

Angus Dunlie had planned well and worked hard, but the results had been discouraging. He was not ready to give up, but he moved more slowly, there was no spring in his step, and there were fresh worry-lines across his high brow. For the second year, the lands he had planted in corn and potatoes had yielded barely enough to feed his own household, let alone having anything left to sell. He'd started to plant a small number of acres in indigo but he was having trouble finding good workers at a wage he could afford.

A few of his neighbors were doing better—conspicuously Orde Barstow, but Barstow openly and defiantly used Negro slaves to work his plantation outside of town.

That I will never do, Dunlie vowed, slapping his open hand against his saddle. Not only was it illegal, it was against God's law. The Trustees, though they had eased some of their other strictures (including the ban on strong drink—now grogshops flourished on every other corner) had wisely continued the prohibition of slaves, though enforcement was lax, and powerful men such as Barstow flouted it every day. Still, men of conscience, Dunlie and Oglethorpe among them, still believed that the institution of slavery would be the final and absolute ruin of Georgia.

Oglethorpe. Dunlie's thoughts lingered on his old friend. The General had taken his defeat at the siege of St. Augustine very hard. For many months after the tattered, exhausted Savannah volunteers had limped back to town, he had not shown his face. He remained isolated, ill with fever, in his house at Frederica.

Only when he had rested and recovered his strength had Oglethorpe begun to think of his responsibilities to Georgia. He knew that Governor Montiano would try to invade Savannah and Charleston as soon as he had amassed enough ships and men, but the task of preparing defenses was frustrating. The South Carolina troops had disbanded, and the legislature was even conducting a humiliating investigation into his competence. England had turned her attention to other theaters of the War of Jenkins's Ear.

So during the past eighteen months, Oglethorpe had worked unceasingly and almost alone to bolster Georgia's defenses and prepare her for the inevitable invasion. Most of his efforts were concentrated on the forts on Saint Simons Island, but he also began a drive to increase the size of his ranger force. For this purpose, he had come north to Savannah this month; he needed every able-bodied man who could be spared, and Dunlie himself was seriously considering enlisting for a stretch. If he did, he would do it soon, for Oglethorpe was convinced that the hour of Spanish attack was near.

But before he could leave his family, Dunlie hoped he would have his personal financial affairs in better order. Perhaps this deal with Davis Strider would accomplish that.

Dunlie tied his horse to the peg in front of the ship's chandler's office on the Strand, where Strider was doing business during his stay in Savannah. He stooped to enter a low, dark doorway, and saw a man seated alone.

"Hello," Dunlie said. "I'm Angus Dunlie and I'm looking for Mr. Davis Strider." His hazel eyes narrowed in response to the dimness, and his face wore a characteristically severe expression.

The man stood up. "Ah, Mr. Dunlie! Good day to you! You honor Strider with this visit, sir!"

Strider was a big-bellied man of middle height with a broad, pock-marked face and an air of bold self-confidence. His dark, greased hair lay flat against his scalp. He pointed to a chair and Dunlie accepted it.

"I've come to see about taking a share in your next voyage," Dunlie said coldly. His first impression of Strider was negative. There was something sleazy and presumptuous about him.

Strider swaggered to a table and filled his pipe with tobacco from a brass urn. "Of course," he said, over his shoulder, "how much have you to invest?"

"That depends, sir, on the details of the venture."

"Strider has two ships being packed for shipping at present," the man said, curiously referring to himself by name. He lit his pipe and blew a cloud of bitter-smelling smoke into the room. This place smells like an Indian's cabin, Dunlie thought. "One is at Charleston, one at Port Royal. Now, Strider thinks the *Celia* is the venture for you. She sails on the first of July, assuming you're interested in haste, bound for mother England, then back to Charleston with a cargo guaranteed to give a more than satisfactory return . . ."

"I heard fifty percent," Dunlie interrupted.

"Ah! Don't know about that, but it's possible, yes, it's possible. Why, sometimes it's even better than that, sir! Yes! There's always risk in life, Mr. Dunlie, why you know that. But Strider's putting his own money into these ventures, as well as your own, and that's your surety that we'll do our very best!"

Strider had more to say, about the dimensions of the *Celia* and her history, about the captain and the schedule, and Dunlie listened impatiently. Why did he bluster so and march about with his belly puffed out? He was clearly a tradesman of the meaner sort, why did he seem so extraordinarily proud to be doing business with him? His attitude, more than anything he said, made Dunlie ill-at-ease.

"Just business like any other business . . ." Strider said. Dunlie caught his words, but not his meaning.

"Why, yes, sir," he said, "all that you say sounds businesslike. I have three hundred pounds to risk on your venture. Naturally, I would like some guarantee."

"Strider can sell you shares in the voyage. He can give you no guarantee," Strider said. "Alas, sir, there is no guarantee he can give you. For your peace of mind, you have to look on Strider—look at me, sir—am I a honest man? And you have to examine the record. Yes, sir, that's it. Examine the record."

"What's your record?" Dunlie asked.

"Better than most. Most of your ventures in this trade bring the cargo through in only one of three voyages. But Strider's record is a fine one. Strider's known for his success. Would you credit, sir, that Strider does it as often as not? Ah, perhaps more often. Strider is confident. He has a faith in the *Celia* and her crew . . ."

"So it's fifty percent for fifty percent," Dunlie said softly. As likely as not, he would lose all his money. But if he did not, he would get a magnificent return of it. He shook his head.

"What's that? What's that?" Strider asked. "It's a matter of business, sir, that's all. A calculated business risk."

"And the cargo?" Dunlie asked. "What is the cargo from Charleston?"

"In Charleston, Strider's agents load the richness of the New World, sir. They load furs and indigo and rice and staves and miscellaneous commodities of that same nature. Full to the groaning, the *Celia* sails off with her precious cargo, sir." Strider paced the small room. He had taken off his jacket and rolled up his sleeves to show arms as hairy as a bear's. His shirt was wet with perspiration and plastered to his bulky frame. Dunlie felt a vague but strong aversion to him. He was surprised at himself.

"And coming back?" Dunlie asked. Why was the man so expansive on some details, so evasive on others?

"First England. *Celia* stops at Chatham, so near to Londontown that the selfsame birds fly past every day, so near that the London merchants hurry down to the wharves to barter for her goods. Then she sails to Bonny with all the commodities necessary for trading there. She takes on her load, fits it into specially built storage, my friend, and whisk . . . she crosses back to Charleston. Now what's the risk in that, eh? Strider promises you—you'll be a richer man come Christmas!"

All of a sudden Dunlie understood. He felt cold rage flow into his vital organs, rise like icy water through his stomach, flow into his heart and lungs. He gasped with anger. "What! What's your damn cargo, Strider?"

"Dear sir, you know the cargo that pays so profitably. You know, dear sir! Strider's cargo is Africans. Watch yourself, sir! What are you doing?"

Dunlie had risen and towered over Strider, his hand clenched into fists and waving belligerently. Blood engorged his usually pale face and his eyes narrowed.

"Damn you, sir! You have been perfidious! I will have no part of your ungodly venture, no part at all!"

Strider backed away. "Stop! Watch yourself there! Eh, eh . . ."

Dunlie longed to punch the big man in his face. He felt his arm draw back as if it were under its own volition, out of his control. He was sick with rage, rage at this puffy pompous rogue who made a living selling other men into slavery, rage at himself for being in this situation, rage at needing money so badly that he had gotten himself here.

"Damn you!" Dunlie thundered, lowering his arm with difficulty.

"Get out if you don't like it! Who dragged you in here, sir? You came on your own, Mr. Dunlie, and it's no fault of mine if . . ."

"I will go, then, but I warn you to get yourself out of Savannah, Strider. There are no slaveholders here!"

"But there will be next year," Strider predicted as Dunlie left. "You'll see! It's just business Strider's in, sir, remember that!"

Dunlie mounted and rode off as if the devil himself were right behind.

Everyone said that Cattie Dunlie had put on airs since she had gone—and stayed nearly a year—to live with the cousin of an aunt in Charleston.

"Did I ever tell you, Rose, about the theater in Dock Street? Imagine, a proper theater, just like in

London. I went with Cousin Mary, wearing ever so fine a dress—you know, my yellow silk, though I never have cause to wear it here . . ."

"Yes, Cattie," Rose said absent-mindedly. Cattie had told her about the theater in Charleston many times, and she scarcely listened any more. Rose had troubles of her own. Her sweetheart, Thomas, had died of a burning fever, contracted, she supposed, from drinking a rum punch, and Rose had been much saddened by the loss. She had lost weight and flesh; she looked much older and had begun to read the Bible for consolation.

Cattie, in contrast, looked prettier and healthier than ever, as though she had suffered nothing in the past two years. Her parents had sent her to Charleston to wait out her inopportune pregnancy, and after torrents of tears and recriminations, it turned out that all Cattie feared was the sea voyage. When that interlude was over, she had delighted in her stay in Charleston, borne the child without any trouble whatsoever, and was perfectly happy to relinquish its care and training to her own mother.

For Angus and Catherine had accepted Cattie's child as a member of the family—he was so close in age to their own little Jemmie. Cattie had been intransigent on one point. She blankly refused to name the baby's father. Angus Dunlie had tried persuasion and he had tried threats, but she would not give in. To the Dunlies, and most of Savannah, it must be admitted, that meant only one thing. Everyone thought the father was Micah Stone, now the husband of Cattie's own sister.

The whole situation, and the gossip it invited, hurt Angus Dunlie most of all. Angus was a sensitive man, and he missed Fayette sorely. He had wept when he found the note she left him, telling her family that she had married Micah Stone. His eldest daughter had

been his favorite; he had cherished her, admired her
modest sweetness, her thoughful nature—so like his
own—and the musical gifts thay shared. Her hasty
elopement had shocked and depressed him; he had
moped about it for many months and tried to send
word after the couple that they were forgiven, but
none of his efforts had elicited any response. They
were gone, swallowed up by the endless wilderness, and
he was left with a sense of loss that was never to leave
him.

Catherine Dunlie was far less bereft, although she
missed Fayette more than she would have missed Cattie, the impudent one, the o'er-lively one, the daughter
with yellow hair and a temper to match her own. She
had whipped Cattie, on the sly, when the poor girl finally confessed that she was with child, but that, too,
had done no good. "What will people think?" she
asked Cattie, trying to instill her daughter with a sense
of propriety when it was far too late, "What will they
think?"

Cattie did not care what anyone thought.

Her child was a boy. She had named him Roland because it seemed a romantic name and called him Dunlie. He was a beautiful baby: blond and blue-eyed,
angle-faced and unusually sweet-tempered, but Cattie
hardly thought of him as her own. She let him grow
closer to her own mother than to herself. Catherine, in
fact, favored Roland above her own son, as if the
memory of his painful birth would forever stand between them. Cattie let Roland call Catherine
"Mamma," when he learned to talk, and taught him to
call her sister. The two little boys were being raised
almost as if they were twins.

Cattie was more interested than ever in being married, but since her stay in Charleston, none of the men
in Savannah seemed to suit her. Savannah's lifestyle

now seemed to her limited, provincial, and poor. She had suitors, but either they revealed themselves to her as rubes, or she seemed too reckless and spirited to them. And there was the problem of her dowry.

Cattie found it cruel, but at this critical point, her father seemed to be short on money. He spent hours with his accounts, but it only made him look worried. Sometimes he complained about costs and his dwindling capital. Having saved himself Fayette's dowry, Cattie thought it especially unjust that he should deny her one. Of course, some men were too rich or too poor to worry about a dowry; Cattie had met plenty of the latter sort, and she was now looking out for a man in the former situation.

"If only I could have stayed in Charleston," Cattie mourned to Rose that afternoon when the two young women were seated together on the kitchen piazza at the Dunlies', their fingers busy shelling peas. "But Papa had to come and get me himself."

"Well, your father is very fond of Roland," Rose commented. She wondered if she would ever have a child of her own. The thought brought a tear to her eye, and she wiped it with a thin, sun-browned hand.

"I wish he were more concerned with me," Cattie said.

"Why, of course he is, Cattie!"

"I want to be married soon," Cattie said.

"Why did you refuse Jack Barstow, then?"

"Oh, Rose! You know. Jack is very nice and kind to me, but what kind of life could I have as a surgeon's wife? Jack has never been the same since he came home from the southern war. He is always so serious, and always riding here and there at all hours of the day and night to see sick people." Cattie wrinkled her nose in distaste. "He'll likely catch the flux or some fever himself!"

At this reminder of the ailment that had carried her Tom away, Rose burst into tears.

"Oh, Rose, I am sorry! Don't take on so! Here! Stop it!" All the peas in Cattie's apron bounced into the grass as she stood up and took Rose into her arms for a hug. "Poor Rosie! You'll be all right, just wait and see!"

Angus Dunlie had finally decided to join General Oglethorpe on his journey to Frederica to prepare the forts and forces there for the expected Spanish invasion. Dunlie felt it was important for Georgia's future that her settlers volunteer to her defense; besides that, Oglethorpe had sealed the bargain with a temporary commission as Captain and a bonus of two hundred pounds sterling.

On the night before he was to leave Savannah, Dunlie called his wife and daughter together to say goodbye.

"I leave the management of the farms and household to your charge, Catherine," he said. "Our good neighbor Robert Whitman will advise you if you feel need of such advice. Above all, your concern should be for the health of our children. And you, Cattie, remember please that a young woman's value in the world is largly defined by her modesty and refinement. I charge you to obey and support your mother in all possible ways."

"And do you still expect you'll be back by fall, Angus?" Catherine asked. She was alarmed at the thought of their separation, and yet she was happy that some of their financial anxieties had been relieved by his accepting the commission.

"By harvest time, my dear. Guard your own health, too, Catherine, for you are the source of all our domestic happiness."

"Thank you, Angus," Catherine said. She nodded and tried to smile. Still ahead of her was the inevitable: Angus would want to lie with her before he left for war. Her feelings on that matter were complex.

"There'll be no men left in Savannah," Cattie complained.

"Let that be of no concern to you, Cattie," Angus said. "I would far rather you concentrated on matters that are within the province of women."

"But does that not include wedlock, Papa? I am only confiding in you my awareness of my Christian duty to wed. Papa, I am already eighteen years old."

"Cattie, we will speak of this when I return. In the meantime, cultivate your womanly qualities, practice meekness and modest decorum."

"Yes, father," Cattie sighed and Angus Dunlie looked distraught. He was upset and confused about what to do with Cattie. Sometimes he suspected she was insincere. How, he asked himself, had he ended up with *two* such independent, disobedient, unruly daughters? Fayette was gone, perhaps even dead by now. He missed her as much as ever. In the two years, they had not heard more from her.

Angus felt guilty. He had never meant to drive Fayette away. Sometimes he blamed himself for bringing his family to America. Perhaps none of this would have happened if they had stayed in Dorset. Life here was hard and there was too much mixing between people of the different social classes. Young women were impressionable and bound to be affected by the proximity of so many reckless, adventurous men.

"And now it is time to go to bed," he said, rising with a candlestick in one hand. "I must leave in the early morning."

Cattie kissed her father enthusiastically and he felt

pleased, despite his concerns for her. "Good night, Papa. I will be up to see you off."

"Come, Catherine," Dunlie said, leaving the room with the two women following him in single file.

Upstairs in their bedroom, Catherine was silent. This matter, long postponed, was about to come to the surface, she felt. Angus sensed her tension. He was tense, too, and determined to have satisfaction.

"I must see to the baby, Angus," Catherine said.

"Very well, my love, and I will watch you. Nothing is more pleasing than the sight of a mother with a child."

James, their son, was old enough to sleep in a small bed in the nursery, and usually Roland slept there, too, but tonight Catherine had carried his wooden cradle into their bedroom. It stood at the foot of their four-poster bed before an open window. A slight breeze moved the thin mosquito netting tied over the cradle.

Angus set the candle on a bedside table and watched Catherine. As she bent over the cradle, her loose cotton dressing gown parted to reveal her large, chalky-white breasts, and Angus felt a stir of desire.

He welcomed it. The most important thing in his life was his family, and he wished it were larger. He wished he had more sons and knew that he was still young enough to sire a dozen of them, but Catherine had been fretful and difficult about sex ever since James was born.

"You are a lovely woman, Catherine," he said softy.

"Ah, no! I am old and already tired," she answered. Her voice had a tone of frustration and resentment. Angus had heard it often, lately, but he still had not gotten accustomed to it. He knew that Catherine's last confinement had been very hard on her; she had been slow to recover her strength, and taking care of Cattie's son had been an added burden.

"To me you are still lovely," he said.

Catherine was still. She fought back tears. *Would* he insist? There was no possible way she could refuse to do her marital duty, and the prospect filled her with anger and fear. Beyond that, she felt guilty. Angus was a good man and a kind father and husband, but she could not bear the thought of more child-bearing.

"In a way, Angus," she said, "it is as if we have two sons now." She rose and crossed the room to stand by the other window. A full moon lighted the sky and everything outside was still. She felt her limbs and organs tighten with anxiety. *If only,* she wished, *I were able to be on that moon, so far away from all this.*

Angus waited for a moment, then he rose and walked to her. Awkwardly, he encircled Catherine's stiff body with his own, feeling her tremble as he put his hands on her breasts.

"Even two sons is not many," he said. "Besides, I am a man and you are my wife. It is our Christian duty to be made one flesh and multiply."

"Are you never satisfied?" Catherine snapped. She winced at the anger in her own voice, then twisted away from her husband and sat on the edge of their bed.

"Catherine, Catherine, what am I to do?"

"I don't know."

"Do you deny me, then?"

I cannot go through that again, Catherine thought. *No, I cannot. I will not.* Angus stood very close to her. He had taken off his clothes and stood naked. She was uncomfortably aware of his physical need. His hands reached out and drew her gown from off her shoulders. It dropped onto the bed, and she sat bare to her waist. In the candlelight, he could see the sheen of her skin and her full, womanly breasts. Her head was bowed and her yellow hair hid her face.

"As you are my husband," she said finally, in a sad, hollow voice, "I have no right to deny you. But I do not wish it."

Dunlie felt something in him turn against her, and for the first time in the twenty years of their marriage he had the desire to strike her.

"I will not rape you, Catherine," he said. "But by being less than a woman, you make me feel less than a man." He turned away.

And Catherine burst into tears of relief.

Chapter Ten

The Spanish Invade Georgia—A Wilderness Scene—Dunlie Renews His Pledge

The scout spurred his horse from one end of Saint Simons Island to the other with the warning: "The Spanish are here! Their ships are in the harbor! The Spanish are coming!"

The news spread panic throughout the island. Oglethorpe pulled back his men from Fort Saint Simons at the island's southern tip, spiked the remaining cannons, freed the livestock and burned the food and supplies. The troops packed themselves inside the palisades of Fort Frederica, the northern bastion. The civilian population of Fredericatown sought refuge inside the wooden walls, the men of the town armed and ready to fight as most of the women and children camped out in the King's Magazine.

The lush, green island was covered with dense forests and acres of marshland. A narrow road ran between tall live oaks hung with gray Spanish moss, ran north to south between the two forts, curving toward the island's eastern shore, skirting the grassy marshes and irregular inlets from the sea.

British scouts watched more than fifteen hundred Spanish soldiers and grenadiers land on the island and march toward deserted Fort Saint Simons. Oglethorpe's men were badly outnumbered and he knew it, but he was fired with reckless courage and a passionate desire for revenge.

"God help us, for we shall face them today," Oglethorpe vowed to Angus Dunlie. The two friends paced the low walls on the inner slope of Frederica's parapets, reviewing the gunners in position. "The damned Navy has not arrived from Cuba, nor the promised gunboats from Charleston. Thank God for the Highlanders."

"Small and his rangers have ridden out to patrol the main trail," Dunlie said. Dunlie was attached to a company of Highlanders, when he was not at the General's side. Dunlie was bound to do his duty, but he felt very isolated from these rough, rowdy, battle-hardened men.

Inside Fort Frederica, the troops were readying for an attack. A battery of cannon faced the river to the west, a moat encircled the star-shaped fort, and Oglethorpe's regimentals, volunteers, Indians, and Highlanders milled about, a mob of red coats, tartans, and war paint. The penned-up horses moved about restlessly and from somewhere came the hysterical crying of a small child.

"The ranger patrol in sight!" a lookout called out from his high wooden tower. Oglethorpe ran to the main gate to meet them.

One of the rangers was missing. The other four gave Oglethorpe the report. "They're within two miles, sir! Small is dead, sir! He was shot by a grenadier and the Indians got him!"

Oglethorpe thought fast. It was nine in the morning. The Spanish would still be getting the lay of the land. The rangers had likely encountered Montiano's advance party. His best hope was to surprise the Spanish somewhere on the narrow road before they had a chance to set up a battle formation.

"Give every man a ration of rum!" Oglethorpe ordered. "And prepare to march!"

The thirty men of the Highland Company were the first out of Fort Frederica. Oglethorpe commandeered a horse and galloped to take their lead. The rangers and Indians were not far behind, most of them on foot, gasping from the heat and the effort of running with twenty-five pound packs of weapons and equipment.

A mile from the fort, Oglethorpe rounded a bend in the trail and caught sight of troops in Spanish uniform. At once the Spaniards started moving into a defensive position near a creek bed. Whooping with excitement, he spurred his horse directly into the midst of the Spanish soldiers, leading the Indians and Highlanders.

"Charge! Charge!" Oglethorpe screamed. Warcries of the Chickasaw, Yamacraw, and Creek filled the air. "Fire!" Oglethorpe ordered, and his troops fired round after round, overwhelming the small advance party and rolling right into the main force.

"Onward!" Oglethorpe yelled, thrilled by the sound of muskets firing and the smell of gunpowder. Leading the attack, he took two prisoners. The chief of the Yamacraw was wounded in his right hand, but he boldly drew his pistol with his left and shot a Spanish officer through the heart. One of the English rangers plunged his horse into crossfire and took the Spanish commander prisoner.

The Spanish panicked and broke ranks. It seemed as

if the British were everywhere. They ran into the woods and up and down the trail, losing their way. Oglethorpe and the rangers pursued some of them south for three miles before calling a halt, and on the return counted thirty-six dead Spaniards lying along the trail.

A few British had been wounded, but only one man had died—from heat exhaustion. Oglethorpe was wild with triumph. "Good work! Fine shooting! A splendid showing!" he shouted hoarsely.

Expecting Montiano to send another attacking force immediately, Oglethorpe directed the men to set up a blockade along the trail near a large open savannah.

Spirits were high as the weary but elated men set up blockade where the trail crossed a spongy marsh on a narrow causeway of brush and logs. There were dense woods on either side of the trail, and Oglethorpe concealed sixty regular soldiers on the east side, in the tangled underbrush, and fifty Highlanders and rangers on the west, also hidden.

Clouds gathered in the sky and a light rain began to fall. Waiting in the silence, the men had time to feel fear. They had done well, they had attacked, they were bolstered by their early morning success, but they knew how badly they were outnumbered. How many Spanish might come marching up that narrow trail? Two hundred? Three hundred or more? The men passed flasks of rum. They had no real rations with them. It was very hot.

Stealthily, some of them heaped up logs and brush into a low barracade to stop musket balls. Oglethorpe rode back to Fort Frederica to collect reinforcements and some of their confidence went with him.

Birds swooped low over the marsh, and the air was heavy with a humid mist. It continued to rain. Too much rain could dampen their powder so that their muskets would not fire.

"God help us," Angus Dunlie prayed. He was crouched among the Highlanders. The first battle had terrified him and left him stunned. He had seen sudden, instant death all around him like Judgment Day. He had fully expected to die and couldn't quite believe he hadn't.

And now the waiting. He feared he had been spared for an even more horrible death. Some of the experienced Highlanders cursed and bragged as they waited. Some of them were very drunk, but Dunlie refused rum and heard nothing said. He had retreated into his own head, and could think only of the horrors that were still to come.

At about three o'clock the first Spanish grenadiers came into view on the far side of the marsh. They stepped cautiously on the narrow, unsteady log causeway. The British troops watched, still hidden, as the Spanish commander called a halt and sent a few men ahead to investigate the odd-looking piles of brush which the scouts did not remember seeing there before.

When the advance party of Spanish neared the northern edge of the marsh, the Highlanders and regulars opened fire. The forests on both sides of the trail exploded with gunfire and smoke. Screaming, drums beating, the Spanish set up a battle formation in the cover of the trees on the south side of the marsh and began to return fire. Both sides fired steadily. The drizzle kept the smoke low and there was little visibility.

Dunlie's mouth was dry as he fired again and again, standing knee-deep in mud. Smoke burned his eyes. The men around him cursed and grunted at the recoil of their muskets. Bullets whizzed over his head and buried themselves in the makeshift barricade.

The Spanish fire was relentless. Some of the regular troops lost heart and left the battle, running back north along the trail to the Fort. The Highlanders and rangers held firm, Dunlie among them. From the shouting and drumming and steady gunfire it seemed they were facing a thousand Spanish.

More of the regulars fled.

Oglethorpe heard the sounds of gunfire from the fort. Ordering the regiment and some other troops of rangers to follow, he rode at top speed toward the marsh. On the way south, he met nearly half of his men in full retreat.

"Ride back, damn it!" he ordered. "Return fire!"

It was nearly four o'clock. The Spanish had no idea that half of Oglethorpe's men had fled the battle. The remaining troops were still firing spiritedly, and the Spanish were nearly out of ammunition. At a crucial moment, their captain made a decision. He ordered the three Spanish companies to retreat to Fort Saint Simons and they obeyed willingly.

Oglethorpe galloped into the battlefield just as the Spanish had withdrawn. Gasping, he took stock of the astonishing situation and let out a cheer.

"God damn! We've done it! We've stood them out!" he yelled. He aimed his musket across the empty marsh and fired, for good measure.

Word of the Spanish invasion of Saint Simons Island had spread throughout Georgia. Mainland settlers from Darien to Savannah panicked, sought refuge in the forts and outlying settlements to evade the attack, rape, and pillage that seemed imminent. In South Carolina, the assembly called the militia to order and repaired fortifications, for Charleston was the real prize, and expected seige and sacking.

But there were other settlers far removed from news

of Oglethorpe's army and their brave stand. Back-country farmers whose land was a half-day's ride from the trading post at Augusta or the German settlement at Ebenezer were as remote and isolated as if they lived on an unexplored continent. Among these settlers were the young farmer Micah Stone and his wife.

For Micah and Fayette had kept their resolve to be married, although the religious celebration of their union had, in fact, followed its physical consummation by six months. Not until Pastor Reinhardt, the spiritual leader of the Salzburghers at Ebenezer, had come to their one-room house in the clearing, as part of his circuit riding of the settlements outlying his parish, had Fayette and Micah joined hands before a representative of the Lord.

But join hands they did, and Pastor Reinhardt had pronounced them man and wife, in the open air and bright sunlight of late fall. After the minister had said the words, the three of them had stood there with bowed heads for a few minutes without speaking. They were much alike: three European-born Americans determined to find a new life on the edge of the wilderness, three who had put shops and society behind them and who had now to put their own hands and backs into the struggle to live on the land.

Fayette and Micah were very thin and brown at the beginning of that first fall, and they made a handsome couple as they were married on the land they themselves had cleared. Eben Reinhardt noticed with pleasure the way her small strong hand clung to his arm, the bold confident set of his shoulders, the true feeling that passed between them with the smallest exchanges. His own English was slow and formal, but he could tell that the green-eyed bride was uncommonly well-spoken.

Who was she, the pastor wondered? She was evidently well-bred, and remarkably pretty, even in her faded yellow-sprigged calico gown. Where had these two met?

Fayette answered his question in her own way, when she confided in her journal the next day:

> Truly, I feel that our Heavenly Father has answered my prayers for a blessed life. Everything is as I dreamed it would be. Micah and I are together and our love grows deeper by the day and night. In many ways this is the most beautiful of lands: not really quiet, for when I listen I can hear that the mockingbird knows many songs, not really wild, for even yellow primroses have taken root in our clearing and the soil sweetly welcomes the seeds we plant in it.

After their wedding, Micah invited the pastor to spend the night, and he accepted. Fayette had cooked a 'possum pie; it was tender and juicy and succulent, according to all three who ate it, and when supper was eaten, in the last light of the day, Fayette unwrapped her violin and played for a while.

"Wonderful!" their visitor exclaimed, half-shutting his eyes, remembering for the first time in a long time the Austrian city where he had grown up. "Ah! This is wonderful!" he exulted.

Fayette played a few tunes very simply, and then passed the instrument to Micah. She was teaching him to play; he learned quickly and easily and remembered an endless number of songs from his boyhood in Berkshire. Their making music together had brought them together in a new way; they played as often as they could, and when the fall changed to winter and the nights were long, they began to play every night. But on his wedding day, Micah remembered an old song, and sang it to Fayette:

> O ruddier than the cherry,
> O sweeter than the berry,
> O nymph more bright
> Than moonshine night . . .

"Don't stop!" Fayette begged. "You are playing so well!" Micah laughed at her enthusiasm, but he complied, with:

> And I would love you all the day,
> Every night would kiss and play,
> If with me you'd fondly stray
> Over the hills and far away.

Fayette's eyes shone with happiness, and that night, with the pastor asleep in their hay-stuffed bed, as she and Micah lay together on a pallet on the dirt floor near the fire, she took his hand to her lips and kissed it again and again, very quietly, as if she could never have her fill.

If that was a night Fayette loved to remember, there were others, in those first few years, that she prayed to forget. One of them was the late winter night Fayette and Micah were awakened by the sound of someone beating on their cabin door.

"Micah!" Fayette had called in a low voice. Micah was a deep sleeper, and when awakened, he was slow to react. Half-dressed, shivering, he stumbled to the door.

A woman, barefoot and crazed and pale as death, fell over their threshold into the house. In her arms she carried a baby wrapped in a bloody shawl.

"Indians!" the woman gasped. "They killed my husband. They stole my daughters. Here! Can you save my baby!"

But the child she held out to Fayette was already dead. His scalp had been cut half off his skull and hung in loose, blood-red folds. The woman was drenched with her child's blood, but her mind could not accept his death. She had walked more than five miles alone, crying and cradling this baby, and she would not give it up. On the second day, Fayette held the woman in her arms, and Micah took the baby away by force and buried it in the frozen ground on the edge of the clearing. That night, the woman had left as suddenly as she had come.

Though not all their Indian neighbors were warlike, they were omnipresent. Without warning, Creeks or Yamacraws would enter the clearing around the cabin, and Fayette had to learn not to scream in fright when she looked up from her weeding or water-getting to see a hunter or warrior standing at her elbow. In the main, the Indians were curious and inscrutable, at least to Fayette.

Fayette was frightened, too, on the rare days when Micah took his horse and rode into Augusta to trade for supplies. Augusta, which had been an Indian trading post and was already showing signs of becoming a town, was a full two days' ride, and Fayette did not always relish long rides, especially now, in the third summer of their homesteading, when her lean body had finally begun to round and swell with child.

"Change your mind and ride with me," Micah suggested, when he was saddled and ready at dawn.

"Ah, no, Micah. I feel I should stay at home. I have so much to do and already my step is slower. By harvest, I shall be too heavy to be much help to you."

"I shall ride home, then, just as fast as I can."

"And I shall keep one ear cocked until I hear the sound of your horse."

Fayette was satisfied to see Micah ride off alone, for although it was true that she felt her body slowed by the weight of their child, and she had many things to do, in fact she had a special plan for the day. Several days ago she had seen some berry bushes, an easy walk from their cabin, just across the creek and up a little hill. Today, Fayette had decided, while Micah was away, she would gather some berries and cook them into a pie.

Enjoying her solitude, Fayette covered her arms against the thorns and brambles, and took a basket with her into the woods. As she left the clearing, she thought suddenly of that poor woman who had come carrying her murdered child. Here, just about here was the spot where Micah had buried him. To be decent, she thought, we should put up a cross. She would remember to ask Micah about it when he came home.

There were so many things to ask and tell Micah, she reflected. In more than two years, she had not yet covered half of them. How surprising marriage was, how surprising the full, fecund feeling of her own womanhood. The time had passed so quickly: clearing the trees, building, and farming. They had few friends, few neighbors, and still when they met—at Sunday meetings, for a barn raising, or hay making, or a wedding to which they were always invited to bring the violin—the fellowship generated seemed to last for weeks.

She paused at the top of the little hill. From here she could look back down onto their farm. From here it looked small and isolated. The sun glinted on the surface of the water in a pail she had left next to the stone front step. From this vantage point she could see the neat rows of the garden, see the pile of wood next to the little stable, see the way the dark green forest rose at the very edges of the cleared land.

Next summer, Fayette thought, there will be a child lying on his blanket next to the garden, perhaps even crawling into the potato patch. She turned away, pleased with the thought, and began to pick the thick dark-blue berries. A flock of blackbirds rose, cawing in protest at her invasion, and settled on the branches of a huge oak tree. The bees were thick in the berries. Their humming was a familiar, soothing sound, but not the low, snuffing, grunting Fayette began to hear next.

At once her brain flashed warning. An Indian? Not a panther? She stopped stock-still and listened. Brush and branches snapped under the weight of the creature moving closer to her. Her nerves tightened. The buzzing of the bees seemed so loud. Should she turn and run? She shivered.

The brush was thick and she could not see whatever was approaching. It came nearer, no more than twenty feet away, still sheltered by the leaves and branches of the blueberry bushes.

Fayette took a deep breath and called out, "Hello! Who goes there?" Her heart was thumping helplessly. If I must die, she thought . . . but a great crashing, thudding sound was her answer and she stepped up on a rock to see a huge brown bear, nearly seven feet tall, she reckoned, lunging and snapping twigs under his weight as he ran back into the forest.

Alone again, Fayette laughed at her fright. Better a bear than an Indian, it seemed. She regretted that she hadn't brought her musket. Bear meat was mild and sweet, and the big bear must have weighed four hundred pounds. She would enjoy telling Micah the story when he came home.

"A toast! A toast!" The cries rang out boldly among the rum-sotted battle-dazed men. Seated at long wooden tables inside the fortified walls of Fort Frederica, the men who had fought blindly and bravely and victoriously for the British flag feasted and refought the bloody battles that already, two days later, were moving into the realm of legend.

"A toast to the King!" A Highlander rose to his feet, wrapped in twelve yards of fine-woven Scottish plaid. At his elbow a pipe player blew a few measures of the royal salute, and every Scot present felt his blood pound.

"To the King! King George! Long life!" a ranger shouted above the bagpipe's droning.

"To the General!" the ranger added, and the rest of his toast was lost in the general shouting.

"Pass the beer," muttered one of the South Carolina volunteers.

It was hard to believe that it was over, but they had seen with their own eyes . . . seen the Spanish fleet slip out of the harbor and sail south. Hard to believe that they had frightened away so superior a force and hard to forget the terrifying ordeal of the battle itself: the trees alive with bursts of flame, the screams of dying men, the damp, low-hanging air choked with sulphurous smoke, the awful, random unpredictability of musket shots and death.

Oglethorpe stood on a lookout platform on the palisade facing the river. He cast a sharp glance southward. Nothing. They had really sailed away. He could appreciate far better than anyone else how fortunate, how fortuitous had been the Spaniards' cautious withdrawal. Hearing the cheers of the men, he looked down and raised his arm to acknowledge the salute. They were good men, good brave fighting men after all. His heart swelled with triumph and he turned to his friend Angus Dunlie.

"By God, Angus, they fought damn well!"

"Aye, James, that they did. We all did." Dunlie was recovering from his own battle shock. Last night he had slept a bit, for the first time free of the booming, crackling, screaming sounds of warfare that had filled his head whenever he had closed his eyes. He was proud to have been at the scene of their victory, but he felt drained and exhausted from it, and more than glad to contemplate civilian life again.

"I have already sent a report to Parliament," Oglethorpe said.

"And now? Will you return with me to Savannah?"

"Indeed, I'd rather see you remain on Saint Simons."

"I might have better luck with planting here, but . . ."

"For sure, my friend. You own . . . how many acres on the island?"

"A Trustees' grant of three hundred, James."

"Well enough."

"But I have a family. I need to build a good house for them. Catherine . . ."

"It is in my power, dear Angus, to reward faithful military service. When it so happens that the man I owe deep gratitude is also a dear friend, so much sweeter is my duty."

Dunlie waited. What was coming? What did he intend to propose? In fact, he was not adverse to devoting his energies to a plantation here on the island. The climate was mild, a sea breeze swept through the marshlands in all but the summer's hottest days, and the land here looked to be far more arable than that he held outside of Savannah.

"You cannot keep me hanging here, James," Dunlie said. "Do you come to the point or not?"

"I am coming to the point directly, dear Angus. Included with my letter to Parliament was a citation of your heroic efforts at the battle and a recommendation that you be rewarded with a grant of five hundred acres here on the island."

Dunlie gasped. "A fine reward, sir!"

"Angus, I know that you will accept it and prosper, and all with the best interest of the Crown and the Colony."

"I will, James."

"Others may crimp and cheat and circumvent the laws, but you will uphold them in letter and in spirit."

"I will."

"Do you take my meaning, specifically, Angus?"

"I do and I shall fulfill your confidence in me. And to keep the laws of the colony for the good of all."

"Good. You are just the sort of man best suited to found a plantation here."

Dunlie stretched out a hand to take Oglethorpe's in a firmhandshake. "You have my pledge, sir, my thanks, and you will always have my friendship."

Oglethorpe smiled. "And now a drop to seal our bargain!"

Chapter Eleven

A Wedding—A Homecoming—A
Surprise Visitor

"Why Cattie Dunlie! I never thought you'd be so mean and cross on your own wedding day!" Rose herself was near to tears. There was less than one hour left before the ceremony, and Cattie had just managed to rip the entire lace border off the white satin bodice of her dress.

Cattie had done it in a temper tantrum which had also resulted in a broken mirror, three broken fingernails, and a coffee stain on her mother's pastel French carpet that would mark this day for one hundred years. Cattie was getting married. In a little more than one hour she would be the wife of Francis Conrad Nickerson, middle-aged owner of a rice and indigo plantation on the Savannah River, but she was far from easy in her mind about what she was about to do.

"Rose, if you don't shut up and sew fast, I'll . . . I'll . . ." Cattie snapped at her oldest friend.

"Come on, Cattie, shrug out of the dress. You can keep the slip on. And why not try to eat something?"

"I won't! Oh, Rose, I'm sorry. I'm not mad at you."

"I know you aren't."

Rose carefully lifted the heavy satin gown so that none of it trailed on the floor, then arranged it over her own lap as she sat down in the rush-bottomed slipper chair to make the emergency repairs. Rose's term as an indentured servant had expired two years ago, and she herself had married. Marriage agreed with her. She looked both serene and vivacious and had lost the tight severity that had once pinched her face. For indeed, time had proved the best cure for her broken heart, though, and Rose admitted it, she still sometimes thought of Thomas.

"I haven't seen you in so long, Cattie," Rose said.

"Well, mother always wants me to stay down there at Sea Groves, you know, though I hate it. It's as boring as can be. You have no idea, Rose."

"I expect I do. Savannah is as lively as ever."

They laughed together. "I know I used to complain about Savannah, but that was before I knew what life in the country was like!"

"So that's why you're not having the wedding on the plantation," Rose said.

"The house is large enough, but oh, Rose. It's not even a plantation, really. It's just a farm. And father works so hard, just like one of the hired men. He won't have slaves, you know, though nearly everyone else does."

Rose nodded. Violations of the law prohibiting slaves were ever more common in the four years since General Oglethorpe had gone back to England, leaving the colony without representation by any of its Trustees. Most of the plantation owners were opposed to the law, and everyone said it would have to be changed before Georgia would really prosper. Still, however serious they might be, her father's problems and principles hadn't put Cattie into such a mood on her wedding day, and Rose wasn't yet sure what had.

"You must be pleased then, Cattie, to be going to live at Nickerson Hall," she ventured.

Cattie stiffened and sniffed. "I suppose. I'm glad to be getting married, Rose. I never thought I'd be such an old maid—you know I'm already twenty-three."

"I always thought you'd marry Jack Barstow, after all," Rose commented.

"Hah! Doctor Barstow, as he calls himself, though he's never had a day's schooling that I know of!"

"That doesn't matter, he's a good doctor. Why he's better at setting bones than any doctor I ever saw in England, and when there was malaria last . . ."

"Oh, who cares! That's enough about doctors and malaria, for pity's sake, Rose!" Snapping her fan angrily, Cattie paced the length and breadth of the room. Finally she paused and looked out of the window into the dark night, remembering Jack as he had been one summer night a long time ago . . . then remembering seeing him last week . . .

He had looked little older but more serious. Perhaps it was his thick sand-colored mustache. When she saw him, he had his head down against the raw wet wind off the river, but she had recognized his broad-shouldered, lanky frame. Then she had noticed that his face was pulled into lines of concentration which at first looked like anger.

But when he had lifted his head and had seen her coming out of Mrs. Parker's bonnet shop, Jack's face had changed and he smiled in delight.

"Why Cattie! Miss Dunlie, I mean! I haven't seen you in . . . so long!"

Cattie had taken in a deep breath, steadying her

nerves, hiding her feelings. "I hope you're not still waiting for me to change my mind, Jack. As to where I've been, I've been living on Saint Simons Island with my family. Terribly dull. Have you heard the news? I'm engaged to be married."

Jack had grabbed her arm and turned her into the shelter of the shop's bay window. "How soon? And to whom, Cattie?"

"Are you sorry, Jack?"

"Course I am. You know I'll always love you."

"You should be married yourself, Jack. Maybe there's still time. Perhaps some grateful patient will give herself to you."

"You've always been the naughtiest, most interesting woman I know, Cattie Dunlie! Now who is to be your husband?"

"I'm quite annoyed that you hadn't heard. Don't you listen for news of me?"

"I work too hard. I never hear gossip, even when it's about me."

"Or about your stepfather? And his concubine?"

"Orde Barstow is doing very well, I hear that. You'd never understand, Cattie, but he really loves Zonah."

"How dare you say I'd never understand? Don't start that again! In the future, if you insult my character, Mr. Doctor Barstow, my own husband will be obliged to defend my honor. So there!"

Jack laughed. "Your honor? Cattie, to me your honor is as untouchable and impossible as my suit for your hand. Do *me* the honor of accepting my most sincere wishes for your marital happiness and my offer to attend you in your first lying-in."

Not my first, Cattie thought, but she only shook her head.

"Never, Jack! You will never attend me in childbirth, I swear it! You only long for a look at my pretty pink skin, you wretched man!"

But both of them had been laughing when they parted, and Jack had called back as Cattie climbed into the waiting carriage, "I look forward to seeing you again, Cattie! Good luck!"

No, she didn't love Francis Nickerson, Cattie admitted to herself, still studying the tree's bare branches shivering in the late December wind. Perhaps in a funny way, she had loved Jack. She had never told anyone that he was Roland's father. It gave her an enormous satisfaction to think that she had kept the secret so well. Not even Rose knew, not even Rose.

"How is your baby, Rose?" she asked, turning suddenly back into the room and blinking. Rose was still bent over her mending, straining her eyes over the lace by candlelight.

"She's just as sweet and pretty as a doll," Rose said proudly. "We call her Penny. Short for Penelope."

"Penny Posey?" Cattie smiled.

"Yes. Doesn't that have a fine ring to it?" Rose asked. "It was Peter's idea. His name is P. P., too, you see."

"Indeed I do," Cattie said.

"Little Roland is as handsome as a prince," Rose said. "Will he go to Nickerson Hall to live with you and your husband?"

Cattie frowned. "No, and hold your tongue about that, Rose. At least till I'm safely wed. I don't really care much what Mr. Nickerson thinks, but mother does."

"Whatever you ask, I will try to comply, Cattie," Rose said. She sighed. "There, now that's as good as new. Try to slip into it without mussing your hair."

"Thank you, Rose," Cattie said sweetly and endeavored to adopt the expression of an innocent, hopeful bride. Her temper tantrums were over and thinking about Jack Barstow had exorcised him from her mind.

The dress she wore for her marriage celebration was the pride of Savannah. It was heavy French satin with a lace-edged bodice and full, puffed, banded sleeves that set off Cattie's plump arms as if they were pink magnolias. The skirt was stiffened with a whalebone to stand out in the manner of the latest fashion, and constructed of tiers of graduated satin leaves, arranged in rows from the waist to the hem. The back of the gown ended in a lace-edged train. She wore gloves, on her blonde hair a silver headdress of filigree worked into robins and roses, and she carried a white satin and silver fan, a gift from her bridegroom.

Thus finally arrayed, Cattie and Rose hugged each other in true friendship and walked together down the narrow stairs to the parlor, where the memebers of the family and a few guests were gathered It was seven-thirty in the evening, Christmas night, 1747, and Catherine Dunlie had combined the few festive touches she could manage for the holiday with the festivities demanded by the occasion of a daughter marrying well.

Actually, Angus and Catherine were of two opinions about Cattie's choice of a husband. Their positions were not entirely divergent, for sure; both of them were relieved to see Cattie marrying somebody. Never had such a good-looking, blatantly nubile, moderately-well-to-do young woman remained so long on Savannah's marriage market. It seemed men were led easily into courting Cattie, many of them even into falling in love with her, but Cattie had no luck in getting a man to the altar.

"Let them talk!" Cattie said, when her mother bemoaned the situation. Cattie had been gossip's darling for five years—even more— and yet few people understood her at all. Least of all did Francis Nickerson, himself a recent widower, who misjudged Cattie nearly as widely as she misjudged him. In fact, Catherine Dunlie had been the active ingredient in their courtship; she had promoted the one to the other and managed to arrange things. The extent of her supporting arrangements would not be comprehended by either of the nuptial pair for some months. Only then would Francis realize he had married the high-spirited, greedy, self-concerned daughter rather than the self-contained, mannered, conventional mother, and only then would Cattie wake up to discover herself wed to a narrow-minded, miserly libertine.

Angus Dunlie had no objections to Francis Nickerson as a man, at least that he was yet aware of, but he frankly despised Nickerson's political persuasions. Nickerson was a slave owner who spoke out in active opposition to the colony's prohibition against the importation and use of African slaves, and it did not soothe Angus Dunlie's resentment that Nickerson's plantation was among the largest and most prosperous on the Savannah River.

But tonight, for the duration of the festivities, all disagreements were forbidden, all arguments postponed. Angus Dunlie stepped forward to give his daughter his arm, and led her to stand next to her bridegroom, in front of the Reverend Bartholemew Zouberbuhler, the Swiss-born Anglican rector. Zouberbuhler pronounced the simple words that yoked Cattie and Francis Nickerson till death, and everyone sat down to a fine supper of roast turkey, oyster pies, crab patties, and a sweet syllabub spiked with rum.

For Byron Barstow, seven-year-old Crown Prince and Heir Apparent, life on his father's plantation was endlessly varied and wonderful. For most of his life that he could recall, Byron had lived on Black-woods Plantation on Saint Simons Island. Orde Barstow rarely returned to his house in Savannah, at first because he was so totally absorbed in the dredging and digging and dike-building of the rice fields and in overseeing the construction of his house and outbuildings. Now he was even busier. Although his overseer, Harley Beene, had charge of maintaining and managing the slaves who worked the rice fields, who had built the three-story wooden house of native black oak, and who populated his life, Orde Barstow had less leisure time than he would have liked.

Only in the winter months did Orde have time to ride out hunting, to arrange fishing and shooting parties with fellow planters, to "dally" with Zonah, and to spend time with his beloved son. For the demands of rice cultivation lessened in these months, after the September harvest and the few weeks of curing the sheaved rice, after the rice had been bagged and carried to the docks, after Orde had traveled with his crop to Charleston and seen it fetch the best possible price. Only then could he reckon up the profitability of the season and by then it was time to start planning and preparing for seeding the squares in early March.

Orde enjoyed visiting the busy port of Charleston with its distinctive city-scaled architecture and its sophisticated social life, but this year he had been marooned there longer than he had planned. He had missed getting home in time for Christmas and barely made it for New Year's Eve, bringing, as usual, ten or a dozen newly arrived African slaves, as well as a black and white pony as a present for his son.

When Orde stepped off the packet boat from Charleston both Zonah and Byron were waiting on the docks at the sheltered, southern tip of the island.

"Papa! Papa!" the boy shouted as Orde appeared on the forward deck of the packet. "We saw your sail and came to meet you!"

Orde smiled and raised his arm in salute. He looked at Zonah. She was dressed all in white, as was her custom, and sat very proudly in her ribbon-trimmed saddle atop her light brown mare. A damn fine-looking woman, Orde told himself. I didn't see any prettier in Charleston. Zonah had bloomed in her maturity. She was still reed-thin and fragile to look at, but her limbs and features had rounded out into soft curves, and she kept her curly hair cut short enough to emphasize the graceful lines of her neck and shoulders.

And she had done well, too, raising the boy, Orde thought. Byron was sharp as a silver knife, and good. Already Orde had thought about sending him away to school—at least to Charleston—to learn that the world was more than riding and shooting and running wild. But not yet. For the next few years, the Virginia schoolmaster he had hired would be good enough. He would teach Byron to read and figure, and tutor the rest of the children on the plantation while he was at it. Harley Beene had five children, and Orde saw no reason why he shouldn't teach Zonah's children, as well—there were four of them now, light-skinned and good-looking and smart, as, Orde said to himself, you might expect, considering.

In its first five years, Blackwoods Plantation had grown and prospered. Orde Barstow owned slightly more than sixteen hundred acres of the island's southern lowlands, not far from the ruins of Fort Saint Simons and the site of the battle between the Spanish and British forces that had come to be called the Battle of Bloody Marsh. Barstow had been granted some of the land before the threat of Spanish invasion had been removed from South Georgia, but only afterward had he begun to survey and block off rice fields and bring in laborers.

Four years ago he had built the house on a point of wooded land. It was a modestly large frame house, with the peculiar masonry foundation native to the island, called "tabby." Tabby was a mortar mixed of burned oyster shells, sand, and whole shells that hardened into a decent substitute for stone. The walls of Barstow's house were three feet thick and he expected it to stand forever. He had chosen its sight carefully: on three sides it was shaded and sheltered by massive oak trees, which kept it cool on the hottest days. On the east side of the house he had built a long, railed porch along the length of the ground floor. From anywhere along the porch and from the windows of the two downstairs reception rooms, the master bedroom, and Orde's own office, you could see straight out to sea.

Now, riding next to Zonah and his son, Orde enjoyed his homecoming. He regarded his home with pride and appreciation. To others the lush, dense vegetation might have been dark and gloomy. To Orde, the silver-gray tentacles of the waving Spanish moss hanging off all the enveloping oaks cast a watery, shadowy spell over the house and grounds. He sighed. It was serene, silent, secret, and that was the way he liked it.

It was early afternoon. As Orde lifted his son off his perch on the front of his saddle, Byron heard the shouting of some of the other children at play and looked up at his father.

"There is an hour before dinner," Orde said. "I want to meet with Mr. Beene for a few minutes as soon as he gets back with the new Africans. Byron, you may do whatever you want, just be sure to be on time for dinner."

"Yes, father."

"Don't you think I brought a surprise from Charleston for you?"

"Did you? What?" The boy grinned.

"You'll see at dinner. Zonah?"

"Yes, sir?" Putting out a hand to Orde for help in dismounting, Zonah managed her slide from saddle to safe ground with a gesture that was both graceful and seductive. When she stood next to Orde, she kept hold of his hand.

"I'll want a bath before dinner. Wait for me in my bedroom, and I will come directly from seeing Beene."

"Yes, sir." Zonah spoke distinctly and coolly. Her stiff white dimity skirts rustled as she preceded Barstow into their house. As they reached the door, Harley Beene came into the front yard driving a slat-sided wagon crammed with shackled sea-sick slaves, most of them only months from African villages and unable to speak a word of English or comprehend any but the basic fact of their new existence.

Zonah did not turn to look at them.

Although Sea Groves Plantation, to which the remaining Dunlies returned a few weeks following Cattie's wedding, was only a few miles from Orde Barstow's home at Blackwoods, it was a plantation on a simpler scale. Angus Dunlie had neither the time nor capital to build a fine mansion with many outbuildings for his family. Their two-story wooden house with its spacious front porch was far less elegant than the house the Dunlies still owned in Savannah.

Optimistically, Dunlie called his plantation Sea Groves. He created the groves himself, planting a hundred orange trees the first spring after the Battle of Bloody Marsh. The next year he added fifty lemon trees, and the year after that he set out a few acres of peaches and dates, next to the mulberry trees, which he grew in accordance with the requirements of the colony's Trustees, who had theorized from the start that Georgia should become one of the world's great silk-producing regions. Unfortunately the mulberry tree native to Georgia, the black mulberry, produced leaves too coarse to be appetizing to silkworms, so colonists were ordered to plant white mulberry trees.

Long before the mulberries matured, interest in silk-producing waned in most parts of the colony. The Germans in Ebenezer were the most persistent and most successful at spinning silk from the filaments contributed by specially imported silkworms, but even on Saint Simons Isle some of the colonists, Angus Dunlie among them, had carried out their pledges to raise mulberry trees for the proposed silk industry.

But silk-spinning was not the most financially impractical stricture of the Trustees, as far as Angus Dunlie and the other island planters were concerned. Resentment against the Trustees' slavery prohibition had grown from a grumble to a howl. Like most of the other planters in Georgia, Dunlie was land-rich and labor-poor. The land was there: rich, dark, and fertile, rolling in well-watered plains, stretching full of promise as far as the eye could see. It was ideally suited for growing rice, as the planters in South Carolina had already discovered. But breaking the land, squaring off the fields, and planting, tending, and harvesting the rice required endless man hours of exhausting labor and constant exposure to the heat and sun. It was no work for white men, more and more of the planters decided, openly violating the law and buying African slaves.

Dunlie's work force was relatively small. He employed nine indentured servants, six of whom were bachelors, and he hired at a daily wage the available men and women who had been servants of the Georgia Trust, but whose contracts had expired and who now lived on small farms and in the town of Frederica. With him from Savannah, Dunlie had brought the Negro Moses, a free man whom he had trained to oversee the other hired laborers. Moses was a good worker and valuable servant, for in addition to being strong and loyal to Dunlie, he had learned the rudiments of carpentry and coopering while in Savannah. Since his unwilling acquisition of the black man, Dunlie had handled the situation in his own way: he ignored Moses's color and treated him like a white worker, a policy that had created problems of its own.

But at Sea Groves, Dunlie worked alongside Moses and the hired white laborers in the groves and fields. So far, they had just begun to put in rice. Their main crops were corn, peas, beans, and potatoes, staples to keep the household alive. In good years, there was a bit extra to ship to Savannah to sell. No year was disastrous, but no year so far had been really good; every year was a bit better than the one before and seemed to promise prosperity just ahead, or perhaps just ahead of that.

Dunlie admitted that his home life was dull. His days, once leisured except for restless concern over accounts and investments, were now filled with backbreaking physical work. He missed the society of his two daughters, especially Fayette, long gone but still acutely missed. His son and grandson were still small enough to live mostly in the world of women, and his wife was dour and strained in her change of life and made that realm a troubled, frantic one.

It was a gloomy, disspirited family dinner to which Angus Dunlie returned that chilly January afternoon.

Winter was the slack season on the plantation. When the wind blew from the sea, it was bitterly cold. Migratory birds wintered in the marshlands, deer came out of the thickets and nibbled on the frost-blackened corn stalks, and some nights ice formed on the inlets and ponds. There were no guests and the pace of life slowed. It was the season for repairing equipment, buying seed, and preparing for the big effort of spring planting.

The family was waiting at the table when he entered the dining room. The table was neatly spread with pewter, and he could smell something spicy from the kitchen—the serving maid Catherine had taught to cook had turned out to be talented. Even the two little boys were subdued, their hair neatly combed down with water and their hands folded.

"Dear Lord," Dunlie prayed from the head of the table, "let us give thanks together for all good things. Let us give thanks for our bodily powers and our spiritual energies, let us remember as we gather together, he who gathered together earthly men in fellowship, that we might all be saved. Let us magnify the Lord and let us exalt his name together. Let us bless the Lord at all times, let his praise be continually in our mouths. Let us cheerfully do His will, let us praise his name every day and forever and ever . . ."

"Amen."

All heads turned to the stranger's voice.

At the door stood a red-faced, round-cheeked, bearded, and bespectacled man. He was bundled up in layers of clothing—a yellow shirt under a red jacket, blue trousers and black stockings. On his head he wore a coonskin cap, round his neck was a green striped scarf, and he carried a large pack, buckled onto his shoulders with leather straps.

All the Dunlies stared. Everything told them he was

indigenous to some region far more remote than Savannah or even Charleston. The man had an exotic, foreign look. He looked curious but harmless, and when he spoke, they all marveled at his accent.

"I'm Oliver Phelps, fellow Americans. I make my way through the world without a musket or matchlock. I'm at your mercy, friends, for so I hope we'll soon be, though it's presumptuous of me to show up hungry at your dinner time."

"Welcome to our table," Angus Dunlie said. "Have a seat, sir, and Catherine, ask Liza to bring another plate. Tell me, sir, how far have you come?"

Deftly, Oliver Phelps shrugged out of his pack and walked to the fire. He swept off his coonskin cap and ran his fingers through his thick black curls.

"Just now, I've come from Sunbury, good sir, though if you're inquiring after my home, it's Massachusetts I'd have to name. Yep, the Bay State'd be my home if I had one, though a peddling man has to bid farewell to all this—a sweet wife, obedient children, the warmth of a fire on a winter's night . . ."

Liza entered the room carrying a plate for the visitor and hid her face; his accent was too funny to bear.

"What brings you here to our island?" Dunlie asked.

"Luck and latitude, I 'speculate, dear sir. Besides, I always wanted to see the spot where the Georgians whipped the might of Spain's army."

Dunlie's narrow face lit with pleasure. "Don't tell me news of that battle has spread to Massachusetts?"

The peddler was eating cornbread and chicken with okra as fast as he could fork it into his mouth. "Delicious! Wonderful! I always look forward to Southern-style cooking. My compliments to you, madam, for your generosity in providing us this bountiful spread . . ."

Catherine smiled slowly. The surprise visitor had brought them all to life. It was amusing to watch him eat. He lifted everything into his mouth with his right hand, waving a bit of cornbread with his left.

"And I dare to say there's a few notions in my pack which may just interest you, dear lady. Jest as soon as I've done justice to this meal, I'll be opening it up for your inspection. Now, young men! Introduce yourselves to Oliver Phelps."

Looking first to Angus, who nodded, James rose and bowed as his mother had taught him. "I'm Jemmy Dunlie, sir, and this is my brother, Roland. He's just five. I'm seven years of age."

"Thank you for the information and very well said, too. So it's the Dunlie family I've to thank for breaking my fast."

"Beer, Mr. Phelps?" Dunlie offered.

"No, sir, thank you but no. I'm not a drinking man. But I've always relished the company of those who like a drop."

"I'm sure you've seen many of them, Mr. Phelps, on your travels."

"That I have, Mr. Dunlie, and heard many tales. I'll gladly fill your ears. I'm a walking newspaper. I've seen it happen. Robbery in Boston. Fire in Philadelphia. Have you heard Poor Richard's latest rhyme? Smallpox, I'm sorry to say, kept me out of Charleston this last winter. There's a lot to tell. The trouble lies in getting it ordered in my mind, sir. Let's see . . . I always like to head south in the fall, jest when the leaves in Massachusetts are turnin' red and the frost begins to pinch my pointed ears."

"Which way did you come through Georgia?"

"November saw me north of Augusta, sir. Seems I walked a thousand miles through your back country. Good land out that way and not too many folks yet, either. Room for more. Seems like I saw a lot of good Americans making a new life out there . . ."

"Did you ever," Angus Dunlie leaned forward and asked a question that had come into his mind with a force that surprised him, "did you ever meet a married woman named Fayette in the wild country near Augusta?"

Phelps paused and scratched his head.

"Fayette? Is she kin you've lost touch with, then? Seems to me . . ."

"My daughter," Dunlie said.

"I believe she *was* called Fayette. I believe that is how she was called."

Dunlie asked eagerly, "Did you really meet Fayette?"

"Mind you, I'm not sure . . ." the peddler hesitated. "Now wouldn't she be the one who plays like an angel on the fiddle?"

"The fiddle! Yes, that's her! That's Fayette! How was she? How did you leave her, sir?"

"Well now, dear me, let me think. I do remember that music!"

"No hurry, Mr. Phelps. We're hoping you'll agree to stop with us for a few days. Give us time to look over the contents of your knapsack, you'd like that, wouldn't you, Catherine?"

Catherine was profoundly startled by the resurrection of her elder daughter by this multi-colored ragtag peddler. She leaned forward across the table and seized Oliver Phelps's arm. Her eyes were shining and her face was open and eager. "You can't leave until you tell us every single thing you remember. Every single thing!"

Chapter Twelve

An Indian Siege—An Encounter—A Dunking at Fishing Creek

"Trouble, sir?" inquired Mae Wilkins, Jack Barstow's housekeeper, poking her white-capped head out of her bedroom door. The sound of Jack coming late nearly always woke Mrs. Wilkins, try as he did to ease open the latch, to still the sound of his boots on the bare board floor, to find his way to the staircase without lighting a candle. No matter, Mrs. Wilkins was there, halfway out her door, her round face open with insatiable curiosity and concern.

"Yes, Mrs. Wilkins, trouble. The same trouble." As long as she was awake anyway, Jack touched a brand to the banked coals and lit a candle. He hung his cloak on a peg near the hearth.

"Those miserable trouble-making Indians! They should shoot them all! And now that they're allowing slaves, it's a bad example. We could all be murdered in our beds!"

"No one's been murdered yet, Mrs. Wilkins."

"Thank God for that, doctor. Where are they now? Where's that fool Stephens?" Mae Wilkins chattered nervously and her scrawny breast heaved.

"I left Stephens and the lot of them in Machenry's Tavern . . . smoking the pipe of peace."

"And drinking? Are they still giving those nasty redskins drink?"

"There's a bit of drinking going on, Mrs. Wilkins, along with the pipe smoking and promise making," Jack admitted, collapsing into a wooden armchair. He was so weary even his mustache drooped.

"Lord protect us! I'm sure we'll all be killed tomorrow! Oh, how will this end?"

"I don't know," said Jack, who feared the worse. The siege had been going on for nearly a month, for a siege it was. Malatchee, the Creek king, had been stirred to this mischief by none other than his cousin, Mary Musgrove, the half-breed interpreter whose fate had been tied up with that of Georgia since the first day Oglethorpe had set foot on Tamacraw Bluff.

This time Mary Musgrove had fired up young Malatchee to lead more than one hundred Creek chieftains and warriors in an attack on Savannah. The Creeks had come down the river in canoes, howling and shooting off their muskets. The heat-exhausted, feversapped citizens of Savannah had panicked. The Creeks demanded money and reparations with all the passion of a people just coming to understand how they had been stripped of their hereditary lands, but the territories were already settled and taken for granted, the Trustees were in England, and the people of Savannah had met the Indians' demands with helpless and empty promises and a firestorm of Indian hatred and fear.

For three and a half weeks the Indians had been camped on the outskirts of the city. Every night they stormed the streets, singing and yelling demonically and demanding drink in the taverns. William Stephens, Savannah's chief magistrate, had adopted a pacification policy—plying the Creeks with gifts of food and drink and leading Malatchee and Mary and her husband into endless negotiations. Stephens had also called out the volunteer militia and some of the young men of town had organized a Horse Guard to ride the streets in a nightly patrol.

"Doctor Jack? Doctor?" A woman's voice, emotional, oddly accented.

Jack and Mrs. Wilkins looked at each other. They were used to late-night visitors looking for the doctor. But tonight Jack was dizzy with fatigue.

"I'm here," Jack called out. "Come in!"

In the dimness stood Mary Musgrove herself, her red dress torn and spattered, her feet in laced moccasins, her hair tousled. Jack had known Mary since the colony's early days, and her trust in Jack had drawn him into the constant and changing negotiations between the Indians and the officials of the city.

"What is it, Mary?" Jack asked. "What more can you say tonight?" He ignored the sound of Mrs. Wilkins's door slamming. "Come on in, Mary. Who else is there with you?"

"Me and Malatchee." Her voice was hoarse and disturbed.

"Come in then, Mary. You're hoarse from screaming, aren't you? Why are you still standing there? What can I do for you?"

"Too late to do anything, Jack, eh? They put my husband in jail. They want to arrest me. Already they have tried it, but I ran away. Now it is too late. We have had enough talk. They talk of treaties. All the treaties are to steal from the Indians, steal our land and that of our sacred ancestors."

"Damn them! Damn them! We shoot all them white men dead!" Malatchee growled. He staggered into the room. Jack could see he was blind drunk.

"Streets full of riders to frighten us," Mary complained. Jack guessed that the horse guards had forced her to his door.

"You have frightened everyone, Mary. They are frightened of war."

"I am Empress and Queen of the Upper and Lower Creeks! No one frightens me!"

"Shoot them all!" Malatchee yelled. He fell into Jack's fireside armchair, dropping his musket. It clattered to the floor. When sober, Malatchee was a strong and regal young man in his early twenties with all the grace and dignity of a natural aristocrat. During these weeks of threats and negotiations, Jack had taken his measure. Malatchee invariably yielded to the last person to speak with him. He was no match for the machinations of his cousin Mary.

But was Mary match enough for her husband, Thomas Bosomworth? He was her third English husband, an Anglican priest who had put aside the sacraments to concentrate on getting rich—through Mary's rights. The two of them had persuaded Malatchee to acknowledge Mary as Queen of the Creeks. Then they demanded more than a thousand pounds payment for Mary's long service as an interpreter and clear title to three Georgia islands: St. Catherine's, Ossabaw, and Sapelo, which Oglethorpe had reserved for Creek hunting grounds. To back up their claims, they had enlisted the Creeks' finest warriors.

"It all belongs to me!" Mary shouted, pacing the room stamping her foot. "Even here! Every inch of this land is mine!" Once-beautiful, dark-haired Mary was still an impressive woman, but tonight she was disheveled and dirty and, like her cousin, she was muddled by drink.

"Mary, you've told them all this," Jack said patiently. "It won't do any good."

"You bet! I've just told them all. They told me to go to jail, and I told them I'd make them sorry. My husband's brother has gone now to get the warriors. Then they'll see!"

"Where has he gone?"

"Gone out to the camp. They're all waiting to fight. He'll bring them in here tonight and tomorrow will be different!"

"Shoot! Shoot!" Malatchee yelled weakly. He looked sick. His eyes were glazed and his legs unsteady. Malatchee had been so drunk and so angry at the tavern that he had foamed at the mouth. Mary was drunk, too; still, she might be telling the truth. Jack pulled his boots back on and grabbed Mary's arm.

"Do you mean what you say? Has he gone to rouse the warriors?"

"Oh yes, he has! They'll come quick!"

"Let's go meet them," Jack said, pulling Mary out the door. "Come on, Malatchee."

Together, the three of them stumbled through the dark, uneasy streets of Savannah. Few slept. It was hot and humid; a ripe-rotten smell rose off the river, the high-summer smell of decaying reeds and low water. The air was motionless, as were the trees. Even the clouds lingered in the night sky, as if too sluggish, too heavy with moisture to shift past the moon and the stars.

"Who goes there?" challenged the watchman at the Yamacraw Gate.

"Doctor Barstow," Jack called out, and the man turned his back on them, marching the limits of his guard station.

"With the Queen of the Upper and Lower Creeks!" Mary muttered unheard. Malatchee bent over a bush to vomit, poisoned by liquor.

"This way?" Jack asked, and Mary took the lead.

The Indian encampment was a mile outside the palisades. As they approached, Jack heard drums beating and excited voices. The Indians had kindled dozens of bonfires, and the sky was bright and smoky. As they drew closer he heard the war chanting, the traditional Creek yells that sparked battle courage.

"Stop them, Mary! Stop them now!" Jack begged. He turned Mary to face him. Her face was blank with weariness and pain. Jack grabbed her arm. "Remember the treaties with General Oglethorpe? Remember?"

"A fig for the General! This is my land!"

"Listen, Mary. Things are not the same as they were. Things have changed since those days. You can't make them the same. The General paid fairly for Creek lands. All the chiefs signed treaties with England. It's too late to go back. If you let your people make war on Savannah, many many people will die, your people as well as the white people. And still, Mary, it will not be as the old days. Still more white men will come in more ships and bring more treaties and more guns."

"To hell with all that!" Malatchee shouted. Mary was silent. A look of sadness had come over her face. Jack knew she had understood.

"If you are owed more money for your work, then you will be paid," Jack reasoned. "General Oglethorpe is in England, but he will send you money. Has he ever tricked you, Mary? You know he hasn't. And these men, nothing can stop these white men. There is no changing that."

"God damn," she said.

"If there is a big war between the Indians and the white men, Mary, you know who will win."

"We win!" Malatchee shouted. "We shoot them all!"

"You know who will win," Jack said, shaking Mary by her shoulders.

Her eyes told him that she knew. "Give me my husband back out of jail. Give me money. And we will stop. For now."

Several weeks after the militia and Horse Guards had entertained the Creeks at yet one more—the last and most spectacular—spree in Machenry's Tavern, after the rum-sotted Indians had left the city and gone back to their homes, Angus Dunlie made the long ride north from Sea Groves Plantation to Savannah. With enormous heaviness of heart, Dunlie had decided to renege, if possible, and only with the General's personal permission, on his oath never to own or employ Negro slaves.

Slavery was now legal in Georgia. The demand for it, widespread from the beginning, had come to be heard from the highest ranks of society, from men including silver-tongued George Whitefield, James Habersham, who had already made a name for himself in Savannah with his trading house and his work with Whitefield on the orphanage, and even Bolzius, preacher to the strict, hard-working, moral Salzburgers. All these men agreed that commerce and development in Georgia had come to a sorry, melancholy state and could not be improved without slavery. Slavery, they argued, would spur Georgia's laggard growth—the colony was sick and in need of a miracle cure.

Georgia was not the garden of Eden, after all. Few planters seemed to be prospering—except those who had cheated on the slavery injunction for years. Much of the land was not fertile—and those who had limited amounts of it wanted more. There was laughably little silk being raised, and no wine; the only steady crops were rice and corn. A few experimented with wheat and indigo, but none of the olive trees the first settlers had planted, under the instructions of the Trustees, were left alive. The exotic tropical plants in the experimental Trustees' Garden had withered away and died.

The colonists had more grievances. The climate was too hot; there was malaria in the swamps and summer fevers everywhere. A lot of discouraged settlers had already left. It was such a simple matter to move over the river into South Carolina, where a man could own as much land and as many slaves as he could afford, and no one required him to plant mulberry trees.

So the Trustees had given in. They set up a system of rules permitting and regulating slavery, tied into the system of indentured servitude, qualified with requirements to teach slaves Christianity and how to wind silk.

The utopia had failed, and for some high-minded idealists, among them Angus Dunlie, it was a bitter disappointment. Dunlie had given Oglethorpe his word, his oath, that he would not use slaves but would uphold the humanitarian principles they had so often discussed and agreed upon. Dunlie was ahead of his time. He honestly felt that slaves were a curse to those people who owned them and that no one had the right to reduce other human beings to slavery.

Almost fifteen years in this colony, Dunlie thought sadly as he rode into Savannah along the Tybee Lighthouse road. Fifteen years and now to have it end like this.

It was a damp fall day, and the steady drizzle and overcast skies intensified his mood. Here along the narrow, sandy road, the live oaks met overhead to filter what light there was. Behind him stretched Guale, the old Spanish mission province—a vast land of grassy marshlands, golden sands and lush forest—all the promise of Georgia's richness, so far, he thought, so far largely unfulfilled.

The sound of a horse approaching at a full gallop excited Dunlie's own mount, and he reined the animal in. When the rider came into sight, Dunlie recognized Jack Barstow.

"Hello! Hey there! Barstow! Isn't that you?"

"Good day, Dunlie! Coming into town?"

"Yes, and there to take ship for England."

"What?"

"Yes, I must sail as soon as possible."

"There's the *Mogador*, sailing tomorrow," Jack said. "But what's your haste?"

"Business. I go on business. Damn sad business, at that."

"What do you mean?"

"I've come to the point, Jack, that I must break my vow on slavery, and for that I'm bound to see the General himself."

"They say, sir, 'tis for the good of the colony."

"Eh! And how do you feel?"

"Like you, sir, I regret it. I would say that like most things, it's for the good of the rich."

"Well enough said. And you? You're riding to a sick bed?"

"Aye, pardon me, I must hurry. I had a message that a workman at the Tybee Light fell from the tower and still lives. God help him! And Godspeed to you, sir." Jack's horse neighed and danced in a circle as he turned it back onto the trail. "And my regards to your family!" he called back as he rode away.

I always liked that young man, Dunlie thought.

Strange, I once thought that he and Cattie . . . or was it Fayette? Oh, well, whoever, it was now a thing of the past.

Fayette, in her backwoods cabin, was now the mother of two, and much the wiser for it. Two children, she could now claim, were ten times the work of one. Both were boys. She was glad of that, and so was Micah, who already took the six-year-old boy, Pittman, hunting. Pittman had a squirrel-tailed cap to show for it. He was a better than fair shot for a boy twice his age, and thought of nothing but hunting and fishing.

Fayette called the second child Isaac, but to her continuing regret, neither had been baptised. The traveling Pastor Eben Reinhardt, who had married her, had been drowned in a flash flood and there was no church yet, even in Fishing Creek, which was what everyone called the little village clustered around the nearest trading post.

Fayette and Micah were far less isolated than when they had first come to settle in the forest. Scarcely a month went by when they didn't see a peddler, or a neighbor didn't ride into their clearing or they to a neighbor's for some reason: Micah to consult about some problem of farming, Fayette to lend a hand in child-bearing or sickness, or just to visit. Sugar, flour in sacks, even lengths of cloth could be traded for at Fishing Creek, and Fayette hoped that by the time the child she now carried was ready, there would be a school.

But for now, the thing worrying her was the children's baptism. She had heard that there would be a preacher coming in to Fishing Creek this Sunday, coming from Augusta, and she dearly wanted to be there. It was a bad time for all of them to leave; it was still harvest time, but Fayette longed to go. As she wrote in her journal:

It has been so long since I found time to write here, that I feel obliged to note that our second son, Isaac, is born and doing well. He is now three years old, and since neither he nor Pittman have been privileged to have a Christian baptism, that is the first thing on my mind these days.

Fayette paused. Isaac was pulling at her skirt as she sat on the edge of their bed to write. He was at a whining age, and not nearly as independent as Pittman had been at three, but still strong enough to be devilish, to tug at hot skillets and fall into the creek, strong enough to bear watching every minute.

"Isaac, dear, bring me my violin now, and I will play for you," she bargained.

It is a great responsibility to be all of church and school, teacher, and priest to my children, but I try not to lose sight of my goals. For if not for me, my sons will grow up here in this unmapped wilderness ignorant of all civilization, even as I knew it as a child. I play music to them and read scriptures to them lest they know only Indians and cornfields, sky and forest and creek and God's own works. Yet I wonder, sometimes, are they less fortunate than many English children for leading simpler lives? Are Micah and I less happy for lack of the pleasures of town? Indeed, the pair who is better satisfied with each other may be hard to find.

Fayette put down her pen and stepped to look out the open door. Isaac had been distracted and had wandered out the door. She saw him at once, a bright-headed little figure staggering across the yard to the woodshed where his father worked and his older brother had climbed to the top of a woodpile. Seeing Micah bare-shouldered in the sunlight stirred Fayette. The sexual bond between them was as strong as the emotional one, and even when she was with child, they made love every night.

Impulsively, Fayette ran out into the yard to join the rest of her family.

"Look! Look!" Pittman shouted. "See how high I am!"

"Take care," Fayette said softly. "And you, too," she said to Micah.

Micah set down his axe and wiped his face. "Fayette, I've been thinking. I don't see how I can spare the time to ride into Fishing Creek for the church meeting, but I know how much you want to go."

"You know I have put my mind to their being christened."

"And you are right to. So can't I send you off with the two boys? Likely the road'll be busy with people goin' in, and anyway, you never minded the ride."

"I wish you could come along, Micah, but if you can't, then I will ride alone. I think it's important."

So early Sunday morning Fayette put both boys together on the good-tempered mare they called Nellie, and the three of them rode into Fishing Creek. Before Fayette had gone more than half a mile she saw that Micah had been right. There were more horses and riders on the narrow dirt road than she had ever seen before. It was almost like a parade. She and the children rode slowly, partly for safety's sake and partly because Fayette wasn't in any rush, she liked the easy gait set by a walking mare, and enjoyed traveling in the open air.

Moving as slowly as they were, most of the other riders and wagons passed by the Stone family, and Fayette got a look at all of them. There were men and women and children dressed pretty much the same as the Stones: their clothing homemade and faded if not patched, the children barefoot and bareheaded, the men most often in buckskin and leather britches. Some Indians rode past. A few soldiers went by in rangers' uniforms, modified for backwoods riding with leather pants under long hunting shirts.

Fayette and her boys stared and stared. The horses' hooves stirred up the dust on the road and clouds of it rose to settle on their clothes, their faces and arms, on the horses until everything was the same clay color. Shouts rang out along the road and someone was singing. Fayette was glad that she had remembered to bring her violin.

When they were just outside Fishing Creek, the crowd was as thick as on a city street. There was an excited feeling in the air. The children could feel it at once, and they squirmed to dismount and run around.

"Now I want you to stay by me," Fayette cautioned. "Isaac, you take Pittman's hand and hang on."

Fayette tied the horses near the trading post and led the children in the direction of the crowd—toward the boat landing where the two creeks ran together. Along the way she saw some familiar faces among the mass of unfamiliar ones. One woman she knew told her that the preacher had come from Savannah. His name was George Whitefield.

Fayette felt a chill of excitement. Of course she remembered Reverend Whitefield; he had christened her brother Jemmy; likely he still knew her father. And he was thought to be the best, most stirring preacher in Georgia and the southern colonies. She had heard, if she remembered right, that he had preached in every colony.

A wooden platform rose at the water's edge and banners of white and blue hung from the overhanging trees. Fayette led the children under the trees and settled them down in the grass to wait. Reverend Whitefield was not here yet. As soon as he arrived, the meeting would start. Fayette fed the children and they all walked to the river's edge for water.

As they waited, more and more people gathered at the river. They came and came and kept on coming. Finally, when there were more people together than Fayette had seen in the nine years since she left Savannah and more than either of the boys had seen in his whole life, a ripple of excitement ran through the crowd. Heads turned and conversation hushed. He was here.

George Whitefield rode his black horse right up to the edge of the platform and dismounted with a graceful leap.

"God bless you, dear people, for gathering here today!" He took a stance at the center of the wooden platform.

"Amen!" someone called out, but Fayette was too dazzled to speak. Whitefield was still youthful-looking. He was slim, dressed all in black with snowy white linen. He was bareheaded and his face shone with confidence. When he smiled it was like the sun breaking through the forest.

"I am happy to be here and to see you all here," Whitefield shouted, "because God is with us today! Let us pray! Let us thank God for his unspeakable goodness. Fall on your knees, citizens, fall on your knees and pray with me!"

"I felt a trembling fear the minute he began to preach," Fayette told Micah later, "it was as if he was dressed in God's own authority. His voice rang out clear as a London bell, a sweet solemnity sat upon his brow, and I felt my heart pierced to the core with remorse for my sins and hope for my salvation."

All around her, people were as moved as Fayette was. Some fainted, particularly young women. One man cried out that he had sinned and began to beat himself with a horsewhip. Voices rose in hysterical shouts. Whitefield preached for over an hour.

"And so I beg you, I invite you, I order you, my fellow sinners, to surrender yourselves, surrender yourselves wholly to Christ! For only then will you be allowed to glimpse the gates of the Kingdom of Heaven!"

I am so glad, Fayette thought, that the boys are able to hear him speak. Both of them were silent, mesmerized by the power of Whitefield's eloquence and the mood of the crowd.

"Dear God, forgive me, for I have done evil! I have sinned," a woman not far from Fayette screamed in a hysterical voice.

"I hear you, good woman, and God hears you, too!" Whitefield called out to her. "I tell you the pain you feel is the pain of a new birth, birth pangs of the spirit. Feel it! Feel the suffering and rejoice in it, for only by being born again and purging your soul of all evil will you be allowed into the Kingdom of the Lord! Amen, yes, Amen!"

In a moment's lull, Whitefield passed the collection plate, calling out for contributions for his work and his orphanage. Fayette was embarrassed that she had no coins to put in the plate. All around her she saw men digging into their pockets.

"For in your natural state, people of Georgia, you are half devil, half beast. I cry for you . . . I cry out in agony for the knowledge of your individual sins, and I cry out for you to give in to the spirit! Feel it! Do you feel it?"

The woman who had cried out was writhing and

moaning. "Cleanse me," she begged, twisting her hands and tossing her head, "scour me!"

"And the children . . . those children whom God has sent to us," Whitefield said, "as innocent as they seem to be, yet if they are not accepted to Christ, they are as a generation of vipers. And will those children, who go through life and die without awakening, will they hate their parents when they feel the miseries of Hell? For if our lives be not a journey to Heaven, then they are but one other journey and that one leads us straight to Hell."

Fayette felt as if Whitefield were speaking directly to her. It was for this that she had come. She rose, taking both boys by the hand, and led them through the people seated on the grass, led them past the woman frothing at the mouth. Whitefield caught sight of Fayette coming and called out, "Yes! Yes, my good woman! Come ye forth and bring forth your little boys!"

He does not recognize me, Fayette realized with mixed feelings. Undaunted, she stumbled forward, Isaac whining.

"Hush, Isaac," Fayette said. At the river's edge two men were dipping those who came forth into the water. She tried to give them the boys' hands, but both of her sons clung to her. "This is your baptism," she said, "you will be cleansed and reborn."

"Noooo . . ." Isaac wailed. He struggled when the dipping man reached for him. The man was wearing a black suit without stockings or shoes.

"Come on in, be born again . . ." the man said. Fayette looked into his watery blue eyes, and the next thing she knew she, too, was in the creek, feeling the cold water bubble up over her head. She gasped, sputtered, swallowed a big gulp, and came up coughing, still clinging to her children's hands.

"God bless you!" the man in black called out. Whitefield reached out and put his hand on Fayette's head. Her children were screaming in fright.

"Hallelujah!" Whitefield shouted, "for she is saved in the name of the Lord! Hallelujah!"

Chapter Thirteen

Cattie Stirs Up Trouble—Zonah Feels
It—An Accident

Using her father's brief stay in Savannah as an excuse, Cattie Dunlie Nickerson had taken her small carriage and ridden into town to spend a while at her parents' house there. She left her husband and Nickerson Hall with great relief and lingered in Savannah after Angus had sailed to England.

In fact, Cattie found her life as the mistress of a plantation both exhausting and tiresome. Francis Nickerson owned more than thirty slaves and employed eight white indentured servants, but Cattie had learned that the responsibilities of labor management were nearly as taxing as the effort of doing things herself. For all the slaves had to be taught and directed and watched over and rewarded for learning something well. On occasion they had to be punished for laxness or laziness or sulkiness or rebelliousness. There was always the fear of insurrection, of direct or indirect revolt.

Everyone told stories of such things. Slaves set fire to crops and buildings, poisoned their masters and their masters' children. They ran away to Spanish Florida as often as they could, stealing horses or boats. It had been ten years since the Stono insurrection in South Carolina which had killed twenty-one whites and twice as many blacks, but people still talked about it. It was difficult to forget when most of the faces you saw were black.

Cattie found her new life hard to get used to. She found that she was at the beck and call of the "people" whom her husband owned, body and soul. She was their nurse, their marriage counselor, their schoolmistress, and their manager. Early in the morning Bessie, the cook, slipped into her bedroom and expected to be told what to cook for that day. Another house slave carried in a carcass of beef or pork and wanted instructions on how to butcher it. Someone was always sick and begging her to run down to the quarters to see to a crying child or an expectant woman who was nearing her time.

After a little more than two years, Cattie was also tired of marriage, tired of Francis Nickerson's endless boring stories, tired of seeing him fall asleep at the supper table, red veins popping out on his coarse-skinned, pock-marked face, tired of sharing his bed.

For it was her sex life as much as anything else that had driven Cattie, albeit temporarily—she intended to return—from her husband's house. Cattie had expected him to be a tired-out, indifferent lover; she presumed that he would have exhausted his passions on his first wife, but after a few months of marriage she was willing to wager that it was Nickerson's insistent and persistent lustfulness that had sent the poor woman to her grave.

Cattie had no idea why she had not conceived yet,

but she knew it was not for lack of opportunity. No matter how tired or drunk Francis Nickerson might be when he rolled into bed next to her, he woke an hour or two later and disturbed Cattie's own sleep, mounting her with grunts and gasps of desire, pinning Cattie to her pillows, and enjoying it. Cattie had been amazed, at first, then distressed and finally, disgusted. But there was no escape; that was life, that was marriage. She adjusted, but it left a sour taste in her mouth and had changed her attitude toward life.

Life, it seemed to Cattie in her mid-twenties, was not nearly as interesting as she had thought it would be. Of course, she disliked work. Reading or needlework had never appealed to her. Sex was a chore and a bore. Motherhood had not moved her—her son still lived at Sea Groves in her mother's care. Grown women did not do the outdoor things, swimming and walking and climbing trees, that she had loved as a girl. And Cattie had few friends, none at Nickerson Hall.

In fact, two years of marriage had changed Cattie considerably, and perhaps not for the better. She had grown mercenary; although she had always been materialistic in an innocent way—disliking inconvenience and unpleasantness in a childish, spoiled way; liking sweets and sunny days and good times—now she had come to view life as a marketplace and human relationships as contracts and barter.

Sex, as Cattie had come to see it, was the price she paid for survival in the world of men. Her husband had her, at his will. She, in turn, had a carriage and driver, a comfortable home, pretty clothes, and all the trinkets and gold that she could wheedle out of him. More and more often, now, she thought that it wasn't enough. In the past few months she had put her mind to the problem of getting a sizable chunk of Nickerson

Hall in her own name, or some goodly number of acres, or at least a decent sum of money. For Francis Nickerson was already forty-nine and he had relatives, including two skinny teenaged daughters. If he should die, Cattie was not sure how much of his estate would come directly to her.

She thought about it, though. She wondered and pondered and had begun to plot. It was very much on her mind. And so was her quest for any other material security she could come across.

It was partly to investigate such matters, that Cattie remained in Savannah after her father had sailed to see General Oglethorpe. Cattie was established in her father's house on Abercorn Street as if it were her own, attended by two female slaves and her driver, a thin Negro, blind in one eye, called Goldie.

A week passed, then a month. Cattie was very content to be away from Nickerson Hall, and when Francis wrote, asking her when she would be home, she replied that she had suffered a fever and was recovering slowly. In truth, she was having the best time she could manage. She had learned to play whist, she had bought herself a pair of golden finches, she drove out in her carriage every day, she visited Rose and her children at their humble house, and she had renewed her affair with Jack Barstow.

The pleasure Cattie got from that relationship was somewhat apart from her usual pattern of male-female give and take. True, Jack was the most solicitous and attentive of lovers, he brought her presents of roses and sugar cakes and wild turkeys—which he was as likely to get in payment from a patient as anything else, but Jack was not a rich man. Rich in promises, he said of himself, though he also had two fine horses, a solid house on King Street, and a cellar full of French wines, the gift of a grateful husband whose wife he

had saved from malaria and who had put miles between his family and Savannah's climate as fast as he
could.

"You've always been sweet on Jack Barstow," Cattie's friend Rose, now Mrs. Peter Posey, said to her
and Cattie agreed. She did like Jack; mostly because—
more than anyone else in the world—he liked her. Jack
made Cattie laugh and feel young and free again. He
had stopped off at her house one afternoon to extract
a tooth for Flora, Cattie's personal slave, and stayed to
take Cattie to bed. Cattie found to her amazement
that sex with Jack could be quite pleasant, especially
when they had shared a bottle of wine.

Jack in bed was quite unlike Francis, of course. He
was young and strong and affectionate, and when she
had gotten used to receiving as well as giving physical
pleasure, Cattie looked forward to seeing her lover and
came to depend on him. It was a situation that was
bound to turn explosive. Jack loved Cattie and swore
he always had and always would. It pained him that
she was married to another man and that she was
openly pleased to have financial security and an absentee husband. Cattie told him nothing about her
love life with her husband, but what he imagined tormented Jack.

Seeing his torment, Cattie turned cruel. Half-angry
that she had traded love for money but nonetheless
devoted to the latter, she turned Jack out of her house
and refused to see him again.

One afternoon, shortly after Jack and Cattie had
quarreled, Cattie had a surprise visitor at the house on
Abercorn Street. She was in her bedroom, napping in
the late afternoon, when Flora came to tell her that a
gentleman, a Mr. Barstow, but "not the usual one,"
was waiting for her in the front parlor.

Hastily, Cattie dressed in one of her finest gowns, a

green and pink flowered silk, and tucked her golden hair up under a lace cap. She ran downstairs to meet Orde Barstow.

"Why, Mr. Barstow! What a surprise! What brings me this honor?"

Orde Barstow bowed and kissed Cattie's hand. "I am delighted to see you looking so well. Illness agrees with you, my dear. You look prettier than ever."

Cattie sighed. Savannah was a small town, a very small town, and she had known Orde Barstow most of her life. Of course she had known him to be the man with whom her father disagreed violently and with whom he had quarreled. As well as anyone else, she knew of his unorthodox family arrangements, how he lived as if married to a black woman and that he had adopted an orphan for a son. But it was not until she had married that Cattie had met Orde socially.

Orde was a friend of Francis Nickerson's, a hunting, card-playing, gambling friend, and he had come to visit at Nickerson Hall on several occasions.

"Francis sent you, then," Cattie said. "How is my husband?"

"Considerably less robust than yourself," Orde commented. He laughed and something moved Cattie to join him, though she had never before imagined Orde as a co-conspirator.

"Fah! I am feeling quite spirited these days," Cattie said. "Perhaps it is the excitement of city life. May I ask you to take tea?"

"With pleasure. I have something in particular to discuss," Orde said and settled himself comfortably into the armchair of the man whom he had vowed to despise forever, the man whose family he had cursed until the end of their days.

Cattie ordered Flora to bring tea and sat down opposite Orde.

"You are looking well," she said. He was fashionably dressed in a new suit and his sky-blue silk waistcoat, and the years had given him an aristocratic dignity. Cattie felt a little chill, thinking how angry her
father would be if he knew she was entertaining Barstow in his house. Really, though, Cattie thought their
old rivalry foolish. Hadn't they quarreled over a
slave—a single slave? As for herself, she rather liked
Orde Barstow. He was surely the most cultured, most
amusing of Francis's friends, and not the less interesting as he was Jack's estranged stepfather. Father will
never know of this, she vowed, but as for Jack, perhaps
she would tell him at once!

Poor Cattie. In her little plots and machinations she
was no match for Orde. Barstow, too, was thinking of
Angus Dunlie and the last time he had been inside this
rather poorly furnished room. More than nine years
had passed already, but the recollection sent a flash of
temper through him; his rivalry with Dunlie was far
from dead. He had kept an eye and ear to all of Dunlie's doings, and he had welcomed every rumor of
Dunlie's financial difficulties.

Still, Orde longed to insult Dunlie in some more
personal way. Visiting his daugher in his house was
one step. Cattie had come to Orde's attention when
Francis Nickerson married her, though he had heard
with delight the rumor that she was not pure at the
altar. In Orde's judgment, and this was no secret, he
enjoyed expounding on it in any tavern at all, his
"friend" Francis Nickerson was both gross and boor-
ish, and Cattie's marrying him was obviously a desperate financial bargain. It was also, obviously, an insult
to Angus Dunlie's proud and preachy political position.

Meeting Cattie, seeing her—a precious jewel of a
beautiful woman in the chaotic commonness of Nick-

erson Hall—had stirred Orde in another way. It had been years since he had slept with a white woman, other than a couple of Savannah whores, and he had a craving to take Cattie to bed. The idea, once implanted at Nickerson's supper table, had taken root and grown into an obsession of sorts.

Watching her now, his mind was filled with lustful thoughts. He admired her shiny yellow hair, so fashionably arranged. He studied the uncommonly pink swell of her half-exposed breasts above her low cut bodice and fancied burying his head in that soft pillow. Now if they were in London, Orde thought, it would be a simple matter. He would take her in his carriage, carry her off to a country inn or one on the west side of town, and . . . But here, in this country town?

Cattie's thoughts, as they drank tea—Orde spiked it with rum from a silver flask—and chatted, were not really far different from his. How unlike her husband was this man, she thought. Barstow was a true gentleman, mannerly, gracious, charming, and also rich. Not for the first time, Cattie thought she had made a mistake in marrying so soon. She was only twenty-five, now, and just beginning to learn what the world was like. Had she managed differently, the society of Orde Barstow, or men like him—no doubt there were others—would be her daily experience.

Cattie's cheeks flushed from the rum, and she looked rosier than ever. A misty, unfocused expression came into her blue eyes. Orde caught sight of it and knew that the time had come.

"But enough talk of business," Orde said. "I think I have bored you. And that was not my intention."

"Oh, not at all. I am very interested in investments! Oh, look! It is so late. It is quite dark outside!"

"Your society is so pleasant I took no notice of the

time!" Orde said. "I apologize. You have been a charming hostess. Perfect in every way."

"Why, thank you, sir!" Cattie rose and whirled flirtatiously around the parlor, shaking her silken skirt over her hips, peering out of the windows.

"But I do have one last favor to ask of you."

"Last?" Cattie laughed. "But what is it?"

"Will you grant it?"

"Surely not until I know what it is!"

"I would like to kiss you."

Cattie's blue eyes opened wider. He was so bold! She was confused. How could he have said what he'd said— a man his age and a friend of her husband's? Was he teasing her? She bent her head to think. It was a thoroughly unconventional way to behave. Francis had never kissed her until after their wedding, and her affair with Jack was a complete secret she scarcely admitted to herself.

On the other hand she was terribly flattered. What it suggested, although Barstow had not actually said this, was that she was so overwhelmingly desirable that he could not resist her. Perhaps no man could resist her. That was a pleasant and stimulating thought. Cattie raised her head.

"And then what?" she asked.

Orde Barstow laughed. What a surprising little baggage she was. "Why then, whatever you like. I will do whatever you like."

"Whatever I like," Cattie repeated. "Well, in that case, it is quite simple. I will do whatever you like and in return, you will do whatever I like. Is it agreed?"

"Agreed," Orde Barstow said and lowered his lips directly to Cattie's silky-soft bosom.

When Orde came home to Blackwoods after his visit to Savannah, Zonah knew something had happened to him. He had a different air. Zonah's happiness, her very survival, depended on Orde Barstow's moods and whims and she was excellent at feeling them; she was atuned to Orde as a sailor to the winds or the soundness of his craft, atuned, indeed, as a slave to his master.

All her life, Zonah had moved back and forth between the world of whites and the world of slavery, of her own race. Unlike most of the black people in the colony, she had been born in slavery. She had been born and raised in the Big House of an Anglo-Jamaican sugar planter, born the first child of the mistress's chambermaid. Although she had learned the language of her Ibo mother as well, and many of her beliefs, she had heard English spoken since she could walk, and she had grown very accustomed to the ways of an English household.

Then the planter and his entire family died of the fever. To pay his debts, Zonah and the rest of his possessions were shipped to Charleston, and Zonah had been sold to Orde Barstow.

Those early days seemed so long ago now, Zonah thought. But it was not her way to look back. She was bent on walking on, and the only way to walk without falling was to look ahead—not too far ahead, just a bit ahead—to enjoy life whenever it was possible, and not to think of maybes or might-have-beens.

For the last fifteen years Zonah had served Orde Barstow. She ran his household, she raised his children, she served as a go-between his field slaves and the overseer, and she slept in his bed. Her life was exceptional and she knew it—she had seen slavery and its attendant miseries all her days: some of what she had seen was unspeakable and some could not bear remembering, but Zonah's own lot had been lucky.

"Luck follows me all my days," she had often told

her friend Saraby, sometimes ironically. Saraby agreed. No other black woman that anyone knew of lived in the big house with the master. No other black woman dressed up in white clothes and sometimes played hostess for the master. Zonah had borne four healthy children, and they lived together with Saraby in one of the dirt-floored huts in a row behind the barn, but they did not work in the rice fields like the other slave children.

Zonah had always been allowed to teach and to mother her children. She spoke to them only in English and taught them to keep out of sight as much as possible, and when the tutor came for Byron Barstow, her children were instructed by him, too. This delighted Zonah, although she was as impassive and inscrutable in her reaction as usual.

Secretly, Zonah had hopes for her children by Orde. The oldest boy, Ira, was shy and brilliant. He was now fifteen, and very soon a trade or an apprenticeship must be found for him. The girl, Mary, was fourteen. She was quiet and tractable, nowhere near as pretty as her mother, but clean-featured and appealingly fragile-looking. She was the best seamstress at Blackwoods and worked hard at it every day.

The younger two boys, Sam and Joe, were just babies: energetic and lively. It gave their mother pleasure, mixed with apprehension, to see them growing and maturing, playing with Byron Barstow and the children of Harley and Bessie Beene—just as if they were free.

When Zonah sensed the change in Orde Barstow, she feared for her children as well as herself. At first, she did not know what had happened to him—just that something had. Never before had he come home and not wanted her body immediately. Never before had he stared at her—quizzically, critically, when she undressed and offered herself to him at bedtime. The sexual bond between them was strong and habitual; Zonah felt his rejection of her as a blow and a strong warning of more trouble to come.

She was right. As soon as he had seen the plantation record book and talked to Harley Beene, Orde had some announcements to make.

"Zonah," he told her, when they were together in his second-floor study. "Something has to be done about those children. They're plenty old enough to work."

"Yes, sir." Zonah agreed. Her heart had stopped and she was breathless. What had he decided? Would they be taken away from her?

"Byron, too," Orde said. "I want him to get off the plantation. He should learn more of the world. I'm going to send him north to school."

"Yes, sir."

"And Ira. Ira is clever. I'd like to see him freed—one day—but it's too soon. He needs training. He'll work side by side with Beene from now on, but I want him to learn about management, too."

"So he'll stay here," Zonah breathed in relief.

"Yes, for the time being. And Mary . . ."

"Yes, Mary?"

"A woman I know, north of Savannah, needs a seamstress. I'll take Mary to her the next time I go."

"Oh!" Zonah trembled. Take Mary away? It was the thing she had feared most. Who was this woman? Why was Mary being sent to her? All her instincts warned her to keep silent, but she could not. In a hollow voice she asked, "Who will be our seamstress, then? Mary works very hard here."

"I can't help it. She'll have to teach one of the other niggers before she goes."

"Oh!"

"Bring me some tea, Zonah. I want to look over these books again. I think Beene is trying to cheat me."

"Yes, sir." Zonah made it out of the room without stumbling, but outside she collapsed on the steps and put both hands over her thumping heart. Then she covered her eyes and cried for a while. Were her lucky days over? Had she lost her appeal to him? She looked down at her slim dark body. Too skinny? Too poor? Too dark?

"Evil days, bad woman, trouble coming," Zonah muttered to herself when she had recovered sufficient composure to run to the kitchen house for her master's tea. She felt as if a deadly poison had slipped under her skin and was running, running through her veins. But what could she do? She remembered something her mother had told her, "When a knife is heading straight for your heart, straighten your back."

Fayette was busy in her kitchen, setting out five loaves of bread for their final rising, when she heard her son Pittman scream. She knew at once that something was seriously wrong.

"Isaac, watch the baby!" she called back. She snatched up a woolen shawl and ran outside. It was cold out and last night the first frost had nipped the grass, browning it. The wind tossed dried leaves and ripped others off the red-gold oak trees. The sky was a dull November gray.

Fayette ran in the direction of Pittman's screams. He and Micah had gone out at daybreak to cut down trees for firewood. By now they might be half a mile into the woods, but Pittman's cries were coming closer and closer.

"What is it? What is it?" Fayette called out as soon

as she glimpsed her sturdy, tow-headed son. His face was white and his eyes wild.

"Oh, Mamma! Papa! A tree! It fell on him!"

"Dear God. Where?"

Together they ran back through the thick woods. It seemed unnaturally silent to Fayette, silent as death. The only sound she could hear was the pounding of the blood in her ears and her own gasps for breath.

They ran and ran. It seemed like miles to Fayette. Pittman sobbed, but neither of them wasted breath on talk.

"Where? Where?" Fayette demanded when they came to a point where the trail disappeared into underbrush.

"Up here!"

From there on, Pittman led the way. They climbed a little hill covered with sweet gums and holly and blackberry bushes. A snake slithered off a sun-warmed stone and some creature rustled the bushes.

Fayette's lungs ached before she saw the signs of Micah's logging. He had already felled a stand of tall pines and had them stacked in the clearing.

"Over here!" Pittman yelled.

Fayette heard the horse's terrified neighing before she could take in the whole situation. A huge pine tree had fallen to trap both Micah and his horse underneath. The horse was pinned lengthwise and his legs were kicking desperately like the legs of a pinned beetle. Foam spilled from his mouth and his head was back, eyes rolled white in terror and pain.

Micah lay still. Both his legs were pinned under the tree, and he had lost consciousness. A trickle of blood ran out of the corner of his mouth.

"How can we move the tree?" Fayette screamed. She pushed at it feebly. Her strength was nothing to the enormous weight of the pine.

"I'll help! I'll help," Pittman sobbed. He had put his shoulder to the tree and could almost move it. He rocked it and Micah stirred.

"Run back for the other horse!" Fayette ordered him. "Go! Run!" She knelt by Micah's head and touched his closed eyes.

"Micah? Micah, darling, please speak," she wheedled. He was still breathing, but his skin was white as parchment and cold to her touch. The horse's groans of agony were painful to hear.

"Micah, just stay alive, please don't die," Fayette begged. Already on her knees, she bent her head and prayed out loud.

"Please God, spare him. Please let him live and I will do your work all the days of my life."

Chapter Fourteen

*Cattie Flees—Byron Barstow Goes Off
to School—Doctor Jack Loses His
Nurse—Fayette Awaits the Call*

By the early seventeen-fifties, it was generally acknowledged that the Georgia experiment had failed. The population of Savannah had declined drastically, and those left complained increasingly loudly. Personal pessimism was confirmed by low property values. A house and lot in Savannah would sell for a few shillings, except that no one who wanted them had any money at all.

Later, a prominent Savannah merchant reflected that in 1751 he could have bought half of the city for twenty pounds sterling, but things were bound to improve, and the first signs of it could be seen even as the Trustee era came to an end in 1752. From the Trustees, Parliament decreed, the colony would come under the direct control of King George, but before they surrendered their charter, the Trustees gave the Geogians an exercise in self-government, and delegates from all parts of the colony came together in Savannah to make certain recommendations for their own betterment.

Angus Dunlie was among them; so was Orde Barstow; and so was Doctor Jack Barstow. Women were not represented, nor were Indians. Slaves were not even mentioned, though the first Georgia Assembly recommended, among other things, that Savannah should have a new wharf and that ships should not dump ballast in the river.

After 1752, the new Georgia began to emerge. The colony had never before had any governor at all, for the Trustees had not managed to appoint one. Within two years, King George had set up John Reynolds, formerly an officer in the Royal Navy, as governor, and established a council, an assembly, and courts. Before that year, Georgia had had no lawyers. In fact, they had been prohibited as an unnecessary scourge to the common man, but the first year of the Royal era brought the first lawyers and soon they were plentiful enough to be referred to as "the bar."

During those troubled transitional years, Angus Dunlie devoted himself to Sea Groves Plantation and his family. In England, he had sold the last of his family's holdings in Dorset and had sought out his old friend James Oglethorpe. The old general was still passionately interested in Georgian affairs, but had mellowed. Dunlie found him enjoying his pleasant country estate, his English beer, and his literary friends who included Dr. Samuel Johnson, Boswell, and Oliver Goldsmith.

Dunlie had felt greatly at odds with London life. He felt old-fashioned and provincial, knew himself to be more concerned with survival than with style, was alarmed by the crowds and the press of city life, and despised the damp climate. He returned to Georgia fully committed to his life there, after suffering en route a dreadful, storm-wracked crossing.

Soon after Dunlie's return to Sea Groves, the character of the plantation began to change. His first stop in America had been in Charleston, where, his conscience cleared by Oglethorpe's personal absolution from his well-meant pledge, he had become a slave owner. Taking the money from the sale of his family seat, he bought thirty African slaves.

In managing this captive work force, Dunlie was luckier than most. He had the assistance of Moses Black, as he now called his overseer, and together they undertook the training of thirty unhappy men and women snatched from their African villages and transported under the most intolerably cruel circumstances to a new continent with an unknown language.

Both Dunlie and Moses Black were at first extremely discouraged. Moses had been born in South Carolina and was himself vastly different from the new slaves, who huddled together out of wretched kinship. Several of them died and one killed himself with an axe while Moses was forcing them to build themselves dwelling houses. Still chained and shackled, the new slaves dug trenches and built dams to convert the low, marshy land at Sea Groves into rice paddies. In the summer they worked naked. In winter they were given shoes and a sparse allotment of clothing. Cracked rice, too poor to sell, was the mainstay of their diet. From that, they made flat rice cakes and flavored them with benne seeds, which they planted at the end of rows of corn and peas for good luck. The slaves at Sea Groves were luckier than most; Dunlie allowed them small plots for their own vegetable gardens, and he gave them meat at least once a week. As soon as it was possible, he intended to teach them to read and write and worship Jesus Christ.

Through work and discipline, the slaves adjusted to their lives. Dunlie was amazed to see that Sea Groves made a small profit on the very first slave-produced rice crop. The next harvest was better than the first, and in the year after that he was about to ship one hundred barrels of rice to Savannah for exporting to Europe. He grossed about twenty-five per cent on his investment in slaves and goods.

"Hurry, Mary! Yes, all my dresses, except the black silk . . . oh, better pack the black one, too."

Cattie Dunlie Nickerson was in a hurry. A desperate hurry. An epidemic of yellow fever had broken out in Savannah earlier in the summer, but only now, in late September, had it reached isolated Nickerson Hall. Ten of the slaves had died this past week, and many more were wracked with the disease.

It's Francis's fault, Cattie thought. She had wanted to leave at once, as soon as the first cries of pain and calls for help had been heard in the quarters, but Francis had lingered against her advice, and now he was sick himself.

"Yes, ma'am. This trunk is all ready to go," light-skinned Mary, who had been Cattie's seamstress and personal maid for three years now, hid her excitement at being on the way home again. For Cattie was taking her, with her maid Flora, as fast as Goldie could drive the carriage south to her parents plantation on Saint Simons Island to escape the fever, and Mary hoped she would have a chance to visit her mother while they were there.

"Don't forget my hatbox!" Cattie cautioned Mary. Though I doubt I shall have cause to wear any fine clothes in the country, Cattie thought. I expect life at Sea Groves is as boring and primitive as ever.

She sighed. There was no more postponing it. She had to go and say farewell to Francis.

Handkerchief pressed to her nose, Cattie tiptoed down the dim, sickness-silenced upstairs hall of the house where she had lived for five years. Propriety demanded that she remain to nurse her dying husband, but Cattie had chosen to defy propriety. After all, she told herself, Francis had two daughters to nurse him, and besides . . .

What Cattie could not admit even to herself was that she felt sure her husband was as good as dead. All remedies for yellow fever were useless, as far as she knew, and since Francis had been seized with the first ghastly symptoms, an agonizing headache and a burning thirst, she had seen him deteriorate swiftly. His delirium and convulsions had been frightful and last night, when the fever had reached its crisis, he had sobbed out to her that he was sure to die and that she should flee.

Cattie had decided at once that he was right. She only hoped that she was leaving in time.

"Sukie? Margaret?" she called, outside the door.

Sukie, the elder of Francis's teenaged daughters, opened the door a crack.

"How is he?" Cattie demanded, stepping back.

"Oh, Catherine, his breath smells bad," Sukie reported. "And the spots are all over his body."

"Dear God!" Cattie murmured. She poked her head into the bedroom. Francis lay limply in the middle of their big bed, his big body swathed in a sweat-drenched linen nightshirt. As she looked in, he gave a choked groan. His face was dyed a dark, dull red color and he opened bloodshot eyes.

"Unnnnnnnnn . . ." he groaned again, trying to frame some word, but his tongue was swollen with mucus, and he could not speak. When he opened his mouth, Cattie saw that his gums were dark, almost black. She shuddered, and Sukie moved forward to lay a comforting hand on her shoulder.

"Try not to cry," Sukie whispered, patting her, assuming that Cattie was stunned with grief. Cattie shuddered again, dislodging the unwelcome hand.

"Stay away as much as you can," Cattie told Sukie. "I must go. You and Margaret should follow as soon as . . . Oh, I feel . . ."

Cattie swayed a bit, feigning faintness.

"Oh, Catherine, please take care of yourself!" Sukie gasped. One of Cattie's maneuvers, in insuring her escape from Nickerson Hall, had been to hint that she thought she was with child, which in fact she did not.

"Yes . . . I shall," Cattie promised, and turned to flee. "Tell him . . . tell him farewell from me!" she called back.

As Cattie's carriage, driven by the coachman who was blind in one eye, made its way slowly along the river road from Nickerson Hall to the coast, Orde Barstow was also on the road, journeying north from Savannah, where he and his family had taken refuge from the fever epidemic. Although Cattie did not know it, the disease had just broken out on the island and all the white people who could manage were fleeing.

With Barstow rode his son, Byron, now twelve years old and on his way to be enrolled in a boarding school in Charleston. Young Barstow was proud to be riding alone with his father but not pleased to be going away to school.

"You promised that I can come home for Christmas," he reminded his father, casting a sidelong glance to check his father's mood.

"Yes, of course," Orde said absently. The boy was so

young; he could see that he was sorry to leave home. Orde cast a critical eye at his adopted son. Really, the boy had turned out very well. He was slim, but strong and wiry and already nearly as tall as Orde himself. Although Byron's fair, sand-colored hair was not like Orde's own dark, grey-streaked curls, they both had blue eyes, and Orde was well enough satisfied that the boy looked English, and even passably aristocratic. He was nothing to be ashamed of.

Orde had never hidden the fact that the boy was adopted. After all, it was obvious. Orde knew that his business and home life had kept alive all the gossips in Georgia for many years, but he had stalwartly ignored them. "A man's private life is his own damn business," Orde had often told his friend Francis Nickerson, and if Nickerson was one of his few friends, why plantation life was by its nature isolated, and when Orde felt the need of society, he made one of his seasonal trips to Charleston. There he had always maintained business acquaintances who were obliged to stay on good terms with him.

Orde had mellowed over the years, and he felt satisfied with most aspects of his life. His plantation, Blackwoods, was the largest and most prosperous on Saint Simons Island, and would have made him a rich man, had he not already been one. Every year he shipped more bushels of rice from Savannah; this past season had been the best ever, and he looked forward to making a good thirty percent on the crop now being harvested.

There is little I regret, Orde thought. I lack nothing—a pleasant home, a loyal and obedient woman, an heir . . . Byron was a good son, he thought with satisfaction. He was even-tempered and level-headed and polite. A lot of credit for him should go to Zonah, Orde admitted. Zonah had been a good mother to all her children——and she had never let her motherhood interfere with his pleasure. From the beginning she had raised Byron carefully and she had done well.

The narrow trail was deep in mud, for the night had brought a fall storm off the sea and both riders were silent as they guided their horses through the dryest parts.

Orde felt a momentary pang of guilt as he remembered how sad Zonah had been over the incident with Mary. Sometimes he had felt he shouldn't have done it—given Mary to Cattie Nickerson—especially as his relationship with Cattie had turned out to be so short-lived. But Zonah had recovered her spirits; she was all right now, Orde told himself. Everything between them was just as it had always been.

"Easy there," Orde cautioned Byron, as a black snake slithered out of the mud, spooking Byron's horse.

"Father?" Byron asked. "How long do I have to stay away at school?"

"I want you to learn everything you can," Orde said. "About figures . . . and history, I suppose. But when you come home you will learn from me. Beginning next summer I want you to ride with me every day and learn how a plantation is managed. Schoolmasters know books, but they don't know everything. Remember that. And remember that you are a Barstow—as good as a Barstow."

"Yes, father. I know . . . that I was not born to you . . ."

"Of course you do."

"But . . . do you know who my parents were?"

"No, I don't. You were an orphan when I took you in. I reckon you were the luckiest orphan in Georgia. And I've raised you as my own."

"I know! And I love you, father . . ." Byron's

throat tightened. It was so hard to talk about it. He hardly ever thought of what might have happened to him if he hadn't been so lucky. Whenever he did think of it at all, he felt that he had been . . . saved . . . by God or some Divine Chance. And yet it gave him an off feeling. It was odd about Zonah, too. When he'd been younger, he had been secretly convinced that she was his real mother, but he was ashamed, now, that he'd been so confused.

"Good," Orde said gruffly.

"I miss you all already," Byron said. "You, and Blackwoods, and . . . Ira and Sam and Joe and Zonah. But . . ."

"But what?"

"Don't you have any idea . . . where they came from? My mother and father?"

"No, son, I don't. No one knows. So let's not speak of it again."

"All right," Byron said.

Except maybe Zonah, Orde thought. He had wondered, from time to time, if she knew more than she had said. Well, at any rate, what did it matter?

For Doctor Jack Barstow, the months of the yellow-fever epidemic in Savannah had been a time of cease-less and saddening work. Hundreds had taken the fever and fifty-two had died. In the first weeks of the summer epidemic, Mrs. Wilkins, Jack's housekeeper, had served him as a nurse and the patients who came to collapse in his house had turned the place into first an infirmary, and later, a morgue. But Mrs. Wilkins herself had succumbed to the disease, and Jack had worked on through hot rainy July and into dry scorching August, hopefully, almost helplessly tending the sick in their homes and in his.

But during those airless, diseased summer days, Jack

had found a new and surprising ally and assistant. It was Joan, the same half-Indian midwife who had attended Catherine Dunlie in childbirth and prescribed an abortive herbal draught for her daughter. More than once, during the years, Jack had come across evidence of her doctoring, and he had developed a respect for her instinctive and not unsuccessful touch with the sick.

For Jack had always been eager to learn more about his craft—any and every way he could. In his first days of doctoring, in Oglethorpe's army, he had learned about bleeding and setting bones from William McDavid, the army surgeon. When McDavid died, Jack had taken over his surgical kit, a simple leather saddlebag with all the tools of his trade: clips, hooks, pins, and sutures; shears, crooked needles, forceps, lancets, probes, scalpels, syringes, catheters, tourniquets, and a trepanning instrument.

Back in Savannah, Jack had tried to learn more about surgery and pharmacy from anyone who knew. The best-known medical practitioner in Georgia was Noble Jones, and this intelligent and practical man had passed on to Jack much of the knowledge of his profession. A doctor's most prized assets were his strength, dexterity, and a keen knowledge of human anatomy. As well as his surgical tools, Jack had compresses, lint and tow to stuff into wounds to stop the bleeding, adhesive plasters, linen bandages, fracture pillows, and various splints. He knew of a few pain killers, primarily alcohol, laudanum, and oil of cloves. Jack had also ordered a few books from Boston, and he knew to prescribe cinchona, or "Jesuit's" bark, yielding quinine, for malaria, and mercury, when he could get it, against syphilis.

But little was known about treating yellow fever. It was a dreadful and puzzling malady. Jack had ob-

served that it was usually seasonal and struck those
in apparent good health without any premonition.
White people seemed even more susceptible to it than
Negroes, though no one knew why.

Jack saw yellow fever as a spasm of the extreme ar-
teries, a condition of nervous excitation. Generally, for
fevers, bleeding was recommended, but during that
dreadful summer of epidemic and experimentation, he
became convinced that bleeding only weakened the
yellow-fever victim, especially in the early stages of the
disease when the patient was in a state of debility.

Joan agreed. "They's thirsty," she told Jack. "They
need more water, not less blood."

Jack took on Joan as his nurse, and they dosed his
patients with a bitter brew she concocted of white oak
bark and rattlesnake root. The two communicated
well with the few words of English they shared. Joan's
wide knowledge and long experience with Indian herbal medicines interested him. He visited her hut and
saw the herbs she dried, and he walked with her in the
woods to see where the plants, trees, mushrooms, and
roots grew. From Joan, Jack learned about using sen-
eca, or snake root, for a purgative, and jimsonweed
for treating asthma. She showed him poke berries,
used as an astringent; sour dock, used to treat the itch;
and blackberry roots, dogwood bark, elderberries, and
goldenrod, all used in treating dysentery. He learned
that juniper berries were good for ridding his patients
of worms, and boneset was useful for treating fever
and consumption.

Nevertheless, most of those who fell ill with yellow
fever either died or they didn't, seemingly regardless of
all efforts to treat them. As the summer waned, there
were fewer new cases, and it seemed the epidemic was
over early on that still, breathless September morning

when Jack stopped in at Joan's hut, after a night ride to the MacBrides' plantation outside of town.

Jack was exhausted and discouraged, for all seven of the MacBrides were ill and their two little sons had looked beyond recovery when he had left them at dawn.

"Joan! Good morning!" he called, but there was no answer.

Jack dismounted and went into Joan's house to look for her.

The hut was small and dark. Joan lived there alone, carrying her water from a small stream and cooking outside in the summer months. Jack stooped to pass through the low doorway and ducked to avoid the bunches of drying herbs she had hung from a branch propped between the rafters.

"Dear God! Are *you* sick?" Jack exclaimed, seeing Joan lying on a pallet on the floor with a pail of water and a dipper by her side.

Joan sat up slowly. "Aye. I feel light in my head and sick in my stomach."

Jack felt a pang of despair. "Do you think it's the fever?" he asked, noting the ominous dryness of her skin and her glazed, fevered eyes.

Joan struggled to her feet.

"What are you doing? Lie down," he ordered.

"I'm sick, but I must go, Doctor Jack."

"Don't act daft, Joan. Where do you want to go?"

The dark-skinned woman swayed, her small square body still as agile as that of a woman half her fifty years. Jack put out a hand to support her. He was truly saddened to feel the dry, papery heat of her arm.

"Doctor Jack, there's something on my conscious from long ago that won't let me rest or die in peace."

Jack stared at Joan's sad, simple face in astonishment. He had never before heard her make such a statement. "Don't speak of dying yet, Joan. I need you for my nurse. And everyone needs you as a midwife." Conscience? he thought, what rubbish! Poor Joan has helped the sick and needy all the days of her life. What fool has been filling her head with talk of conscience?

Joan struggled out of Jack's grasp and wrapped her shivering self in a rabbit-skin shawl. She staggered toward her door.

"Stop! I'm not letting you go wandering off somewhere. Joan, what's troubling your mind?"

"To Barstow . . . " she muttered. "I must go."

Jack followed her out of her hut. The red-yellow sun hung threateningly in the sky, burning his face, but Joan shivered with the fever.

"Barstow?" Jack asked, and Joan nodded. Could she mean his stepfather and not him? "Who? Orde Barstow?" Joan's eyes showed her relief that he had understood, but Jack understood only that the fever must be affecting her mind. Yellow fever patients often suffered delirium and frightful delusions. She had an *idée fixe*, he acknowledged, but she had to be stopped. He doubted she could walk ten paces in her condition, let alone the five miles to his stepfather's house in town.

"No, Joan," he said, putting his arm on her shoulder, "forget him. Forget it, whatever it is. Lie down and I will bathe your face."

"I must go!" Joan screamed with an amazing fierceness. Her eyes were bloodshot but wide-open with determination. "I must tell it!"

"All right," Jack agreed, for his respect for the woman would not allow him to deny what might be her last wishes. "Come, then, I will take you astride."

"To the Barstows'," Joan commanded. Her ears rang painfully and her tongue felt thick and dry, but she could think only of putting that old wrong to rights.

Jack lifted Joan onto his tired horse, and she clung to him weakly as they rode slowly into town. He could feel her trembling and hear her agonized breathing, but when he tried to stop, she begged him to go on. The day grew steadily hotter as they rode together. It was an intense, choking, late-summer heat that had slowed all life and business. Few people were out on the streets of the town when they rode through it toward the Barstow house, and those who were looked up lackadaisically at the odd sight of the doctor with the Indian midwife on his horse.

"Perhaps it will rain," Jack guessed, judging the hazy sky.

"No," Joan said, "not while I live," and Jack did not waste breath arguing with her.

At last they reached the lane leading up to the rear of Orde Barstow's house. Although Jack had once lived here, he had not entered the house in many years, not since the day his stepfather had cursed him.

"Stop," Joan ordered. "Now, I go alone."

"What? Let me help you, Joan . . ."

"No. Please, Jack, I want to go alone. You wait, now." Jack protested as she slid off the horse and ran toward the Barstow house, but he obeyed her. Dear God, he thought, what an incredible will she had. Why on earth is she determined to see old Orde? He tied his horse and followed Joan. She should not be allowed to go inside; he would make sure she didn't. Of course all the occupants of the house would have already been exposed to the fever, but it was possible that Joan could bring new contagion.

The thought sped his steps, and he ran around the stables. It was all familiar, and yet unfamiliar. Everything was hushed in the barnyard.

"Joan!" he called out. His voice rang, echoed.

Then he saw Zonah, dressed in white, peering around the edge of the kitchen shed.

"Zonah!" Jack cried with pleasure in his voice. "Where is she?"

Zonah did not answer. Her dark face was stern and her hands hung at her sides. Jack approached. He sensed that something was wrong. Then, at Zonah's feet, he saw Joan's crumpled body.

"She's dead," Zonah said.

Fayette felt that her prayers had been answered. She crossed her heart as she recalled that terrible day . . . she had been frightened blind that Micah was dead—he had *seemed* dead, trapped under the fallen log, lying there white and still.

Sobbing, consecrating to God the rest of her life, Fayette had strained helplessly, trying to move the log, then had given up and kneeled at Micah's head, rubbing his head and heart to bring the blood to them, waiting the unendurable minutes while Pittman ran to fetch Nellie.

At last he had returned, and together they had hitched Nellie to the log and pulled it off Micah's legs.

Fayette's lips had still formed prayers and promises as she had slung Micah over Nellie's back like a sack of flour and had carried him back to their cabin.

"Pittman, get the musket and shoot the horse," she had directed her eldest son when they had spread Micah out on the bed.

"Please, God, let him live," Fayette had begged. Tears streamed out of her eyes, and when she saw his eyes flutter open, she screamed in joy.

Micah had broken both legs and could not yet, perhaps never would, walk with a normal gait, but that

November day was now just a terrible memory. For all that winter and into the next spring, Fayette had done the work of both a man and a woman, all the cooking and cleaning and housekeeping for Micah and the three children, and then as much of the outside work as she could manage. She had piled on Micah's winter clothing on top of her own, and she had run out, before dawn and after dark some days, to feed the animals and chop firewood.

Fayette sighed. It was November again, three years since the day of the accident, and she had thoughts she longed to confide to her journal. In the last few minutes of daylight she went to the low chest where she kept it and opened the book to write:

How very much that one day three years ago has changed our lives. In all this time Micah has just managed to walk again and still has pain, I know it from the shadow that comes into his eyes when he is tired. But, in truth, I did intend, at the time when I foresaw the loss of my love and the bleak desert life without him would be to me, to see my own life changed even more. For I did promise to God Almighty, Our Heavenly Father who saved Micah and spared him to live in my love, that I would do his work all the rest of the days of my life . . .

Fayette stopped for a moment to comfort her baby daughter, Jenny. Green-eyed curly-headed Jenny was her father's favorite, a plucky, cheeky toddler who hated to be left behind by her brothers but was still too young to keep up.

"Mother! Isaac run off and left me!" Jenny sobbed.

"Hush, dear. Both of your brothers will be coming in soon for supper. Just stay here and you will be the first to see your papa," Fayette said to her.

And to this day, I have not kept my promise," Fayette wrote. "Indeed, I do not yet know how I am to keep it. I want to serve God, of course not through neglecting my duties to my family, but I am not called to any particular task. Oh, I have not forgotten my promise, I have not denied it, and do not mean to postpone it any longer than my strength may permit, but though I long to hear the voice of God, though I listen for it with my heart open, I do not hear a Call and do not know which way I will be allowed to serve. Perhaps I am impatient. If so, if time will clarify my Way, I can only wait, and wait I will.

Troubled, Fayette closed her dairy. Her head spun as she stood up and she realized she had not eaten all day. As ever, these days food was scarce—even now, when she had just harvested the potatoes and corn from the garden—for the supply had to last all winter, but tonight they would all fill their bellies, for Pittman had shot a doe, and Fayette had set a venison stew on the fire at midday.

"Jenny, run out and ask your brothers to shuck some corn!" she directed. "And keep an eye out for your papa—he's coming in from the milking just about now."

I will wait, Fayette thought as she stirred the rich, aromatic stew, I will wait for the call and when it comes, I will be ready.

Chapter Fifteen

*Savannah Celebrates—Cattie Dances
with the Wrong Barstow—Orde Gets
Out of Hand*

All Savannah turned out to celebrate the arrival of
Georgia's first Royal Governor, John Reynolds, in
Christmas week, 1754.

It was a gala day in the town, where any unusual
event attracted a crowd. The taverns opened at dawn,
ale and rum flowed, and reunions, toasts, new friend-
ships, quarrels, brawls, hasty weddings, and jubilation
were the order of the day. There was a rifle match
with prizes of swords, saddles and bridles, rifles and
money, all contributed by the new governor. Some
spirited young men set fire to the militia's guardhouse,
perhaps recalling miserable nights spent in its dank,
vermin-infested walls, and nearly burned the old council chamber as well.

Despite a few charred timbers and a chimney that
had collapsed during a session held to discuss building
new chambers, the council house, the largest public
structure in town, was to be the site of an exclusive

"entertainment" with dancing and supper to honor new Governor Reynolds.

Only Georgians of "the better sort" were invited to attend the governor's entertainment, but everyone turned out for the procession and official ceremonies. It was a fine, cool, late December day. As on the King's birthday, the public celebration began in the morning with a ceremonial flag-raising. Cannons roared. There were speeches and more speeches. The assembled crowd toasted the new Governor, the King, the Royal Family, and Oglethorpe, and the militia drank to them all, still in marching formation.

After the ceremony, everyone with any claim to official office paraded through the streets of town, stepping in time to the military drummers. The procession was the most elaborate ever held in Savannah. The militia showed off their new uniforms and fired off rounds with their muskets. Thirty schoolboys, organized into military ranks, wore neat red hats and jackets and sang a patriotic song as they followed the militia. All the officials of Georgia's government marched with their wives.

Angus Dunlie had been chosen speaker of the Georgia assembly. He and Catherine, plump and breathless in a new lustring gown of olive-colored silk, marched close behind Governor Reynolds and the judges. The rest of the assemblymen, including Orde Barstow, followed Dunlie.

At the sight of Angus Dunlie with his cold, prim little wife, Catherine, Orde felt a familiar pang of resentment. He had known the Dunlies for twenty years, now, although they had encountered each other only rarely in the recent past, and Orde felt that he had bettered Angus Dunlie in every one of life's important ways, but their rivalry was still active, in Orde's mind.

He had never forgiven Dunlie for his absurd, insulting behavior in giving refuge to his slave, Moses, or for alienating his stepson, Jack, which he had come to blame on Dunlie. Of course, Orde had seen Jack over the years, but since that final quarrel and Jack's stealing Moses, they had never again been friends, and Orde had come to regret the loss.

Through the years, Orde had heard much about Dunlie's financial struggles and enjoyed them. He had heard with satisfaction of Dunlie's family troubles—everyone knew his older daughter had eloped with a common workingman and all about his wild daughter Cattie—Orde had relished the gossip about her illegitimate child and taken particular pleasure, some years ago, in seducing her himself. But despite his problems, Dunlie had a reputation in the colony for being honest and high-principled, and despite Orde's campaigning against him, he had been elected speaker of the assembly by his fellow planters.

This rankled, and so did Orde's realization that nothing he had done—either publicly or behind the scenes—to harm or insult Dunlie had really attained its desired effect. Seeing Angus Dunlie's tall, spare frame walking ahead, marking the proud set of his thin shoulders next to his diminutive blond wife, Orde cursed Dunlie for his stiff-necked stubbornness. In the assembly their differences had already begun to emerge: at the first meeting they had both stood in heated debate about the provisions of the new slave code. Orde wanted to see a slave code for Georgia at least as strict as the one in South Carolina. If Dunlie had his way, Orde thought bitterly, Georgia's Negro slaves would be cared for like Whitefield's coddled orphans at Bethesda. Ridiculous.

And then, standing on the sidelines, waving, Orde spotted Dunlie's son, James, and Cattie's love-child. All the Dunlies looked happy and proud—of their high-and-mighty papa, Orde assumed. For the hundredth time, Orde wished his own son had come home for the holidays. Byron had done well at his Charleston boarding school, and on the advice of his masters, Orde had sent him on to the new College at New Jersey, at Princeton. Byron was bright and Orde was pleased to see him succeed in his studies, pleased to see him mature and grow man-like, but the truth remained. He missed him sorely.

"Hurrah!" James Dunlie cheered as Orde passed close to him.

"God bless the Colony of Georgia!" Cattie called out. Orde caught Cattie's eye and he enjoyed seeing her blush. Orde admitted to himself that his secret affair with Cattie had been mainly for the pleasure of compromising Angus Dunlie's daughter—not that he didn't deem Cattie an extremely handsome and spirited woman. She was a widow, now, but Orde felt sure she wasn't grieving over Francis Nickerson. In fact, he, who had enjoyed drinking and gambling with Francis, probably missed him more than Cattie did. She looked far from sad, Orde observed, elegantly dressed in tucked black silk and as pink-cheeked and pretty as she had been at twenty.

A shame her father never knew, Orde thought. Seeing blond, vivacious Cattie made him feel lustful. It was a welcome feeling. Orde was fifty-seven but felt damn well—perfect, in fact, except for a slight weakening of his vision. There's fight in Old Barstow yet, Orde told himself, and he did look far younger than his years as he stepped along in the procession, his dark curls only streaked with gray, and his stocky, muscular body as solid as ever. Not dead yet, he thought. Old Lanky Dunlie will not find it easy to lord it over me in that assembly.

Orde grinned. Perhaps I'll ask Miss Cattie for a

dance tonight, he vowed. How can she refuse an assemblyman at the Governor's Ball?

"Don't they look fine, Cattie?" James O. Dunlie asked his sister. Fifteen now, James was already a man. He had inherited his father's looks, and to some extent his mother's temperament. James was tall and leggy, had a shock of light hair above a long, big-featured face and resembled his mother. But in addition to his family traits, James had some peculiarly his own. He was by turns silent and moody and explosively hot-tempered.

"Aye . . . What?" Cattie mumbled. She had caught Orde Barstow's expression as he passed, and she, too, had remembered the time when they had been lovers. Since that time, Cattie had had other lovers—all in secret, of course, for she was the widow of a respectable planter—and still, she was unmarried. Her son, Roland, stood between Cattie and her brother, James. Cattie was fond of Roland—he was a good-looking likeable boy, but he was now nearly grown, almost thirteen, and Cattie had a new plan. Now that she had plenty of money—oh, enough, anyway, including title to half of Nickerson Hall, and her own slaves, including blind Goldie, her driver, and Flora and the mulatto Mary, her personal maids, Cattie was considering telling Jack Barstow that he was Roland's father and marrying him, after all, to legitimize Roland's birth.

In truth, Jack Barstow seemed the best solution to her problem. For Cattie had begun to look on it as a problem. At the age of thirty-one, she found herself a woman alone—a mother, yet not motherly—a widow, yet unscarred by grief. She was too old for the young men she saw about her—the young militiamen in from the backwoods or freshly arrived from England were too inexperienced to interest her—and yet she had no inclination to marry an older man. Her marriage to

Francis Nickerson had taught her that much at least, and she deemed herself lucky to have escaped from it as early as she had.

Naturally, she thought of Jack. He was of the right age, still in good health, and he had always amused her. Their on-and-off involvement had given Cattie a good deal of pleasure over the years. He was still unmarried, and he had gained a good reputation for his doctoring. And besides, Cattie felt sure that deep down, Jack still loved her. She liked to think that love was eternal.

Perhaps tonight at the ball, Cattie mused. Surely Jack will be there. Perhaps tonight I'll talk to him. The idea stirred her.

"Let's go!" Roland said in a low voice to James. The two were closer than twins, and although James was two years older, it was Roland who always took the lead in their games and pranks. Roland was a small, wiry, confident boy with pale blue eyes and a complexion as freckled as a bird's egg. Behind his pale eyes was a shrewd, practical intelligence that secured him the position of leadership—seeing as a small boy that in contests of physical strength James would always win, Roland had become subtle and learned to "manage" James's strength, bullying tendencies, and outbreaks of temper to his own advantage.

Poor James, who had never been anyone's favorite. A thin, colicky baby, he had grown up to be a nervous, whining boy. His mother, perhaps unconsciously recalling the trauma of his birth, had openly favored Cattie's handsome baby, Roland, and Angus Dunlie had been so scrupulously careful not to spoil his natural son that he had been cold and strict. James was afraid of his parents, especially his sharp-tongued mother, and had become devious and sly to cope with his fearful world.

"Where?" James asked, still absorbed by the passing procession.

"Down to the Market Square. There's going to be a slave auction. Don't you want to see it?"

James's eyes, hazel like his father's, widened in excitement. "Yes!"

"Well, let's go." Roland turned to Cattie and put on the polite and shy expression he used for dealing with authority. "Auntie, we have to run an errand for Papa now."

Cattie nodded, still lost in her own thoughts. A distressing idea had occured to her. Perhaps Jack would not want to marry her. Why had he never married? Perhaps he had a woman somewhere, or . . . Nonsense, Cattie thought. Jack had always loved her, he would be the happiest man on earth to have another chance. Cattie nodded as she turned into the crowd.

"God bless King George!" a yellow-toothed drunken trapper shouted, lurching toward Cattie. "Pardon me, ma'am," he coughed when he saw her outraged expression. Cattie sniffed and stepped around the trapper. She would go home and prepare herself for the evening. It was important that she look her very best.

The ramshackle council house had been completely transformed for the Governor's ball. A committee of Savannah's good wives had supervised its cleaning and decorating. The pine board floor gleamed, candles burned brightly in every available candleholder, and garlands of holly with its bright berries and shiny leaves had been twisted around the bare rafters to give the room the look of a bower.

At the head of the room, three long trestle tables had been covered with white linen and spread with a sumptuous and elegant supper. Slaves had worked outside all day, turning a steer and three sheep on spits above open fires, and wild turkeys, geese, and chickens were now browning next to the juicy, delicious-smelling roasts of meat.

According to the custom, an especially ornamental dish, or "grand conceit" as the goodwives described it, was used as a centerpiece for the table. Tonight it was a Tansy Pudding, a huge molded dish made with two quarts of cream, forty eggs, and a pound of almonds, flavored with orange-flower water and tansy, colored with enough spinach to make it a lively green, and decorated with almonds, citron, and sliced sugared oranges.

It was just dusk, and the guests were arriving. Among the first were the three Dunlies.

"La! Look at that pudding!" Cattie whispered to her mother. Catherine Dunlie had contributed several dishes from her own kitchen, and she looked down the long tables for them. As her figure suggested, Catherine was increasingly fond of rich foods and she had sent along two kinds of pie, one buttered apple pie and the other a tempting giblet pie, rich in cream and laced with brandy.

"Mind you don't touch the stewed spinach," Catherine cautioned her daughter. "I don't trust it." She looked down the table, past the Salamagundy, a dish of cold chicken, anchovies, eggs, and onions, past the Scotch collops and boiled mushroom sauce for fowl, past the cakes and tarts and pickles. There she spotted her own apple pie and she smiled. It was large and golden brown and she knew it was tasty for Annie had made another, and they had eaten it at midday.

But Cattie had little interest in the table. Her eyes scanned the room, looking for Jack Barstow. She had spent hours fixing her hair, powdering and dressing herself for tonight. Although she must wear mourning for five years at least, she was determined to look gay, and had fastened her golden locket around her neck. Her black silk gown was fashionably low cut, and its short sleeves and scallop-edged petticoat were trimmed in dark green. Thank goodness I look well in black, Cattie had decided earlier. It made her clear, delicate skin look even whiter and set off her golden hair.

The supper was to be served at ten, but the dancing had already begun when the Dunlies entered the room. It was crowded, and all ages were represented from shawl-swathed grandmothers lined up on benches to babies in the arms of their mothers. A few strangers from Charleston and London attracted attention—but aside from them, everyone knew everyone else.

"Good evening, good evening," Angus Dunlie called out to neighbors and old friends as he moved into the crowd with Catherine on his arm to pay his respects to Governor Reynolds.

A quartet of Negro fiddlers provided the music, playing the familiar tune of a lively minuet that set Cattie's foot atapping. She studied the couples out on the floor, many of them militia with their sweethearts. Jack was nowhere to be seen. How young they all looked, Cattie noted in dismay. Well, not all. She saw Robert and Sarah Whitman, her parents' friends, and recognized many others: Lachlan McIntosh, the planter; James Habersham, the merchant, and Harris, his partner; Noble Jones, Captain of the Militia, and Bartholomew Zouberbuhler, the rector of Christ Church.

Cattie saw a crowd of men clustered about the kegs of rum and beer at one end of the room, and she moved slowly in that direction. As she passed an open window she looked into two faces: her son, Roland, and her brother, James.

"Hisssss . . ." she whispered. Then louder, "What are you two naughty fellows doing? Come in, if you will . . ." But they were gone, and Cattie did not care where they went.

Her attention had been totally captured by the appearance of Orde Barstow at the door. Cattie was not the only one whose eye was drawn to Orde. A rustle of skirts and a hush in the conversation accompanied his entry.

Even for a man who had a long-standing reputation for dandyism, Orde was splendidly turned out. His square, stocky frame was clothed in a sober gray suit of the newest cut, which only set off the gorgeous sunset orange of his embroidered silk waistcoat. Silver buttons ran the length of his top coat and frills of fine white lace flourished at his cuffs and on his shirt front. Above the brightness of his waistcoat his face was serious, stern, and his intense blue eyes glittered mockingly, even belligerently.

Cattie saw all this and caught her breath. Orde was the handsomest man in the room, better looking than men half his age, and yet . . . his expression alarmed her. She sensed some trouble was coming.

Wielding her fan, Cattie stared at Orde and wondered what he would do. Would he dance? She had never seen him at a social function before; most men of his age and stature were accompanied at such functions by their wives, but of course, Orde Barstow had no wife. Cattie had not long to wait and wonder. With mixed feelings, she realized that Orde was walking in her direction, heading straight for her where she stood near the window.

"Good evening, Miss Cattie," he said, bowing, his voice rich. "Or should I say Madam Nickerson? I have never had the opportunity to express personally my condolences at your loss."

"Good evening," Cattie said. She smelled liquor on Orde's breath and felt her nerves tighten. She covered her face with her fan and said in a low voice, "What you call me does not interest me as much as that you speak to me at all. It will distress my parents, sir!"

Cattie tried to turn away from him, but Orde put out a restraining hand and stopped her. "As long as everyone is watching us already, my dear, why not pretend that you are glad to see me?"

"I am not glad to see you. Oh, that is, I like it well enough—to look at you, for you shine in this drab gathering, but Mr. Barstow, we cannot continue this conversation. Everyone, as you have already said, is watching us."

"In that case, let us give them a show." Orde grinned and bowed again. "May I have the honor of leading you in this dance?"

Before Cattie could answer, he had pulled her onto the floor, into the line of partners behind Robert and Sarah Whitman, her parents' friends. Cattie noticed that Sarah Whitman was frowning and her husband glowering. She felt a pang of annoyance and embarrassment—they were all such gossips—she oughtn't be dancing with a man she knew her father disliked—but on the other hand, he was a gentleman and a member of the assembly, and he had been a friend of her late husband's—to break away would cause a scene—so wasn't it better to do it gracefully?

The motions of the minuet separated Cattie from her partner for the first few minutes, then brought them back together, hand in hand.

"There, aren't you enjoying yourself?" Orde asked her.

"Well enough, thank you. But I have not yet met my father's eye."

"I shall meet it for you. Angus Dunlie must be proud of his lovely daughter, so much the prettiest woman present that even the wickedest man is drawn to her side."

Cattie frowned. How could she chastise an ex-lover she had never openly acknowledged? "I have not seen you in nearly two years," she said.

"Years of prosperity pass so quickly," Orde said.

"That is true," Cattie said, curtsying. It was not in her nature to look back; she had no interest in the past at all, but she was becoming more concerned about her future. Dancing with old Orde was of no use to her—where was the other Barstow—Jack? What would he think if he came to see her dancing with his former stepfather? Why, no one in Savannah counted Orde Barstow as a friend, she realized, though everyone was glad to do business with him.

"What wayward thought has crossed your pretty face with such a dark cloud?" Orde asked. His eyes were the bluest on earth, Cattie noticed, and his curly salt-and-pepper hair very wild for a man of fashion.

"That dancing with you may ruin my reputation," Cattie said, "and how glad I am that you have never adopted an ugly powdered wig!"

"I have never understood," Orde said seriously, "of what earthly value is a reputation. I have gotten along splendidly without one for fifty-seven years."

"It's easier for a man, I assure you," Cattie said. "And did you lose yours immediately upon birth?"

"Immediately. For the day I was born my mother died. My father never forgave me."

Cattie watched her feet as she put them through the most intricate part of the dance. She wondered if he was speaking the truth. Why did Orde Barstow always distract her so? He was so different from most other men she had known. So different that none of the usual rules of behavior or conversation could apply to him, or to her while she was with him. But later . . .

she would suffer for this foolish dancing, which was bound to look like a flirtation, no matter what it really was.

"*Your* father!" Cattie said. "I'm sure he's dead by now, but mine still lives, and I hope he will forgive me!"

"Courage, my dear," Orde mocked as he turned Cattie in a sedate circle and transferred her small white hand to his elbow. "This dance is nearly over and then I shall return you to the society of our smug, safe neighbors. I have enjoyed this interlude, but I must go."

"Go? Aren't you planning to stay for supper? And after the supper more dancing, you know."

"Oh, I'll be back. It's just that I have thought of something that will clarify my position and reputation as well . . ."

The music ended and Orde bowed elaborately again, holding Cattie's hand a fraction longer than necessary, long enough to send a slight tremor up her arm.

"Good-bye, then," Cattie said, fanning herself vigorously. I wish he'd go, she thought. Orde Barstow is a troublemaker, no matter what else he is. And isn't it just like him to arrive, set all the tongues awagging, and then leave!

"Thank you, madam," he said, "You are so kind."

Cattie cast her eyes around to see who was listening. As far as she could tell, everyone was. She lowered her eyes demurely. "Thank you, Mr. Barstow."

On his way to the door, Orde stopped to shake hands with the new Governor. He heard the hush in the conversation as he crossed the room and felt the animosity toward him with short-tempered amusement.

"Damn them all," he muttered as he left the council house. His carriage was waiting and he took the reins from the driver himself despite the evening's chill. He was in a hurry to get home and get back.

The streets of Savannah were clogged with men and women celebrating the occasion.

"Stand aside!" Orde's driver yelled. Orde took a drink from the jug of rum he kept under the driver's seat. Everywhere he looked he saw people: sailors and soldiers, whores and Indians, Negroes and bemused frontiersmen dressed in skins and furs. They passed a bonfire in Percival Square. The flames leaped to the sky and the crowd cheered. Orde took another drink and felt his spirits soar. He was delighted with his idea for upsetting the good, solemn gentry of Savannah, so proper and sedate at their exclusive gathering in the council house.

A few minutes later Orde's carriage stopped in front of his house in St. James Square. Only a few small lights burned inside, but Orde leaped from his perch outside the carriage, swung open the front door and called out.

"Zonah! Zonah, where are you? I want you!"

Zonah, who had passed a lonely evening doing mending and needlework, missing her children whom she had left behind at Blackwoods, was upstairs. She appeared at the door of Orde's bedroom wearing only a petticoat and corset cover as Orde bounded up the stairs.

"Yes, sir?" she asked. Her voice was tremulous. She had no idea what he wanted now.

"Get dressed," Orde commanded. "We're going out."

In her late thirties, Zonah had gained weight and she was more beautiful than ever. Her skin was clear and shone with health; maturity had slowed her and added to her natural dignity and grace. To Orde's eye, she was luscious—a rare, ripe beauty as succulent and marvelous as an exotic fruit. Seeing her partly undressed stirred his appetite, and he reached out to stroke her breasts and pat her full buttocks.

This, Zonah understood. She smiled, and her large, dark eyes widened.

"Mmmmmmm . . ." Orde groaned as he kissed her. "I said, get dressed, Zonah!" he said. "And light some candles in here!"

"Yes, sir," Zonah said, carrying a lighted taper to the wall sconce.

"Wear your new dress. The one I brought you."

Zonah fought back confusion and fear. He wanted her to dress, now, so late at night? The silk dress had been a present, and she had never worn it out of the house. What on earth was happening? She stood still, motionless, still too astonished to obey.

"Come on!" Orde laughed. "Dress at once." He spun her around toward the door. Zonah kept her clothes in the little attic room off the stairs.

When she returned carrying the dress, Orde had taken off his jacket and waistcoat and was sitting on the bed. Zonah recognized the light of passion in his eyes, and it stirred her just as it always did.

"Sir?" she asked, pausing just out of his reach. Her eyes fixed on his and she let him see that she admired and desired him.

"Come here, darling," Orde said, "before you dress, let me love you." His arms reached out for her and she slipped' into them. His hands caressed her smooth brown shoulders, stroked her graceful neck as she reached down to unbutton her own petticoat, then his breeches.

"I never tire of you, Zonah," Orde said. It surprised him, but it was so. Her breasts, so round and weighty and full, fell into his open palms and he touched them softly.

Sometimes Zonah's helplessness, her total, natural submissiveness stirred Orde to dominate her sexually, ignited his cruelty, but other times, like this night, her sweet openness soothed him. He was overwhelmed with gentle feelings as he kissed her face and breasts and entered her slowly, sighing with pleasure, and then, as he reached his climax, groaning with satisfaction.

Afterward, he lay back while Zonah obediently dressed.

The dress she put on had been made in Paris, and Orde had paid more than twenty pounds for it in Charleston. It was double-embroidered ivory satin, fashioned with a dramatically low neckline, whimsical puffed sleeves trimmed with Brussels lace, and opened over a petticoat painted with pale pink tea roses.

Next to the creamy silk, Zonah's skin glowed like mahogany. She covered her short hair with the high, white wig and pulled on long white silk gloves. Her shoes were white satin with high red-painted wooden heels and she carried a silk fan decorated with scenes of Italian lakes.

When she was dressed Orde looked at her proudly. "You'll be the finest lady there," he promised.

"Where?" Zonah asked. She had no notion of what Orde was planning, but whatever it was, she was completely in his hands. Indeed, this had been the reality of her life ever since Orde Barstow had bought her on the block in Charleston twenty years ago, and Zonah had come to accept the framework of her life and security there was in Orde's caring for her.

Orde struggled to his feet and settled his flame-colored waistcoat. He pulled on his topcoat and took

Zonah's hand. "We're going into society," he answered. "Can you dance?"

"No, sir."

"No matter. We'll be arriving in time for supper, anyway. You can eat."

Cattie was determined to confront Jack Barstow, and she spotted him the minute he entered the council house. Anxiously, she patted her bouffant golden hair and smoothed the skirts of her black silk gown. Thank goodness Orde Barstow is well out of here, she thought. It would have been a tactical error to have Jack see her dancing with Orde. Or perhaps not. Perhaps it would have stirred his passions.

She swayed on her toes, restraining herself with difficulty, longing to rush across the room and speak to Jack, but forced by convention to wait for his approach. Like a spider eyeing its prey she watched him remove his long black wool cape, exchange greetings with the men at the punchbowl, and pause to admire the Tansy Pudding at the buffet. Jack looked very well, in Cattie's estimation. He was soberly dressed, as was his custom, in a dark wool coat and breeches, but wore a waistcoat of a rich burgundy twill, which pointed up his still-slim figure, his blond mustache, and the ruddy glow of his skin.

Finally he caught sight of her, and Cattie noted a spark of excitement in his eyes. She hid her expression behind her black fan and waited impatiently.

Jack approached and bowed. "Good evening, Miss Cattie, if I may call you so . . ."

"You always have," Cattie replied. "Good evening, Jack."

"You look . . . as usual . . . wonderful. We have not met for a long time."

"I know. And have you missed me?"

"I've thought about you, Cattie. I've often thought of you." Jack gave Cattie his arm, and together they strolled to one side of the room where they could speak without being overheard.

Cattie considered his last remark. What did it mean? Was she too hasty in guessing it meant that he loved her? How happy he would be, she thought, to know that she had decided to say yes when he proposed.

She smiled flirtatiously. "Have you, Jack? You've thought only good things, I do hope."

"You know that I've always been fond of you. Why, there was a time when I thought we would someday marry."

Thought? Cattie was taken aback. His use of the past tense was alarming. It wasn't a bit too late, not as far as she was concerned. Why did he say *thought*? Nervously, she slipped her arm through his and squeezed his wrist.

"In faith, it's pleasant to see you, Cattie!" Jack vowed, stroking his light mustache. "When I think of the old times! But never mind what's done. You are looking as pretty as ever."

Cattie's spirits rose a bit. This was what she liked to hear. She shifted her weight, turning half way then back so her silken skirts rustled and billowed. Her new dress, though black, was so prettily styled and trimmed that no one could fail to admire it.

"Fie, Jack!" she giggled. "So you have thought that we would marry?"

"Surely you have not forgotten those days, Cattie?"

"No," she said truthfully. "I have not forgotten. But do you no longer think of marriage at all, dear Jack?" She looked up with deliberate charm, widening her eyes flirtatiously.

"Never. I acknowledge that I am too old and settled in my ways. And, as it has turned out, my life has other . . . compensations. I have been denied the comfort of a wife and a snug home, but I have managed to do without them, you see."

Oh, dear, Cattie thought, even as she smiled. What on earth could he mean by compensations? She lowered her eyes, lest he should be able to read in them any of the urgency she felt. This conversation was not going as she had planned, not at all.

"I myself," she said confidingly, "have thought that perhaps I will marry again."

"You have? Ah, Cattie, you are a woman made for marriage. Are you betrothed to some fine young man, then?"

"No . . . not yet."

"Well, who will he be this time?" Jack laughed and leaned forward to peer into Cattie's clear blue eyes.

"Stand back, Doctor Barstow! You examine me as if I were a patient! Have mercy, I am not ailing!"

"Not at all! Not at all! You have always been the healthiest woman I know."

"Well, why don't you marry me, then?"

Cattie's question fell into a pause in the music, and she was dismayed by her boldness as soon as she realized what she had said. To hide her blushes, she fluttered her fan. What could she do? Why didn't he answer? Now she would have to pretend that she was jesting, unless he responded at once with a real counter-proposal.

But he did not.

"Oh, Cattie! If only! But we should never be happy together. We are too different, I fear. You are a rich woman, used to luxury, and still a coquette. I am just a plain surgeon, and as I have confessed, I have reconciled myself to die a bachelor."

Cattie was upset. She had expected so much of this encounter, and everything was going wrong. Either

Jack Barstow was stupid and did not understand her, or he did not want her. Neither prospect was satisfying. She felt anger at the very prospect of rejection, and her voice was edged when she spoke next.

"A plain surgeon! A bachelor! Ah, what a grim fate you have elected, sir!"

"Grim indeed." Jack studied Cattie. He was genuinely puzzled. She sounded almost angry. What was wrong with her?

Desperately, Cattie decided to play her strongest card. There was no question but that she would win with this one. How surprised he would be! How delighted! Perhaps he would fall on his knees to her . . .

"Do you never think, Jack, that you may already have familial responsibilities . . . that you have never accepted?"

Jack stared. "No," he said. "I do not take your meaning."

"I mean, sir, that perhaps you have not escaped, only postponed, your responsibility toward . . . a family."

"You will have to be plainer-spoken with me, Cattie. I still cannot understand."

Cattie took a deep breath. She had never been one to avoid confrontations or settle for defeat. Her eyes met Jack's boldly.

"I will put it plainly, then. Jack Barstow, my son, Roland, is your son as well."

Jack's jaw dropped. He stared at Cattie, whom he had known for so long. His mind was racing. It wasn't possible. She was teasing him, as she always had. He remembered the summer before he went south to St. Augustine to fight with the General. Of course he remembered Cattie as she had been then—so exquisitely young and innocent, so beautiful. He remembered making love to her under the willow. When he returned she had gone to Charleston to visit some relative. He knew she had a son. But she had never, ever, suggested that he . . . So many years had passed since then, years when they had been involved again and parted again. He remembered the scandal about Cattie's feelings for Micah Stone, then the worse scandal about Fayette eloping with him. He remembered how she had jilted him, years later, for his own stepfather!

Everyone had said that Cattie's love-child had been fathered by Micah Stone. Everyone had always said so. What Cattie suggested now could not be true.

"I do not believe you, Cattie," Jack said flatly.

"You . . . what?"

"You are teasing me. As you have so often done. I do not believe you."

Rage choked her. I think I shall faint, she thought desperately. This cannot be true. Her face went white and she swayed.

"Are you all right?" he asked. He put out a hand to steady her.

But the outrage of the moment had strengthened Cattie. "Do not touch me," she snapped. "If you touch me again, I shall scream."

"But Cattie . . ."

Inside the carriage, Zonah sat silent, but Orde was elated. He sipped more rum and sang a song about spies and soldiers with a chorus of "ta-tum, ta-tums." Zonah looked out at the people in the streets and marveled at them. As well as the arrival of the new Governor, Savannah was celebrating Christmas, a holy day as well marked in the taverns as in the churches. Tomorrow would be Christmas Eve, and a hush would fall over the town, but tonight everyone who could possibly afford it was drunk.

"Here we are!" Orde shouted when the carriage

halted before the council house. He tumbled out and helped Zonah across the muddy sidewalk. She trembled on his arm and for a moment he looked into her eyes with an expression of tenderness.

"The truth is, you're better'n any of 'em," he said.

The windows of the council house blazed with light, and Orde heard excited chatter and the sound of violins as he stepped up to the door with Zonah. The eighty most powerful citizens of Savannah were seated at dinner with the new governor of Georgia.

As they entered, everything stopped.

Everything stopped. All conversation, all the clatter of dishes and service and knife and fork against china. The musicians stopped. A woman's laugh broke off in the middle. Then someone gasped, and someone else dropped a plate.

"Play on, play on," Angus Dunlie called to the fiddlers. Someone must act, he told himself. I suppose I must. He rose from the table, leaving his seat next to the new governor. Looking strained and weary, he started walking toward Orde and Zonah at the door.

Zonah looked around the room. To her everything was a confusion of white faces and bright lights. She clung to Orde's arm and swayed on her high heels. Orde saw empty seats at one of the long, linen-covered tables and headed for it, taking Zonah with him.

Cattie, steadied by more rum punch than she had ever drunk before, was seated near the end of one of the tables. She turned her chair around to have a better look. Why, she's dressed up like a bride! Cattie marveled, delighted by this new scandal, the only thing imaginable to take her mind off her own disappointment. What an incredible dress! But Orde Barstow must have lost his mind to bring her here!

Angus Dunlie intercepted Orde and Zonah in the middle of the dance floor. The three of them faced each other just in front of the musicians, who were scraping through the same tune they had tried to play before.

"Mr. Barstow!" Angus Dunlie said in a low, shocked voice, "What in hell are you doing?"

"Doing, sir? Why I have come to dinner. And I have brought my mistress along with me!"

"You cannot. You cannot bring her here, sir. It is an insult to the ladies."

Orde grinned. "Zonah is more of a lady than any whore in this room!"

Angus Dunlie winced. "Barstow, I cannot tolerate this. If you wish to insult me personally, then I must respond personally, but 'tis late in the day for quarrels. I ask you to go at once, without making any more trouble."

"I am not making the trouble. Now stand aside and let us dine."

"I believe you are drunk, Barstow. I cannot permit you to stay."

Orde tapped his foot to the music. "Pity you can't dance," he said to Zonah. She fixed her huge dark eyes on Orde, then at the tables laden with food and at the people seated around them. Cattie fancied she looked right at her, and shivered.

"It was just so awful," Cattie told a friend later. "You can't imagine. Everyone was looking and pretending not to look. Nobody was talking, for everyone wanted to hear what was being said! Oh, my soul, I was frightened! Orde Barstow looked crazed. I was afraid he would fire at us all on the spot. But father stood up to him and . . ."

"Barstow, we cannot further disrupt this gathering," Angus Dunlie said, taking Orde by his elbow. Orde tried to shake off Dunlie's hand, but the taller man held firm.

"Let go! I warn you," Barstow muttered. He shook his big, curly head as if trying to rid himself of a pain. He suddenly felt very drunk. He felt the room spinning, felt a weakness in his legs. Why was everyone clinging to him? They were weighing him down. Zonah was on one side and Angus Dunlie was tugging on the other. "God damnit! What the hell . . ." he said in a loud voice.

"I warn you . . . you must go! Let's step outside," Dunlie suggested. I must get him out of here, he thought. He is dangerous.

Orde staggered, and Zonah saw how drunk he was.

"Come now," she whispered to him. "Let us go home."

And obediently, swaying crazily, his blue eyes glassy and wild, Orde let himself be led by Zonah, led meekly as a child. Dunlie took half Orde's weight, and slowly Zonah guided the two men out the door.

The cold, damp air outside shocked Orde out of his stupor and he turned on Dunlie.

"You have insulted me, sir!"

"You are drunk."

"Drunk or sober, you have gone too far this time. My honor—and that of my lady—is outraged."

Dunlie held his breath. *He* was outraged that the man would bring his slave, dressed up like a Paris doll, to an important social event, but he did not want to handle Barstow's insanity personally. All he wanted was for the man to go; if he never saw him again he would be content.

"I advise you, sir . . ." Dunlie began, seeing the crazy glint in Barstow's eye.

"I want none of your advice. None of your pompous prescriptions! Do you miss my meaning, Dunlie? Is your mind so dull as that? I say, you have insulted us—and I demand satisfaction!"

Dunlie had never faced another man in a duel and never wanted to. He was no coward but it was not his style—duels were for hot-headed young fools. Of course he could use a sword and he could shoot, but he did not want to.

"Go home," he advised Barstow, and his voice was weary. "Go home and forget your anger."

"Please, sir, please . . ." Zonah begged. "Come now."

Barstow clung to Zonah's arm, but his face was bright with anger and twisted with spite.

"I'll not forget this insult, Dunlie!"

With effort, Dunlie held his tongue. Behind him in the council house he heard the sounds of the fiddlers and a wave of excited chatter. His hands gripped into fists and the minutes that passed as Zonah and Orde climbed into their carriage seemed as long as hours.

Finally they were gone, Orde calling back insults, and Angus Dunlie slumped against the hitching post, weak with relief. He had avoided bloodshed and gotten rid of the man, but he feared he had only postponed an inevitable confrontation.

Chapter Sixteen

Fayette Acts the Good Samaritan—
Cattie Advises the Lovelorn—Orde and
Byron Barstow Go Shooting

Fayette left her three children asleep and went out alone at dawn to feed the chickens. Micah had been gone since the day before on a long ride into Augusta to buy supplies. She had not slept well, but the cool, fresh air pleased her. It was a bright summer morning. Her feet followed the worn dirt path instinctively, and she lifted her gaze to admire the blueness of the sky and the yellow sun shining through the hilltop pines.

Just in front of the chicken coop she saw the first bloodstains on the dirt path. Fresh blood. Had a fox gotten in after the chickens? She felt anger, and she expected trouble as she opened the door to the coop. She never expected the sight that lay before her.

All the chickens were huddled together in one corner. Stretched out to fill the coop was the body of a thin, lanky mulatto on his back, his arms outstretched, his head lolling forward on his chest.

Dear God, Fayette thought, what is he doing here and dear God, he looks dead. She was amazed but not frightened, for the black man's wretchedly gaunt body, his stillness, and the blood told her he was likely beyond violence. And her attention was caught by something else. On a leather throng around his neck hung a shiny metal cross.

Breathlessly, Fayette stepped forward. Few Wilkes County families owned slaves, but this man had the look of a runaway. Perhaps he had come all the way from South Carolina. And he was hurt. Her sympathy was stirred.

He looked so young—scarcely more than a boy—and did not react to her approach. His eyes were closed and she could not hear him breathing, but as she watched, she saw his chest rise and fall slightly. So he was still alive!

Whoever he is or wherever he's come from, he's a Christian, Fayette thought. She leaned forward and touched the silvery cross. A sign. She had never before seen a slave wearing a cross. His chest was warm. I must help him, she thought. If I don't, he'll die. Perhaps God has sent him to me to test my charity. She had vowed to serve God, and Jesus had said that to help the least of men was to help him. The idea took hold in her mind. Perhaps this is the call to duty I waited, she thought. I'm sure it is.

When she had made up her mind, Fayette moved very quickly. With Pittman's help she lugged the unconscious man into the house and stretched him out on the big bed. The children watched with awe as she bathed the bloody wound on his leg and tried to feed him warm milk.

"Hush now," Fayette said. "This poor man is tired and very sick. You take some corn cakes and eat outside. Then, Pittman, take Isaac and Jenny with you to do the chores, just as usual."

Fayette overheard the children talking on the step outside the door. "Where did he come from?" Isaac asked his older brother.

"I don't know," Pittman answered. "Our mother found him. I think he came out of the woods."

Out of the woods, Fayette thought. Yes, or from beyond the woods. She could see that he had walked a long way—his bare feet were hard with callouses—and he had been badly treated. There were scars from a lash on his back, old ones and fresh ones only partly healed. His right leg had been caught in a shackle or a trap and was dark with poison.

Gently, Fayette bathed the infected leg and wiped his hot skin with a cloth wrung out in water. He lay so still that she was constantly afraid he had already died. His lips were cracked and his brow burned with fever. Still, he did not rally to drink the milk or even to open his eyes.

All through the day Fayette nursed the sick man. As the day grew hotter she propped the door open to let in air. She fanned him and brushed away flies. Nothing roused him from his sickly sleep.

While she nursed him, Fayette studied his face. It was a well-formed face, long and delicate with the features of some Caucasian ancestor. His skin was a creamy medium brown, his eyebrows thick half circles above deep-set eyes. She had never touched a Negro before, never even seen one so closely, but his helplessness appealed to her.

While she nursed the mulatto, Fayette prayed for his recovery. She had no fears for herself, but she kept the children outside. From what she had seen of fevers, she judged that he was close to reaching a crisis. In a few hours, surely by nightfall, he would take a turn toward life or toward death.

Then, in the late afternoon, she heard men's voices outside. She rushed to the door. Across the clearing she saw Micah, whom she expected home from Agusta, but Micah was not alone. With him were two strangers on horseback, carrying rifles.

"They will not have him," Fayette said to herself. Beyond a doubt she knew that the two men were slave catchers and that they were hunting this poor sick man. She thought desperately of what to do. She must hide him. She would not give him up to them, no matter where he had run from, no matter what he had done. He was too sick to move, and it was her duty to save him. She saw it clearly.

Fayette quickly wrapped her quilted coverlet around the man's body and rolled him off the bed and under it. He was hot to the touch but as still as a corpse, and she prayed he didn't wake to think himself in his coffin.

"Fayette!" Micah called from outside. With shaking hands she smoothed her hair and straightened her skirt. Even if they searched the cabin they wouldn't find him easily, but she would do her best to keep them outside.

Then she thought of the children. They would tell Micah! Oh, how could she stop them!

Ashen-faced, Fayette ran out of the cabin calling her children. They were already running across the clearing toward their father, but her frantic scream stopped them.

"Come back here at once!" she ordered. "Do as I say!"

The three children turned to face her, looking frightened and confused. "I don't want you here," she said, collaring Pittman. "Now run along. Run up to the pasture! All of you! Do as I say!"

"Fayette?" Micah questioned. Since his accident he had come to rely heavily on Fayette—on her strength and her judgment, but he had never seen her so tense.

"I don't want them to see or hear the slave catchers," she said. "You know I think it's wicked."

"But Fayette . . ." Micah said. His voice was weak and Fayette realized that the ride into Augusta had tired him.

"Pardon us, ma'am," the bigger stranger said. "We don't want to scare you or your youngsters, but we're looking for a mean mullato called Luke. He's run off from Mulberry Plantation near Zubly's Ferry."

"He's not here," Fayette said flatly. God forgive my lies.

"Of course he's not here," Micah said. "But Fayette, can't we give these men some refreshment?"

"I'll draw some fresh water," Fayette said, moving reluctantly toward the well. It was close to the cabin. The men followed and she felt as if she were drawing them toward an awful confrontation. What if the poor man woke and called out?

"Mighty grateful to you," the smaller man said. Both men were dressed like trappers in brown homespun hunting shirts and leather breeches. The big one wore a long, shaggy beard, nut brown and glistening with sweat. "But take care, ma'am. Keep an eye out for this fellow. We tracked him all the way to Fishing Creek, and he may be headed this way."

"Best be gone, then," Fayette said softly.

"You'll know him if you see him," the bigger man said. "He's a light-skinned mulatto with one blue eye."

"I've never seen a blue-eyed Negro in my life," Fayette said. She did not meet anyone's eyes as she drew water from the well and passed it to the men. They drank slowly, and it seemed to her that the bearded one eyed her suspiciously.

After drinking the men thanked them and said good-bye. "We'll ride on now, but likely be back this way. Keep an eye out for Luke Blue. Five pounds to the one who finds him."

Five pounds, Fayette marveled. How could one slave be worth that much?

She took Micah's arm as the men rode away and clung to it.

"Fayette, is something wrong?" he asked.

She tried to still her thumping heart. Never in her life had she lied to anyone as she had lied to them. It was wrong and she was sure she would be punished for it. But there was no hope of keeping it from Micah. She had to tell him at once, no matter what.

"Micah, I lied. I have seen that mulatto. He's hurt and sick with fever."

"What are you saying?" Micah asked.

Fayette trembled. What if he called the patrollers back and . . . she had to be strong. It was her duty to God.

"I took him in. He's hidden inside."

"Fayette!"

"He's so sick and helpless. And he's just one of God's creatures."

"The man is dangerous!"

"He doesn't look dangerous to me. He's too sick to open his eyes."

"Fayette! He's a runaway slave. He belongs to some man in South Carolina. You heard the man say he's mean."

"He doesn't look mean to me. And I won't give him up to them. He'll die if he isn't cared for—probably die anyway."

Micah stared at his wife, dumbfounded. She faced

him squarely, her trembling hands the only outward sign of her nervousness. He had seen her determined, but she had never opposed him before, although he knew she was strong-willed and that she despised slavery and all that it involved. But to take in a runaway . . . it was dangerous!

"What if he had hurt you . . . or the children?"

"I know that he could not." She clasped her hands together fervently. "Micah, I think he was sent by God to test my devotion. Because you were spared and I promised . . ."

"No!" Micah said. "Fayette, it's not right!"

"I feel it is, Micah dear. I feel it is my duty to nurse him till he's well."

"And then? And then turn him over to the patrol?"

Fayette did not answer, but she smiled with relief, taking the question as his permission to nurse Luke Blue until he was well.

Together, they collected their children and went into the cabin. Micah helped Fayette lift the man back onto the bed, but he was silent and his mouth set in a tight line. It was wrong, he felt. It was dishonest and would only bring trouble. When he saw the thin, sick brown-skinned body he felt only revulsion, and he was surer than ever that he was right.

Cattie found Mary crumpled up into a heap in the little sewing room off her second-floor sitting room at Sea Groves. Mary was crying, sobbing so hard that Cattie was afraid.

"Mary! What on earth is the matter?"

But Mary was crying too hard to speak.

Cattie had been at Sea Groves all the spring and summer, visiting her family, and she had brought her personal servants, Flora, her maid, Goldie, her coachman, and Mary, her seamstress. Mary had been an especially welcome addition to the staff at Sea Groves, for she was an exceptionally fine seamstress; she could copy any style, work over an old garment till it looked as good as new, and do plain sewing as well and as fast as any woman in Georgia.

Catherine Dunlie had set Mary to work on new clothes for herself and Angus, then on shirts and breeches for the boys, who were still growing so fast they needed new clothes every few months.

Mary's head, covered by a neat muslin cap, was still bowed. Cattie bent over and rapped on it.

"Sit up, Mary, and tell me what's wrong!"

"Yes, ma'am . . ." Mary tried to obey, but when she lifted her pretty, cafe-au-lait face, Cattie could see that it was reddened and swollen from crying, and her voice was hoarse and scratchy. "I'm . . . ashamed to tell."

"Nonsense. Tell me at once," Cattie ordered, suspecting some household catastrophe. Really, Mary was a fine servant; she was modest and shy and obedient as well as sweet-tempered and pretty to look at. Cattie was prepared to forgive her almost any misdemeanor.

"Oh, Miss Cattie, I didn't mean to do it! I couldn't help it!"

"What?" Cattie snapped impatiently. "What didn't you mean to do? What did you do, you little fool! Tell me at once!"

Seeing Cattie's famous temper rising, Mary grasped for breath and tried to wipe her face on a very soggy handkerchief she had balled up in her long-fingered brown hand.

"Oh, Miss Cattie, please forgive me! I've fallen in love!"

Cattie laughed. Love! Was the whole world love-struck?

Mary looked stricken. Her tear-streaked face wore

an expression of confusion and pain. "Miss Cattie! Please don't laugh! I'm so miserable!"

But Cattie laughed harder. The idea was very amusing to her. Darkies falling in love! It was preposterous. Next thing they would be writing love letters, arranging rendezvous, holding weddings . . . Why that last wasn't such a bad idea. Mary could make herself a lovely wedding dress, and it would be quite a pretty scene.

"Well, Mary, don't take on so. Why don't you marry your sweetheart?"

"Marry him?"

"Why not? Who is he, Mary?"

"It's . . . it's Moses, ma'am."

"Moses Black? Papa's overseer?" Cattie was surprised. Moses was much older than Mary . . . but he had never yet taken a wife, as far as she knew . . . and besides . . . Cattie grinned. The irony of Mary's choice was bound to be hurtful, at least annoying, to Orde Barstow, Mary's father. For Moses was the slave Angus Dunlie had given refuge—many years ago—and Orde Barstow had never forgiven him that episode. To marry that slave to Orde's own daughter Mary . . . Cattie resolved to encourage the match, and to make sure Orde Barstow heard about it, too. "Why, there's nothing so terrible about that," Cattie said to Mary. "Do you think he fancies you?"

"Oh, yes, ma'am," Mary said.

"Hmmm . . ." What a sneaky, secretive people they are, Cattie thought. Just imagine: Mary and Moses being in love, and Mary so miserable about it. "Well, Mary, would you like me to speak to my father about it? If he approves the match, why then you may marry . . ."

"Oh, yes, ma'am! Thank you, ma'am!" Mary's tears

had fled and she turned a face full of hope and gratitude toward Cattie.

Cattie was pleased, too.

A light knock on his bedroom door awakened Byron Barstow before dawn on that early September morning.

"Mister Byron! Mister Byron!" Effie, one of the house slaves, called when he did not respond to the knocking.

"I'm coming, Effie," Byron called out. He lay in bed with his eyes closed for a few more moments. It was his last day at home. Tomorrow he would take a packet ship back north to college after three months spent on the plantation.

Although he would miss his family, Byron was glad to be leaving Blackwoods and going back to school. He knew it was his own fault—he was the one who had changed, but it hadn't been a happy summer. He had found himself at odds with a lot of the things he had to do and see and still powerless to change them or even to complain.

Yawning, Byron swung his legs out of bed and reached for his riding boots. He and his father planned to ride into the marshlands and shoot birds this last morning. If he didn't get up at once, he would be keeping Orde waiting.

Even those planters who usually spent the winter in their Savannah townhouses, the Dunlies and the Barstows among them, returned to their plantations in time for the spring planting. Both families had been on Saint Simons Island since March. The rice was planted in the early spring—in March and April. By May all the seed had been sown, the squares were flooded, and the green shoots of the rice plants were weaving under the clear water.

Byron had come home in June. Then, and throughout the months of summer, the field laborers drained and reflooded the rice fields, working the ground and pulling weeds when the water was off. There was a rhythm to the work, hard though it was, and a slow, steady, inexorable rhythm to the long days and hot nights of summer.

But this year, for the first time, Byron hadn't fallen into the rhythm. He rode out, as usual, with his father—nearly every day. Although Harley Beene was still Orde's right-hand man and the overseer at Blackwoods, Orde himself always kept a close eye on everything that went on. Every day during the busy seasons, he rode out to the fields to supervise the slaves working there. And Byron had ridden with him. But he had hated it.

Tomorrow, Byron said to himself as he dressed and left his bedroom. It was five o'clock. Breakfast and his father were waiting downstairs in the dining room—a full breakfast of grilled meat and fried eggs and cornbread served with waxy yellow butter kept in a stone crock in the coolest part of the pumphouse.

"Sorry to be late, sir," he said to his father and sat down to eat. When they had finished, the two men left the room together—one very young but tall and lean as a man with tousled sandy hair—one noticeably grayer since the last winter. Their horses, already saddled, and dogs waited outside, and the groom handed both Barstows their riding crops.

Byron felt happy despite himself. It felt fine to be up in the cool of the morning with a good horse under him, felt fine to be riding out for a day's hunting. He gave a yell of pleasure and jumped his horse over the boxwood hedge at the foot of the lawn.

There was a strong breeze blowing off the ocean, a breeze that anticipated fall, and Byron and Orde enjoyed their ride north along the eastern shore of the island. The sun rose while they rode to the vast salt marshes, where wild ducks and marsh hens abounded. They tied their horses at the edge of the marsh, called to their three long-eared dogs, and walked a mile to a quiet spot where they had hunted before.

It was a gray day with hazy clouds in front of the sun and they settled in a canebrake, waiting for the interruption of their arrival to be absorbed again by the quiet of the marsh. Byron waited quietly, as he had been taught, but he was aware of some uncommon tension that existed between himself and his father. Several times he felt Orde looking at him, and finally he smiled at his father, as if encouraging him to speak.

After a while, Orde did speak. His voice was low and Byron had to lean toward him to hear.

"Tomorrow you go back to school," Orde said.

"Yes, father."

"You are nearly a man, now, Byron."

"I am already sixteen, sir."

"Aye. It's the very beginning of life, son. Just the beginning." He smiled.

"I guess so, sir."

"You like it at school, don't you?"

"Yes, sir, I do."

"Well, when you finish up there, you'll come home, though. You are my heir, you know that. You'll own Blackwoods and all the rest and take care of them all your life and pass them on to your sons, I hope."

Byron nodded and neither man spoke for a few minutes. Then Orde cleared his throat and began again.

"There was one more thing I wanted to say to you. Just to get it off my mind. Some advice for you."

Byron turned wide-open eyes toward Orde, and at that moment he looked far younger than sixteen years.

"Son, when you see a woman you want, take her.

That's my advice. Don't hold back or ask a lot of questions, don't shillyshally around. That's my advice to you. You understand?"

"Yes, sir."

"Take her, son, if you want her. Get her somehow—it can always be done. Everything's fair. You see . . . as far as I know, anyway . . . women are the finest thing in life. There's other things that are necessary, of course: a man's pride, money, and all money gets. But women—they're the finest of all. Make sure you mark my words."

"I do, sir." Byron nodded vigorously.

"Then hush up now and let's do some shooting."

But during the next few hours, though both men took aim and fired at the wild ducks and marsh hens that rose out of the depths of the marsh, fluttering and calling out alarms to their fellows, only Byron's shots brought down any birds. Orde shot again and again, and again and again he missed his targets. Byron was surprised at first, then embarrassed, then upset. He didn't want to beat his father in a shooting contest, and it was increasingly clear that Orde did not want to lose to his son. His poor shooting annoyed him. At first he swore, then his face went red. Finally, he went white.

After Byron had brought down two big ducks and a half-dozen hens, another hen, a plump golden brown bird, rose from the break nearly in front of them. Both men took aim and fired. It was impossible to tell whose shot had gone true, but Byron turned at once to his father.

"Good shot, sir. You got it."

"Have you had enough?" Orde asked with a weariness in his voice that had not been there before.

"Yes, father," Byron said.

Without further conversation they gathered the

dead birds and packed them into their saddlebags. The dogs danced around the horses' hooves. It was early afternoon and the sky was still gray, and there was still an unseasonably cool wind off the ocean.

Byron was lost in thought. What had happened to his father's aim since the last time they had hunted? Orde had always been a crack shot, admired all over the island for his accuracy at the hunts.

Then, as he passed close to his father, between the horses, Byron was able to look into his father's face from a distance of only a few inches. And he saw . . . or thought he saw . . . a grayish film over his eyes—a film like a gray lens. He looked away.

So that was it. Orde was losing his vision. Byron rode home beside his father without speaking. There was a lump of sadness in his throat that would have choked him if he'd allowed it.

Chapter Seventeen

Scandals, Sins, and Sorrows—Orde Explodes; Fayette Loses Her Patient— Zonah Acts in Time

Orde Barstow did hear about the match between his daughter Mary and Moses, Dunlie's coal-black head man, and it caused him pain and rage. "Why the girl's almost white!" he fumed to Zonah one morning when they were together in his bedchamber. Orde had finished drinking tea and writing a letter, and now he was dressing for the day ahead.

"Poor Mary. I hate to think of her being with those Dunlies," Zonah said simply. She held Orde's starched and ruffled linen shirt for him to pull on. Zonah had the same concern for Mary she had for all her children—she prayed for their survival and their success, not success on the scale permitted to white people, but any limited success permitted to black people in this white society. Zonah still mourned for Mary—her eldest child, gone now for many years, and she wished her well, most fervently. Some day we will meet again, she promised her daughter, in her dreams.

"He's done it to insult me," Orde complained, overlooking the fact that it was he who had given Mary to Cattie Dunlie. "Damn it, I won't suffer this insult! I'll make the man pay!" He buttoned his breeches and sat down to pull on high leather boots.

It was late fall, and Orde and Zonah were back in their Savannah townhouse. The rice harvest was in and Georgia's planters had returned to town, seeing to the sale and shipping of their product, and to the administration of their civic affairs—the Colonial Assembly was meeting in the council house.

"Yes, sir," Zonah said. She was thinking of the night when she had worn her silk dress and Orde had taken her to the Governor's Ball. She remembered how bitterly Angus and Orde had faced each other there. The real cause of their long-standing feud was not important, she sensed. The two men had opposed each other for so long and disagreed on so many matters that the one's very existence aggravated the other. It was a bad situation, and, of course, it was more complicated than either man realized. Zonah sighed. Seeing Angus Dunlie at the party she had been powerfully struck by something that she alone had so far seemed to notice—how closely Orde's adopted son, Byron, resembled his natural father. Why had she the only eyes to see this, Zonah wondered. It gave her an uneasy feeling . . .

I am the only one who knows, Zonah had thought many times since. The only one who knows, now that Joan is dead. The secret did not rest easily with her, for she was still deeply superstitious about the survival of both the twins. How much of the trouble that had come to her since had been the result of her stealing the twin? Was it in punishment for that act that she had lost Mary? Was it because of the evil she had stirred up, that her life and Orde's were still caught up with the Dunlie family?

And now Zonah had a new fear. She could tell that Orde's sight was failing. She had noticed it long before Byron had, and she suspected that it was getting worse. Orde's health was the mainspring of her life; she was totally dependent on it. Without Orde as their protector, anything could happen to her and their children.

"Well, dear woman, I must go." Orde stood up, stamped his feet solidly in his boots, and reached for the coat Zonah handed him. "Another day at the assembly. Likely another debate with Dunlie, the bloody fool!"

"Take care, sir," Zonah begged.

Orde was caught by the emotion in her voice, and he gave her a hug before he swaggered out the door.

Zonah straightened up the room after Orde had gone, and on his writing table she discovered the letter he had just written to Byron at school. For sure, she had heard him say he had intended to send it by the packet sailing this afternoon. Now it would miss the sailing, and this was the last until next week. Zonah picked up the letter and as she studied the address, a sudden idea came to her.

She opened the envelope. The letter, a single sheet of stiff paper, was folded inside. She pulled it out and took up Orde's pen to add her own message before she sealed the envelope and ran with it to the ship dispatcher's office and gave it to him to take aboard the mail boat.

Two months had passed since the day that Fayette had taken in the sick mulatto runaway, and the time had brought changes, although the poor man still lay abed in the small cabin, still weak and needy.

Fayette, who had given herself wholly to the care and tending of the young fugitive, had become aloof and spiritual. She looked upon her nursing as a special duty for God, more than physical nursing. If I hadn't found him, he would surely have died, she told herself over and over again. But I have saved him for the Lord. Even when the worst of his fever was over, the man was very fragile, and Fayette sat by his side for hours, praying and trying to coddle him into accepting bits of food.

Micah resented the time and strength Fayette gave the runaway.

"You care more for him than your own children!" he accused Fayette one day.

Fayette was shocked. "God forgive you, Micah Stone, if you think me guilty of neglecting my children!" she vowed. "I would never do that! I have strength enough for all of you. Please, Micah, try to understand! Husband, what is wrong? We have never quarreled like this before."

In fact, there was something wrong. Micah had never fully recovered from his accident, and they had not lain together as man and woman for more than a year. At first, they had both assumed that the cause of his impotence was the injury to his legs, but now Micah seemed well, and he was still unable to respond to Fayette as a man. She confided to her journal-book:

He has become melancholy, and although I will always love him, I cannot blind myself to the truth. He has changed, hardened toward me. His heart and mind, which used to be turned toward me, are now turned away. I fear we shall exchange bitter words over my caring for Luke Blue, for he has made it plain that he does not approve of what I believe to be my Christian duty. But God knows that my pity toward the poor man's suffering is pure and in falling from me, gives me my only spiritual peace.

Fayette closed her diary and leaned over to stroke Luke's brow. He was sleeping, and she studied his handsome, now familiar face. Never was there a better-tempered, more appreciative patient, she thought. As she watched, his sleep was interrupted by a dream, and he groaned, as he so often did.

"No! No! No!" he cried out. Fayette reckoned he was having the dream of running away again; she knew all his nightmares, and the story of his life. Luke had been born on Beau Terre, a huge indigo plantation across the river in South Carolina. His father was his master, his mother a maid in the big house. Sickly as a child, Luke had been taught reading and writing with the master's white children, and when he was old enough to work, given a job as a patroon, or boatman, a coveted position on river plantations.

It was then, working the river boats, coming to know the constantly shifting channels, the depths and the shallows, and the ever-changing currents, that Luke Blue had become religious.

"Sometimes, in the water, I thought I saw the face of God," he had told Fayette, and she felt a pang of awe. He was so weak and helpless, so soft-spoken and sincere, that she could not help but trust him. And like him. She came to like him very much, and as the weeks passed, they became very close.

"I came to think, ma'am, that God never meant for us to be slaves," he whispered to Fayette one afternoon when they were alone. His voice rose with fervor. "I had the thought that it was all a mistake, and that I could just go! Go away! God freed me, ma'am, he led me out of slavery . . . but then the men started to chase me. They came after me with guns and dogs abarking—came fast. I was only four or five miles from my plantation when they came upon me in a very dark part of the swamps . . ."

"Hush, now, don't rouse your fever again," Fayette pleaded, knowing the desperate excitement that possessed him whenever he spoke of running away. It wasn't good for him, she knew it.

"I was scared to death, for I knew if they caught me they'd whip me bad, but there was no place to hide! I climbed up a tall tree, but one of the patrollers saw me there and shook me down and took me back. Oh, then they did whip me!"

"Don't speak of it!"

"But I waited. Oh, I hadn't changed! I knew I still had to go, so I waited till my back healed up and then I slipped out again, this time going out in the dark of night, in a big storm. I knew I had to go, and I knew it was my last chance—'cause if they caught me again they would whip me to death. I'd seen it happen. This time I took a little boat, and so they guessed I'd crossed the river, but I left the boat then and started to run. I ran and ran! I had to go through some wild country and that's where I caught my foot in a bear trap.

"Oh! It did hurt! And I was scared, for I thought I might bleed to death, but God saved me, ma'am, for God led me right to you and that proves it, I guess."

"It's all right, hush now," Fayette said soothingly.

"God bless you, God bless you," Luke whispered over and over again. Fayette was moved beyond words. She leaned forward to comfort him. Her strong feelings for Luke Blue were very complex and confusing to her. Nursing him had aroused in her a tenderness that was unlike any she had experienced before. She had such power over him . . . he was so helpless and so grateful. Oddly, she grew jealous of him, and refused to let her children or Micah do anything for him.

She fed him herself. She bathed him, lingering in horrified silence over the streaked and speckled skin of his back where the seams and ridges left by his beatings stretched from his neck to the base of his spine.

"Oh, Luke," she whispered back, as he blessed her, "I am so sorry . . ."

He shivered. His fever had never entirely left him, and when the chills gripped him, there was nothing she could do to get him warm.

"Are you cold?" she asked. He nodded.

Wordlessly, naturally, Fayette put her arms out and wrapped them around Luke's body. She felt him tremble and held him tighter. He was so thin. She felt his involuntary shivering throughout her own body as if it were her own, and it ignited in her a new warmth.

He clung to her, and she rubbed his bare back with her warm hands, touching the awful roughness of his abused skin. He buried his head, covered with such soft, densely curly dark hair, in her breasts, and as he clung to her, she cradled him there.

"Poor, poor Luke," she crooned, bending her head so her own dark, curly hair escaped its pins and fell forward like a veil. In the warm dark cave formed by her body stretching over his reclining one, his hands sought her breasts and coaxed them out of her calico gown.

Fayette started to pull back, but his mouth fastened on her breasts, and he suckled at them like a baby. She was touched. If only she *could* sustain him with her own warmth and strength, succor him back to strength and health.

"No," she murmured, but he did not stop. His mouth was greedy and insistent and it excited her.

"No, Luke," she said more insistently, taking her hands off his back, but he did not heed. Instead, his hands locked around her and he pulled her closer to his body. She struggled to get up, but his strength was melded of lust and spirit, and it surprised her.

"*Please* let me go," she asked firmly, still not quite aware of what he was doing. She felt his face against her chest, felt the wetness of his mouth and of his tears. For just a moment, she shut her eyes, but in the darkness, her feelings were too large, intolerable, and she opened them again to struggle harder against his fierce grip.

Fayette felt her blood pounding in her ears, and felt, beneath her body, the stirring in his. He was so thin that the hot thrust of his organ made itself known to her at once. She felt it between their bodies and flushed. She struggled harder, but his grip was relentless.

"Luke! Luke!" she begged, but he did not answer. For the first time she was frightened of what was happening. It could not. He could not. She tensed, went rigid, but he took his mouth from her breast and easily flipped her over into bed, next to him, then beneath him.

Her skirt and petticoat were wrapped tightly around her legs, binding her, and he tugged them free. His breath was coming in short gasps. His bony chest poked into her and his elbow hurt her. She knew his thin, dark, long-fingered hands so well, and now they were forcing apart her thighs.

His probing fingers shocked her into momentary silence. It could not be . . . not be true. He pulled up her skirts and kneeled between her legs, holding them apart as his hands held her shoulders down. Fayette opened her eyes and looked up at Luke's face. It was the same face she had sponged and caressed so often, the same face—unchanged. She opened her mouth in a scream, but he moved his hand to smother it.

"I love you," he said in a low voice.

She saw his dark, swollen member, then felt it plunge into her body. His hand filled her mouth, tasted dry and salty and the feeling between her legs was not pain.

Nor were the tears that streamed down her face tears of fear or sadness, for after all, she loved him, too.

Byron Barstow, now in his third year at the College of New Jersey, founded in Newark, now at Princeton, returned from a supper of oysters with two of his classmates to find the letter from his father with the odd postscript in Zonah's shaky, unfamiliar hand.

"By God," he swore in the manly way he adopted with his friends, "what am I to make of this?"

Peter Coffin and Zachary Day, two young men from Connecticut, as devoted as was Byron to the classic collegiate pursuits of gambling, horse racing, and drink, swayed unsteadily, and sat down together on the steps of Byron's boarding house. All three young men were rather more drunk than not.

"Give it here, old friend, and I'll settle it for you," Zachary vowed.

"Trouble at home?" Peter Coffin inquired.

"I don't understand," Byron said. "It's a letter as usual from my father, giving me the news . . . all as usual. Then, here at the end is a note from my stepmother."

"Didn't know you had a stepmother," Zachary Day said.

"What does she say?" Peter asked.

"She writes: 'Best come home. He needs you.' "

"That's all?"

"Yes, all." Byron shook the letter. "Damn! Of all the times to leave school . . ." His thoughts had flown south and it depressed him. His life here was so different . . . it was a world apart, a world of men with

many different backgrounds and points of view:
churchmen and classicists, young men from wealthy
families bred to ride and shoot and carouse, and sober
young scholars. There was every sort of new idea
afoot: new notions of science, literature, the arts, politics: Byron had met men who advocated the colonies,
breaking away from England and others who wanted
all slavery abolished.

But this note from Zonah . . . He was surprised.
Zonah had never written to him. He hadn't even realized she was able to write. Byron had never advertised
his unusual family situation to his friends, not that he
was ashamed of his father . . . in fact he loved him
and felt increasingly protective toward the irascible
man—almost an outcast in his own society—who had
adopted him and brought him up with all the rights
of a real son.

And he had been distressed, on his last visit home,
to see that Orde's eyesight was weakening. Perhaps it
had been the first sign of another, more debilitating
illness. He sighed. Whatever the explanation, he could
not in conscience ignore Zonah's appeal.

"I must go home," Byron announced to his friends.

"When?" Peter Coffin asked.

"And miss the races tomorrow night?" Zachary Day
asked.

"At once. In the morning." Byron said. He would
ride to Philadelphia at first light and take the packet
ship to Savannah. It was the worst time of year for
ocean travel, the season when gales and storms beat
around Cape Hatteras, and hurricanes raced up the
south coast, but with luck he would be in Georgia in
four days' time.

Orde Barstow entered the council chamber to hear
Angus Dunlie, in his capacity as speaker of the assem-

bly, reading aloud portions of the South Carolina slave code. The slave code of their northern neighbors was being adapted for use in Georgia, and many of its tenets had aroused bitter debate among the assemblymen.

The South Carolina slave code, as Dunlie's reading reminded the planters and businessmen who represented the colony, was based on the principle that Negroes were "of barbarous, wild, savage natures, and such as renders them wholly unqualified to be governed by the laws, customs, and practices of this province." As such, of course, they had to have laws and regulations of their own.

White Georgians regarded their slave population in varying ways. Typically, they considered them crafty, child-like, capable of being taught mechanical skills by rote, incapable of real thought, and possessed of a special physical endurance. Slaves were generally believed to be unreliable in character: at one moment faithful and affectionate toward their masters, and at the next rebellious and stubborn and possessed with an evil rancor toward the men who bought and sold them.

Orde bowed to his fellow assemblymen as he crossed the small chamber to his seat. Habersham, Harris, Macintosh, Noble Jones, John Graham, Thomas Vincent, Charles Watson—they were all there. Orde knew them all and was on good terms with none of them. At the head of a massive mahogany table sat Henry Ellis, the new governor. Ellis, like Reynolds a military man, had been sent by the King in response to the strains and stresses of the French and Indian wars—as yet no threat to Georgia. Ellis was an explorer who had once tried to find the Northwest Passage. He found Savannah's climate enervating, and though he had only endured it for a few months, Orde noted that the man already looked sickly.

The drafting of the slave code had occupied the assemblymen for some time. Its measures would apply to all slaves—black, Indian, and those of mixed blood.

In Georgia, a slave could expect death for any of a number of crimes: killing a white person except by accident or in defense of his master or overseer; insurrection or attempted insurrection; enticing another slave to run away; willfully burning or destroying rice, corn, or other grain; setting fire to tar kilns or naval stores; stealing another slave; or poisoning another person, slave or free. A slave could die for maiming or wounding a white person upon the first offense, or for merely striking him upon the third.

For lesser mischief, for behavior deemed disobedient or disrespectful, slaves might be whipped, put in irons, or locked up. According to the code, masters were allowed to discipline their own slaves, as long as they did not endanger life or limb, but provisions were also made for the colonial government to do some of the punishing. Money was allowed in the colonial budget to execute at least one slave per year.

The law would also impose some restrictions on slave-holders. They were not permitted to work their slaves on Sunday, except for household servants or emergencies, or for more than sixteen hours a day, and masters were required to feed and clothe their slaves adequately or pay. For murdering or cruelly abusing a slave, a white person could be fined fifty pounds.

"Passing laws is one thing, enforcing them another," Orde muttered to no one in particular as he stalked to his seat. Everyone heard him, and most of them men knew it to be true. There was a certain futility in these sessions, in all the proceedings of the assembly.

Some of the men were hopeful that with the new governor, things would go better. John Reynolds, whose arrival had caused such celebration, had gone in less than two years, although he had made himself bitterly unpopular in less time. Reynolds had dissolved the assembly when it failed to do his bidding, had openly favored his friends, especially William Little, and had tried to move the capitol of Georgia to a new town on the Ogeechee River called Hardwicke. In trying to cover up his illegal maneuvers, Reynolds had gone so far as to alter the legislative minutes.

"Wasting time, imbeciles, the whole lot of 'em," Orde said. There was a stir among the other assemblymen, but no one spoke.

Clearing his throat, Angus Dunlie frowned in Barstow's direction and said, "May I please have your attention, gentlemen; we have many points still to discuss."

Barstow glared, but did not speak further.

"In continuation, then, gentlemen, I put before you article thirty of the code: that marriage or carnal relations between members of the white race and the Negro race shall be illegal and punishable by a fine of ten pounds, for the white person involved, and public flogging for the person of the Negro race."

Barstow jumped to his feet. "Sir! I object."

"Object, Mr. Barstow?" Dunlie drawled. Dear Lord, he had hoped Barstow would be absent when this article came up. Every man present knew that Barstow was time and time again a criminal if miscegenation were against the law.

"Yes, sir, I object. The article you have just proposed is insulting, unnecessary, and violates privacy. It is beyond the province of law, sir, to tell a man where he may lie abed!"

A stony silence was abruptly followed by titters

from among the young clerks seated at the base of the speaker's platform.

"Perhaps that is your opinion, Mr. Barstow," Dunlie said reasonably, "but is it the opinion of the entire body of assemblymen?"

"No man here knows more about the matter than do I," Barstow vowed.

Bolder titters came from the direction of the clerks and a murmur of incredulity from the Governor's.

"Silence!" Angus Dunlie shouted. He was very nervous. Orde Barstow looked wild-eyed and choleric. Would the man insist upon making this article a personal issue? Would he insist upon making a fool of himself in front of the whole assembly?

"May I speak, Mr. Dunlie?" Orde asked, sneering.

"If it is to the point," Dunlie answered.

"I shall be the judge of that," Barstow said. He paused. "I thank you, sir, for the opportunity to speak. This is a matter upon which I have strong feelings."

Barstow's rich voice trembled.

"Hear, hear," taunted some young fellow among the clerks.

"Silence!" Dunlie roared. "Mr. Barstow addresses us."

"For more than twenty years," Orde said, "from the first day when I set foot upon the sandy bluff that is now our Strand, this land of Georgia has been plagued by weak-minded men, hypocritically parading themselves as virtuous, who have taken it upon their consciences to tell other men how to live. All present take my meaning. I refer, in part, to churchmen who themselves indulged in gluttony, avarice, and fornication. I refer to leaders as well as absentee Trustees, who kept our colony down, kept it *down*, I say, by prohibiting the sale of rum and slaves when the two were necessary for our success—our survival!"

"Get to your point, Barstow," Angus Dunlie said. This was most irregular. Was Barstow drunk again? Did he thrive on causing scandals? His speech was absurd.

"I will do just that. I oppose article thirty as you have read it, sir, and I propose that we, as a body, reject it! All men have follies, sir, even men who limp and stagger through life without taking the pleasures and privileges due a gentleman. You cannot legislate against passion, Mr. Dunlie. You may as well ship every nigger in Georgia back to Africa, for men will be men, and women women, sir!"

Dunlie was white with embarrassment and struggled to control his temper. "Are you through, Mr. Barstow?" he asked.

"I'll be through when you scuttle that damn fool article," Barstow shouted.

"We are all gentlemen here, Barstow. You need not scream like a Cherokee on the war path."

"Like a savage, is that it? I swear by my faith, you still do not understand me! Does your blood run so cold, Dunlie, that you can not comprehend the natural workings of a man's desires? Is passion a commodity beyond your experience? Surely you have read . . ."

"*Will* you make this a personal matter, Barstow?"

"Indeed, if that will help you to see my point."

"I see your point, sir, and I see beyond it. I see the necessity of prohibiting unnatural, immoral behavior. If such behavior should occur, even be common, it is nonetheless regrettable, and it is our duty as lawmakers to fix the law against it."

"Excuse me, sir. Are you calling *me* immoral and unnatural?"

"Why, Barstow, must you make this a personal matter?"

"I am becoming increasingly convinced that it is one, Dunlie."

"Whatever grievances we have between us are not the concern of this assembly," Dunlie said in a flat, fearful voice.

"Shall we, then, plan to settle them elsewhere, Dunlie?"

"Wherever you say."

"Indeed. Will you meet me, Angus Dunlie, at the east end of Hutchinson's Island at dawn in two days' time?"

Dunlie shuddered, but he hesitated only a minute. A confrontation with Orde Barstow, though anathema to him, had long seemed inevitable. If the time had come, it had come. He could no more refuse to defend his honor, especially when insulted before the entire assembly, than he could stave off his fate.

Orde Barstow, red with anger, hissed at Dunlie, rising on his toes and leaning forward like a maddened animal, "What do you say, Dunlie, what do you say?"

What else can I say, Dunlie thought. "I accept, sir," he said in his soft, slow voice. "I am not afraid of you, Barstow, or of your threats. And I will meet you as you ask . . ." He looked around the assembly. All present were dumbstruck with the turn this debate had taken. The bad feeling between Barstow and Dunlie had burned so long at a low ebb that its sudden burst into flames had caught them by surprise.

"By God, they mean to fight," one of the assemblymen gasped.

"Excellent," Orde said, an expression of mixed malevolence and triumph on his square, flushed face. The article in question, the debate, the entire proceedings of the assembly were forgotten in the face of his prom-

ised opportunity to settle Angus Dunlie for once and
for all, and he strode through the council chambers
without a moment's hesitation. "I relish this challenge,
sir! For what is unbearable can no longer be borne.
Please send me, at my home, notice of your choice of
weapons, and I will meet you in two days' time. My
honor, sir, craves this satisfaction."

A cold wind blew into the council house when Orde
Barstow passed through the outside door. Angus Dunlie slumped in his seat. "A recess, gentlemen," he said
weakly, "At this point, by your leave, I call a recess . . ."

Fayette lay alone in the cabin for some hours after
Luke Blue had left. At first she cried as if she would
never stop, mourning for him, for what had happened
between them, for what would happen to each of them
for the rest of their lives, and for the sad likelihood
that she would never know what it was.

When the first, fresh grief wore off, shock set in.
The unspeakable had occurred. She could not take it
all in at once. Her mind was a cold, empty place where
colder winds blew. She was not herself at all. What
had happened to the self who had been before Luke
Blue? What had happened to that woman—wife,
mother, handmaiden of the Lord? She must be no
more, for that Fayette could not have experienced
Luke Blue.

Perhaps I am already dead, Fayette thought, almost
hopefully. Stunned, she rose from the tousled bed
where Luke had lain for those weeks and wandered
outside. She felt numb, weightless, utterly without
strength. Her dress was torn, her bodice immodestly
askew, but she was impervious to herself. It was unseasonably cool outside, a westerly wind blew dark clouds
which threatened rain, but she welcomed the gray
bleakness of the sky.

The wind buffeted her as she wandered without de-sign among the cabbages and corn in the garden patch, past the baby hogs which ran in a narrow enclosure, past the chicken sheds, past the sheep grazing near the sluggish stream. Her face was blank, her throat dry, her eyes empty and unseeing, and her fingers twisted together helplessly.

It was so that Micah found her when he came down from the woodlot with his sons, and, seeing her, he knew at once what had happened. Fayette's disheveled state, the dumb agony of her expression were all the proof he needed.

"Take the children inside and stay there," he or-dered. He picked up his rifle, which he always kept near him, and saddled a horse. "When I find him—I shall shoot him, Fayette," he said.

"Please," she said weakly in a voice that frightened the children into silence, but she could say no more. What did she want to ask? That he not go, that he come home safely, that she be forgiven?

But she could not ask and Micah did not stop to listen. When she was alone with the children, Fayette dropped to her knees and clasped her hands in prayer.

"Dear God," she prayed out loud, "Forgive me and forgive him. Please let him live, let Micah come home safely, and let you in your Infinite Wisdom show me the way to go on . . ."

"Where's Luke?" Jenny asked. "Where? Where?" but Pittman knew the answer. "He's run off again, sis-ter, run away just like he come. Can't you hush? Mam-ma's praying to God."

"Guide my steps and strengthen me, Lord," Fayette prayed, "for I am struck down with the weight of my sins and sorrows. Dear God, our Father, who art in Heaven . . ."

Chapter Eighteen

Fathers and Sons Make Arrangements—
Fayette in Despair—A Good Man Dies

Angus Dunlie woke the next morning with a sour, bitter taste in his mouth, but at first he remembered nothing of what had happened the day before. Then he remembered his dream. He had dreamed of having to fight a duel . . . with pistols . . . of taking aim, of squeezing the trigger, then having it fail, of struggling, sweating, being desperate to fire the pistol and save his own life . . .

He groaned and sat up in his curtained bed. "Oh, dear God," he said aloud, suddenly remembering that it was no dream. It was true. He did have to fight a duel. That vile man, his long-time enemy, had actually challenged him to a duel. And he had accepted. "Dear Lord," he said again, "Why? Why has it come to this?" Why had he agreed to it? He sank back into his pillows. What else could he have done? He had no choice. Barstow would have it no other way; he had wanted this duel for years, and now it would be.

Angus lay without moving for a few more minutes, reviewing his situation. Catherine had already left the room, as was her custom. Although they slept in the same bed, there was little tenderness left between them . . . and less love. He had not made love to her in many years, for she did not wish it and he refused to compel her, but he had no other source of physical pleasure, and he resented it.

Increasingly, through the years, Angus Dunlie had turned inward. He was close-mouthed and circumspect. He was civic-minded, but kept his troubles to himself. His diversions were few, and though his financial situation was much improved since his introduction of slaves to Sea Groves, he took little satisfaction even from that.

And his family. He sighed. Years ago, he had looked to his children for meaning in life, but of late, he had found only disappointment. What did it mean that one daughter had disappeared while the other lingered at home, a widow who did not grieve, a mother who had no natural feeling for her child? Not that it was Roland's fault. Roland, in fact, was the main hope of Angus Dunlie's mature years, for Cattie's little boy had grown into a promising teenager, blue-eyed and handsome, well-spoken, reliable and honest and kind.

Whereas Dunlie's own son, James Oglethorpe, was another, and most profound, disappointment. Dunlie scowled as he faced the fact that James was a problem. Like his mother, he was prone to temper tantrums and moody silences. He was as cold and emotionally inexpressive as Dunlie himself, and although Dunlie realized that the boy seemed to have inherited the worst of his parents' natures, he had no explanation for James's predeliction toward violence, his cruelty toward animals and slaves, his constant attempts to

bully Roland, his dishonesty. He had caused Angus
Dunlie great pain.

That it should come to this, Dunlie mourned. To
have come so far for this! He who had so wanted a son,
to nurture such a bad one. How had it come to be?
He, a proudly rational man, to be involved in an emotional duel! He knew that Orde Barstow had hated
him for years, but had he not suffered enough?

"Angus?" Catherine asked, coming into the bedroom. "Are you getting up? Oh, dear God, what shall I
do if you die? By my faith, I am quite hysterical! I am
sick to death! Oh, Angus, what shall we all do if you
die?"

"Let us at least hope for the best," Dunlie said,
swinging himself out of bed. "Don't kill me off yet. I
am a good clean shot, at least as good a shot as that
damn Barstow, and I shall do everything in my power
to shoot him before he shoots me."

"Oh, Lord! I can't stand it! I can't stand to think of
it!" Catherine burst into tears.

Dunlie patted her arm stiffly, but he had no heart
for empty promises. It was true, he might well die tomorrow, but he would do his damnedest to prevent it.
I will not die if I can help it, he vowed. I'll meet that
troublemaking scoundrel and shoot him through the
heart. The world will be well rid of Orde Barstow.

"Find James and send him to me," he ordered Catherine. "He will stand up as my second. I want him to
go to Barstow with a note. We will fight with pistols.
Pray God, my first shot will go true."

Puffed up with the importance of his errand, James
Dunlie swaggered through the wooden gate and up
the steps of Orde Barstow's town house. A skinny,
wide-eyed black maid admitted him and he stood
alone for a minute in the front parlor, impressed de-

spite himself by the richness of the room's furnishings and the fine proportions of the house itself.

A few minutes later he faced Orde Barstow, his father's arch-enemy, and for the first time in his life, found himself face to face with Barstow's son, Byron.

The two young men had known each other since childhood—Savannah was small enough to make it inevitable—but they had steadfastly avoided each other out of unanalyzed feelings that started with family loyalty and custom and went far beyond. Of late, Byron had been out of town during the school years, and both boys had been on their family's plantations in the summer, and they had not even glimpsed each other in years.

"Mr. Barstow," said James, looking into the man's square, florid face and blazing blue eyes, "I have a note for you from my father. Here."

Orde took the folded note from James's hand and read it. James looked at Byron and Byron looked at James. James was seized with a strange feeling that young Barstow reminded him of someone, but couldn't remember who. He scowled. Why, Byron Barstow had powdered his hair. How foppish. And he was dressed like a dandy in a frilled white linen shirt and a golden-brown velvet waistcoat. James straightened. Young Barstow seemed a bit taller than he was, but no, perhaps he wasn't. If he straightened his shoulders they were amazingly like in size, except that he, James, was a bit thinner. Wiry, he liked to think of himself.

"So you are to be your father's second," Orde Barstow commented.

James Dunlie nodded.

"Oh, father, then may I not serve as yours?" Byron asked. "It's only fair and I want to—so much."

His voice, thought James Dunlie, is affected. No

doubt all those fancy schools he's gone to. I bet I could lick him. He's a bit soft-looking.

"Damn, I don't like·it," Orde Barstow said. "I told you before, I'd rather have Beene."

"But if Dunlie is to have his son . . ." Byron begged. "I am not afraid."

"If you're not, then you're a damn fool," Orde snorted.

"Father, please!"

Orde laughed. "I supposed I might as well give you something to do while you're here. But I wouldn't let you if I thought there was the slightest chance . . . just a minute, Dunlie. I want to write a few lines in reply." He strode to a high cherry writing table, dipped a pen in ink, and hunched over to write.

James Dunlie and Byron Barstow eyed each other suspiciously. Byron spoke first.

"How old are you, Dunlie?"

"Eighteen," James lied, his eyes avoiding Byron's. "And you?"

"Seventeen," Byron replied.

James felt his face twitch nervously as he waited for Orde Barstow to finish. Someday I'll have a house as fine as this one, he vowed, no matter what I have to do to get it. He shifted his weight from foot to foot on the rich, dark red patterned carpet. A clock struck the hour with deep sonorous notes.

"The arrangements are satisfactory, and I have written your father so," Orde said in his deep voice. He handed Byron the paper he had written on, and Byron crossed the room to hand it to James who took it without thanking him and turned to go.

"Let me show you to the door," Byron suggested, and shoulder to shoulder they left the room.

"Good-bye, Mr. Dunlie," Byron said at the door.

"Good-bye," James said through clenched teeth,

thinking, I hope I get to take a shot. I'd relish shooting this rogue right in his face. He paused on the doorstep, and as he drew a deep breath, he heard Orde called out to his son, "Unmannerly runt, eh, Byron?" and he went white with anger and shame.

I'll show them, James Dunlie vowed. I'll make them both respect me, and fear me before I'm through. I hate them, and I'll never stop.

He paused halfway down the walk to the gate and picked up a stone to fire at the horse tethered at the side of the house. His aim was good. The stone caught the horse just above its eye, and he was rewarded by the animal's whinny of pain.

Two months had passed since Luke Blue had left Fayette and Micah's home, since the day when the unspeakable had happened, and Micah had set out after Luke with his gun. Micah had returned alone on that day, returned home without finding Luke or any trace of him in the woods or on the roads, but when he had entered the cabin that night, tired and silent, Fayette had seen at once that he had taken a turn for the worse.

And since then, during those two months, she had learned that she was right. Micah left her alone only to do the most essential tasks outside—for a few hours each day he tended the animals and the gardens and chopped firewood. Then he returned to sit without speaking in front of the fire, watching her without looking at her, without speaking to her. Nothing she could say would rouse him to his old spirits. He was utterly glum, utterly despairing and unresponsive, either to her or to the three children.

Micah's mood had put Fayette into a similar state of despair, which she suffered the less easily for thinking it a sin. But worse than that, as the days and weeks ticked by, like the gradual coiling of a spring, she had tightened up with the growing knowledge that it had happened, that which she had dreaded above all, that which had seemed too gross a punishment for the Lord to send her.

For she was increasingly certain that she was with child. Only she and Micah knew that it could not be his child, that it was surely a child conceived in that moment of forbidden intimacy between Fayette and Luke Blue. Fayette bore this new horror alone. She was afraid to tell Micah, afraid that it would move him toward violence, but she knew she could not keep her secret forever.

I have little time, Fayette thought, on a cool fall morning which hinted of winter to follow. Soon it will be too late to travel, and here nothing is likely to change. Alone, I can not bear this much longer. This is the time to turn back to my family for help. She looked over at Micah. He was seated before the fire, whittling without purpose on a length of forked beechwood.

"Micah," she began, "what shall we do?"

He did not answer.

Fayette tried again. "Micah, I have been thinking. I must have help. I cannot manage alone."

Micah looked at his wife and Fayette shuddered before his gaze, which seemed to her full of boundless hate, but still he would not answer. Fayette had come so far before with Micah, often before, but today she was determined to go on.

"So, Micah, I want to leave here now. I have thought about it and I can see no other way. I will take the children and go back to Savannah. What do you say of that? Will you come with us?"

Micah set down his knife and waited.

"You never knew my father, but it has come to me

that he alone can help us with what we must do. And
there are doctors there. Perhaps a doctor . . . your
legs . . . and the children . . . At any rate, Micah, I
have decided so, and unless you have another plan, let
us go as soon as possible."

Taking his silence for assent, Fayette bent all her
energy to preparations for the trip. She packed up
clothes and food enough, and planned that they would
go by horseback to the river and there wait for a boat
going downstream to Savannah by the sea.

Fayette had little hope for salvaging any happiness,
but when she had started making progress toward
their journey, she felt a measure of relief and accepted
it gratefully. On a sunny morning Fayette and her
three children left the clearing where they had lived
for so many years, and at the last minute, Micah
mounted his horse and rode with his family.

According to the arrangements agreed upon between
Orde Barstow and Angus Dunlie, the two men were to
meet at five in the morning in the pasture at the easternmost end of Hutchinson's Island. Each man would
be armed with a fine Italian pistol, the distance between them would be twelve paces, and the first man
to draw blood would be declared the winner. The appointed day dawned cool and gray; a heavy fog hung
over the island.

Doctor Jack Barstow, summoned by Dunlie, was the
last to arrive on the scene. He saw the two parties at
some distance apart, waved to both, then rode up to
Dunlie and his son James.

"Good morning, if it can in any way be considered
such. How are you, sir?" Jack asked.

Dunlie's face showed the strain and pallor of insom-
nia. "Well enough, Jack. I am ready, ready to die if so
it will be. My son, James, is my second. But I ask you,

Doctor, to look unto my rival there. Go see to him, sir. Is he faint?"

Jack Barstow made his way to the Barstow contingent, under a tall live oak tree. Orde Barstow was pacing unevenly beneath the tree, taking support from the arm of his son, Byron. Jack went to him at once.

"Good morning. Mr. Barstow, what is wrong, sir?"

Orde staggered and bent his head. He lifted it with effort and shook it as if it were weighted. "Damn it all! I don't know, I am damned if I know, but I am as staggered as if drunk, sir, though I have taken no alcohol!" He weaved, swayed, and his eyes shut, seemingly involuntarily.

"Doctor, I think he's too sick to defend himself. Let me take your place, father," Byron suggested.

"No! A thousand times no! I relish this chance to take on Dunlie! I won't miss it as long as I can draw breath. But, what . . . Damnit, sir!" Orde's eyes closed again, and he swayed in a faint, falling to his knees.

"How long has he been so?" Jack asked Byron Barstow.

"It's just come over him."

Jack removed his gloves and felt Orde's pulse. "He's faint, very faint. I don't see. . ."

"How can he fight? I must take his place. 'Tis clear."

At that suggestion, Orde rallied and shook his head fiercely. "No! I won't have it! I'll fight this duel myself!"

Jack Barstow stepped back and watched Orde struggle to his feet. He had seen men so—but only in the last stages of life or the crises of fever. As he watched, Orde's eyes closed, despite his apparent effort to open them, and he tumbled forward into a heap at Jack's feet.

"He cannot fight," Byron said firmly.

"He cannot fight," Jack agreed.

"Will you tell them so?" Byron asked Jack, "and that I will take his place? If it is agreeable, then I am ready at once." Byron had bent as he spoke, and dragged Orde's limp body to rest against the trunk of the tree.

Jack Barstow nodded. "I will," he said and walked slowly back to the spot where Dunlie and his son were waiting.

Tenderly, Byron Barstow stretched out his father's legs and settled them in a natural position. Orde was drawing deep, tortured breaths and snoring with a long rattle. His body was as limp as if dead, but in fact, he was only heavily drugged, drugged with all the laudanum Byron had been able to buy at Savannah's two pharmacies.

"It's better this way, Father," Byron said to the unconscious figure. I only did what I had to do, he reminded himself. His eyesight is far too weak for him to meet anyone in a duel. It would be murder. Although I am not a famous shot, at least I shall have a chance.

Angus Dunlie and his son, James, listened without comment as Jack Barstow explained to them that Orde Barstow was quite definitely ill, and would be unable to fight for himself. "However, his second sends his word that he is prepared to take his place," Jack said, "and, unless you have good reason to object, we will begin at once."

James Dunlie took the news with a sneer. "So you must face that young dandy," he said to his father, after a fleeting thought that perhaps he should offer to replace his father. "God speed your bullet."

"I am ready, and would like to proceed at once," Angus Dunlie said coldly. He was far from calm, but had settled into a grim fatality of mind. Young Barstow was only a lad—he had no will to shoot at children, but indeed he had no will, or intention, to shoot at all. Perhaps I will wing him, he thought, wondering if he could do even that . . . Since it must be, he thought, only let it be at once, and over quickly. "Show him the pistols, please, let him choose, and I am ready to take my position."

So Jack Barstow, who had served in this capacity in countless duels, several of them in this very pasture, a popular spot for Savannah's hot-blooded young men to settle disputes, took the set of matched pistols in their case to Byron Barstow for his approval.

Byron looked over both guns, examined them, and selected one. Each pistol held but one ball and each man would be allowed but one shot. Jack loaded Byron's pistol and returned to Angus Dunlie with the remaining pistol.

At a signal from Jack, both men walked toward each other and took a position back to back. Byron was nearly as tall as Angus Dunlie, and at a casual glance they looked as like as kin, but Jack noticed nothing save the dull resignation on Angus Dunlie's long face and the bloodless pallor of Byron's.

"Each of you is to take twelve paces," Jack Barstow directed, "stop on the signal, then turn and fire at will. If, after a fire, either party is hit, the duel is over; if neither man gets a hit, the second of the man challenged, namely, Angus Dunlie, will approach the second of Mr. Barstow, who is, of course, now representing his principal, and ask him if his honor be satisfied. Gentlemen, are you ready?"

Jack looked from young Barstow to old Dunlie, a man whom he had revered and respected for many years. Both men nodded.

"Then count off your paces. One, two . . ."

Each man took twelve paces, slowly and carefully, holding his pistol at his right side. Orde Barstow lay without moving under the live oak at a distance of about thirty feet. James Oglethorpe Dunlie watched tensely. Jack Barstow ran to fetch his medicine case from his saddlebags, turning just as the two men had reached the appointed distance.

Angus Dunlie took a deep breath. He stopped, turned to the right, and aimed the pistol at the young man his rival had adopted and raised as his son. The gesture froze his blood, he felt a powerful horror, and he knew he could not shoot at the innocent boy.

Byron Barstow tossed his head when he had taken twelve paces. Sick with fear, his hand trembled as he turned to face his father's rival. He raised the pistol and took aim. Dear God, he prayed, help me, steady me, somehow spare us both . . .

Impulsively, Angus Dunlie changed his aim. He raised the pistol and fired it into the air. I cannot shoot that young man, he thought, and a sense of relief as welcome and strangely like happiness flooded him in the seconds before he felt a huge, dull, and spreading pain in his lower chest cavity. It is over, thank God, he thought. He looked down at his own body, smelling it, seeing a red-ringed hole, seeing his death wound as if it were not his own.

The sound of the two shots was followed by a moment of silence. Then, seeing Angus Dunlie lurch forward, seeing his knees crumple and his face go whiter yet with shock, Byron Barstow cried out in horror. Jack Barstow rushed forward to the wounded man.

"Father!" James Dunlie called out. He was shocked. His father hit! His father wounded . . . perhaps dead. James Dunlie had not allowed himself to speculate upon the possibility of his father's being hit . . . it had seemed unlikely . . . why his father was a good shot . . . but he hadn't even aimed at young Barstow. In realizing that, James Dunlie felt a stab of resentment at his parent. Why hadn't the old man fired at Byron Barstow? Could it be seen as cowardice? Damnation! Why must his father be so? Always he had chosen the passive, neutral act. He could have shot young Barstow, in a way even more satisfying than shooting his father . . . but he had not even *tried* . . .

Slowly, like a sleepwalker, James Dunlie strode forward to his father's aid, his thoughts still tangled. Why had his father . . . and how like him . . . but why, why . . . and now . . .?

Byron Barstow stood horribly alone, the victor, but forgotten. No one looked in his direction. He felt no triumph. His shot had gone true. He had hit his mark. And now? Unsure, still shocked, he hesitated, remembered his father. He turned and ran back to Orde's side. The duel was over, he had done what he felt he must, and now there was nothing more he could do but try to rouse him and get him home.

"How bad is he hit?" James Dunlie asked Jack. Jack had cushioned Angus's head and was probing his wound with a lancet. Blood spurted from the wound and covered Jack's right hand.

"Bad. It's gone in all the way. He's punctured clean," Jack commented.

"Dear God! Father? Father, speak to me," James begged. He knelt, cradled Angus's head and looked into his eyes, but they were hazel blanks, empty of recognition.

James felt as though he were looking into the face of Death itself. In the waxy stillness of Angus's face there were no answers, no advice, no admonitions, no instructions. James felt at once angry and bereft and cheated.

"Father! Speak!" James demanded, shaking his father's head.

Jack Barstow felt tears sting his eyes as Angus Dunlie's pulse slowed, then stopped.

"Yes, he is dead," he said after a minute. "So dies a good man . . ."

"Oh, Goddamn!" James declared.

"Let it end here," Jack pleaded. He looked toward Byron Barstow and his father, and his voice echoed in the stillness, "He is dead. Let it end here, I beg of you." Jack was distressed and grief-stricken far beyond professionalism and tears blurred his voice. Still kneeling, holding Angus Dunlie's lifeless arm, he looked from Byron Barstow to James Dunlie, both young men standing rigidly by the still bodies of their fathers.

The young men were locked in each other's intense gaze, and Jack Barstow had the feeling of being excluded as from a powerful and private passion.

"Let the mourning begin and the conflict end," Jack Barstow begged, but as he watched, James Dunlie's face went ugly with spite.

"Byron Barstow!" he shouted, "He's dead! You've killed him! God damn you for it!"

Byron shuddered. He was choked with guilt and horror. His father had been the challenger, not himself, and he had acted according to the conventions of the code duello, and yet, he felt that James Dunlie was right. How could any man forgive his father's murderer? Silenced, he bowed his head.

"I'll get you, Barstow!" James Dunlie threatened. "I'll have my chance at you, and laugh to see *your* life's blood seep into the soil!"

"No more!" Jack Barstow shouted. "This is no time or place for such words. No right is made by doubling wrongs. James Dunlie, get your father's carriage and bring it here. You, Barstow, be gone. I will visit your father at home tonight. See that he is made comfortable until then."

Both young men obeyed the authority in Jack Barstow's voice, and with trembling hands he closed Angus Dunlie's eyes. "Farewell, my friend," he said softly. He had known and admired Dunlie all his life, known him as a father and a military colleague, admired his principles, his stature as a force for good in the community, known him as a strict, patient, moral man.

It is the end of the beginning, he thought. The death of Angus Dunlie is the end of Georgia's first days, the end of certain peaceable hopes and possibilities. He wept.

Chapter Nineteen

Zonah Fears What She Knows—A
Funeral—And an Ill-Timed
Homecoming

Zonah had followed Orde's carriage out to the gate, and she waited there, praying to the gods of fire and life all the while Orde and Byron were away and the duel was being fought on Hutchinson's Island. She stood and she paced around the huge live oak by the gateposts, too anxious to sit down or to wait inside the house. At the first sight of Orde's carriage, she ran forward to meet it, and saw that Byron was holding the reins.

"Where is he?" she asked anxiously.

Byron looked up, startled by Zonah's sudden appearance. His head was spinning with shocked misery. He had killed Angus Dunlie. Oh, yes, he had done it for his father, but how much did that lessen the crime? Byron's hands shook and he felt sick with guilt and sadness. At first Zonah's voice did not mean anything to him; it did not reach him.

Then Zonah saw Orde Barstow stretched out behind

Byron, lying on his back, and she opened her mouth in a wail of genuine agony. "Ohhhhhhhhhhh! Oh, no! Oh, no!" Zonah grabbed the side of the carriage and lifted herself onto it, swayed, and fell forward. She screamed louder and higher and Byron was shocked out of himself.

"No! Stop, Zonah! See, he is not dead!" Byron promised. His voice was rough with emotion. She really loves him, he thought, and so should a man and woman love, but the thought was lost in the confusion of the moment.

Zonah had scrambled across the carriage on her knees to Orde. She cradled his head in her lap. Tears streamed down her face as she bent over him, kissing his hands, slapping his face.

"He is not dead! He is sleeping in a strange sleep! What happened, what happened, Byron?"

"First let us put him to bed."

"Why so still? He was grazed, then, by a ball? He was hit!"

"No, no, he was not hit at all," Byron answered. A groom ran forward, then the houseservants, all shouting and surrounding the carriage. Byron was only vaguely aware . . . they were all black faces . . . some strange to him, but all his father's people.

Zonah took charge. "Carry him to his bed," she commanded. "You, Tom, take the young master inside. You, take the carriage away. Hurry!"

Feeling out of place and helpless, Byron brushed off the slave women who offered him food, drink, who tried to lead him into the parlor. He climbed the stairs behind Zonah and his father's still body, borne aloft by three huge black men.

"There! Put him down carefully, so . . ." Zonah ordered them. When Orde was flat in bed he began to snore deeply, as he had on Hutchinson's Island, and

Zonah turned to Byron, not at all surprised to see him standing meekly at the end of the bed.

"Why does he sleep?" she demanded.

Byron ignored the question and muttered, "I took his place, Zonah. He could not shoot, so I took his place against Angus Dunlie."

Zonah froze, suddenly anticipating the full horror of what had occurred, understanding the full horror of the taboo. She faced Byron, the tall lanky young man she had held as a baby, whom she had raised as carefully as if he was her own son, the gentle, intelligent young man who had grown into all the promise of his boyhood, who was so much the son and heir Orde Barstow had wanted. Zonah began to tremble.

"I faced Angus Dunlie," he stammered, "I . . . had to . . . I shot him."

Zonah shut her eyes. She shuddered. In some awful way, she had feared this. It was all a punishment, a working out of the evil born with the twins. Nothing she had done over the years had stopped the evil or put an end to it. It still lived, it had made its way back into their lives, it had grown to bear bitter fruit, to poison lives, to strike down healthy men . . .

"And?" she forced herself to ask, "And is he dead?"

Byron nodded miserably, but Zonah did not see him.

"Is he dead?" she demanded again. "You shot him?"

"Yes," Byron said.

Zonah dropped to her knees and covered her face with her hands to protect herself from the evil. She felt it swirling about them, felt the air rustle with spirits, felt a cold wind blow through the door and raise the hairs on her arms, felt her blood tingle in warning. Such powerful evil! Oh, she could never settle it! She could never atone for the evil of stealing the twin, of hiding it, of letting both boys live! Wringing her hands, she wailed miserably.

Byron, choking back tears of grief and guilt, could not understand Zonah's reaction. "What is it?" he begged, "Why are you crying so, Zonah? Why?"

But Zonah could not answer. She cupped her hands over her ringing ears. She heard worse sounds, worse cries of mourning inside her head. The infinite was outraged. It was the most powerful of taboos. The son had killed his father . . . and in innocence. He who seemed so blessed among men was hopelessly cursed.

"Please, Zonah," Byron begged in a shaking voice. "Stop! He's all right! Stop! Speak to me!"

But Zonah would not pronounce such evil out loud, would not give it the life of words, could never explain it, or if not never, at least not yet. She raised her head and saw Byron's pale, shaken figure, saw his innocence and his unhappiness. He was still young; perhaps with Angus Dunlie he had killed the evil for his lifetime, she thought hopefully. Perhaps the evil had died today, and it was that death she felt in the air. But even as she struggled to her feet she knew the weight of an awful dread that it was not so, not over yet.

"Tell me, Zonah," Byron asked again, but she shook her head.

"Not now, not now," she said in a voice that was nearly her own again, "See! He wakes! Ah . . ."

Orde Barstow stirred. He raised his big, square head and blinked his blue eyes. His gray and black curly hair was wild about his face and he looked shocked.

"What happened?" he demanded. "Where is he?" He saw Zonah, Byron. "Where's Dunlie? Where am I?" he bellowed.

In accordance with Savannah's custom, Angus Dunlie's funeral was held the next day in early evening.

Bells tolled as the funeral procession made its way from the services in Christ Church to the cemetery. An open carriage at the head of the procession carried Angus's long body, laid out on a black-covered bier in his best suit, and his widow, Catherine, dressed in black and heavily veiled, walked behind.

Beneath the veils, Catherine's face was dry, her expression set and stoical. She had cried before Angus left home to fight the duel, she had wept hysterically as she waited to hear the news of the duel's outcome, but since Angus had been brought home dead, she had shed not a tear.

Catherine was shocked, profoundly shocked, and angry. It was the anger that had dried her tears. To her, it seemed outrageous and unforgivably heartless of Angus to have gotten himself killed. Stupid man, he had led her along the path of life until this point where, now that she was nearly an old woman, she was far from home, burdened and beset with family and financial responsibilities she had never been raised or taught to accept, two large, demanding households, and countless near-savage darkies.

Catherine swore softly to herself. Her only consolation was that at least she would have her own way. She would never marry again—oh, no—she would not think of it. A new husband would demand new intimacies, bring new problems, and added duties. No, she was well rid of Angus in that respect, and now that she was alone, she would take charge.

"Tomorrow," she had told her family before the trek to the church and cemetery began, "tomorrow we return to Sea Groves."

Cattie had opened her mouth to protest, but her mother's look stopped her.

"If you do not care to come along," she said sharply

to her daughter, "stay. I don't care. But James and Roland come with me."

Cattie had stirred uneasily, remembering the scene she had witnessed the night before. It was something that she and her mother were never to discuss and never to forget. Cattie had heard odd laughter from inside her parents' bedroom and had stopped before the closed door.

"Mother?" she had called, surprised, curious.

There was no answer.

"Mother, are you all right?" Cattie had called again, and then, receiving no reply, she had eased the door open a few inches and looked inside.

The room was dark except for a single candle on the bedside table and the light thrown off by the fire in the shallow fireplace. Catherine Dunlie was standing, naked, in the middle of the bed where she had slept for so many years with Angus, her blond hair loose and tousled, her full, voluptuous figure shining a pale ivory.

Cattie had gasped. She could smell wine and the odd, acrid odor of burning fabric. She met her mother's eyes, then her gaze slipped to the fire, and she saw the sleeve of one of her father's shirts, saw the flames lick the buff satin of his favorite waistcoat.

"Mother!" Cattie had cried, frightened and horrified.

"Get out! Get out, you sneaking, spying chit!" Catherine had shrieked and Cattie backed away, all too willing.

In the morning, Catherine had not spoken of it. She was cold and aloof and paid her daughter no particular attention.

With James and Roland on either side, Catherine had endured the long, melancholy funeral service in Christ Church. Everything there had been hung with black crepe: the pulpit and desks of the church, the organ loft, the pews occupied by the Governor and members of the council. Friends of the Dunlies, their neighbors, members of the militia, and many people Catherine did not recognize gathered to mourn. A young cleric visiting from England played a dirge on the new organ, the first in Georgia.

Through it all, Catherine seethed with anger and hardened her heart toward the memory of the man she had lived with for thirty-four years. Two funeral sermons were preached, and in each Angus Dunlie's memory was praised and his life called out as an example to young and old, to all the living. Sarah Whitman sobbed in the pew behind Catherine and leaned forward to place a steadying hand on Catherine's arm, but she looked at it coldly and felt relief only when Sarah had taken it away.

Will this sermon never end, Catherine asked herself as the Reverend Mr. Zouberbuhler read from St. Matthew:

> Then shall be two in the field; the one shall be taken, and the other left. Two women shall be grinding at the mill; the one shall be taken, and the other left. Watch, therefore; for ye know not what hour your Lord doth come . . . .

The black-coated minister intoned and his voice broke with sadness, but Catherine was unmoved. Only let me endure this day, she asked, and rose gratefully to follow the hearse to the cemetery in the southern-most part of town. There she would endure more eulogies and the militia would fire muskets, but when darkness settled on the mourners, she would be able to go home, free at last.

Orde Barstow, fully recovered by the next after-noon, insisted that Byron should return at once to school.

"There's a packet sailing at dusk for Charleston, my boy," he told Byron, "and I want you on it. The sooner you put all this mess behind you, the better. I never meant to put you in such danger, I hope you believe me, but I was fortunate to have you, as it turned out. Damn it! What luck to be visited with such a strange and sudden spell—I never had such a strong fever—and when I think that it might have been you instead of that miserable Dunlie . . . Why, thank God your shot went true."

Byron had not recovered. He was silent and moody, deeply disturbed by the experience, the fear, the ten-sion, the shock of killing, and still shaken and puzzled by Zonah's reaction.

Orde Barstow saw Byron's anxiety and distress and was not unmoved by it. "I'd be glad to keep you home, son, but it's best that you go."

"Yes," Byron repeated, "it's best that I go."

"Let's go together to the docks, then, son. And look, here's a few pounds to speed your way." He handed Byron a sack of coins, twenty pounds in gold, but By-ron took it without counting it.

"Thank you, father," he said soberly.

"Not so glum, not so glum. You've done a man's job and I'm proud of you! You're a good son, Byron Bar-stow!"

"Thank you, father."

"All this will blow over and be forgotten by your next return, you'll see. Now let's be off!"

Byron looked for Zonah to say good-bye, but she was not in the kitchen or the laundry or the quarters, and he gave up. "Please tell Zonah I bid her farewell," he asked his father as they walked together out of the gate and down the familiar lanes that led to the river.

"Zonah? That I will," Orde promised. He was always surprised by Byron's attachment to Zonah, but thought it harmless.

Both men heard the bells tolling for Angus Dunlie's funeral as they crossed town, and Byron's stomach churned with guilt and despair. To think that he had killed the man they tolled for. Would God forgive him? He remembered how Dunlie's son, James, had cursed him and vowed vengeance. Please God, they had been empty threats in the heat of the moment. He had no stomach for further duelling, no stomach and no heart. He would never do it again in his life. Of that he was sure. Before heaven, he would never again shoot a man.

"Put it out of your mind," Orde advised. "Do not think on it further. You acted as you had to. You saved my life. Remember that, son . . ."

The sun had set and the sky was dimming as Orde and Byron stood near the customs house on the Strand. They were waiting for the small open boat that carried passengers out to the packet ship anchored in the middle of the river. Sea birds flew overhead and circled, cawing, looking for food. Byron felt beaten and exhausted, but Orde was in fine spirits.

"By my word, I almost wish I were sailing off with you, son. There's something invigorating in taking passage at dusk and sailing by the stars! You'll have a fine voyage . . . Dear me, look at that crew!"

The sight Orde Barstow called to Byron's attention was that of a poor, ragged backwoods family making their way up the Strand. They had apparently just disembarked from a river ferry, for they looked bewildered, and carried with them bundles and boxes and sacks, which appeared to contain all their worldly belongings.

At the head of the little procession was a dark-haired woman past her prime, perhaps once pretty, Orde judged, but so scrawny and ragged and over-worked that it was hard to say for sure. Behind her straggled three children, the youngest a girl, each smaller than the last by a head or so, each staggering under the weight of baskets and bundles. Following the boys was a disheveled blond-bearded man, more alarming for the madness in his blue eyes than all of the others for their poverty-stricken appearance.

Byron's attention was immediately caught by the look in the man's eyes, caught and held. His eyes were as empty as the sky . . . what could befall a man to make him look that way? Byron was about to point out this oddity to his father, but the woman ap-proached them steadily and he was stopped by her voice.

"Excuse me, good sirs," she asked in an old-fashioned way, and her voice was neither rough nor unpleasantly accented, "but we are just arriving in town." She set down the basket she carried, and some chickens inside squawked in protest.

Byron looked at her curiously. Her deep-set eyes were a frank, intelligent green color, though ringed with exhaustion. Poor woman, what could have made her husband look so? He felt sorry for her.

"May I direct you to some lodging house?" Orde Barstow offered, wondering if this family could afford any lodging at all. Perhaps the Widow Peeker's place . . .

"No, no thank you, sir," the woman said. "We have family to go to. But can you tell me, sir, why the bells toll so mournfully?"

"Why those are the funeral bells," Orde explained. "Look sharp, Byron, here is the boat . . ."

Byron shivered to be reminded of the funeral and looked away from the ragged family. "Good-bye, father," he said, "God keep you well."

Orde shook his son's hand vigorously, ignoring the woman who stood so near them, "God speed you, son, and bring you safely home again . . ."

"I'll not detain you," the woman said. "But who has died?"

Byron stepped back, leaving the answer to his father.

"A man named Angus Dunlie," Orde said shortly, "killed in a duel. Now, I beg your pardon, madam, but I have a few more words for my son . . ."

But Byron's eyes were on the poor woman, and he saw her stagger as if she had caught a blow to her head. "My father!" she gasped, and swayed as if she would faint.

I cannot stand it; I must go, Byron thought. I must go at once. "See to her, father!" he called out and jumped into the open boat.

And Orde Barstow, clumsily, reluctantly, did what he could for Fayette, calling for water from the staff of the customs house, bellowing at her husband, "See here, my good man! What is wrong with your wife?" In a few minutes' time, Fayette's hysterical sobbing had gathered a sympathetic crowd, and Orde slipped away at once.

"Unfortunate," he muttered to himself as he turned into Machenry's Tavern for a bracer of rum. "Unfortunate, but none of my fault. Why that man looks to be as mad as a hatter!"

Darkness fell and the bells ceased their relentless tolling, but Byron's ship had already left the harbor and Orde was tossing back a third glass of rum punch as Catherine Dunlie turned away from her husband's grave and started to make her way home.

For Orde Barstow, who kept his post in Machenry's well-furnished tavern and continued to drink rum until he was helped home to bed by the two menservants sent by Zonah, the dockside incident was just that—an unlucky coincidence to be put out of his mind, and with the aid of alcohol, soon forgotten.

But for the Dunlies, riding home from the burying ground in Cattie's carriage, the day's surprises were not yet over.

Roland, seated up front with Goldie, was the first to see the crowd outside the Dunlie house. He leaned forward in amazement. Three children sat on the steps of the empty house, a bewildered-looking, blond-bearded man hovered behind them, and, in front, though it was nearly dark and the grass was wet with dew, a dark-haired woman lay stretched out on her back. Around this family, for they had the look of a group joined together by blood, clustered several of the Dunlies' neighbors, still in their church-going clothes—donned out of respect to the dead—and some others Roland knew only by sight as waterfront riffraff, men who hung around the docks, making a scanty living loading and unloading ships and ferrying passengers across the river.

Everyone turned as Goldie slowed the carriage, and it moved up the narrow lane to the side of the house.

"Hey! Who's there?" James called to Roland from inside the carriage, where he sat with his mother and sister.

"I don't know . . ." Roland said. A blur of moving light caught his eye and he turned to see Doctor Jack Barstow hurrying toward the house, accompanied by his man who was carrying a torch.

"What's wrong?" Catherine Dunlie demanded in a tired and tremulous voice. The carriage stopped and she poked her head out, taking in the entire unlikely scene without comprehension. "Who are all these people?"

George Owen, a neighbor who was a friend of Roland's, ran up to the carriage and shouted to Catherine Dunlie. "It's your daughter!" he cried. "It's Fayette—and her family—come home!"

"Dear Lord in heaven," Catherine mumbled. She put her hands over heart. It was thumping wildly. Oh, it had all been too much of a shock, now she was ill of it! Oh, how could Angus have died and left her with all these troubles? Fayette? Alive? Home after more than a dozen years? No, she didn't believe it.

"Fayette!" Cattie screamed. Scrambling past James Dunlie, she jumped out of the carriage and ran to the woman lying on her back. She arrived just as Jack Barstow did, the crowd opening up for her, and fell on her knees before the prone figure.

"What's wrong with her? Is it really Fayette?"

"Of course it's Fayette," Jack said sensibly. "Now stand aside, all of you, and let the woman have some air. Stand aside and let me have a look at her."

"What are you doing here?" Cattie asked Jack, with whom she was not currently on good terms.

"Shouldn't I ask you why your sister is not inside in bed?" Jack replied. "I was summoned, madam, when she fainted in town and was carried here by these men . . ."

Cattie surveyed the crowd and shuddered. "Go home now, at once . . ." She stopped, arrested by the sight of Micah Stone, who was still standing by his sons without speaking a word or seeming to understand anything that was going on.

"Micah!" she gasped. "Oh, good Lord, what's wrong with them, Jack? Can't anybody tell me what's wrong?"

"I can tell you she needs rest . . . and quiet," Jack said. He rose and bowed to Catherine Dunlie, who had made her way from the carriage on the arm of her son, James, and stood, frowning, at Fayette's dark, tousled head. "My condolences to you, madam. In the face of this development, may I ask your permission to carry the patient inside?"

Catherine nodded, speechless with shock, and pointed the way with a gesture of her arm. Roland, with the aid of his friend George Owen and Jack Barstow's man, carried Fayette into the house and upstairs to the room where she had slept as a girl.

"Who're you?" Cattie asked the oldest boy. In a halting voice he answered her, "I'm Pittman, ma'am, and next is Isaac. Our sister Jenny's the baby. But ma'am, please, our father is sicker than our mother . . ."

Poor lad, Jack Barstow thought, herding the boys and their father into the Dunlie house, and waving for the crowd to disperse, but he made an effort to put heart into his voice. "Nonsense," he said, as cheerfully as possible, "you've likely had a hard journey. Fix him up with a good drink of rum, Cattie, and mark my words, little Jenny won't be the baby for long. Cattie, I believe that your sister is with child, and if that's all that's wrong with her, she'll be telling us all the news by tomorrow."

And Cattie tried to believe him, calling for food and drink to be served in the dining room to the three boys and their father, but although he ate hungrily, Micah Stone did not speak a word, and Cattie escaped as soon as she could, leaving Roland behind.

Upstairs, Cattie ran from her mother's bedroom to

Fayette's, finding Catherine numbly sipping at the toddy Doctor Jack had prescribed for her, and Fayette murmuring prayers, but she could not put the sight of Micah Stone out of her mind.

"He's daft, isn't he?" she asked bluntly of Jack Barstow in Fayette's room. Shaking his head in warning, Jack led Cattie out of earshot.

"There are things it is not given to us to understand," he replied, "They have both suffered some shock . . . some trial or terror that has flattened them. You will have to treat them kindly, Cattie . . ."

"Treat them kindly?" Cattie stamped her foot in a flash of temper. "And who is to treat me kindly? Honestly, hasn't there been enough trouble around here, what with duels and dying and funerals. Without Fayette choosing this day to drag herself home to make us all take care of her!"

"You'll manage," Jack said, smiling at the thought that Cattie still acted as if she were sixteen years old.

"Yes, I expect I shall," Cattie sniffed, "I always—"

"He's gone," James Dunlie announced, bounding up the stairs to confront Cattie and Doctor Jack.

"Who is?" Cattie asked.

"You know—their father, her . . . husband!" James grinned in amusement. "The simple one!"

"Don't say such things!" Cattie complained, reaching out to give her brother's ears a box. "What do you mean he's gone?"

"Owww! It's true, you know! He just put down his fork and ran out the door . . ."

"Well, likely enough he'll be right back," Cattie said, privately adding, "although I'd be glad to see the last of him."

But Micah Stone did not reappear that night, or all the next day, and when at the end of the week Cather-

ine and her children and grandchildren made the trek
south to Sea Groves plantation, Micah had not returned and they had to resign themselves to go on
without him.

Chapter Twenty

*James Dunlie Rebels—Mad Micah
Stalks the Island—Fayette Gives Birth
for the Last Time*

James Dunlie was frustrated and angry. It had been
six months since his father's death, or murder, as he
thought of it, at the hands of Byron Barstow. During
those six months the Dunlie family had settled into
plantation life at Sea Groves, but it was a life that did
not suit James.

During his lifetime, Angus Dunlie had worked tremendously hard to build and develop Sea Groves—its
groves of oranges and lemon and mulberry trees, its
big house and many outbuildings, including the small
huts where the slaves lived, and most importantly, its
rice fields. Angus had worked side by side with Moses
Black, his Negro overseer, and had seen Sea Groves
grow and flourish. Had he lived, Angus would have
taken great pleasure in having the plantation's control
and management pass into the hands of his son
James—though Angus, in his fair, precise, and kindly

way always included his grandson, Roland, in his dreams for the future of Sea Groves.

But Catherine Dunlie had taken over Sea Groves completely. Catherine had put wifehood and bereavement behind her without a backward glance and had accepted full authority and command at the plantation as if it were a role she had waited half a lifetime to play. She plunged herself into the work of planting, raising, harvesting, and selling rice with a fierce strength and determination that astonished her family. She rose early, breakfasted alone with her ledger books, and rode out with Moses to the fields, leaving supervision of domestic work to Fayette—who accepted the responsibility willingly but clumsily—and competent, light-skinned Mary Black, Moses's wife who was now general housekeeper.

Catherine lost weight and appeared younger. In fact, she was being transformed by the feeling of power. Her energy and endurance were remarkable, but her temper was short, and whereas before she had indulged it only in moody silences and half-smothered tantrums, she now gave it free rein.

Catherine became a tyrant and ruled Sea Groves absolutely. None of her family had the strength or will to oppose her; in fact, she was generally benevolent to them, except for her son, James. Catherine acted unself-consciously, but she had never really loved the son she had so longed for and so suffered over. As a child, he had been colicky and fretful, and she had been weakened and ill and had resented it. She had openly favored bright, sweet-tempered Roland; James knew it and had always suffered from the rejection.

As Angus Dunlie had noted, James and his mother were much alike, and the ways in which they were like set them against each other more strongly than differences might have done. Both were impulsive and hot-tempered. Both enjoyed power, and for both of them, compromise was difficult and hatreds not soon forgotten.

One April morning, as James still lay abed after a riotous night of possum hunting and drinking with Roland and two of the sons of Marswell Eaton, their nearest neighbor, he was awakened by loud and angry pounding on his bedroom door.

"Roland? What the hell?" James shouted, but before he could even reach for his nightshirt, his mother had burst into the room, fully dressed in black silk, her eyes blazing with anger, and her right arm swinging a leather riding crop.

"Get up! Get up, you lazy scamp! Lying abed with the sun already high! With your poor mother hard at work for hours!"

James was furious and had a dreadful hangover. He jumped out of bed and dashed for the chair where he had piled his clothes in the middle of the night. Catherine advanced, switching the crop and landed a smart blow on her son's bare white bottom.

"There! You deserve a good thrashing, James Dunlie!"

"Ow! Mother! What's wrong!? It's only . . ."

"It's not the first time, James! Oh, why do I have such a lazy, slow-witted son? Oh, why do I find myself so burdened? A woman of my age should be surrounded by the comfort and support of her children!"

She loves it, James thought to himself, white with anger and embarrassment at being beaten by his mother, she loves running Sea Groves and ordering all of us around as if we were no better than darkies . . .

"James! Are you listening? I found the bridle and reins you whipped that boy Riley half to death for stealing—left by accident in the small well-house! You idiot! Oh, how can I trust you to go to market in Savannah! Have you already forgotten you were to go today?"

"Of course I haven't forgotten." Damn her, James thought. Not for the first time, he thought—if Father were alive, this could never happen. His mother treated him like a wicked, stupid child. She seemed to want to see him bungle jobs, she enjoyed chastising him. She was quick to excuse Roland's pranks—why could she never overlook his? He shut his eyes against the pain of his headache.

"Are you ill?" Catherine demanded. "Dear Lord, why am I cursed with a sickly son?"

"I am not ill!" James shouted. "Oh, pardon me, mother. I do not mean to shout." Hopping away from her on one leg, he struggled to pull on his second boot. His spirits were rising rapidly, now that he remembered he was going to the slave market in Savannah. How I would love to get away from her for good—away from Sea Groves, too, until the day she's dead. Why, that day can't be so far off, he thought, for she is an old woman . . .

Looking at Catherine—vibrant, trim, and black-bonneted—James was not confident of her imminent mortality, but he was cheered by even the thought of its possibility.

Catherine had retreated to the doorway. "I wonder if I can trust you to do this errand for me," she said. "Do you remember what we discussed? I want ten healthy field workers—young and strong and docile. Look at their teeth. And their feet. Walk them up and down before you bid for them. Do you think you can handle it?" she asked suspiciously.

"Yes, mother, of course." James buttoned his waistcoat and reached for his jacket. "Of course I can do it!"

"Very well, your horse was saddled an hour ago. I

will give you the money when you have breakfasted."

As soon as his mother had left, James dug a flask out of his chest and drank some rum to steady his head. He smiled as the liquor hit his stomach with a jolt and spread a slow warmth over his body. She has no respect for me, he thought resentfully. I am a man of eighteen. I ought be running Sea Groves, not being ordered around by an old woman. Why, I have half a mind to take that money to Savannah and do what I will with it.

Braced by thoughts of escape and of avenging himself on his mother, James left his room and strode through hallways busy with women slaves doing the morning housekeeping. He passed Fayette's closed door. Poor odd Fayette, he thought. Her time is near. She has never been the same since her husband disappeared, though I would think she's well enough rid of him.

Impulsively, James turned into the bedroom his parents had shared. He paused, took a deep breath, then removed his father's gold watch from the inlaid casket where it was always kept. No one saw him, and he smiled with pleasure as he tucked it into his own waistcoat pocket.

It's mine by rights, anyway, he thought. That old crow should have given it to me when he died . . . she's probably waiting to give it to Roland. Well, I shall prevent that and give myself a bit more operating money in town. The idea of leaving Sea Groves for good had taken root in his mind and was growing unchecked as he approached his mother's office for her final instructions and the money set aside for field hands.

"Carry this note also to Governor Ellis," Catherine commanded her son. "Ride carefully, guard the money well, and do not tarry in town. I beg you, take care and use the wits God gave you. I daresay they are well rested. I shall expect you . . ."

"Expect me when I return, Mother," James said impertinently and turned on his heels. "Nagging old witch," he muttered as he cleared the front steps with a leap and mounted his horse with the graceful ease of a man born to ride, dizzy with drink, and utterly glad to be leaving his home behind.

In the years since General Oglethorpe's glorious victory at the Battle of Bloody Marsh, the village and garrison at Fort Frederica had been allowed to fall into ruin. The fort, once regarded as Georgia's main bulwark against the Spanish, was neglected once it appeared unlikely that there would be any more warfare on the southern frontier. Many of the soldiers and officers who had lived at Frederica in the 1740s settled in other parts of the colony, leaving a small foot regiment to protect empty houses, barracks without soldiers, guns without carriages, and streets grown over with weeds.

When large rice plantations worked by slaves began to characterize the settlement of the island, some attempts were made to repair parts of the fort, but much of it was in a condition beyond repair. The fortifications were falling down and decayed; many of the houses were destroyed in a fire; and the cannon that had not been removed to Savannah lay around in the sand and grass and were spoiled by neglect.

Runaway slaves sometimes found refuge in this melancholy ghost town; fugitives often hid out there for weeks at a time; rough woodsmen looking for land or temporary work passed through, and thus, the arrival of Micah Stone attracted no attention at all.

Micah had spent the winter in the woods near Sa-

vannah and had walked the eighty miles along the
Golden Coast to the mouth of the Altamaha River. He
had worked for a blacksmith in Darien for a few
weeks; the smith remembered him as a quite, gentle
man with a bad limp, "not all there, if you know what
I mean."

Indeed, Micah was quiet. He rarely spoke a word
except to arrange for food and lodging. He had grown
thin and scrawny and dressed more like a trapper or
Indian than the farmer he had been. His blond hair
and beard were long and tangled; his feet were shod in
moccasins, and he had a red felt hat he pulled low
over his vacant blue eyes.

And behind those blank eyes Micah lived his life.
He shot game, skinned it and cooked it; he worked at
odd jobs and spent the money he earned in taverns; he
slept in haylofts or empty houses or unrolled his blanket and slept in the woods, but his real life was all
lived in his troubled mind. In his mind, Micah relived
his years of happiness with Fayette and the children
and the abrupt changes that had split the family and
driven him away. He talked to his lost sons, silently,
endlessly, for hour after hour, counseling them, advis-
ing them, teaching them everything he knew and
learned during his months in the woods. When he
thought of Fayette, blackness filled his mind, squeezing everything sensible out, leaving only pain. And
when he thought of Luke Blue, he exploded into a
murderous rage.

More and more often now, the rage extended to all
black people, and the pain welled up at the sight of
any woman—especially a mother with sons. It was the
blacksmith's shy, hard-working wife who had driven
him from Darien, for she had tried to be kind to
Micah, and her gentle voice—with its English country
accent—was very like Fayette's.

Micah's mind was wildly unfocused. His attention could not catch on a single thought, he had no plans or coherent memories, but his mind returned with increasing force to a couple of facts and ideas. Fayette, his love, had betrayed him. His life was ruined. That he knew unshakably. Fayette had turned from him. And she carried the child of a runaway slave! He shuddered, remembering, and twisted his hands miserably. His heart pounded. He could never stand to see her again . . . never . . . and yet—he had inquired until he learned from people in Savannah where Fayette and her family lived—he had come here to be near them, he was drawn closer and closer.

One afternoon he walked through the dense woods from Frederica to Sea Groves. For hours he prowled around the plantation. He saw slave laborers in the fields, saw the groves of citrus trees, saw the road leading up to the house, and followed it a few hundred yards before he felt his feet as weighty as stones and turned back into the woods.

That night he could not sleep. Fayette appeared to him in his dreams, smiling at him with her deep-set green eyes, tempting him with her soft voice, her lush, full-breasted body. Then he saw that she was swollen with child, and he woke howling. She was unworthy, unworthy to raise his sons, unworthy to live.

After that dream, he knew better why he had come to Saint Simons Island and what he must do. He felt sure that the time for it was near—no calendar told him, but he felt it as surely as an astronomer knows the coming of a comet. He felt it draw closer, closer, and one day he woke knowing that it was the day he would go to Sea Groves and find Fayette.

Micah was half-hidden in the holly bushes along the access road when James Dunlie galloped away from his home that morning. Micah drew back, waiting, but neither James nor his horse sensed any hidden presence. James's haste excited Micah, and he hurried on toward the house, now absolutely sure that he had chosen the right time.

Fayette's labor had started at midnight. She lay alone in the room where she had slept since coming to Sea Groves and her mind wandered as her body alternately struggled against the thrusting infant and rested. By candlelight, she read a few pages in her Bible and said a prayer for a safe delivery. She dozed during the dark hours, but by early morning she was fully awake. She heard her mother pounding on her brother's door to waken him, heard their quarrel, and later, James clomp down the stairs in his heavy riding boots.

Soon after that she called to one of the maids who sent for her mother and the midwife.

Catherine was the first to arrive. "Well, Fayette, so your time is here. I've sent your boys off hunting with Roland, so they'll be away all day. How are you feeling? You look strong enough."

Fayette smiled as bravely as she could. She was afraid of her mother, who seemed so changed in her new role as head of the household. And she felt embarrassed that she had cast herself back upon her family in this condition—deserted by her husband, and too far gone in pregnancy to be much help. Fayette wept whenever she thought of their homestead, left so far behind. Would she ever see it again? Would she ever again see Micah? As for her worst fears for the pregnancy and the child, she had kept them to herself.

For what could she do if the child looked black? She could do nothing. She could only ask God for help and trust in Him, and that she had.

Sighing, Fayette began to murmur prayers, but half

under her breath as she was well aware that her devoutness did not please Catherine. Authority had changed her mother, Fayette sensed. Or perhaps the gradual passage of the years—had her mother been so hasty and critical before? Fayette clenched her teeth against the sudden pain and opened her eyes to see her mother frowning at her.

"Well," Catherine said, "the midwife will soon be here. Sukey has delivered all the babies at Sea Groves for years. You can trust her."

And Catherine turned and left.

Fayette was almost happy to be alone for a time. "Dear God," she prayed out loud, "deliver me from this travail and restore my strength so that I may serve you for all the rest of my days. Protect my life and the life of this your unborn child, I beseech you. For you are capable of all, you know all, you will all and control all and it is in your hands that I place my life."

When Sukey arrived, she could see at once that Fayette was only minutes from giving birth.

"You're doing real good, Miss Fayette," Sukey encouraged her. Stepping quickly around the room, she closed the curtains to shut out the light and some of the increasing heat, then sent one of the house servants for hot water and some towels. Sukey gave Fayette a rope to pull on, knotted one end of it around one of the bedposts, and brushed away the flies that fought to settle on Fayette's sweaty body and the perspiration-soaked sheets.

Fayette moaned. The room was as hot as an oven, and she felt the muscles of her legs clench and cramp as she pushed with the contractions of her body. She remembered her other babies being born—Micah had always been there, and they had seemed to come faster than this one—or had she lost track of time? "Dear Father, dear God, dear Lord, our Father, Who art in Heaven," she chanted and unbidden, Luke Blue's thin, handsome face bobbed into her mind.

The remembrance made her writhe with guilt and agony. She twisted from right to left, from left to right. When she opened her eyes it was so dark she thought it must be night, but then she saw the sunshine around the edges of the shutters like a golden rim, and she fancied that it was a glimpse into the light of heaven.

"Here comes that baby, Miss Fayette," Sukey said. "Here comes that baby's head. Now you just keep on pushin', you're doing good, so good!"

Fayette felt extreme, extraordinary, illuminating pain as the baby's head emerged. Then she felt a wave of hope. It was coming! Soon she would be rid of this pain and have the little baby and then . . . then perhaps . . .

"Here it comes, here it comes," Sukey chanted. She moved close to Fayette and put her strong, experienced hands around the baby's neck and shoulders, quiding its passage into the air.

Fayette screamed and gave a tremendous push.

"Good! All's well now. God bless him!" Sukey announced, holding the tiny, infant high in the air, still attached to Fayette by the long, ropey umbilical cord. Deftly, Sukey cut the cord with a knife and wiped the baby with a cloth.

"A beautiful boy, this here is a beautiful boy child," Sukey murmured. She was struck by how much the infant looked like her own newborns had, like those of other slave women, but she dismissed the identification of its race. It was not possible, so it was not true. How funny that all newborn babies looked alike. This one was light-brown-skinned with matted kinky hair.

His small face scrunched into a howl and as soon as Sukey lifted him high and patted his backside, he cried out with a lusty insistence, and Sukey handed him to Fayette.

"Now you hold that sweet baby, Miss Fayette, and I'll just be right back," Sukey promised, slipping out of the room to get a clean sheet for Fayette's bed.

Fayette held the squalling, squirming infant gratefully and panted. A wave of the relief from extreme pain that so closely resembles ecstasy washed over her, and she cried tears of happiness. Instinctively, she held the baby between her breasts, its heart next to hers and fondled it, examining its tiny perfect arms and legs.

"Blessed child, what will become of you?" she whispered. "I can only assign you to God's protection . . ."

Fayette blinked and looked up. Someone had entered the room. It was not Sukey, but in the semigloom, she did not know who it was. Then, as he moved closer, she could smell an outdoor man's odor, the odor of skins and sweat and fresh air and wood smoke.

She gave a little cry of surprise. The looming figure moved closer to her, and she gasped.

"Micah! Husband!"

It was Micah, Fayette realized, but Micah gone wild. His hair was dirty and tangled and as long as a trapper's. His hunting shirt, a kind of loose frock that reached half-way down his thighs, was torn and soiled and belted at the waist with a rawhide thong that carried a fringed pocket and his hunting knife.

Fayette was struck with fear. Micah looked possessed. His eyes glinted with anger and evil, and his dirty hands reached out for her. She sat up and shrank back, clutching the baby to her bosom, too frightened to scream.

"Don't come nearer, Micah," she warned. "Don't touch me, or him. In God's name, I tell you—stop!"

Micah spat on the floor. "Whore!" he shouted, "Worthless cheating bitch! Vagrant fleecer! Slattern!"

"Go away, Micah!" Fayette begged, trembling with fear. "Call me any name you choose, but leave me alone. I can't help what happened. It's all over now and you just have to . . ."

"Harlot! Damned strumpet! Give me that child!"

"No! No, you shan't touch him! By God, Micah, you are mad!"

Micah reached out and with a merciless strength ripped the naked newborn baby from Fayette's arms. He held it up by its feet with his left hand and let it swing back and forth. The baby screamed and Fayette struggled to rise.

"Help!" she screamed, "Help! Sukey, come at once! Oh, someone, please help!"

There was a strange silence outside the room, only a momentary silence. Sukey had lingered in the kitchen for a bite to eat with the other women. They were all out of earshot.

Micah laughed horribly. Fayette, on her knees, crawled across the room and grabbed his legs, but he drove her back toward the bed with a powerful kick.

Still the baby screamed as Micah swung it back and forth. Then, he carefully removed his hunting knife from the loop on his belt. Fayette choked on her screams and she fought to regain her feet, but she was stunned and weak and she swayed, blackness nibbling on the edges of her vision. Everything seemed to lose definition in the gloom; all she saw clearly was the glint of the knife.

Carefully, as calmly as skinning a rabbit, Micah touched the tip of the knife to the baby's throat and slit its chest from neck to navel. Then he worked the knife around in the tiny cavity and cut out the baby's heart. He replaced the knife in his belt and tugged at the twin lobes of the heart with his fingers, loosening them, pulling them free and then hurling them into Fayette's face.

Chapter Twenty-one

*Rosalind Drayton Meets the Liberty
Boys—Byron Won't Duel—Catherine
Dunlie Rules the Roost—And James
Takes a Wife*

"Miss Drayton! You can't go out there alone!" Eliza
Parker's face was white with fear as she pulled her
head back inside her dressmaking shop and slammed
the door. "There's a mob crossing through Reynolds
Square! You won't be safe! Please stay here."

"Nonsense, I must go home," Rosalind Drayton
said, pulling on her gloves. "The Sons of Liberty! Uncle calls them the Sons of Licentiousness, but they
can't actually do a thing. He'll worry if I'm not home
by dark, Mrs. Parker, so thank you, but I'll go quickly
and send my maid for the dress first thing in the
morning."

Rosalind pulled the hood of her red velvet cape up
over her auburn curls and dashed out into the street.
As soon as she had left the quiet of Bryan Street and
entered Reynolds Square, she feared that she had
made a mistake. The square was choked with a full two

hundred milling, marching men, most of them young and roughly dressed, all of them shouting epithets and scowling with anger.

"Liberty! Property and no stamps!" the crowd chanted, and "We won't have stamps, we won't!"

"Burn 'im! Burn 'im!" a white-haired man shouted right into Rosalind's ear. He carried a torch and waved it menacingly at the sight of her bright red cape.

"Don't come near me!" Rosalind said in a low voice, her blue eyes cold and her jaw set. The man stepped back a pace.

Two men at the head of the mob carried a full-sized straw effigy of what Rosalind recognized as a stamp-agent. So that was it. The mob was out to protest the sale of the King's tax stamps, due to begin day after tomorrow. Since the stamps had arrived on the *Speedwell*, Savannah had awaited the arrival of the agent who would sell them and talked of nothing else.

"Down with the Tyrant!" "No taxation without representation!" "Burn those stamps!" "Burn the agent!" The cries were deafening and darkness descended almost at once. Torchlit the mob seemed even more frightening.

"Let me pass!" Rosalind demanded, but her voice was lost and she was swept helplessly into the center of the mob as it moved along Duke Street. Rosalind was frightened, but she was determined not to show it. These Sons of Liberty, as they called themselves, were nothing but riffraff; it was only a political dispute, she reminded herself, and the lawbreakers would end up in the stocks or in jail.

But the mood of the mob was ugly. Some of them were armed with cutlasses. She felt the half-restrained violence. She smelled liquor. Some of the men were clearly drunk.

"Burn the bastards!" "We won't have it!" "On to Government House!" they yelled. Government House! Rosalind felt a sudden hope. If she let herself march along with the Liberty Boys she would end up at home more surely than if she resisted. And pray to God, when they reached St. James Square, her uncle would deal with them, and it would all be settled and forgotten by the morrow.

Rosalind was particularly concerned for the tranquility of the morrow, for it was to be her wedding day, a day long awaited and happily anticipated. She could not savor the thought now, but earlier, even an hour ago in Mrs. Parker's shop, she had been very happy.

"Yes, tomorrow," she had told the dressmaker, "tomorrow I will be Mrs. James Dunlie."

Rosalind had known James Dunlie, and admired him, for more than two years, but her uncle had refused to hear of her marrying until she was nineteen. At the time, two years had seemed forever to wait; what if James could not, but found another suitable woman with a more permissive guardian? Or what if her uncle had carried out his threat to send her back to England—away from the increasing danger of the "Bonfire brethren," as he called all these ungrateful rabble-rousers who stirred up trouble and complained about every new proclamation from Parliament?

But neither of these calamities had occurred, and the day was nearly here. Rosalind was in love and her pink cheeks glowed with pleased anticipation. Her uncle was also pleased, for James Dunlie was solidly Tory in his politics, from a good family, and so acceptable that he had given Rosalind a dowry of two thousand pounds. James Dunlie was also pleased, for the dowry would aid him substantially in his business as the marriage allied him with the most prominent Tory family in Georgia.

For Rosalind's uncle and guardian was James Wright, Georgia's governor since 1760, American-born, and the most popular and successful royal governor the colony had ever had. Five years had passed since Governor Wright had come to Savannah, and in that time he had managed remarkably well to soothe both the hotheads and the redskins. In the Cherokee War, the southern phase of the French and Indian wars, Wright had negotiated with the Creeks and helped to forge a peace treaty between the five Indian nations and the four southern colonies that gave Georgia peaceful western borders for the first time ever, and launched an era of growth and prosperity. During his tenure, Wright was to increase the size of Georgia almost fivefold, acquiring rich, rolling lands that drew new settlers at a good rate.

Wright did not exempt himself from the new prosperity. He was the second richest man in Georgia, the owner of eleven plantations with nineteen thousand acres and more than five hundred slaves. He had been a widower since Rosalind's aunt had drowned two years before on a voyage to England, and Rosalind had enjoyed sometimes acting as his official hostess in Government House, as Georgians called his residence in St. James Square.

"Although I sorely miss you, and wish with all my heart that we could be together on my wedding day, I am pleased enough with colonial life . . ." Rosalind had written her cousin Rebecca the night before. "These Georgians seem a hearty, honest folk, and I approve their style. Adornment and display are the exception rather than the rule, as in London, and everywhere the people live close to nature."

Rosalind had closed with kisses and an entreaty for her cousin to come for a visit, for soon after their marriage she would go with James Dunlie to his plantation near far-off, unknown Augusta. Rosalind was blinded by love, and could not see that she did not know her prospective husband very well, but she knew vaguely that he maintained only distant ties with his family on their island plantation, and had made his own name and fortune as a slave dealer in the newer city upriver.

In fact, James Dunlie had taken the money his mother had given him to buy field hands, seven years ago, and had bought and sold newly landed Africans to build up a business in Georgia to rival that of the Charleston slavemongers, who had supplied Georgia planters for years. It was through this business that he had met the Governor, for by the time Wright arrived in Savannah and started to accumulate land and property, James Dunlie had already begun to make a name for himself as a man of the better sort who could handle the details of a business that was commonly felt to be offensive, although essential. Rosalind herself had never in her life seen a member of the Negro race before coming to Georgia, and she had only just begun to comprehend this American institution, but James Dunlie was impressively wealthy—and ever more so—as well as stirringly handsome, and she was inclined to suspend any judgments on his professional activities.

With a howl, the mob surged into St. James Square, carrying a scared, white-faced Rosalind with them. "Hang 'im!" "Hang 'im!" someone shouted, and she saw that a crude wooden gallows had been erected in the center of the pleasant tree-filled square. "Liberty and no Stamp Act!" "Liberty! Liberty! Liberty!" the mob howled. Rosalind's eyes filled with tears. What would happen now? How could she get away? Would they break into Government House after her uncle?

A roll of drums turned all eyes to the front door of Government House. The door opened and flanked by six armed rangers in lobster-red coats, Governor Wright emerged. Wright wore a black suit and a black cocked hat; his powdered white curls hung down to his shoulders. His face was deadly serious, but unmarked by fear, and Rosalind felt a tremor of family pride.

"Gentlemen!" Wright shouted. "By coming here you violate the law. The law forbids all riots, routs and tumultuous assemblies!"

"To hell with the law!" a man shouted, and the mob roared its approval. "What about the stamps?" another voice asked.

"The stamps are not here! Gentlemen, you have been led astray by unscrupulous leaders. Disperse, disperse now, before there is bloodshed . . ."

Another roll of drums smothered the low roar of the mob.

"It is my duty to protect the honest citizens of Georgia," Wright said. "Protect them against law-breaking mobs!"

"Get 'im! Hang 'im! Burn 'im!" a few voices called out, but the majority of the men were hushed.

"Friends!" a young man's voice called out. "This is no moment to hold back! I charge you . . ."

"Barstow! Is it you?"

Rosalind recognized the voice of her beloved James Dunlie. She turned in surprise to see that he had appeared at the edge of the guard flanking her uncle and now leaned down off the steps, nearly losing his balance, determined to confront the man he had called by name, the young man who had marched near the head of the mob since Reynolds Square.

Before Rosalind could call to him, James jumped off the steps and shoved past a torch bearer. "Damnation, Barstow!" he shouted, "I wouldn't expect it, even of you!"

"James!" Rosalind called weakly, but her voice was lost in the tumult of the mob. A torch had been touched to the straw effigy, and it was crackling and burning, shooting sparks off onto the heads and clothing of the nearest men. The mob's courage had risen again . . . they pressed forward toward Government House, and Rosalind was helplessly separated from James and the other man.

"This is no time for us to talk, Mr. Dunlie," Byron Barstow said, "There are larger matters at stake here today."

"I don't want to talk!" James said, "I have waited years to avenge my father's death. I want revenge!" James Dunlie's teeth were clenched, and he seized Barstow by both arms just below the elbow and forced him apart from the mob, to the side alley of Government House.

Byron felt the murderous tension in James Dunlie's grip, saw the hatred in his face, and his heart ached. Seeing young Dunlie brought back all the feelings of guilt he had about that unfortunate duel. How could Dunlie fail to hate him? He who had killed his father? Byron felt no animosity toward Dunlie, no anger, only sadness and guilt . . .

"I despise you!" James Dunlie spit out the words. "I'll make no secret of it. I want to kill you—I want to face you in a duel, Barstow. I want my chance at you— one shot at you as you had at my poor father!"

Barstow winced. "I am no coward, Dunlie, but

'twould be no way to settle old hatreds. Our lives have changed; we are grown apart. We cannot follow violence and anger with more violence . . . it will solve nothing."

"I have my own solution in mind, Barstow. Nothing less. I am asking you to defend your honor, sir! Have you no honor, then?"

"I recognize no code of honor. I am opposed to duelling, for myself and for anyone else. 'Tis a barbaric practice; I refuse."

At that, Dunlie, who was out of his mind with rage, lunged at Barstow with a knife, but Byron Barstow side-stepped the attack and ducked out the alleyway back into the mob. He was shaking with emotion, but swallowed it. "Later," he said to himself, "I will deal with it later, not now!"

The mood of the mob had deteriorated in the few minutes Byron Barstow had been out of sight, and he walked into a hand-to-hand fight between one of the rangers and one of the Liberty Boys which was already out of hand. One man had a cutlass and stabbed the other behind the ear. Blood spurted out in a deadly spray, and a woman beside Byron screamed hysterically.

It was Rosalind. "Help! Help!" she shrieked, her voice rising and tightening in panic and horror. She flailed her arms wildly and the hood of her cape fell back, revealing her neatly curled hair and her small heart-shaped face. "Why it's a girl!" one man cried out in surprise, and Rosalind realized that she had been carried along unobserved.

"Of course I'm a girl! What did you expect?" she braved, ignoring the tears streaking her cheeks.

"Let her pass," a man shouted, and Rosalind took advantage of the moment's hesitation in the pressure of the mob to make a break for Government House. She darted past two scuffling men and up the steps.

"Give us the Stamps!" "Burn 'im!" a drunken man still called out.

"It's his niece," a man shouted, but too late.

"Rosalind! Dear heaven! What are you doing out here?" James Wright asked angrily, but Rosalind's courage had expired. She ducked under his outstretched arm and ran inside to safety.

Catherine Dunlie folded the letter from her son and removed the tiny spectacles she used for reading and figuring. Her son, James, had written—as he so seldom did—to inform her about his intention to wed Rosalind Drayton. He had mentioned the date of the ceremony without particularly inviting any of his family to be present.

It's just as well, Catherine thought. I don't enjoy traveling and anyway, there's too much work to do here. Perhaps Cattie would attend; Cattie remained in the Dunlie house in Savannah where she lived alone, enjoying her life by all reports. Her relations with the rest of the family were cordial, if distant.

And as for James . . . Catherine had recently come to terms with her feelings for him. On the other hand, he was a renegade—he had left Sea Groves seven years ago without so much as a farewell, and she had not seen him for two full years after that. Nor had she seen the money she'd given him that morning . . . the same unforgettable morning Fayette and her newborn baby had been killed. That had been a terrible, tragic time. They had never caught the murderer or found out who he was, although people said only an Indian or a Negro was capable of such savagery. Life had seemed so crazy and hard to fathom. I wished then,

Catherine recalled, that I had the faith Fayette did, but after all, what good did it ever do poor Fayette? Even the darkies had been disturbed by the violent murders, Catherine recollected, and had got the idea the murders were a curse on the family. Their quarters had echoed with eerie singing and drummings until she had to put a stop to it, and the midwife, Sukey, who had found both the bodies, had been regarded as something of a witch ever since.

But that was long past, now, Catherine assured herself. At first she had been so angry at James for his selfish desertion of the plantation and his responsibilities to his family that she had refused to speak his name. But in truth, James had never been handy or hard-working; she, Catherine, had never liked him, and—above all—there was Roland. Roland, so steady and sweet-tempered, so hard-working and dependable, and still so handsome and mannerly.

Catherine sighed. Because of Roland, and of course Fayette's children, she had been able to carry on. Characteristically, Roland had urged her to forgive James, and when he returned home, finally, with the money he had originally taken and reports of his fabulous business successes, she had grudgingly offered him her cheek to kiss.

So now James was marrying. Obviously, he had taken pains to make a good match—both financially and politically. It was just like him, Catherine thought without realizing that her son was as practical and calculating as herself. It was the season for marrying, or so it seemed, for Catherine had heard that Blackwoods Plantation had been the scene of a lavish wedding for Byron Barstow and his bride, Kate Musgrove; and now Fayette's oldest son Pittman, was engaged to the daughter of another plantation owner—Sally Ann

Martin—and Sally's father, Samuel Savage Martin, was determined that the wedding for his daughter would outshine the one at the Barstows' plantation.

All that is well enough, Catherine thought. I am an old woman, now, although I have never felt better in my life. The future belongs to them—the children, my children's children—and they are welcome to it. I wonder what Georgia will be like when they are sixty . . . Catherine smiled sadly, for it was impossible to guess at such things, and because she had remembered that it was her birthday, her sixtieth, and none of her progeny had remembered it.

A child's stifled giggle outside her sitting-room door caught Catherine's attention.

"Who's there?" she called out. It had been such a quiet Sunday afternoon. She had wondered where all the young men had gone, but she hadn't thought to miss them, for they were all fond of fishing and hunting and seized every free hour to ride off and enjoy those diversions.

"Happy birthday, Grandmother!" called Jenny, Catherine's only granddaughter, and the little girl burst in through the door. "They're all waitin' downstairs! There's to be a party!"

Despite herself, Catherine was pleased. "A party? Why Jenny, you shouldn't surprise an old lady so!"

"How old are you, Grandmother?" Jenny asked. She was a shy, serious child of nine years, already very like her mother with sparkling green eyes and thick, dark, curly hair tied up now with yellow silk ribbons.

"Never mind that, Jenny! Now you all will just have to wait while I change my dress and fix my hair!"

"We've having a spice cake!" Jenny announced, "so please hurry, Grandmother."

"I will," Catherine promised.

And later, after the family party, after the spice cake had been eaten, after Roland had spoken the toasts for Catherine's birthday, a good harvest, to the Colony of Georgia and the health of King George, Catherine slipped upstairs to take a little nap before supper, the men walked out to the stables to look at a new colt, and Pittman took his fiancée, Sally Martin, for a walk around the gardens and grounds.

There was a chill wind from the sea as the young people walked down the tree-lined road from the house. Crows were perched on the long, leafless arm of a sycamore like teeth on a comb. Sally shivered and admitted that she found the sight depressing.

"Just wait till spring, Sally," Pittman explained as they turned into the first of the orange groves. "There is no more glorious sight on earth—you'll see! 'Tis a magnificent spectacle—shiny green leaves and golden fruit with silver flowers! And the smell!"

"What was it like in Wilkes County, where you were born?" Sally asked, slipping her arm through Pittman's.

"Very different," Pittman said, "In Wilkes, the forests are thick and silent and the land seems endless. Here I have the sense of being confined because of the sea—but there, a man can possess all that he can see . . ."

Sally shivered. Pittman had spoken to her of someday moving back to that part of the colony, but she preferred not to think of it yet. Sally was a slim, impulsive eighteen-year-old, with the freckles and flaming red curls of all the Martins, and she was very much in love with tall, handsome Pittman.

"Oh, look! It's your family burying ground," she said as they neared the grassy plot fenced in with split rails. "Shouldn't you show me your mother's grave?"

"It's over here," Pittman said, leading her to the corner where Fayette had been buried. Her grave was marked with a tall granite slab ornamented by an open Bible, worked by a stonemason in Charleston and sent down the inland waterway by boat.

"What a handsome tombstone," Sally said shyly. She felt odd and sad. Why, she couldn't *imagine* either of her parents dying; poor Pittman. And then she caught sight of the tiny stone next to Fayette's.

"Who lies there?" she asked curiously.

Pittman bent and ripped a tangle of vines and weeds off the smaller stone. "They never keep it up! Why does no one care for it?" he said angrily. He threw fistfuls of grass and leaves over the fence, and cut his hand on a thorny vine.

"Why, whose grave is it?" Sally asked again.

"That of my little brother who . . . died when my mother did," Pittman answered in a troubled voice, and for a moment he looked the image of his father, though Sally did not know it. There was something so odd about his face that Sally was reminded how many strange, sad things had happened to Pittman's family. She resolved to be a good wife, to love and cherish him all the days of his life; for now, she would make him forget death and sadness.

"Come away, now, darling," she said. "Let's walk down to the rice mill."

In Savannah, on her wedding night, Rosalind undressed very slowly and hesitantly. When James left their bedroom for a minute, she hastened to slip into her embroidered, tucked, and lace-edged linen nightgown. Rosalind was a virgin; she had never been naked in front of a man or seen a naked man, and she was terribly nervous that she would not be able to please her new husband.

Governor Wright had invited all the best people in Savannah to Rosalind's wedding, and nearly fifty guests had returned to Government House for a reception with all the rum and Madeira anyone could drink. The whole house had been bright with candles, and the Governor's English butler had set out enough delicacies to please royalty, including huge silver dishes of fresh creamed oysters and deviled crabs, roast game, a side of beef, and Rosalind's favorite: sugar coconut cakes.

Rosalind remembered it as if it were a dream. She had been transported with excitement, flushed and utterly fashionable in her dress of stiff white China taffeta with tiers of lace and stays embroidered with pink and white rosebuds. A trio of Negro fiddlers had played dance music, and when James had taken his bride in his arms for the first waltz, Rosalind had fancied herself living in a dream.

It would have been perfect, Rosalind thought, if not for the menace of the Liberty Boys and their outrageous demonstrations. Her uncle's courage in facing the mob yesterday had been nothing less than heroic, everyone said, but they also said there would be more trouble before the matter was settled. Rosalind could not bear to think of the event, and she had resolved not to let it cloud her wedding day.

But the other guests had not forgotten the rowdy mob so easily. In fact, at the reception, Rosalind had thought more than once that it was she and her wedding which seemed to have been forgotten. The more her uncle and his friends drank, the more they talked politics and stormed endlessly about the Liberty Boys.

"How can they argue that the tax is unjust?" James's

friend, planter Roderick Mackintosh, had asked rhe-
torically. "Georgia has been subsidized by Parliament
from the beginning—last year they sent us four thousand pounds!"

"Why, they believe themselves to be beyond the
powers of Parliament," James Wright answered. "But
they shall learn that they are not."

"Indeed they shall," Mackintosh had said, "and
learn respect!"

"I suspect our Georgians have been stirred up in
this feckless protest by outsiders," Wright had said.
"They had never thought of rebellion till spirited on
by our northern neighbors, who never let them rest, or
gave them time to cool off."

Such heated political discussions, Rosalind felt, were
quite out of place at a wedding reception. She was no
better pleased when talk turned, as it so often did in
James's company, to the problems of slavery and slave
management.

"Another band of fugitive slaves has been seen
camped in the swamps just across the river," Roderick
Mackintosh had said. "They are armed, by God, and
ride on murderous raids at isolated plantations."

"Surely their number is small," Governor Wright
said.

"Of course they are few—so far," Mackintosh said,
"But they must be subdued absolutely. They are savages, crazed and desperate, and none of us is safe while
they still live."

"Let us speak further of that," James had said, and
led Mackintosh toward the punch bowl.

Rosalind, left standing alone with her uncle and his
elderly friends, had begun to feel neglected, and she
was alarmed to see how much her new husband put
down. Finally, she saw Mackintosh leave and per-

suaded James that it was time to leave the Governor
and the last few guests below and retire to the low
bedroom, as the largest guest bedroom in Government
House was called.

"So there we are, Rosalind," James said as he entered the bed chamber. Rosalind moved to brush out
her long auburn hair.

"Yes, husband," she said and if her voice shook, he
did not notice it.

James was quite drunk and in no mood to waste
time. He had long lusted for Rosalind, although tonight he had other things on his mind. "Come here,"
he ordered her.

Rosalind set down her silver brush. She hesitated.
James reclined on the feather bed, and the candle on
the night table flickered. "Come here!" he called impatiently and she crossed to him.

Rosalind trembled, looking down at him, and he
sensed her fear. Fear and vulnerability stimulated ag-
gression in James's mind. He reached up for her and
drew her down to him, sliding his hands up under her
voluminous nightdress and squeezing her slim waist
before his fingers found her breasts.

"Ah . . ." he sighed, and drew her mouth to his in
a kiss. His hands, cold and insistent on her nipples,
shocked her. She twisted and tried to pull back. Her
resistance challenged him, and he touched her more
roughly, probing between her legs before he ordered
her to take off her nightgown.

"What're you afraid of?" James asked. He pulled off
his silk hose and knee breeches and fumbled at the
buttons of his starched, ruffled shirt. Rosalind
reached to help him. Her pale, slim body aroused
him.

"You'll make a good wife . . ." James mumbled. He
thrust his fingers between her legs.

She was too shocked to answer. How roughly he handled her! She felt like crying. Was this what all women endured in their marriage beds? She shut her eyes to keep back the tears, and in that moment he entered her.

"Ohhhh!" Rosalind gasped. She had never dreamed of such a thing! He had turned her around so that the full weight of his torso and legs was behind him as he slammed into her again and again until he climaxed and groaned his pleasure.

Everything stopped.

James panted heavily. Rosalind lay as if wounded and kept her eyes closed. Her mind was spinning. What would he do now? She waited only a minute.

Amazingly, James rose and pulled on his clothes again. "I have to go out," he said. Rosalind opened her eyes in surprise. Still, she hoped he would tell her he loved her, how pretty and desirable she was, but when he did not, she asked, "Where are you going?"

"Out. I have to go out."

"But where?" Rosalind wailed. How had she disappointed him? How could he leave her—on their wedding night?

"People don't understand the difficulties of my business," James complained. "It's chancy and demanding. They have to be broken in; most of them don't take to slavery naturally. In every new shipment I lose a few to fever, a few to melancholy, and some of them just run off. Why a couple of them got as far as the ocean and built canoes to sail back to Africa. Some of 'em would rather be dead."

Rosalind shivered and pulled her nightgown over her head. Of course a man's business was important, but she was becoming convinced that James's was dangerous, and brought him into contact with an unsavory sort. She hadn't liked that man Mackintosh at all.

"I still don't understand why you have to go out at night," she said.

"Ten of my new ones have broken away," James said. "Big healthy men. They're hiding out in the swamps, and I'm going to ride out with Mackintosh and get them back. There's a full moon tonight, and dead or alive, we're going to bring them in."

Chapter Twenty-two

*Byron Barstow Drills the Blackwoods
Boys—James Dunlie Vows to Stop
Him—Zonah Confesses at Last*

"Steady! Steady, boys! Now just hold that line
steady!"

Twenty of the finest, youngest, healthiest hands on
Blackwoods Plantation formed in two lines in the pasture next to the big house. Each of them was holding a
wooden pole the size and weight of a musket; each had
a grimly serious expression on his face, and they all
looked to their master's son, Byron Barstow, for orders.

"Fix bayonets!" Byron ordered, and the twenty men
simulated the fixing of bayonets.

"Ready, aim, and fire!" Byron charged them. "Excellent! Now, Ira, you march 'em down the road and
back—double time."

"Forward, march!" Ira called out, and the twin lines
of apprentice soldiers headed away from the house toward the rice mill and the docks.

Byron walked back to the big house from the pasture and called to his father, Orde, who was sitting on

the piazza watching the maneuvers from his chair. Behind him hovered Zonah, who was never far from his side since the fever that had broken his health ten years before. Orde was old enough to retire and relinquish control of Blackwoods to his son, but his spirit was unbowed. He was as ascerbic and hasty as he had ever been, and allowed Byron only secondary command, although in truth he doted on his clever, capable son and approved nearly everything he suggested.

"What do you think of them, father?" Byron asked.

"I think they look like a passel of slaves playing soldier," Orde said.

"Perhaps. But we shall need every able-bodied man we can find. I want to march them up to Savannah and use them as an example of what can be done with black soldiers. That is, with your permission, sir."

"Humph. Glad you got around to that. I don't like it, not at all. Especially not your taking Ira. Ira is the most important man we've got! But if what you say is going on in Savannah is true . . ."

"It is true, father! And you know about the massacre in Lexington. Resistance is growing in all the colonies. Americans will not bear more oppression. We are our own men. There's going to be a war, and Georgia must be part of it."

"Sometimes I think I made a mistake sending you north to school," Orde said.

Zonah stood behind his chair, a middle-aged woman now, but one who looked no older than she had twenty years ago, still slim, still inscrutable, still dressed all in white. As Orde spoke, she stroked his shoulder soothingly with one long-fingered hand and listened to Byron with grave attention. In their later years, Orde and Zonah were closer than ever. They were rarely physically apart and seemed to communicate without words. Byron had long marvelled at the

oddly successful union; he himself had been married
for almost ten years and had three small children. His
wife, a native Georgian, born Kate Musgrove, had
stayed in the townhouse in Savannah after their an-
nual trip to sell the plantation's rice crop, and Byron
looked forward to joining her as soon as he took the
black militia north.

"Learning is never a mistake, father," Byron said.
"And besides, I would be happy not to ever leave
Georgia again; my travels have made me appreciate
our life here all the more. It is for love of Georgia that
I am determined to fight!"

"Fighting for love of some tract of land? You sound
like a damn fool. War is no glorious venture—war is
dying and dysentery, fleas and mouldy bread, and
some men getting rich, no matter what the war's
fought about; though I don't suppose I can tell you
that. The young have to learn for themselves."

"For love of liberty, then, father! Can you understand that?"

"Liberty? I have noticed that you young Georgians
have a strange idea of liberty . . . but no matter. I
am too old to interest myself in ideas. I value only my
family; but that is my own outlook. Times change.
You must live your own life, Byron."

Byron was struck with admiration and respect for
Orde. All over the colony, men were taking sides over
the move to resistance and rebellion. Many families
had quarreled bitterly among themselves—father
against son and brother against brother. Most of the
old men—men born in England who had come to
Georgia in the service of their king—could never condone disloyalty to the Crown and the mother country,
but those whose minds looked forward instead of backward, who had been born Georgians, opposed the

royal domination, which they had come to think of as unfair oppression.

Both Orde and Byron knew some of the prominent families split over the matter of the growing resistance: Noble Jones, patriarch, planter, physician, was an intimate of the Governor and a confirmed loyalist, while his son, Noble Wymberly Jones, was already a leader among the patriots. James Habersham could never turn against the King and had served as acting Governor while Wright had recently visited England; but his three sons, James, John, and Joseph were ardent Liberty Boys.

"Father," he said to Orde with emotion in his voice, "I thank you for the advice and for your support. You have always been generous to me . . . and I appreciate it more than I can say."

"Nonsense!" Orde snapped, visibly stirred and embarrassed. "You're my son, that's all! And damn it, such conversations are for women!"

The news of the battles of Lexington and Concord reached Savannah on May 10. In reaction, the Liberty Boys, led by Noble W. Jones, Joseph Habersham, and Edward Telfair, broke into the public powder magazine and stole about five hundred pounds of gunpowder. Then they sent it, along with a shipment of rice and some money, to Boston. Governor Wright ordered the culprits arrested and offered a reward of one hundred fifty pounds for their capture, but public opinion was strong in support of the Whigs, and no arrests were made.

Emboldened by their success, the patriots determined to spoil the usual celebration for the King's birthday on June 4. On the night of June 2, they spiked the twenty-one cannons on the battery and threw them down the bluff into the river. With the fading enthusiasm of a harrassed man. Wright had some of the cannons dredged up, drilled out and fired to celebrate the royal birthday. He appeared to drink the King's health under the flagpole, then invited officals and assemblymen to a "genteel entertainment" at the courthouse.

From the courthouse window, the Governor's guests could see the patriots erect Georgia's first Liberty Pole in the square and fire cannon in their own celebration. Later, they held an elegant dinner at Tondee's Tavern, where they drank and toasted American liberty, American rights, American leaders, and a speedy reconciliation between America and the mother land.

Wright was less optimistic about a speedy settlement. Support for the patriots was rising all over the colony, and he was weary of daily insults and his increasing helplessness to put down illegal revolutionary activities. "To be Plain, my Lord," he wrote to Lord Dartmouth in London, "I see Nothing but a Prospect of a General Rebellion." His friends were turning patriot—more every day—and he warned the most stalwart of them to leave the province if they could.

James Dunlie was alarmed about Wright's warning and came down river from his plantation near Augusta to Savannah to appraise the situation. He arrived in time for the largest rally yet of the Sons of Liberty. Three or four hundred strong, they paraded the sandy streets of Savannah and put up a Liberty tree. Dunlie was horrified and alarmed.

The next morning, he left for Saint Simons Island to warn his family at Sea Groves of the frightening increase of mob violence and the threat to the property of landed Tories.

James arrived on the very afternoon Byron Barstow was exercising his black militia at Blackwoods. It was a hot, airless afternoon. At the Dunlie plantation, he found his mother sitting in an armchair outside the house on the wide piazza, erect and severely dressed in a high-collared, long-sleeved black silk dress. The diminutive silver-haired matriarch was dozing, her tiny white hands folded in her lap, while a young slave girl stirred the air with a huge fan woven of palmetto fronds.

Catherine blinked awake and swallowed quickly to clear her throat when she heard her son's horse cantering up the tree-lined road from the docks.

"Who's that?" she asked peevishly, "who is burning a horse on such a hot day?"

"I don't know, ma'am," the girl said softly. James was so often absent from Sea Groves that he was a stranger to many of the slaves who lived there, although he had never relinquished his claim to the plantation's inheritance.

Catherine swayed as she rose for a clearer look at the rider. "It's my son, James," she said without enthusiasm. "Serafina, go tell Mary to send up a tray. I expect he'll be hungry after the trip." She watched James dismount and hand his reins to a groom.

"What brings you here?" she called out.

"Greetings, Mother," James said. He bowed low over Catherine's hand. At thirty-five, James looked older. Prosperity had thickened his waist and coarsened his features, but in his maturity he resembled Angus Dunlie more strongly than he had ever before. Catherine was struck by the likeness. His deep-set eyes, his freckled-and-sandy coloring, his bold nose and somewhat stiff carriage . . . it was enough to turn Catherine against him.

"You look wonderfully well, mother," James said politely, assessing Catherine's condition as he spoke. "Rosalind, my wife, sends her love and respects. But I come on urgent business of a less amiable nature, I regret to say."

"What's wrong?" Catherine demanded, sitting down and smoothing her silk skirts. She let James stand. If he has come to borrow money, she thought, I shall definitely refuse.

"I feared that in your isolation here, you have not fully understood the threat those Whig mobs are raising. Madam, they are ruling Savannah with violence and terror, and in Sunbury and Midway I understand the situation to be equally bad."

"Then they are both ungrateful and disloyal!" Catherine snapped.

"Undoubtedly, mother," James replied. "But what of our neighbors? Have you solid support among the other planters?"

"Most of them will always remain loyal to the Crown, but—of course—the Barstows!" Catherine put all the weight of a lifetime's hostility into her voice as she pronounced the name.

"The Barstows?" James asked. Why in all possible logic would an old, rich man like Orde Barstow side with the Liberty Boys?

"James, I am disgusted and outraged to tell you what he is doing now," Catherine said energetically. "That family has turned against everything we believed in when we came to the colony! I fear I shall need a regiment to defend myself against them! Son, I have heard that—everyone says it—some have seen it with their own eyes . . ."

"Seen what, Mother?"

Catherine gasped. Thinking of it had exasperated her and reddened her face. Behind her chair Mary Black, the near-white housekeeper who had been the cause of so much spite and suffering between Cattie, Orde, and

Zonah, had appeared, and paused just inside the doorway with a tray of food. Serafina followed her with a pitcher of lemonade, but as she heard the hysteria in Catherine's voice, she stopped suddenly and let Serafina sail on out ahead of her.

"Give her a drink at once, you stupid girl!" James bellowed.

"Let me speak!"

"Of course, mother . . ."

"Byron Barstow has armed a passel of their field hands and is drilling them like a militia. And I tell you this—he intends to take them to Savannah to oppose the government there! Outrageous!"

James felt a slow rage suffuse his bones and blood at the idea. How long, how much longer, he asked himself, must I suffer over that wretched family? They have plagued us Dunlies since before I was born! In faith, I wish I had gotten Byron to the duelling field and had it over with ten years ago. Since then I have longed for another opportunity. I swear, I shall not rest until I see him lying dead.

"Mother," he said slowly, "perhaps it is for this reason that God guided me to the island just north. Nothing on earth could bring me to tolerate that—not while I have strength to stop him."

"James," Catherine said warningly, "you cannot trespass at Blackwoods . . ."

"Indeed, I shall not. But a troop of niggers marching to Savannah along the coastal road . . . I swear to you . . . by my father's memory . . . he shall never get there alive!"

A pause followed James's oath. Catherine frowned. She felt exhausted by this interview with her intense, hot-tempered son. Perhaps he would succeed in killing young Barstow; she hoped by God he did, but as for herself . . . she felt almost faint. Where was that wretched Serafina, lazy girl. She looked around. Serafina stood rooted, still holding the pitcher.

"Lemonade? Bring me some sherry. And where is the food?"

"Here, Miss Catherine," Mary Black said in her sweet, low voice. James looked up in surprise as she glided onto the piazza carrying the tray, for at a first glance Mary Black looked just like an exceptionally pretty white woman. "Welcome home, Mister James," she said. She set down the tray, smiled impassively, and added, "I'll send some sherry and glasses, too, Miss Catherine. Serafina, you take up that fan again."

But when Mary Black left the piazza, she ran straight through the house to the stables. There she saddled a horse, mounted it, and rode across roads and fields straight for Blackwoods as if the devil were after her. Mary had but one thought in mind: to warn Zonah of the danger to Byron's life.

In later years, the secret knowledge of Byron Barstow's lineage had begun to weigh heavily on Zonah's mind. Sometimes, when she tried to fall asleep, she could think of nothing else, and very often, when she dreamed she saw twins, boy twins, reaching out for each other with widespread arms, howling, openmouthed, to be joined together.

Zonah had become increasingly superstitious. She feared the evil force that had made two babies where there should have been one, had let them be separated, made them hate each other, and then made itself known, time and time again, in blood-hungry vengeful ways. That force had made Byron unknowingly commit a terrible, unnatural crime. She could never blame Byron; she could only pity him.

Always, Zonah had prayed that the evil would wear itself out. But from the start, she had known, she had

known. Because both twins had lived and both had
grown up, the evil spirits had nowhere to go. When
Angus Dunlie had died, she had hoped that the evil,
too, had died, but although Orde's jealousy of Angus
Dunlie had come to an end, and Orde was well satisfied with his son, Byron, the other twin, James, was
said to be a bad man—a slave trader, and Zonah was
sure the Barstows had not seen the last of him.

One good, one bad, Zonah thought. What would
have happened if she had taken the other twin to give
to Orde? Zonah thought of her own children. Ira and
Mary, the oldest two, were doing well. Mary, of
course, was living at Sea Groves, but after many years
of separation, she and her mother had met secretly one
day five years ago, and since then they had met again
many times. Mary was happily married to that man
Moses, a good man, and had children of her own. Ira,
now in his thirties, was the head driver at Blackwoods,
and Zonah knew that he was valued above all the other
slaves.

But secretly, in her heart, Zonah had longed that her
children should be not slave, but free. The desire had
been the master passion of her child-bearing, child-
rearing years, but as she grew older and the size of
the slave population at Blackwoods, on Saint Simons
Island, and in the whole colony had increased, Zonah's
highest hopes had gradually dimmed. One of the conditions of her prolonged alliance with Orde Barstow
was her isolation from the other slaves, her estrange-
ment from her own people and yet her complete
ostracism from white society. Saraby had been Zonah's
only friend for many years, but now Saraby was gone,
and Zonah had been very lonely.

Zonah knew the other slaves at Blackwoods resented
her privileged position, and she knew, too, how preca-
rious was that position. While Orde lived—and she re-

mained in his favor—Zonah was the unoffical mistress
of the plantation, she dressed in white and directed all
the other slaves. But the day Orde Barstow died—what
would she be then? And what of their other children,
the teenaged Joe and Sam? Zonah did not know, she
did not know . . . and she worried about it.

Zonah's only possible philosophy was one of resignation and fatalism. Her world was full of forces that she
could not control; her destiny was not in her own
hands. Externally, Zonah was calm and serene; she
moved about the house like an inscrutable goddess,
aloof and removed from daily disputes, but in truth,
she was moody and solitary, and more and more of
late, she was obsessed with a mounting sense of impend-
ing doom.

On the afternoon, then, when her daughter Mary
came riding to Blackwoods, Zonah accepted, immediately and completely, the grim implication of Mary's
warning. Zonah saw Mary riding across the west pasture and ran to meet her under a huge willow tree by
the front gate.

"James Dunlie has heard of the men your young
master is training," Mary gasped, still holding her
horse's reins, "and I heard him vow to kill him. I
heard him say he'd ambush them on the coastal road
to Savannah. Oh, Mother, he must take care! They all
must! I heard him say that Byron will never get there
alive!"

With a hatred stronger than love . . . Zonah
thought. He loathes, despises his twin brother and
must fight to cast him out. She felt sick with dread
and despair.

"You were right to come to me at once with this
warning," Zonah said to Mary. "Go home quickly now
before you are missed."

Zonah stood alone under the willow after Mary had

ridden away. She held her face in her hands and prayed for guidance, but no good spirits came to her. Instead, her head was filled with spinning blackness, and she heard the snarling and snapping of the rival dog gods. In her mind's eye the howling red-eyed dogs became the two brothers, Byron and James, and she saw them locked in a desperate battle to the death, biting at each other's limbs, gouging out eyes with sharp teeth, scratching at each other's genitals, and finally each taking the head of the other—incredibly—in his wide-stretched mouth.

They will not rest until one of them is dead, Zonah thought miserably. He—the other one—will finally kill Byron, unless I can stop him. I can stop him only by speaking the truth, letting the truth sound out into the air, letting it have its day . . . Sorrowfully, mournfully, she clenched her hands at her sides and walked into the big house to do what she had decided she must.

Zonah found both Orde Barstow and Byron in the ground-floor sitting room where Orde liked to spend summer afternoons because it was open to the piazza that ran along the side of the house. All the windows and doors stood open to admit any available breezes, and Zonah entered the room silently from the open door behind Byron's chair. She faced Orde and he knew at once that something was terribly wrong.

"Zonah! What is it?"

Zonah's face was frozen into a mask of resignation. She knew that what she was about to do would change her own life forever, but she could not stop. Tears ran unheeded down her brown face as she spoke, and she was clearly in a dazed condition.

"Many years ago you wanted to have a son," she began.

"Here I am," Byron joked, turning to see Zonah. "Zonah! You are so upset! What is wrong?"

"Hush. I have a story to tell," Zonah said. "A true story. You, sir, you wanted a son."

"Yes, of course," Orde said. He was bewildered, but alarmed.

Zonah's eyes focused somewhere beyond him. "I found you that son, but he was not born to a woman on a ship. He was not born to a woman in the House of Strangers in Savannah. On the day that Byron Barstow was born, a woman in Savannah gave birth to two babies—two baby boys—and one of them was stolen from her and that baby was Byron Barstow."

Orde's voice was harsh and emotional. "So you lied to me. Who was the woman, Zonah? Do you know her name?"

"Oh, yes, I know her name. No good comes of hiding the truth. No good comes of two babies where one should be. Both babies lived, both babies grew up and became men, but there is still no good of it!"

Byron was listening to Zonah with incredulity and fear. He dreaded hearing it . . . something frightening and foreboding had entered the room with Zonah. Feeling dizzy, he rose and crossed the room, away from Zonah, away from the chair where Orde sat, fists clenched.

"Get to the point, damn it, Zonah! Who the hell was it?" Orde demanded. He waved his fists. "Who stole the baby? From whom? Who gave him to you?"

"The babies were born to Catherine Dunlie, wife of Angus Dunlie," Zonah chanted, as if unconscious to all but the story she must tell at last. "The first child born was Byron; the next his twin brother, now called James Dunlie. I tell you this because I must. Joan the midwife who is now dead put the first baby in my arms. I gave that baby to you, and . . ."

"Stop!" Orde shouted. "In God's name, Zonah, is this the truth?" Swaying, he stood up. His face was bloodless, his eyes bulged. "Is this the truth? If you are lying now, I shall have you beaten!"

"Oh, yes, Zonah is now telling you the truth. The truth is telling itself, sir. Oh, yes, yes, yes . . ."

"God—damn—you!" Orde howled. "I am the most cursed of men! All my life I have been nurturing other men's sons! How I have been tricked! And by you! I have taken to my bosom the son of my worst enemy! I have raised a goddamn Dunlie as my own!"

Orde crumpled back into his chair, gasping and retching. His head fell forward and a stream of spittle ran out of his mouth onto his knees, but no one moved to help him. Then he began to twitch and writhe in convulsions, but even as he did, he raised his voice again in anger, "Zonah! Zoooonah!" he howled, as he had so often for so many years, "How . . . could . . . you . . . do this to me? Why? Why did you do this?"

Zonah had no answer. A bee entered the silent room through a window and settled on Orde's inkwell. She was rooted to the spot where she stood, listening to the voices in her head, still seeing the black dogs fighting each other, still hearing the awful howling of evil forces.

Byron stood a bit apart from Zonah and Orde, and he, too, was unable to move. He was shocked beyond speech, beyond action. His mind raced. If I am the son of Angus Dunlie . . . if I am the son of Angus Dunlie . . . then I . . . I have killed my own father! Once again, Byron remembered the scene of the duel, that awful morning he had tried so hard to forget but which returned, unbidden. Before him, as clearly as a scene in a painting, he could see Angus Dunlie's thin, tall frame, his pale, freckled face, his gun pointing up to the sky, his refusal to fire . . . as if he had known.

The muscles of Byron's face worked and he wept. There was no other sound in the room.

Minutes passed before Byron had come back to the present enough to be aware that Zonah had left the room and that his father was toppled forward in his armchair, weakly gasping for breath.

"Father!" Byron called out, as was his habit, and he ran to Orde's side to help him. His cry echoed in the stillness.

Chapter Twenty-three

A Visit to Sea Groves—A Beating—
A Funeral at Blackwoods

Less than an hour later, Zonah and her son Ira drove up to the big house at Sea Groves in a small open carriage pulled by two black horses. Zonah had never been to Sea Groves in her life; neither had Ira, though they had lived less than five miles away for many years.

"I'm not going to let you go there alone," Ira had said, when Zonah asked him if he would drive with her to the Dunlie plantation. Zonah refused to explain her errand to her son except to say that she had to settle some old grievance for Orde, and Ira, who knew very well that his mother could not be dissuaded when she had made up her mind about something, had quickly harnessed the horses to the carriage and helped Zonah into her seat.

It was late afternoon and the heat had increased. A heavy stuperous silence hung over the island and the little coastal road they drove along. Zonah sat straight-backed and speechless, her lips set and her white-gloved hands folded in her lap. Ira abandoned his efforts to engage his mother in conversation and fell into contemplation of the land they drove past.

For the first half mile or so they rode through the rice fields of Blackwoods, past workers bent over, knee deep in the water of the stretch flow, the late spring flooding of the just-sprouted rice plants. They passed the reed-choked salt marsh, passed the huge rice mill turned by the tide, crossed dikes guarding the rice squares, passed a little creek lined with thick and luxuriant evergreens and giant cypresses covered with parasitic pendants of gray Spanish moss.

Finally they reached the boundaries of the Dunlie plantation and Ira's strong sense of trespassing tightened his nerves. Here again were fields of rice, dikes, and pastures. They drove along a tree-lined road and glimpsed the big white house at the end of it, across a stretch of green lawn where a few sheep grazed.

"Where do you want to go now, mother?" Ira asked.

"I want to see Catherine Dunlie," Zonah said firmly.

Ira stopped the carriage directly in front of the house and waited. A parade of wide-eyed house slaves filed out of the front door and appeared from around the edges of the house and Ira looked for Mary among them, but she was not there.

"Hello there!" Ira called out, masking his apprehension, "we have come from Blackwoods to see Mistress Dunlie." He helped Zonah down from the carriage.

The Dunlie slaves were speechless at the sight of two black people alone in a carriage at the front door, amazed by the sight of Zonah in her elegant ruffled white dimity dress, her high white bonnet, her white lace gloves.

"Show us the way," Ira said, and Serafina stepped

forward to lead Ira and Zonah around the open gallery toward the wide south piazza, where she knew that Catherine Dunlie still sat with her son, drinking sherry.

The afternoon's stifling heat, the sweet strength of the sherry, and her son's endless business stories made Catherine Dunlie drowsy, and she thought at first that she was dreaming when she looked up to see Serafina leading two strange Negroes onto the piazza. James stopped in mid-sentence.

"So you see, mother, an investment of three thousand . . ."

Both of them recognized Zonah at once. It had been years since they had seen her, except in Orde Barstow's carriage at a good distance, but she could have been no one else.

Zonah nodded and began to speak in an odd, far-off voice. "Catherine Dunlie, I have come to you because I must." Zonah's heart felt as heavy as a dead thing in her chest. Although she had not seemed to see, Orde's anger, his outrage, and his physical collapse had hurt her. She could blame only herself, but she could not stop; she felt compelled to go on with her long-overdue confession. Still the black voices howled in her ears, still her mind was oppressed by the evil spirits; she had no choice.

"Many years ago, a wrong was done to you," Zonah said, "When you lay in childbed for the last time. Not one boy child but two came forth from you that day."

"What are you talking about?" James Dunlie demanded. "Who sent you here?"

"Hush, let her speak," Catherine said. She leaned forward in her chair, wide-awake, sensing that she was about to hear something of the utmost importance.

"I alone remember," Zonah said. "For I came to your house and met the midwife, Joan, at the foot of the stairs. I carried away your first-born son, carried him to the house of Orde Barstow, where he grew up and is now known as . . ."

"Byron Barstow!" exploded James.

"Are you telling the truth?" Catherine asked, rising, gripping the arms of her chair with trembling hands.

"Yes," Zonah said softly, "Yes, it is true. Byron Barstow is your firstborn. This one was the secondborn twin."

Catherine gasped. She put her hand on her heart. "Somehow I know you are speaking the truth," she said. "By my faith, it all rings true. How well I remember the day . . ."

"That loathsome Whig my brother!" James spat out. I hate him anyway, perhaps even more, he thought, and I shall never accept him as a brother or a Dunlie.

Catherine Dunlie eyed Zonah with unmasked hatred and disgust. "You outrageous, dressed-up, lascivious nigger!" she screamed. She reached into her pocket and found the whistle that summoned her bodyguard, Major, the biggest Negro on the plantation. She blew it. "You filthy black whore! You were not fit to touch a Dunlie but you stole my baby and ruined his life! So help me, you will be punished for this! I'll have you whipped till you scream for pity."

Ira stepped forward to protect his mother, but Major and two other giant black men arrived at Catherine's side.

"Major, tie her to that tree. Him, too. Tie them both up and whip them until I tell you to stop."

Ira grabbed Zonah and started to pull her away, but before he could move the two men had overpowered him, stunning him with a blow to the head.

"Beat them—her first," Catherine said coldly, only the edge of her voice showing her passionate anger.

Astonished, yet somehow gratified, James Dunlie watched as the slaves did his mother's bidding, tying both Ira and Zonah to the thick trunk of the willow. Major produced a braided leather whip and brought it down across Zonah's back, slicing her sheer dimity dress with the first blow. She screamed once. Again and again he slashed at Zonah's back with the whip; James saw her dress cut to white ribbons, saw red welts rise and saw the brown skin split to spurt blood. Throughout it, Zonah did not cry out again.

"Stop for now," Catherine ordered, and Major obediently moved to the other side of the tree to beat Ira. The smell of blood was hot and sickening. James felt his stomach heave, but Catherine did not seem to notice. Coolly, she picked up the half-empty sherry bottle and walked up to the willow tree. Raising her arm, she shook the bottle over Zonah's bloody, mangled back and Zonah winced as the alcohol burned into the raw flesh.

When Byron Barstow realized that Zonah had gone and that Orde was alive, if very seriously shocked, he called for two men to carry Orde upstairs to his bedchamber. There Orde lay, ashen-faced, propped up on a heap of feather pillows, and from there he looked at the young man he had raised as his son with a numbed expression of pain and confusion.

"Father . . . I . . ." Byron tried to speak, waiting to offer some words of solace and comfort, but the irony of his calling Orde father stopped him.

Orde reached out for Byron's hand and held it in his withered, age-spotted grasp. Orde's hand trembled.

"It's not your fault, Byron," Orde croaked, "none of it is your fault. You've been better than a natural son to me. But she . . . she . . ."

"I know," Byron said simply, "but try to rest now.

You must try to regain your strength." Such a colossal betrayal from Zonah, of all the world, had shocked Orde even more than the news itself, Byron guessed. He had an idea of how much Zonah had meant to Orde, how long and completely he had trusted her, and how incapable he had thought her of any lie or deception.

Orde's grip was powerful and relentless. "How could she? How could she keep it from me . . . for so long?" Orde asked, and his voice trailed off into a pained cry. Byron's heart ached for him, but he could not answer.

"Father, I have to go out now . . . for a bit," he said, disengaging his hand, "I feel that I must be alone to think about this. Try to rest."

And Byron left, saddling his most spirited horse and giving him his head as soon as he had left the stable-yard behind him. Despite the heat, he rode hatless, and as horse and rider galloped north along the ocean road and then along the silvery sand beach, tears mixed with perspiration to streak Byron's face and neck, and he threw back his head to howl his pain and frustration into the sea wind.

For, mercifully, a wind had risen in the east and swept over the deep Atlantic waters to soothe and cool the Island with a stirring, salty breeze. Byron felt the wind and was calmed by it. After all, he thought, my life must go on. I am no more a Dunlie than I ever was, and I was never a Barstow except in name. What does it matter what name I call myself? Barstow is a fine name, a good American name. And as for the duel . . . well, I cannot think any more about that now . . . I must think about that later, not today . . .

Catherine and James and all the people at Sea Groves felt the rising breeze, but it failed to quell the restless excitement that had swept over the house and the plantation during the afternoon of arrivals and surprises, quarreling and brutal beatings. In fact, James and his mother were still quarreling—she with an endurance and strength that seemed super-human.

"What difference does it make, mother?" James asked Catherine querulously. "I am still your son. He is nothing to you."

"I have often felt," Catherine said sadistically, turning all her unhappiness, her pained outrage, against James, "that indeed *you* are nothing to me. I have never felt that you are my real son. God only knows. Perhaps that wretched whore stole you from the orphan house. In a lifetime of lies, who can discern the truth?"

They were interrupted by Roland. "I came as quickly as I could, madam. Oh, James . . ." Roland, who was no longer on the best of terms with his young uncle, his boyhood playmate and companion now grown apart from him, bowed to James coldly, then faced his grandmother. "There is terrible unrest in the fields and the quarters, madam. The people are agitated! I've never seen them so restive! In truth, I feared for you alone at the house. What has happened?"

Catherine forgot her annoyance with James; forgot everything that had happened in the light of this new threat. Like every slaveholder, she was terrified of insurrection. Stories of slave rebellions spread fear and panic among plantation owners. Catherine knew that only six months earlier a group of slaves newly arrived from Africa had gone on a rampage in St. Andrew Parish, slaughtering their overseer in the field, killing three more whites, and wounding others before they were stopped.

And Catherine believed, would always believe, that her daughter Fayette had been brutally murdered by a maddened runaway slave, although none had ever been caught. Catherine shuddered. The slaves themselves, she knew, held that Fayette and her baby had been killed by evil spirits. She could never understand these Africans, never feel comfortable with them or trust them, no matter how long they lived in her house. Theirs was a world apart . . .

"Where's Moses?" she asked, clutching Roland's arm. "Keep him by your side at all times. Where's Major? Get the rest of them into their cabins and give them extra meat for supper. Blow the night horn at sunset tonight. Oh, dear Lord, save us from those nasty brutish savages!"

"Let me handle this, mother!" James interrupted. "This is no time to show weakness or fear!"

"You! I want no help from you! No help or advice, if you please. Get out of here! Haven't you caused me trouble enough?"

"I? *I* have caused trouble?" James stumbled, backing away from Catherine, a white-haired virago in black. She raised a fist, he felt her hostility, and for a crazy moment James thought she might have him beaten. She hates me, he realized. She has never loved me and she is capable of doing anything to hurt me. Finally his own anger stirred, but with it a cold feeling of despair which kept his temper in check as he said very stiffly, "Very well, mother, I shall go, and I wish you very well with all your affairs."

"Indeed, that's what they are. My own affairs. Not yours. By God, you shall never have a penny of my money or an acre of Sea Groves. I shall give it all to Byron Barstow first! How high and mighty you think yourself, coming down here and causing all this uproar!"

I? I caused this? How am I at fault, James asked himself helplessly, but he forced himself to turn and walk away. If I stay, he thought, I shall strike her in the face, and she is naught but a nasty old woman. No court of law on earth will support her disinheriting me, and as for my so-called brother, Byron Barstow, I shall see him dead, too, long before I am reduced to begging for this dreary God-forsaken plantation.

"Grandmother!" Roland demanded, "What has been going on? What has James done to upset you so?"

At Blackwoods, the same breeze stirred Orde Barstow, who had dozed off in exhaustion. The wind from the sea blew the curtains of his bed and those on the easterly windows and their billowing whiteness reminded him, as he slowly drifted back to consciousness, of the white dresses Zonah always wore.

"Zonah . . ." he murmured to himself before he came awake enough to remember that something dreadful had happened, something that must change things between him and Zonah forever.

The breeze stimulated him, and dizzy but driven, he sat up in bed and swung his legs over the side. His stirring brought one of the young house slaves, Tessie, running to his side.

"Easy now, Mister Barstow. Byron told me not to let you get yourself out of bed till he came home."

"Where is he?"

"He went ridin' off, Mister Barstow, and he gave me orders not to let you . . ."

"What's that?"

"I don't know, sir."

Both of them had heard the slow, steady clop-clop and creak of a horse carriage coming up the front driveway, coming closer and closer to the front of the house.

"Well, run and look, you silly girl!"

"Yes, sir." Tessie ran to the south windows, the ones that faced over the driveway and the lush green lawn.

She parted the curtains and leaned out an open window. What she saw made her scream.

"What is it? What is it?" Orde's voice was weak and choked with emotion.

"Oh, Mister Barstow! I . . . I cain't say!"

With a super-human effort, Orde stood and staggered to the window. Tessie stepped aside and one story below he saw the horse carriage Zonah and Ira had driven away in. It had come home driverless. Ira was slumped in the driver's seat, lying on his back, his eyes shut, with a bright red-burned "D" branded on the flesh of his chest. And behind him, heaped in the back of the cart, was the crumpled body of his love, Zonah, a mangled horror of shredded white dimity, bleeding flesh, and naked skin.

"Zonah! Zonah! Zonah!" Orde screamed. His voice was a high, pain-honed knife and it cut through Zonah's stupor. She was not dead. She lifted her head in time to see Orde pitch forward out the window, his arms spread wide, his face a white mask of shock and horror.

He landed on his neck with the full impact of his weight behind the landing. He died at once.

Because Zonah insisted, Orde Barstow was buried that night. Zonah had lain for an hour as Celeste, who was the midwife at Blackwoods and proficient at healing with herbs and poultices, had bathed her wounds and bound them loosely in strips of cotton. Celeste had also given Zonah a draught of a powerful painkiller, brewed of mandrake and rosehip tea, and Zonah had made Ira and Byron drink some of it, too.

While Celeste had been tending to Zonah, Marcus, the cooper who was also one of the twenty men in Byron's militia, had built Orde's coffin out of black oak. Two other men were sent to ride around Saint Simons to inform some of the neighboring planters about the funeral service that night. Byron, incapable of action, lost in thought, sat in stunned silence in the front parlor, where Marcus brought the coffin when it was finished and where the women bathed and laid out Orde.

No matter how he thought of it, Byron felt that his father had been as good as killed by the Dunlies. He blamed them. He blamed himself, too, for riding off, for not staying by Orde's bedside to watch after him. There was no point in blaming Zonah for her part in things—anyway, she was so obviously heartbroken that he was aware that she would not outlive Orde by long.

"I hope this is the end of it," Byron said to Samuel Savage Martin when the planter came in at dusk, hat in hand, to pay his respects. "Pray God this is the end of it."

"He was a brave man," Martin said. "He had an individual way about him. He was a man who thought for himself, and some of his conclusions weren't the same as other folks' conclusions, but before Heaven, he was a *man*."

"He was a wonderful father," Byron said.

Byron had insisted that Zonah should be present in the parlor while the funeral guests were assembling, and as she was too weak to stand for long, he had seated her in a high-backed wooden chair at the head of the coffin. For the first time in her life, Zonah looked old. She wore a voluminous black silk dress, hastily and poorly fitted to her by its rightful owner, one of the fattest slave women on the plantation, and her face was tightened up with pain, her lovely dark eyes mere slits and her lips set in a thin miserable line.

Awkwardly, Samuel Martin nodded to her. The other neighbors ignored her, but most of the prominent Island families were represented, including James and Margery Spaulding, who came from "The Gener-

al's Farm," where James Oglethorpe had once lived.
Because there was no regular minister of the gospel on
the island and no time to send to Midway or Savannah
for one, the island planters took turns praying aloud
and Samuel Martin read some passages from scriptures.

Just as the twilight was thickening into darkness,
the funeral procession, with Orde's coffin borne on
the strong shoulders of his mulatto sons, Joseph and
Samuel, made its way from the house to the burying
ground on the edge of the swamp. All the slaves at
Blackwoods joined the procession, carrying lighted
pine knots as torches and singing in unison a high,
mournful wailing dirge.

The sound gave Byron Barstow a strange chill. Byron was exhausted, half-crazy from the long and tragic
day, and had the sense that the darkness now falling
over the island was somehow permanent—that days of
sunshine and brightness had ended forever with the
death of Orde Barstow, that dawn and daylight would
never come again.

Zonah, too weak to walk, was carried in a cane set-
tee, and lapsed from time to time into unconsciousness. She woke when the two men bearing her chair set
it down at the side of Orde's grave, and cried out with
such heartfelt sadness that Byron moved instinctively
to her side.

"Take heart, Zonah, for he will rest in peace," Byron said, but he wondered if it were true. At the grave,
the assembled people sang a hymn—the deep bass voice
of Marcus the cooper holding the weaker voices together—and then Orde's coffin was lowered into the
hole dug for it and already seeping in with brackish
water, some of it standing six inches deep.

When the coffin had been settled into its soggy resting place and covered over with the sandy and mouldy

soil, the slaves of Blackwoods drew closer, forming a big ring around the new grave. "Good-bye, good-bye," the slaves called out and a silence as profound as the darkness fell over the rest of the assembled mourners. The slaves held high their lighted torches and then, in unison, threw them backward over their heads as far as they could throw them, and then left the gravesite quietly, only a few muffled sobs coming back to the ears of the neighbors, who walked with Byron back to his father's house before dispersing for their own homes, solemn and silent as the night.

Chapter Twenty-four

Georgians Take Sides—Sir James in Trouble—Independence Is Declared

The late summer and fall of 1775 were characterized throughout Georgia by good weather and a bumper rice crop, by ever-increasing strength among the patriots, and desperate efforts by both Whigs and Tories to keep the Indians neutral and to prevent their joining the other side. In Savannah, James Wright, powerless, still held sway at Government House. A second provincial congress met and became the de facto legislature of the colony. Georgia chose delegates to the Continental Congress in Philadelphia and ranged herself with her sister colonies.

Sir James Wright, knighted during his visit to England in 1772, wrote to his friend Lord Dartmouth in England, "The Powers of Government are wrested out of my Hands . . . It is really a wretched state to be left in . . . not the least means of protection, support, or even personal safety, and these almost daily occurrences are *too much*, my Lord." Control of the militia passed out of Wright's hands in July and control of the law courts in December. Wright and his friends watched all these developments with horror, despair, and indignation.

The patriots and their executive arm, the Council of Safety, did not tolerate dissenting opinions. They recruited troops, took steps to obtain arms and ammunition, issued money, and saw to it that nothing unfavorable to their cause was printed in the *Gazette*. A tunesmith on York Street chanted the doggerel: "Tories with their brats and wives, Should flee to save their wretched lives." When a man named John Hopkins insulted the Sons of Liberty and drank a toast to "Damnation to America," he was taken from his home, tarred and feathered, and paraded through the streets of Savannah. At the liberty tree, he was told that he would hang if he didn't change his toast to "Damnation to all Tories and Success to American Liberty." He changed. Hopkins was one of many who shifted allegiance. Numerous Tory sympathizers left Georgia, taking with them whatever belongings they could.

In January, 1776, two English war vessels sailed up the river and anchored at Tybee. The men-of-war had come to purchase supplies and had already been turned away from Charleston, but the sight of them off Cockspur Island, bristling with arms, enraged Savannah patriots, particularly the Council of Safety, who came together in Tondee's Tavern to plan swift and appropriate action. Among them were Joseph Habersham, Major in the newly formed battalion of Georgia troops, eight companies organized that month under Lachlan McIntosh, the good doctor Jack Barstow, and Byron Barstow, who had returned to Savannah to throw himself into the revolutionary cause.

"I say we must take him prisoner at once!" Byron vowed.

"We are endangered by the men-of-war," Habersham agreed. Joseph Habersham, whose famous father, James Habersham, had died the month before, his death mourned by Wright as a "heavy blow to the Royal cause," was, like Byron, a militant patriot.

"It will be dangerous, he is well-guarded," Jack Barstow warned.

"Do we stand united on this matter?" Habersham asked.

"Aye."—"We do."—"Let us go at once!" Council members voted.

"Let me go alone . . . or with one other man, then, to Government House," Habersham volunteered.

"I will go with you," Byron Barstow offered.

And so, as boldly as if invited to dine, the two men proceeded to the Governor's house, passed the sentinel with the cry "Habersham to see the Governor," and entered the council chamber, where Sir James was seated with two of his closest advisors and his nephew by marriage, James Dunlie.

At the sight of Habersham and Barstow, Wright rose. Wright was the very perfection of an English gentleman and was dressed in a lavendar satin waistcoat, trimmed with gold braid and buttons with lace ruffles spilling out of his sleeves and a lace jabot at his throat. His round dark eyes widened with astonishment and his voice shook.

"Gentlemen? By whose authority do you enter my council chamber?" he asked. He recognized both Barstow and Habersham, and he could see Joseph Habersham or his brothers James and John without thinking of his former ally, their father.

Without hesitating, Joesph Habersham walked to the head of the long mahogany table and laid his hand on the Governor's shoulder. "Sir James, you are my prisoner!" he exclaimed.

Wright's face worked with indignation and anger. "By whose authority? By whose, I ask you, sir?"

"By the authority of the people of Georgia!"

During this exchange, two of the Governor's advisors had fled precipitately, unheeded by the two patriots, but James Dunlie had stayed, facing Byron Barstow with single-minded resentment.

"By God, Barstow," he said to Byron in a voice tightened with the effort to control anger, "politics as well as personality pit us against each other. We may be brothers, but 'tis no bond! To me you are a murderer, a coward, and a traitor. I despise your cause and shall oppose it to my last breath—and the sound of yours will be music to my ears!"

"Leave personal issues aside!" Habersham ordered. "Sir James, upon your oath of honor, I will permit you house arrest, provided that you make no effort to leave this house, or to leave town, or to communicate in any way with the war ships in the harbor. Have I your word?"

Byron Barstow lifted his musket. There was a tense silence in the room, and when Byron let his eyes drift to James Dunlie he saw his brother's fingers creeping toward the bone-handled paper knife on the table before him.

"Stop!" Byron ordered. "Do not touch that knife, James!"

"The situation leaves me no choice," Wright said, "I acquiesce. You have my word, Mr. Habersham, Mr. Barstow . . ."

Wright's voice trembled and Byron Barstow felt a stab of sympathy, but James Dunlie heard nothing of what was said. His body rigid, Dunlie stared at Byron in wordless hate.

The planters of Saint Simons Island, like most Georgians, were reluctant to take sides on the loyalty question until relatively late. The Islanders were, in the main, American born, but most of their land had been granted to them, and they knew their prosperity had been launched and sustained by the support of the Crown. They were relatively isolated from the fiery Liberty Boys in Savannah, but isolation often fosters independence of mind, and they had come to think of themselves as thoroughly American with their own rights to be safeguarded, a position that leads naturally to the demand for political independence. On the other hand, the Islanders were well aware of their proximity to the British garrison at St. Augustine and their long, exposed, unprotected coastline.

" 'Tis foolhardy to declare against the British," James Spaulding said to Catherine Dunlie. He had invited most of his neighbors to his plantation to celebrate the christening of his son Thomas.

" 'Twould be treasonous," Catherine Dunlie vowed, "but what is a poor widow to do? Daily I hear reports of Whigs stealing cattle and of British ships sighted off the island. We have no means to defend ourselves against ruffians of either party. My loyalty to the Crown is undiminished, sir, but I must think of my own safety and that of my property."

"And mine, also, madam," Spaulding assured her, but some weeks after the christening, Catherine learned that the Spauldings, like many other loyalists, had moved to Florida and the protection of the British military detachments there.

"There is no hope for it," Catherine told Roland on the gray December afternoon when she realized that the island was practically deserted. "We must flee."

"Leave Sea Groves?" Roland asked.

"Leave it all—but only temporarily. We shall ship the last of this season's harvest, hide the seeding rice, and move the healthiest darkies to the small plantation outside Savannah. We will leave Mary and Moses here with the rest. You and I and Isaac and Jenny will go to live in Savannah. We will be safe there. If anyone can keep the rebels in line it is Governor Wright."

And so, loading the finest household goods and supplies and leaving most of the rest of them locked into the cellars and attics and storehouses of the plantation's outbuildings and the main houses, Catherine Dunlie set out on the dangerous and exhausting journey to Savannah. She sent most the slaves and their goods on ahead with Roland in a fleet of twenty flat-bottomed piraguas, which would make their way north through the inland passageway passing Sapolo Island, St. Catherine's, and Ossabaw.

Catherine herself took the road which had been surveyed along the coast by General Oglethorpe. The road was in fairly good repair, but crossed three rivers which had to be forded. In the carriage with Catherine rode her two youngest grandchildren, Isaac and Jenny, who reminded her more every day of their mother, Fayette.

Jenny, now a full-breasted young woman of twenty with lustrous green eyes, had not left Saint Simons since her arrival as a baby, and she cried helplessly as the carriage slowly rolled down the tree-lined driveway and passed the familiar rice fields and salt marshes.

"There's no good in crying," Catherine said stoically and unsympathetically. In truth, she was numbed by the shock of leaving her home. It was more than incredible to think of beginning again after the war, for war seemed more and more inevitable, and she had no appetite for the quick-paced city life of Savannah.

"But grandmother, I confess I am afraid! What will happen to us all?" Jenny wailed.

"I ain't afraid," Isaac, a broad-shouldered young man in his twenties, said firmly. Since his brother, Pittman, and Pittman's wife, Sally, had moved back to Wilkes County to live, Isaac had taken over most of Pittman's work, but he, too, longed to see the wilderness again, although he was too afraid of his grandmother to express his fondest wish, which was to run away and join the Georgia militia. "War is for men, Jenny, that's why you're crying. You just stay out of it. Leave it to the men."

"Leave it to the scoundrels," Catherine advised. "And as for leaving life itself to the men, Jenny, don't be a fool. You are old enough now to do your share; no man can do it for you. Life is full of changes—it seems we are never too old to suffer them . . . but never mind, there is no good in talking to the young, no good at all."

"Grandmother!" Jenny gasped, for though she was used to Catherine's outbursts of temper, she was not accustomed to receiving advice from her grandmother.

I amaze myself, Catherine thought, staring at the winter sun glinting off the swollen creek they skirted in the carriage. I always thought old age was a peaceful, dormant time, but I am more passionate and fervent than ever. I hate leaving Sea Groves. If the young men weren't determined to fight a war, perhaps I could have retired soon, left all the toil to Roland and the boys . . . I hate the thought of going back to Savannah. It was always a wretched provincial town, and I am sure my daughter has made her own life there which will not easily accommodate me. But I have no choice, no choice . . . how often life has denied me a choice! Once again I am alone and must move on.

Catherine Dunlie found, indeed, that the Savannah she re-entered in early February, 1776, was very different from the town she had lived in more than fifteen years earlier. Governor Wright, to whom she had looked for protection, was under house arrest. Haddon Smith, the rector of Christ Church had been harassed by the mob until he fled to England the summer before. Noble Jones and James Habersham, whom she remembered as old friends of Angus's, had died. The young and the revolutionary were everywhere. Everyone talked of war. Two weeks after their arrival in Savannah, her grandson Isaac, a strapping blond-bearded young man, ran away to join the Georgia militia, and Catherine washed her hands of him.

Her daughter Cattie was not much better. Cattie, a slim, handsome, unwrinkled, sharp-tongued woman of fifty, was a patriot-sympathizer, if not actually a patriot herself, and Catherine Dunlie had arrived to find that she had opened the Dunlie family home to board two young officers of the Georgia battalion. The two officers, Lemuel Turner and Patrick McQuestin, were raw, boisterous, inexperienced country boys in their twenties, but Catherine was not too old to percieve what Cattie saw in them.

And as for her son, James . . . She had arrived to find James actually sharing the house with Cattie and the officers, although a confirmed loyalist. James's wife, Rosalind, and their children were waiting for him at their plantation near Augusta, but he lingered in Savannah.

"Madam, I must make arrangements to protect my property—and yours as well," James told Catherine. James had no choice but to overlook the venom with which his mother had dismissed him from Sea Groves after the shattering incident with Zonah, and Catherine had no choice but to treat her son with some re-

spect. Times had changed. The hovering threat of war
had changed and altered many lives, dissolved old al-
liances and created many new ones. Georgians, whatever their position, were making desperate "arrangements." Catherine eyed old friends with suspicion, and
every day learned of neighbors and acquaintances who
had left Georgia for England, Canada, or Florida.

She herself would not hear of leaving. With her
daughter Cattie and her granddaughter Jenny she settled into the familiar, roomy house on Abercorn
Street. The three women—each of a different generation—were like somewhat bewildered boarders in a
crossroads tavern: the two patriot officers came and
went—cheered and cajoled by the ever-flirtatious
Cattie; James spent long hours in his ground-floor office—once Angus Dunlie's study—and slipped out at
night on unexplained clandestine errands; Jenny,
whose education had been neglected at Sea Groves, had
been hastily if belatedly enrolled in a school for young
ladies kept by an Englishwoman on Barclay Street.
Catherine, idle and unhappy in the city, had herself
driven out to the small plantation outside of town every day. She had put her grandson, Roland, in charge
of that small farm, which had lain fallow for fifteen
years. With a force of about thirty slaves Roland began the work of plowing the fields he would plant,
come spring, in corn and peas.

Although Catherine was known to be a Tory-sympa-
thizer, the presence of the two Whig officers in her
house guaranteed her and her family some protection.
Indeed, it was for this reason, rather than any desire to
live under the same roof with Cattie or Catherine, that
James had chosen to stay there.

For James needed a cover. With a few other loyalist
friends, he was deeply involved in a plot to free Governor Wright. Their first attempt was on the night of

February first. James, following the program set up by the conspirators, approached the guard at Government House and offered the doltish provincial lieutenant twenty pounds of gold. When the man accepted, James knocked him out with one brutal blow of a heavy Spanish cutlass and slipped into the familiar mansion. He found Governor Wright asleep in bed.

"Dress. Come at once," James had ordered the distraught, depressed man.

Wright had struggled to follow James, but at the side door, where a carriage was waiting by prearrangement, they were met by a company of twenty cavalry guards who seized Wright and clapped him into arm and leg irons. Wright had sobbed with disappointment as well as physical discomfort as he was led back into the house. James managed to wound one patriot with his cutlass and shots were exchanged by the Georgia volunteers and the King's men. In the confusion James escaped; the guard who had accepted James's bribe was hanged the next day, and his corpse displayed publicly for a week.

After that, Governor Wright was plunged into despair. "I fear for my life," he wrote a friend in Charleston, "for all these patriots are so rabid, so savage in their cry for what they think will be liberty that life itself is cheap to them."

James Dunlie was outraged to learn that Wright was not only being kept in irons but denied any visitors, correspondence, or outings. He devised another, even more dangerous plan to help Wright escape. On the night of February 11, he stole into the big bedroom in the Dunlie house where the officers, Turner and McQuestin, lay snoring, and removed their regimental coats and hats.

It was a cold, miserable night. Thick clouds masked the moon and stars. A light rain was falling, and the wind off the river was icy and raw. James bundled himself up in both coats and pulled one of the black cocked hats down over his face. He tied his horse, hitched to a small open cart, in the alleyway near Government House and crept along the sandy, unpaved street without making a sound. There was only one man on guard outside Government House, a fresh-faced young Salzburgher, shivering with cold.

James studied the guard for a moment, then approached. As soon as he was within earshot he groaned and staggered toward the guard as if badly hurt.

"Who goes there?" the sentry called in a sleepy voice. It was long past midnight and he was more than ready for the change of watch which would not come until dawn.

"Oh! I am wounded!" James cried in a half-muffled voice. He bent over as if in great pain. Seeing his uniform, the guard dropped his musket and ran to help him. James uncoiled, drew back his arm, and stabbed the sentry twice with deadly accuracy. The man gasped and paled. His life's blood gushed forth from his heart, and he crumpled, dead without making a sound.

James rolled the body to the side of the street and ran through the open door into Government House. He encountered two more sentries, both nodding in sleep, and slit their throats. When he found the Governor, he bundled him into the extra regimental coat.

Wright's legs were cramped and chafed against the leg irons. He hobbled painfully and so slowly that James Dunlie had to half-carry him through the house. At the sight of the dead sentries, the Governor cried out in fear.

"Dear God, Dunlie! They will hang us both!"

"Not unless they catch us," Dunlie said grimly. "Make haste!"

Outside, it became obvious that the Governor could not walk either far or quickly. He panted heavily while James Dunlie ran for the cart and horse and brought them around to the door of Government House.

"Where are you taking me?" Wright asked plaintively as the rough cart slowly carried him toward the east side of town.

"To the marsh. There we will take a small boat to your friend Mullryne at Bonaventure."

"Easy! Ugh!" Wright cried out. The cart lurched and trembled. The rain had turned the white sand of the streets into a quagmire. Twice James Dunlie had to push the cart while the horse was pulling to move it out of a ditch.

Suddenly a figure on horseback loomed out of the darkness just before them. Governor Wright ducked his head and hid his face. I must challenge him, Dunlie thought, lest he challenge me.

"Who goes there?" he called out boldly.

"Doctor Barstow . . ." Jack replied, his wide, dark woolen cloak wrapped around him as usual as he rode home from delivering a baby on an outlying plantation.

"Pass on, Doctor . . ." Dunlie called, and to his relief, Jack did, his suspicions unaroused.

A few minutes later they reached the edge of the marsh. The path to the river through the marsh was longer and more difficult than that down the side of the bluffs, but it gave a man a far better chance to slip into a boat without being noticed. James Dunlie helped the Governor out of the cart and, taking his arm around his neck, began to drag him along the narrow path.

It was raining harder and the path was slippery and difficult to see. Both men knew the swamp was full of

snakes, alligators, and quicksand. For the shackled
Wright, each step was agony. Their progress was so
slow that Dunlie feared it would be dawn before they
reached the river. By daylight, the river patrol would
see them at once, and it was likely that the Governor's
escape and the murdered sentries had been discovered
by now.

I was a fool, Dunlie realized, to leave the cart and
horse in the open.

"Faster! We must hurry!" he urged Wright. Wright
was weak with the effort of walking in leg irons; he
was drenched with perspiration even as he shivered in
his rain-soaked clothing, but he set his jaw stubbornly
and would not cry out.

Just as the first faint rays of daylight lightened the
sky they started down the last slope to the river's edge.
James Dunlie stopped and cocked his head. Distinctly,
not far behind them, he could hear the excited barking
of a pack of hunting dogs and the crunching of the
reeds under the weight of a horse.

"They're coming after us!" Wright gasped.

"We're almost there!" Dunlie said with more confidence than he felt. "We'll make it!"

Halfway down the last slope Wright crumpled and
fell forward, dragging Dunlie with him. "My leg!" he
cried, "Oh, God! I think . . . it's broken, Dunlie."

"Don't stop! Come on!" Dunlie said desperately. He
heard a dog barking so close by that his stomach
churned and he tasted bile. Wright was helpless now,
and he had to take the older heavier man's full weight
onto his back and carry him the last hundred yards,
splashing and stumbling through the half-frozen reeds
to the tiny boat he had hidden near a bend in the
river.

Gasping, Dunlie heaved the Governor into the boat
and began to row with all his strength. Wright

slumped forward and in the strengthening light Dunlie could see that his stockings were soaked with blood from the cruel manacles. When Wright gained consciousness he leaned over the gunwales to vomit into the river, while James Dunlie struggled to get the boat into open water as his pursuers' dogs barked furiously and helplessly on the river's bank.

"I did it!" he exulted, "Good-bye to you, you filthy ruffians! Good-bye!"

Laughing, he flexed his aching arms and rowed even harder as a rifle shot cracked the air and the ball skipped across the water between the boat and the shore.

Six months later, almost to the day, the news of the Declaration of Independence reached Georgia. The date was August 10, 1776. Archibald Bullock, a Savannah lawyer who had been chosen President of Georgia and Commander-in-Chief of her forces, read the document aloud in Savannah to the Council of Safety in the long room at Tondee's Tavern. "When in the course of human events it becomes necessary for one people to dissolve the political bonds which had connected them with another . . ." Bullock read, and the legislators and officials present listened with mild premonitions of what was to come.

Afterward, Bullock stepped outside the tavern and read the Declaration to the crowd that had gathered in the public square. "We hold these truths to be self-evident," Bullock read, "That all men are created equal, that they are endowed by their Creator with certain unalienable rights, that among these are Life, Liberty and the pursuit of Happiness . . ."

The crowd was excited and jubilant. Among them were Jack Barstow, who had lived in Savannah for rty-three of his sixty-odd years; the three Dunlie women: Catherine Dunlie, her daughter Cattie Nickerson, and her granddaughter Jenny Stone; and Kate Barstow, Byron Barstow's loyal wife who lived with her children in the big house in St. James Square that Orde Barstow had built more than thirty years ago. It was a hot, humid night. "Hurrah! Hurrah! Hurrah!" the crowd cheered. Doctor Jack thought of war—war meant suffering and death, awful wounds and gangrene and epidemics and fevers. He hoped that it would not be a long war. He prayed that it would be over by spring, and that there would be no fighting in Georgia.

Catherine Dunlie was amazed at the size of the crowd and the passion with which they cheered for Liberty. Years ago, she thought, this sort of feeling was reserved for cock-fights. Her own fervor was retained for the management of her estates—it was the height of the growing season, and her grandson, Roland, predicted a good harvest. Roland was not in Savannah; Catherine insisted that he live outside of town, on the small plantation worked by the slaves from Sea Groves. Catherine started and slapped at a sand fly. She wondered what Angus would have made of this. Angus had dreamed for a great future for Georgia, but no one could have been more loyal to his King than he.

"I am going home," Catherine said. "The mosquitoes have fed on me long enough. *You* should cover your shoulders, Cattie." She beckoned to Major, who as always was hovering within earshot of his mistress.

"Good-bye, mother," Cattie said civilly. "I will come along in a while." Cattie had caught sight of Doctor Jack Barstow on the other side of the square. Cattie was still given to fond feelings for Jack, still visited by the twin demons of pride and desire. If only . . . she thought, if he and I had married after all, if we had

given in to the love we once had for each other . . .
how different my life now would be . . .

Bullock was moving on. Taking most of the crowd
with him, he paused at the Liberty Pole in front of
Tondee's Tavern. The tavern was doing a flourishing
business, and the noise of the cannon on the river
bluffs echoed through the town. After thirteen salutes,
the word spread through the crowd that it would be
read again at the battery on the riverbank and the
celebration was carried along to the battery.

Cattie and Jenny fell behind, as the cheering crowd
headed for the Strand, but Kate Musgrove Barstow
took her twin sons by their hands and let herself be
swept along. "I want you to remember this day all
your lives," she told Andrew and Adam, "and tell your
father about it when you see him next."

Kate Barstow knew better than most of the real difficulties and dangers of war. She knew that her husband, Byron, risked his life daily in his undercover efforts to secure supplies and munitions for the patriot
troops. Just now, Byron had gone south through
British-held territory to see to the plantation on Saint
Simons Island and to bring the black militia north to
Savannah.

Kate was a Georgian through and through. She was
the granddaughter of none other than Mary Musgrove, the half-Creek interpreter who had terrorized
Savannah on another exciting night. Kate, descendant
through her grandmother's first marriage—a liaison
with a British fur trader, had grown up on an uncle's
small indigo plantation on the Savannah River, had
gone to George Whitefield's Bethesda school, and had
fallen in love with Byron Barstow on her seventeenth
birthday, seeing him for the first time at her uncle's
ll plantation, where he had come to join a hunting
. They had married one year later.

Kate was a full-breasted, robust woman whose dark hair and eyes and high cheekbones attested to her Creek blood. She was a good-natured woman who liked a bit of fun, and she let herself get into the mood of celebration that swept Savannah that night.

Bullock read the Declaration for the fourth and final time under the cedar trees in the Trustees Garden. Kate lingered there to drink a toast with some of Byron's friends, a toast to "The Prosperity and perpetuity of the United, Free, and Independent States of America," then went on with them to follow a mock solemn funeral cortege. Two black horses wearing black plumes drew a hearse, draped with black cloth upon which rested an open coffin holding an effigy of King George III. Spectators cheered as fife and drums played *The Rogue's March*.

"It's brilliant," Jonathan Reid, Byron's friend and fellow patriot, exclaimed to Kate Barstow, "but who has designed it? It is so splendidly done!"

And then the tempo of the drums changed to beat a solemn dirge. Reid and Kate Barstow joined the procession following the coffin to the Courthouse.

"The King is dead! Long live the Free States of America!" the crowd chanted. "The King is Dead! The King is Dead!"

Kate wiped away a mock tear and smiled at Jonathan Reid. "They're going to bury him!"

Dressed as a clergyman, a man who looked a lot like Joseph Habersham took his place at the head of the coffin. "Unto Almighty God we commend the soul of our brother departed . . ." he intoned, and a few women in the crowd gasped at the sacrilege before a wave of cheers and laughter drowned their shocked protest.

The mock clergyman read a burial service, and the coffin was lifted off the hearse. "For as much as

George III . . . hath most flagrantly . . . tramped upon the constitution of our country . . . we therefore commit his political existence to the ground— corruption to corruption—tyranny to the grave—and oppression to eternal infamy . . ."

"Hurrah! Hurrah! Hurrah!" shouted the crowd.

Chapter Twenty-five

Savannah Invaded!—Ira Saves Byron—
James Visits His Family—
Jenny Grows Up

During the next two years, the citizens of Georgia lost much of their enthusiasm for the war. Although most of the important battles of the war's early years took place in the northern colonies, the British navy controlled and harassed Georgia's coastline, the Creeks continued to wage wars against her western counties, and the rivalries between Patriots and Tories inside the state were constant and savage.

In the fall of 1778 after their staggering defeat at Saratoga, the British developed a pincer movement, coming from the south as well as from the north to catch Georgia in a squeeze. The British military strategy was simple: they would seize Georgia, which was notoriously weak and divided, and move inevitably northward, gaining loyalist aid as they went.

A fleet of British ships under the command of Colonel Archibald Campbell sailed south from New York and arrived at Tybee Island in the Savannah River on

December 23 of that year. Campbell expected to be met by Lt. Col. Mark Prevost, who had in fact been turned back from Savannah and was retreating to Florida, devastating the coastal towns and burning the landmark church at Midway and pillaging en route.

Campbell arrived in Georgia with about two thousand men. He had been instructed to wait at Tybee until he received a visit from a native Georgian who was a highly trusted loyalist. This spy approached Campbell's flagship in a small open boat rowed by two huge black men. Campbell met with him in his tiny, chart-filled cabin at dawn.

"Good morning, Colonel Campbell! Long live King George!"

Campbell smiled at the man's curious accent. "Good morning, Mister Dunlie. What is your news?"

James Dunlie spoke proudly, "Good news, sir. The Carolina troops have left Savannah. I have it on good authority that there are no more than about five hundred troops and militia inside the city. But I warn you, Savannah has excellent natural defenses. The bluffs above the river are as high as your Dover cliffs." James paused, remembering that Sir James Wright had often made that remark. Sir James was now exiled to Halifax, but eagerly awaiting the recapture of Georgia. "The town is surrounded by a maze of swamps and rice fields. There are only a few possible routes through them. I will show you the one I think will be the best. But mind, it will be dangerous. At this time of year the water is very high."

"Show me the best route," Colonel Campbell urged. "Here are my maps of the town. Show me the best route through the swamps . . ."

Inside Savannah, General Robert Howe, in charge of the Continental troops, was at odds with Colonel Walton, commander of the Georgia militia.

The sight of the British war ships anchored in the river spread panic in the city. Howe took immediate steps to defend the main road from the east and posted brigades to guard the entrances to the swamps.

At daybreak on December 29, the British forces landed about two miles east of Savannah on a plantation belonging to a man named Girardeau and advanced along a narrow causeway toward Brewton's Hill. The British advance party was made up of a company of Highlanders. The company met fire; two were immediately killed and five others wounded, but the bulk of the British forces under the direct command of Campbell came up behind them.

Colonel Campbell was relying heavily on James Dunlie to guide him. Dunlie advised Campbell to conceal his artillery behind Brewton's Hill.

"There is an opening near here," Dunlie gasped. He had never been in battle before; it was exhilarating as well as frightening. He felt sure they would taste victory, but so much depended on getting the troops through the swamps. "The bridge across Lamar's Creek has been destroyed and the tide is rising. By God! Where is that channel?"

For a few agonizing moments, James Dunlie hesitated. Three hundred feet west of the devasted bridge, a trench had been dug and had already filled with swamp water. He was confused. He had lost sight of some landmarks he remembered from his boyhood in Savannah. Then he caught sight of a grizzled old Negro, half-hidden in a holly thicket.

"Hey, you, there!" he yelled. "Come here!"

The old black man obeyed. "Do you live near here?" Dunlie asked him.

"Yes, sir!"

"Do you know the hidden path through the swamps? Of course you do! Show us where it begins!"

"Yes, sir," the man said, eager to give no offense. His name, Colonel Campbell learned, was Quamino Dolly. With Dunlie and Quamino Dolly at his side, Campbell started to make his way through the flooded, muddy marshland. The wet, sandy path penetrated dense, thorny underbrush. The men marched double time, sinking to their boot tops with each step, trying to beat the tide.

In less than an hour, the British troops emerged from the swamps, and came upon the Americans from the rear. Campbell opened rapid fire while his lieutenant, James Baird, brought the flank movement down on Walton's militiamen. Between the two fires, the Americans could only retreat. Many of them, farmer-soldiers, fresh from the forest and fields, lost their heads and panicked. Some of them broke ranks and ran; in the streets of Savannah it was every man for himself.

Byron Barstow was part of the brigade under Colonel Elbert. Before noon on that December day he had seen chaos and carnage that would haunt him for the rest of his life. This brigade was under the general command of Colonel George Walton and had met the offensive of the British army when the first troops rolled back in retreat.

Then they had held their fallback position bravely, under terrific crossfire, for what seemed like hours. Byron was entrenched in a small wooded hollow; just to his left were the familiar faces of the twenty black foot soldiers he had brought from Blackwoods, and in charge of them was Zonah's son Ira, whom Byron knew and loved better than a brother.

To the east of the black troops were the rice paddies that had been Governor Wright's plantation; to the ere dense swamps. In the early morning Byron had been confident that they would stand off the British—although it was rumored that they would be badly outnumbered—but when the redcoats started coming from the right flank, having somehow got through the swamps, the American troops had been under fire from both directions.

There were so many of them! Grimly, Byron looked at the long lines of infantry, of cavalry, of artillery. He looked at them with the eye of a hardened soldier, appraising their strength. It was depressing, but not frightening. Byron had inured himself—as much as possible—to fear. He had hardened to fear, grown accustomed to it, for he had been frightened so often in the past few years. He had been frightened of death, of injury, of failing to act in crisis, of acting too boldly so that others would die. Fear had become familiar and lost its power to cripple him. But more and more often, of late, he had sunk into a black despair which was more desperate and more devastating than his old active fears.

For Byron had become more philosophical. He had come to view all this fighting, this bloodshed, these sacrifices, as an obscene and flagrant waste of human lives and potencies. He, who five years ago, even ten years ago, had been among the most radical, most outspoken, most daring of patriots, had changed

In his heart and mind he had changed. But it was too late. He had cast his lot with the fighters for independence, and now that they were involved in a real war, it was too late to turn back, to argue for a negotiation, to work for a compromise settlement that would bring peace to America without spilling more blood.

"You were right, father," Byron had said softly to himself that morning as he lay awake in the darkness, cold, stiff, unwashed, and felt the now-familiar despa creep over him. Asleep, he had lived in another world, a soft sunlit world where Kate and his children stood by his side as he looked out over the green fields of Blackwoods, so far away. Blackwoods . . . Byron remembered that bright, hot afternoon at Blackwoods when he and Ira had marched the hands up and down with all the innocence of boys playing at the game of soldiers.

"War is dying and dysentery, fleas and mouldy bread and some men getting rich," Orde had said, and Byron knew now that he had been absolutely right. He blamed himself, too, for getting the men from Blackwoods into this war—what was it to them, anyway? He could no longer believe that their lives would be any different, any better, whichever white men had charge of the government.

Just let me last through this, let me endure till the end of the war, Byron thought, still loading, firing, and reloading on command, shoulder to shoulder with a red-faced brickmaker from Savannah and the sixteen-year-old minister's son from Sundury, and I will take of all of them . . . Ira and his brothers, Sam and Joseph, all of them in the militia, the other black people at the plantation, and his own family. Byron knew that his wife, Kate, had often been in danger because of him, and he worried what would happen to her if the British took Savannah now. Kate was herself a staunch patriot, as well as the wife of a known rebel, and violent and vengeful retaliations—often bearing no connection with the Revolution itself—were more than common in this war. Above all, Byron feared that his brother James Dunlie—how strange it was to think of him as a blood brother—would seek out his family
t on them his persistent, murderous desire for
Oh, Kate, my love, Byron's heart cried out,
o you, God save you!

"Captain Barstow? Byron? Are you all right?"

It was Ira's voice. Byron looked up and realized that he had temporarily lost all sense of the present. How much time had gone by as he aimed and fired at the red blur across the hollow without really seeing either bodies or faces, without really admitting that he was firing at men—and that they were firing at him?

He blinked and focused on Ira's concerned face. Ira's hat was missing and Byron saw a scorched powder burn on the shoulder of his linsey-wool waistcoat.

"I'm all right," Byron said finally.

"The order, sir, didn't you hear the order to retreat?" Ira asked. His eyes, blue as Orde's had been, searched Byron's.

"By God, no!" Byron stumbled forward. At his feet was the lifeless body of the Sunbury minister's son, face in the mud, his arms outspread, one hand still clutching his musket.

"The commander has ordered a general retreat!" Ira shouted. He seized Byron's arm and shook it as if to wake him up. Everything around them was in a state of confusion: men were running in every direction, the air was loud with screams of pain and firing rifles, a dense cloud of smoke rose from the direction of the British army, and then out of it ran seemingly hundreds of red-coated men waving fixed bayonets.

"Run! Run! The swamp!" a voice called out. and some of the Americans tried to flee along the same narrow swamp path the British had followed in. It was well covered by Tory artillery, and Byron heard the first men scream as they were hit.

The bulk of Elbert's brigade turned about face and ran through the rice fields and into the town where many were shot and bayonetted. Byron and Ira were among a score of the retreating men who cut across the burying ground. It was now mid-afternoon and the white winter sun shone through the dense cedar trees that surrounded the simple tombstones of the first settlers.

Ira looked west, into the sun, and saw a hulking red-coated soldier half-hidden by a tree. He was taking careful aim in their direction.

"Watch out! Duck!" Ira shouted. He dropped to one knee and took aim at the British soldier.

"Bam! Crack!" Both rifles had gone off at once. The British soldier toppled over dead, but Byron had been hit in his left arm. Ira rushed to help him. The wound looked deep and was bleeding profusely, already soaking Byron's shirt sleeve, his coat, blood gushing down over his hand.

"Don't stop! I'll be all right," Byron said. "Make a run for it! Head for the creek!"

"You all go on ahead," Ira ordered the others. They were a mixed lot: black men and white, men with powder-blackened faces, all tired and desperately frightened. Obediently, they stumbled on toward Musgrove Creek, where the water was so high that thirty of them and their comrades were to drown trying to swim across to safety.

"Go, Ira," Byron begged.

"Not without you," Ira said flatly, "Got to get you out of this graveyard. You're not dead yet!" He jerked off his rawhide belt and tightened it around Byron's upper arm to cut off the flow of blood. Byron winced in pain. He had lost so much blood so fast that he was light-headed, dizzy.

"Can you walk?" Ira asked.

Byron nodded and stumbled to his feet. Ira tied his limp useless arm fast to his chest with another length of leather cord and took Byron's good arm around his shoulder. Byron was much taller; Ira had his father's short, stocky build and his mother's fine bones, but he was well-muscled and amazingly strong. Byron's weight slowed him hardly at all. Ira had a vague idea that the militia's barracks and field hospital were just to the west of them, outside the city's gates by a half mile or so. He headed west, keeping the city's palisades on his right.

Despite the tourniquet, Byron's arm still bled, and he slipped in and out of consciousness. "Leave me, damn it," he ordered Ira when he was aware. "Leave me to die, that's all I want."

"No sir, I won't have it!" Ira replied. Then he felt Byron go limp again. Twice he let him slide to the muddy ground and splashed his face with water from a pool. When Byron sputtered and snorted back to life, Ira picked him up and set off again.

As they neared the militia's camp, they faced a steady stream of American soldiers and officers fleeing in the other direction.

"What news? What news?" Ira asked.

"Savannah is captured!" "Run for your life!" "It's every man for himself!" "They are killing all prisoners!"

Ira looked at Byron. He was very weak and needed immediate medical attention. "Is there a doctor?" he begged, seizing the arm of a tow-headed German in the uniform of the South Carolina militia.

"Back there! But they'll kill you if they catch you!" the man called out, heading for the swamps.

I won't turn back now, Ira decided. He was as good as carrying Byron and he was very tired, but with aching legs he forced himself to run the last distance. They were crossing farm lands, trampling the soggy cornfield. They passed a burning house and barn, heard the agonized whinnying of trapped horses. Ira shuddered, then he saw the first barracks—ramshackled frame huts thrown up last fall by the volunteers—and the fires of the field hospital, and he knew thay would make it.

"Doctor! Doctor!" Ira shouted as soon as they neared the fires. The field hospital was salvation, but it looked like a vision of hell. Ira heard the screams of the wounded, saw men lying everywhere—on blankets, on stretchers, on the cold ground. Women of all ages who served as nurses and camp followers moved among the men, giving them water and food, hearing prayers, holding the hands of the dying. The muddy ground was slick with blood, and on the edge of the camp Ira saw a hideous pile of severed arms and legs.

He gasped, felt a wave of nausea. He closed his eyes and bent over to brace himself.

"Easy, soldier," said a cool voice and Ira felt a steady hand on his arm. "Set him down over here. Do you know his name? How long ago was he hit?"

Ira opened his eyes to the most beautiful woman he had ever seen. She was an angel, an angel with clear green eyes, masses of black curls, a rosy heart-shaped face. She wore a short navy blue nurse's cloak and a long dark skirt looped up to her boot tops. Despite the hell around them, Ira felt his heart jump and loved her immediately.

"Barstow . . ." he stammered, "Captain Byron Barstow, ma'am. Took a ball in his arm about an hour ago . . ."

"Barstow? I'll get Doctor Jack right away," the woman said and disappeared between a row of stretchers.

Ira set Byron down and knelt by his head. "Water? Water, Byron?" he whispered; he unbuttoned Byron's shirt and jacket and tried to peel them off his wet, blood-spattered body.

Almost at once, the woman was back with Doctor Jack Barstow in tow.

"Is this the soldier named Barstow?" he asked.

"Yes, sir," Ira answered. "He is . . . and I am, too. Ira Barstow."

Jack looked into Ira's blue eyes, at his pale brown skin. He looked at the wounded Barstow and recognized Byron, the heir who had supplanted him, his fellow patriot, and in a vague way he understood it all.

"Well, Ira, it has been many years since we've met," he said, "I am Jack Barstow, myself. A good name . . . good as any. Let's see here . . ." Skillfully, without any hesitation, Jack slit the sleeve of Byron's coat and shirt and probed with a sharp steel blade inside the messy wound for the lead shot. Byron stirred, groaned.

"Easy now," he said. "Abby, give him a shot of rum. This must hurt. Or you, Ira. Abby, hold this probe. The hole's as big as an inkwell."

Abby, Ira thought. Her name is Abby. He dribbled some rum into Byron's mouth, still watching the woman, studying her face, drugging himself with the incredible excitement he felt at being near her.

"Hold tight. I've got it now," Jack Barstow said softly. "Abby, pass me some lint to stop this up. More than that. A lot more. All right, now you bandage it tightly, but he won't be safe here. The British will be coming through this hospital in an hour's time. Captain Barstow has got to be hidden."

"I know where his wife lives," Abby said.

"That will be the first place they'll look for him. Ira, I want to send you and one other man into town with him. Don't take him to his own home. Take him to the Dunlies' house on Abercorn Street. Take him to the kitchen door and ask for Miss Cattie. Tell her I sent you and to hide him well. I'll look in on him tonight if I can. And Ira, then you come back here. We can use you."

"Yes, sir!" Ira felt dizzy, gay, light with hope. He

would see her again! He jumped to his feet. Jack Barstow saw the look on his face and followed his eyes to Abby's face, flushed, trembling with emotion.

"When you finish the bandaging, come to me, Abby," Jack said in a gruff voice. I must warn her to be careful, he thought. The mulatto has clearly fallen in love with her.

Jack was very fond of Abigail de Lyon, the young sister of Abraham de Lyon, one of Savannah's foremost Jewish citizens, a patriot who had come to Georgia from Portugal and knew wine cultivation. Savannah Jews were, almost to a man, patriots; in fact, Governor Wright had described them as "violent rebels and persecutors of the King's loyal subjects."

Orde Barstow's son is very handsome, Jack thought, but of course, it can not be. He is legally black. Abby had been living with the Sheftall family, and they were known Whigs . . . but whatever happened, he felt responsible for her. He must look after her himself; and she was so lovely, and despite her intelligence and courage, so vulnerable . . .

During the next month, the British troops who had invaded Savannah took full possession of the city and invited Georgians to sign a loyalty oath. The proclamation, which promised full pardon for past offenses and warned that opposition would be severely dealt with, also informed inhabitants that Parliament had given up any attempts to tax the colonies. Those who refused to sign were called "ringleaders of sedition," and loyal citizens were urged to turn them in to army headquarters for punishment.

Savannah was shocked by the invasion. Her citizens were battered and hungry; many of them had lost kin in the invasion or had friends or relatives who were among the four hundred and fifty American prisoners taken. Some Savannah residents fled to Charleston. Many of the prisoners were being held on cramped prison ships, where starvation and cruelty were the rule. Every day bodies were removed from the ships and slipped into the waters of the river.

The British had lost only seven men in the invasion and reported a mere nineteen wounded. They were exultant victors and they rolled on the conquer other Georgia towns: Ebenezer on January 2, Sunbury on January 10. Augusta was Colonel Campbell's next objective. He planned to set out for Augusta on January 24 with about one thousand troops.

James Dunlie, who had served as a special-information advisor to Campbell and remained largely behind the scenes during the first month of occupation, wanted to go with Campbell. His wife, Rosalind, was on their plantation near Augusta; so were his children, and he wanted to be their liberator when the British army marched into the frontier capitol. Both he and Campbell expected an easy victory upriver.

But before he left Savannah, James Dunlie had one last piece of personal business to conduct. He wanted to locate his brother, Byron Barstow. Before he left town, he wanted to satisfy himself that Byron was not there. He had been searching for Byron ever since the day of the invasion. He had checked the lists of American held prisoner and the lists of Americans killed. Byron Barstow was on neither of these lists, and yet James knew—he had it on the testimony of several members of the Georgia militia—that Byron had been part of Colonel Elbert's brigade.

Perhaps Byron was dead, dead and lost, swept away in the creek or mangled beyond recognition and buried in an unmarked grave. James derived some pleasure in contemplating the possibilities, but he longed to be sure. One day in mid-January he had visited the Barstow house in St. James Square and talked to Byron's wife.

"Believe me, I do not know where he is," Kate Barstow had said, pale with worry, her dark eyes sad, her voice tight with emotion. "I swear to you, I have not heard from him since two days after Christmas, and I have not seen him in longer than that."

"Women always lie," James Dunlie had said. It annoyed him that Byron had such a buxom, fine-looking wife. He had searched every room and corner of the Barstow house with an armed guard, poking into mattresses with a bayonet and smashing open a locked wardrobe cupboard, but they had found nothing to contradict Kate's testimony. As he searched the large, solid house, richly and tastefully furnished, James had recalled the only other time he had been inside: the day he had come to deliver the note from his father about the arrangements for the duel. It gave him an odd, resentful feeling, and when he returned to British headquarters, he asked that ten Hessian officers be stationed there to scar the floors with their heavy boots and drink up the last of Orde Barstow's imported wines.

Although James knew that many Savannah households were short on food and firewood, he had made no attempt to visit his mother's house until just before it was time to leave for Augusta. James had never admitted it to himself, and likely never would, but he was afraid of his bad-tempered, spiteful mother; indeed he had reason to be. Yet, some complex sense of filial loyalty combined with an irrepressible desire to be loved by her brought him back to her time and time again.

Accordingly, late in January he went to the house on Abercorn Street, accompanied by a Negro manservant carrying a sack of flour and a basket of provisions straight from the British officers' kitchen shed. As he approached the house, he noticed Doctor Jack Barstow, wearing his distinctive dark woolen cape, mount his horse and ride away.

James knocked politely at the door of his family's home and asked to see his mother. At once, Catherine descended the stairs, dressed as usual in black. She paused several steps from the bottom landing so that she could look straight into James's eyes.

"Well! Of course, we had heard that you were in Savannah, but how dare you endanger us by coming here?"

"I endanger you? But madam, we have a Tory government now."

"Tory today, Whig tomorrow, for all I know. I want nothing to do with this nasty business. I long for the end of it all so that I can go home to Sea Groves."

"Indeed, we all want an end to it, mother, and I believe the tide is turned. Our victory is near. Look, I have brought you some flour and foodstuffs . . ."

"Send it into the kitchen. God knows we need it. This has been terrible, terrible! James, some troops set fire to the storehouse on the small plantation and set free the blacks living out there. What can be done about it? Where are my reparations? I am a loyal British citizen, I'll have you know!" Catherine slumped dramatically and clung to the bannister.

"Here, mother, let me help you into the parlor," James said awkwardly, as usual at a loss to deal with his mother.

"Thank you, but I can walk!" Catherine snapped. She strode into the parlor with her head erect.

"You do look very well, mother. But I was alarmed to see Doctor Barstow coming from your house. Is someone unwell? Cattie?"

"Cattie is just as she has always been. We are all well enough. Jenny . . ."

"I am very well." Jenny had appeared in the doorway, rosy-cheeked, dressed in one of her aunt Cattie's old frocks, a red-and-white striped poplin which suited her all the better for being a bit too tight. "Good day, Uncle James. Thank you for bringing us the basket of food. We have had no sugar at all in a long while." She smiled.

How pretty and sweet she looks, James thought, so unlike mother and Cattie, who are both so sharp-tongued and hasty with men. Jenny, with her dark-brown curls and dark-lashed green eyes, her full-breasted sturdy figure, stirred him. James, wholly absorbed in the world of men and military affairs, had not looked at a woman in months, and Jenny appealed to him in a direct, lustful way.

"I shall send you another one directly," James said gallantly. "Of course I do not want my own family to be in need."

"Thank you, Uncle James!" Jenny exclaimed. "Do you suppose we could have some fresh meat—there is nothing like a consommé for restoring health!"

James stopped. Despite his pleasure in the sight of his niece, despite his mother's relative kindliness to him, he was suddenly suspicious. "Why," he asked, "who is sick?"

"I *told* you," Catherine said decisively, "no one is sick, we are all well."

But Jenny spoke at the same time, "Aunt Cattie. Aunt Cattie is not strong."

These women are up to no good, James thought, instinctively convinced of it. He saw Jenny flush and look at her grandmother with an expression of alarm. She can hide nothing, he thought, try as she will. Another man would have left it alone, but James put little stock in good manners, and he was by nature suspicious and resentful. He hated to be deceived, especially by women, and he always pressed his advantage when he discovered weakness in another.

"Cattie is not well?" he asked. Neither woman spoke and he continued, "I am sorry to hear it. I must see her. Poor Cattie, I must look in on my dear sister. Is she upstairs in her bed chamber?"

"No! I mean, she is, but you must not disturb her," Jenny said excitedly.

"Why not? She will be glad to see her only brother. Is she contagious, then?"

"No, she is not," Catherine said peevishly. "Jenny, you leave this to me. As usual, James, you have to burst in and disturb the entire household. If you must interrupt Cattie's rest, why of course you must. I shall take you up myself. You shall tour every cupboard and bedchamber in the house, if you so wish, I suppose. You have always been selfish and demanding, and I have always given in to you—I expect that is why you have turned out the way you have!"

James gasped at the injustice of his mother's accusations and then felt a stab of remorse as his usually aloof, self-contained mother burst into tears.

"Please, mother . . ." he begged, feeling angry and manipulated and helpless all at once.

"Oh, what have you done?" Jenny whispered to him, "she is so old, Uncle James! She shouldn't be upset so!"

"I do beg your pardon," James said stiffly and moved toward his mother. She had risen from her armchair and swayed as if to faint. Tears were running down her pale, faded cheeks.

"I will run for her smelling salts," Jenny said and left the room.

"Please, mother," James begged. "I am sorry. What can I do?"

Catherine lifted her chin. "You can go. Go at once. My heart cannot take any more excitement today."

James nodded, bowed and left, beckoning to his uniformed slave, a giant black man called Africa, who stood just inside the front door. He shivered. It was a gray, gloomy afternoon. A light rain was falling and there was a damp, cold wind off the river. Whatever else he wanted, James did not want to be the cause of his mother's death, and her swift transition from virago to supplicant had shocked him.

It wasn't until he had ridden across town and tied his horse before the army barracks, where he had a small room, that he realized that he had—once again—been rejected by his family, he had been outwitted—there had been something or someone in the house that they had not wanted him to discover—he had been duped and turned out into the cold. James frowned, spat at the ground in helpless frustration, and headed for a tavern for a drink and a chair by a warm fire.

When Jenny Stone heard her uncle James slam the door she slumped, weak-kneed with relief.

"Praise God!" she said to herself. I nearly ruined everything, she thought. She forgot her grandmother's smelling salts and ran to her own room for a moment's privacy, a moment to find her composure again.

Poor Jenny, she was so ashamed of her lack of guile; she had lost all control and blurted out the wrong thing. It was not at all what she had meant to do. Jenny's life had changed utterly since she had moved to Savannah with her grandmother; her girlhood at Sea Groves had been so different—utterly straight-forward and innocent. There, she had never needed to think before she spoke. Here, she was learning, everyone had secrets. She had so many intrigues to keep apart from each other that it honestly made her poor head ache.

Of course, the foremost secret, that of life-and-death importance, was the presence of the wounded Byron Barstow hidden in the small bedroom under the eaves. Doctor Jack had brought him here, and grandmother and Aunt Cattie had agreed to hide him and enlisted Jenny's aid in nursing. It was their secret—that of the three women—and it had brought them closer together.

For, in fact, Catherine and her daughter did not always get on well at all. Perhaps they were too much alike, Jenny thought, for both were high-strung and willful, both sharp-tongued and critical, and she tried hard not to incur the displeasure of either. Actually, Jenny was a general favorite, both of the older women confided in *her*—for Jenny's sweet, faithful nature attracted trust.

And other's secrets.

Jenny's brother Isaac had written her in secret and given her welcome news of their older brother, Pittman—both young Stones were members of the Whig militia in Wilkes County. Her cousin Roland had confided in her, too, sharing with her his frustration over being expected to work so hard on the plantation outside of town, when more and more he felt he was called to join the Liberty Boys himself. But that, Jenny feared would likely kill grandmother, she who was already distraught that her favorite son, Byron, was not only a patriot but a captain in the militia whereas her son James, whom she admired for his political and business acumen, displeased her in every other way.

Jenny was very much in awe of her grandmother. She loved her and respected her but as much as she

loved and respected her, she found her hard to understand. Of course, the same was true of Aunt Cattie.
Aunt Cattie was so pretty and charming and looked so
much younger than her age—whatever that was, for
she refused to say—that her sharp tongue and occasional temper tantrums were oddly like those of a
spoiled child. Aunt Cattie was more concerned with
parties and pretty dresses than anyone Jenny had ever
known before—she still had lots of well-dressed friends,
who were always taking her out riding in carriages and
coming to the house on Abercorn Street for tea, and
yet, Aunt Cattie often seemed sad.

It was hard to understand just why, but Jenny felt
that she was on the verge of understanding, and if she
just tried harder, listened more closely, and kept her
own counsel, she would understand that, and everything else, in time.

Apart from family intrigues, Jenny had a secret of
her own. She had found, in a locked chest in her bedroom on the second floor, the journal-book that had
been kept by her mother from the days when she had
first come to Savannah until her last stay here, just
months before she had died, when they had stopped
here in this house before going on to Saint Simons Island.

Reading Fayette's diary had completely changed
Jenny's life. At first it had made her feel tremendously
sad and sorry for herself that she had never known her
mother, but she had decided that she need not feel
guilty for that very reason. True, her mother hadn't
written the book to be read by anyone else, but since
fate had deprived her of the chance to raise her own
daughter and to teach her about life, it was as if the
journal had come to Jenny as a substitute.

Jenny had wept over the diary, prayed over it, read

and reread it, and, holding it in her hands as she slept, dreamed that she was able to talk back to Fayette and tell her about her own life. From the journal she had learned about love, about motherhood, about loneliness, and about the inner life. "I love you, mother," she whispered whenever she read from the journal, and "I thank you for reaching down from heaven to put this book in my hands."

More than anything else, reading her mother's journal had made Jenny think for herself. It was her first solitary experience, her first independent project. It had made her self-reliant, for most of the questions she had were not the sort she could ask either Aunt Cattie or Grandmother; indeed she didn't want either of them to know that she had found the diary. What if they decided she shouldn't have it and tried to take it away from her? She couldn't bear it. It would be like parting with a friend.

So Jenny went about her daily life, her schoolwork, her needlework, her meals with the two older women, with all the past—her mother's past—humming in her mind. She relived her mother's romance with her father, relived those early days in the wilderness, the excitement and weariness of young motherhood, and the growing spiritual awareness and concern for her husband's sanity that had plagued Fayette's last years.

And then, inspired by her mother's example, Jenny had taken the gold coin her grandmother gave her for her twentieth birthday and had gone to the stationers in Broughton Street to buy a journal-book for herself. She held it now, a red leather-bound book with her initials, J. S., pressed on its front.

"How my life has changed," Jenny said out loud, admiring her own diary and the last entry she had made, chronicling the arrival of the weak but handsome patriot captain. Then she shivered, for the dampness of a Savannah winter could penetrate to the very bone.

I nearly ruined everything, Jenny whispered to herself, and then she closed the journal, put it away, and ran to see if the patient, ignorant of his near-discovery, was resting comfortably. With three such devoted nurses, Byron Barstow could not help but recover.

Chapter Twenty-six

*Troops March Up the River Valley—
Cattie and Jack Meet Again—
Savannah Besieged—A Shot Settles a
Rivalry*

The British commander, Colonel Archibald Campbell, set out for Augusta on January 24 with about one thousand men, including James Dunlie, and arrived there on January 31, having faced some opposition along the way from Whig militia but without losing a single man. As his troops rolled up the Savannah River valley they picked up considerable support among the up-country settlers. Howe, the American commander, had retreated into South Carolina, where he turned his troops over to General Lincoln and left the South. At the start it looked very bad for the patriots, but even as the Tories frolicked in Augusta, the Whigs were gathering strength in surrounding Wilkes County, enlisting men under the back-country Colonels Elijah Clarke, John Twiggs, and John Dooly.

Colonel Campbell was more than disappointed with the state of affairs he faced in Augusta. He had anticipated that the Creeks and Cherokees would rally round his men when they entered the town, but he saw few Indians, and the ones he did see were concerned only with getting presents. He had hoped for a total capitulation of the population of Augusta, whom he presumed were all Loyalists just waiting to be liberated, but he found that most of the really ardent Tories had long since slipped away to Florida or South Carolina. And he was even more disheartened to find that Augusta was such a poor, primitive frontier town—why it made Savannah look as grand as Rome.

James Dunlie had offered Campbell quarters at his own plantation, which he called Green Acres, where he had left his wife and family at the beginning of the war. They arrived there to find that Dunlie's family as well as his slave trading business had suffered both injury and indignity during the Whigs' control of the town.

"James, you must not leave us here again," Dunlie's faithful wife, Rosalind, had sobbed when her husband had ridden into the front yard of Green Acres—expecting to find a snug, cozy home and a good dinner and finding instead that his children were sickly, his wife isolated and frightened, and all his slaves gone, run away or stolen by the Whig militia. "You must not leave me again! James, it is class warfare—none of us are safe. These people are not Englishmen, they know nothing of their King nor any government. They are clay-eaters, they murder for sport, they steal everything . . . James, our good neighbor Thomas Brown was tarred and feathered and carried through the streets . . . and, James, Mr. Brown could not walk for six months!"

But James was more concerned that he had lost his capital—his cadre of slaves, twenty strong men whom he had hired out as day laborers and twenty women of child-bearing age, "breeders," as he called them. He had left them in the charge of a white overseer named Warren McGee.

"Where is McGee?" he asked Rosalind.

Rosalind's face twisted in anger. "That vile man ran off with Elijah Clarke—and all my jewelry. Two days after he left all the Negroes disappeared."

"All? All gone?" James fumed.

"Except my maid, Dotty, and the cook. But what have we to cook? Dear husband, I am so glad that you have returned to take care of us!"

But Rosalind was to be disappointed. When Archibald Campbell realized that he was not going to get his expected reinforcements and that the patriots were gaining strength in the back country every day, he withdrew his troops from Augusta to Hudson's Ferry, a frontier station twenty-four miles from Ebenezer. Although Augusta was still under uneasy Tory rule, James Dunlie left with him, promising the long-suffering Rosalind that he would return for her as soon as he could.

On the same day Campbell left Augusta, the Americans surprised about seven hundred Tories under Colonel Boyd at a Wilkes County landmark called Kettle Creek. The Patriots defeated them overwhelmingly. Boyd was killed, the rebel militia fought more effectively than ever before, but the encounter marked the beginning of the really nasty part of the war, savage guerrilla warfare between neighbors. For the next three years, the back country was ruled by violence. Bandits and thieves roved the wild and devastated countryside, killing isolated settlers, burning farms, and stealing everything they came across. Sometimes the raiders claimed to be Whigs, sometimes Tories.

Both sides fell victims to hunger and smallpox, but in many cases they were woodsmen whose private wars bore no connection to the Revolution itself.

For a time, Wilkes County was all there was of rebel Georgia, and the up-rooted state government took refuge there. Savannah still belonged to the British. Colonel Campbell returned to England, but Sir James Wright came home in July, although he expressed his private doubts that many of those who had taken the loyalty oath could be trusted. It seemed no one really thought so, for loyalist converts were mostly used not as advisors or warriors, but as laborers for the King's men. In Savannah their Whig neighbors twitted them in a popular ballad:

> Come, gentleman Tories, firm, loyal and true,
> Here are axes and shovels and something to do!
> For the sake of your King,
> Come labor and sing.

Throughout the state, the spring and summer were uneasy. The British controlled a small area for twenty-five to forty miles around Savannah. The patriots often raided within a few miles of the city, and the British in reprisal raided the Whig areas. The border area, a no-man's land, was badly devastated; meanwhile, the Creeks harassed the state's frontiers.

For those patriots trapped inside British-occupied Savannah during the long, hot summer months of 1779, life became a matter of survival with the constant fear of attack or reinvasion. Nearly all those who stayed took the loyalty oath, "for what else could we do?" Jenny Stone asked her diary.

Food was scarce, but soldiers and spies were not. De-

tachments of square-headed Hessians in blue coats,
British infantrymen in red and white, and green-
jacketed New York Volunteers patrolled Savannah's
sandy, unpaved streets, keeping watch on civilians; but
Georgian patriots slipped in and out of the city often
in woodsman's garb, moving in hay carts, in small
open boats, or on foot under cover of darkness.

News of the war outside Savannah and in the other
colonies was always delayed and accounts garbled and
exaggerated, but in all the stories of warfare and pillage, raids and rebellions and Indian atrocities in the
back country, there had to be some truth.

And if one tenth of all the horror stories that we hear
are true, [Jenny Stone confided to her journal that
summer] then I fear for the state of civilization, for in
this war, families are set against each other, and good
men on either side are asked to kill in the name of
liberty and law. I pray to God to look after Captain
Barstow, who has now left us, and my brothers Isaac
and Pittman who are fighting somewhere up-river.
Dear Grandmama, if what she says is true, would like
to see the Tories stay in Savannah; Aunt Cattie wants
America to be independent of the Crown; and I myself
have pledged to help nurse in Doctor Barstow's clinic,
which is open to all . . .

By mid-summer, Jack Barstow's clinic, which General Prevost permitted him to maintain on the prem-
ises of the former silk-winding filature—by virtue of
his age and status in the community and because of
the obvious need for some medical facilities for the inhabitants of Savannah—was an unofficial information
center for the resistance as well as a hospital. Its public purpose made possible its secret function, for the
British were glad enough to send fever-stricken sol-

diers out of their own quarters, and summer fevers of
every known kind besieged Tory and patriot that year,
rising from the swamps and rice fields as surely as the
mosquitoes and sand flies.

Jenny Stone was one of the many Savannah women,
young and old, who volunteered to help nurse in Doctor Jack's clinic. It was there that she met Abby de
Lyon and the two young women became close friends.
Cattie Dunlie Nickerson was another volunteer
worker.

When Jack Barstow had first caught sight of Cattie
among the women, he had cried out in pleased surprise.

"Cattie! How glad I am to see your fair face here!"

"Good morning, Jack. How things come around,
eh?"

And smiling, they had walked away from the others
for a private word.

"We have seen it all, haven't we, Cattie?"

"A great deal. Who ever would have thought?"

"No one. And you look wonderfully well. I hear
your mother is still alive."

"She will never die of old age, she's too determined,
too hard-hearted . . ." Cattie smiled, "like you, Jack."

"Pray God we will both outlive this war and linger
in peaceful old age."

"Pray God for that."

"Cattie, when you smile at me so, I feel twenty years
old again and that the world is new . . . that Georgia
is just our village on the edge of America."

"So it was . . ."

"Doctor Jack! Doctor Jack! Come at once!" a man's
voice, high with excitement, interrupted them.

"And never will be so again," Jack said in parting,

"but, Cattie, let's be friends! There is no reason why we should not be—the best of friends!"

"No reason on earth," Cattie agreed. "Come see me again, soon, Jack!"

And Jack and Cattie did see each other, and found a new intimacy, even in a city occupied by enemy troops, a city rife with betrayals and counter-betrayals, hungry, tense, and with an uneasy air of imminent disaster, and blown by the crosswinds of hope and despair.

And so the summer passed, while Savannah still hoped for deliverance.

Ever since the capture of Savannah, General Washington and the congress had considered the possible ways to regain the city, but Washington felt he could spare no troops. It was widely held that the only hope for reconquest was with French or Spanish aid, and behind the scenes, Congress debated asking Count d'Estaing, commander of the French fleet, to help liberate Savannah. The French minister squelched this plan; d'Estaing, he said, was busy in the Caribbean, but the Governor of South Carolina, John Rutledge, ignored congress and sent a private entreaty to d'Estaing.

Count d'Estaing, a courageous, well-born, somewhat incompetent Admiral-General, had enjoyed some easy victories in the West Indies and was anxious to add the reconquest of Savannah to his roster of accomplishments before he sailed triumphantly back to France. Accordingly, he accepted Rutledge's invitation. There were two governments in Georgia, after all—the royal one at Savannah and the rebel one in the back country—but he consulted neither. Both the British and Americans in Savannah were greatly surprised to see the French fleet—twenty-two vessels of the line and ten frigates, with about four thousand of France's finest appear off the Tybee bar in early September.

Hurriedly, the Americans near the city scrambled to amass support troops as the British hastened to bolster the city's fortifications. The British knew the French guns could not reach the city but feared a direct land attack. Their commander, General Mark Prevost, summoned outlying forces back to the city and sent word to the troops, Maitland's Highlanders and Hessians, waiting in South Carolina. Even so, he had only about twenty-four hundred men and ten guns.

Americans rallied to assist d'Estaing's troops—Georgians, South Carolinians, and Virginians; among them were Francis Marion, not yet the "Swamp Fox," the Pickney brothers from Charleston, and Count Casimir Pulaski, the dashing and flamboyant Polish officer who commanded a beautifully equipped cavalry detachment.

Savannah was wild with excitement. Rumors and reports were on every tongue. D'Estaing and the American troops had the British outnumbered. D'Estaing had already taken several British vessels at the mouth of the river and had captured the Fort at Tybee. D'Estaing had the same armament as at Newport last year, except that now his troops included mulattoes and Negroes from the West Indies. The British had been caught napping, never expecting the French fleet so close to the hurricane season.

But why did d'Estaing not attack? What was he waiting for?

"What is he waiting for?" Cattie asked Jack Barstow. Jenny Stone asked Abby de Lyon, "How long will he wait?" Patriot sympathizers all over town asked each other. Days passed and the British made good use of them. James Moncrief, an able British engineer, commandeered hundreds of Negro slaves to solidify the British lines, fortify them with redoubts, set up cannon, and block the river with logs and sunken ships. The British worked day and night.

On September 16, elegant, aristocratic d'Estaing finally demanded that Prevost surrender. He gave the British commander twenty-four hours to make up his mind, but in those critical hours, Maitland slipped through the French blockade with his troops—eight hundred fighting Hessians and Highlanders to supplement the British fighting force. Prevost told d'Estaing he had decided to fight.

"I fear he has waited too long," Jack Barstow confessed to Cattie. They had ridden to the highest point inside the city's fortifications, from where they could glimpse the French flags flying against a gray, cloudy sky and assess the new British fortifications.

"The weather is beastly and will hardly improve," Cattie predicted pessimistically. "They can find no anchorage in such rough water. They do not know the shoals and sandbars."

"But I hear that Lachland McIntosh has joined General Lincoln and that they are only ten miles to the west," Jack said. He looked at Cattie quizzically, hardly daring to trust the new intimacy that had grown up between them in the last few months. Usually, they were both so busy they had no time for private conversation, but there were things between them . . . Jack hesitated, but he believed that they must discuss them now . . . before it was too late.

Cattie's eyes met Jack's. She, too, was determined to have him understand certain things. She spoke deliberately.

"Our son . . . known as Roland Dunlie . . . is with Lachlan McIntosh."

Jack paled. He reached out and grasped Cattie's arms almost fiercely.

"I know now that you are telling me the truth," he said hoarsely. "Do you despise me . . . for failing you . . . all these years? Is there anything it is not too late for me to do?"

"Despise you? I do not despise you, Jack. My feelings are more complex but less vengeful than you imagine . . ." Cattie's blue eyes wandered past Jack, toward the sea beyond the river bluffs. "Look! It is almost possible to see the French camp . . . at Beaulieu where they have landed. Our saviors . . . perhaps. When we are saved, Jack, then shall we see? Pray to God that our son is saved, too."

For three weeks after that, the French and American armies laid siege to Savannah while the British perfected their defense. The French moved with Gallic thoroughness and took little interest in their allies. D'Estaing ordered his massive siege apparatus, all his heavy guns, ashore and began to approach, still at a snail's pace. He dug entrenchments in swamps. He placed his guns deliberately. His men begged to go home.

"Why do they not hurry?" Jenny Stone asked her friend Abby de Lyon.

"I have heard that the Frenchmen are weak and sickly," Abby said. "They say they have only two-year-old bread in their ships, that most of them are down with scurvy and that thirty-five dead men are slipped off the ships every day."

"But the American militia . . . why don't they attack?" Jenny wondered.

"They are too few . . . they are disorganized . . .

and some say they are barefoot . . ." Abby whispered in a voice of gloom.

Late at night on the fourth of October, the French-American bombardment began. Savannah was surrounded. D'Estaing fired at random from the land and from the water, and hit homes and helpless civilians. General McIntosh sent a flag of truce to Prevost, asking that women and children be evacuated—among them were his own wife and family—but he was refused. Houses all over Savannah were destroyed and their inhabitants killed, but the British fortifications stood firm.

For the first time, Doctor Jack Barstow had more wounded women and children in his filature hospital than soldiers.

"Dear God, it's Mrs. Lloyd," Jenny Stone exclaimed in horror, recognizing a neighbor being carried past on a stretcher.

"Her house was burned to the ground," Abby de Lyon said in a low voice, "and Mr. Laurie's, on Broughton Street. Two women were killed last night. And three little children and all the Negroes. Some families are being taken to Hutchinson's Island in hopes of being safer over there, but I can't see that we will be safe anywhere!"

"Poor Grandmama! She will not get out of bed," Jenny said. "She says she will die abed, whatever the cause. And she is angry that . . . my Uncle James has come back again."

"Is he staying in your house?" Abby asked sympathetically. Everyone knew that James Dunlie was a Tory of the worst kind, an intimate of Governor Wright's and likely a spy, and that he didn't get on at all well with the rest of his family.

"Oh, no. He's staying at General Prevost's headquarters on Broughton Street. I think Uncle James is afraid of Grandmama." Despite herself, Jenny smiled, but her smile faded when she saw a house near Barnard Street go red with flames.

Savannah took five days of constant bombardment. Many lives were lost, many buildings were destroyed, but the British defenses remained intact. "We have no impact," Benjamin Lincoln complained to his aids. Both the allies and the British knew they must change their mode of attack. D'Estaing was ready for a last, desperate effort. He planned to storm the British lines; Lincoln agreed. The assault on Savannah would begin at dawn on Sunday, October 9.

General Prevost knew the weakest spot in his fortifications—the Spring Hill redoubt, between Musgrove Creek and Yamacraw Swamp—and he bolstered the area with extra troops. D'Estaing knew it, too, and advanced here, supported by the South Carolina troops and followed by Pulaski and his cavalry. The Irish brigade of the French army got lost in Yamacraw Swamp.

The first allied attack was easily repulsed and the scattered troops fell to hand-to-hand fighting. It was still early morning, before full light, and a heavy fog was rolling in from the sea. Desperate fighting raged in the swamps and wooded marshes.

Among the American cavalrymen riding with Count Pulaski was Byron Barstow, who had attached himself to the mounted brigade after the fighting in South Carolina. Byron was vastly changed by his military involvement; he was weary, embittered, even more fatalistic than when he had been hidden in the Dunlie house recovering from his wounds. Now, he had only one object—to get inside Savannah again, to find his own family, and to get them out to safety—somewhere, somehow.

Because he was an expert horseman and knew the terrain, Byron had been assigned to ride with Pulaski's detachment. In the tense, sleepless hours before the attack, Byron had talked to the Count, an intense, irascible aristocrat with deep-set soulful eyes and a tiny dark mustache.

"After we take Savannah," Pulaski had said, "then we shall take Charleston. The war will be over soon . . ."

"Perhaps . . ." Byran had said. "I was born here . . . I have lived here or near here all my life. How odd it is that you have come so far to fight for my city."

"I no longer have city . . . or homeland of my own," Pulaski had said. He took a pinch of snuff between his fingers from the silver snuffbox that General Washington had given him. "And it was only when I had lost them that I began to care for liberty for other men . . ."

Liberty, Byron thought the next morning when he mounted his silver-gray horse for the assault on the British defenses . . . of what use is such an idea when a man is cold and tired and frightened? Only the thought of Kate's warm arms and the faces of my children could move me this morning. I have to believe that in an hour we will be inside Savannah, marching victoriously down Bull Street to the Strand.

But in two hours time, Byron was only halfway across the open land before the Spring Hill redoubt. The French infantrymen who had led the attack had suffered heavy casualties. D'Estaing himself had been wounded. The wounds were of the nastiest sort—the British muskets fired scrap iron, bits of the blades of knives and scissors, even iron chains. Wounded men screamed in pain. Byron saw a man from Saint Simons Island, among the Georgia regulars, staggering straight into enemy fire, a dazed expression on his face. His right hand had been shot off.

"Get back! Get back!" Byron shouted, half-choked with horror, but the man took another blast of grape-shot and pitched forward, dead.

All around them, guns roared. Byron's horse was whinnying insanely, side-stepping over the corpses.

"We charge!" Pulaski yelled. Pulaski's coat, stiff with gold braid, glittered in the pale light. He had seen an opening in the British earthworks and resolved to lead his detachment and the Georgia cavalrymen through it, to enter the city and confuse the enemy. It was a risky plan, but what was not?

Byron rode up to Pulaski's right side.

"God Almighty, ride with us today!" Pulaski shouted, "Forward!"

Two hundred strong, Byron and the others rode at full speed after the heroic Pole. The earth trembled under the beat of their horses' hoofs. For the first few minutes, incredibly, it looked as if they would make it. There was a surprised lull in the British fire. The first horsemen passed between the two British batteries, and then a tremendous crossfire, like a torrent of lead and flames, drenched the rest of the cavalry. Screams of wounded horses and men drowned out the roar of the guns; the riders panicked, broke ranks, rode straight into the batteries, some up over them, most toppling backward.

In all the terrible confusion, Byron saw that Count Pulaski had been hit, felt himself, incredibly, spared. Am I still alive, he asked himself? All around him was carnage of the most ghastly, bloody sort. He felt his mount under him, trembling in fear, but solid. He felt his legs and arms intact, his eyes clear. Dear God, he thought, perhaps I am meant to live through this charge.

Impulsively he rode to Pulaski's side, seeing as he did two of the Polish Count's lieutenants fall as they tried to reach him.

"You are hit!" he screamed over the din of battle. Blood was flowing from Pulaski's thigh where a cannister shot had pierced him; another wound on his shoulder was spurting gore.

Byron leapt from his horse and fell on his knees to raise the Count.

"Jesus! Maria! Joseph!" Pulaski cried in a weak voice.

Byron locked his arms around the Count's neck and lifted him. He slung his limp body over the neck of his horse and caught the reins.

Just then he felt the sharp point of a musket between his shoulders.

"Stop! Halt at once! You are my prisoner!" a British officer said, and Byron dropped to his knees, giving his horse a slap and sending it cantering off toward the woods as he did.

"Let him go," the British officer said. "We don't want that one—he's half dead. Healthy prisoners only. Come along, rebel trash!"

A blow to Byron's head with the musket handle silenced his protests. His vision blurred, he stumbled, then found he could still stand. Blood trickled down his neck as he staggered forward to join a line of other captured cavalry men.

James Dunlie stopped before the military jailhouse on Broughton Street and listened to the gnarled old tunesmith hawking his new songs.

To Charleston with fear
the rebels repair;
D'Estaing scampers back to his boats, sir;

Each blaming the other,
Each cursing his brother,
And—may they cut each other's throats, sir . . .

James laughed. "Hear! Hear! Jolly good lyrics, my
man!" He flipped the wizened balladeer a coin. The
old man took it, bit it, and slipped it into his pocket.
He had other songs for other parts of town, but none
of them had earned him a gold coin in many months.
Happily, he headed for Penrose's Tavern.

James turned into the jailhouse and faced the two-
man guard.

"I have special permission to see the rebel traitor
Byron Barstow," he said, handing the men his papers,
signed by General Prevost.

"He's down at the end. I'm afraid it's a bit raw in
there, sir," one of the guards, an enormously fat Cor-
nishman, apologized, "and a bit dark."

"Give me the lantern," James said. He could not
keep his excitement from showing in his voice. He had
waited for this day for so long, so long.

"I'll show you the way . . ." the guard said,
jangling the heavy ring of keys.

"Make haste! I am a busy man," James said impatiently.

Each blaming the other, each cursing his brother,
James thought as he followed the fat guard down the
narrow passageway to the depths of the makeshift jail.
And so it had turned out, he thought; the allies had
lost at least eight hundred men, about six hundred
and fifty of them French, but British losses had been
trifling. D'Estaing, twice-wounded, had sailed away;
Lincoln had limped off to defend Charleston; Pulaski
had died on the frigate *Wasp* and been buried at sea.

Some of the prisoners stirred hearing the guard's

steps, seeing the swinging lantern. James heard feeble, frightened cries for a doctor, for water, to send messages, but their smell repulsed him. It was the raw stench of men without water to wash or decent food to eat, men left alone to despair and freeze while they waited to starve. James lifted his sleeve to cover his nose, fearing disease. Finally, they reached the end of the line of cells. He had arranged to have Byron confined in solitary; he had prevented his wife from knowing that he was here; and he had anticipated their meeting eagerly.

"Here he is, sir!"

James peered into the dark cell. There was a narrow vertical slit for a window, a dirt floor, a small wooden table and chair. Byron lay on the floor on a single banket. At the approach of the lighted lantern, he had lifted his head and his eyes met his brother's.

"Thank you and be off with you," James said to the guard. "I want to have a private talk with this prisoner. When I want you, I'll summon you."

"Yes, sir," the guard said, lumbering off. "Shut up that wailing!" he called to some other prisoner, who was crying uncontrollably in a very young voice.

"So . . ." James said to Byron. He hung the lantern on a nail and stepped sideways, never taking his eyes off his twin. Byron rose. The two men were of nearly an equal height, but Byron's homespun "uniform" hung loose on his wasted frame, and he was shod in worn moccasins, while James was rosy and robust in a dark blue coat of new cloth, with a row of silver buttons.

"I have long awaited this meeting," James said.

"Aye."

"You have heard . . . the black woman's story . . . that we are twins, sons of the same parents, born together?" James asked.

"Yes," Byron said. "And I believe it to be true. But what does it matter? I know also that the man I shot in a duel was my father. But what can I do for it now? I know that the woman, Zonah, who raised me as if I were her own child, died of the beating she was given by our mother. It saddened me. I mourn for her. But what amends can be made?" He paused and James looked into deep-set hazel eyes, his lightly freckled face, grown over with a stubbled of beard, as if they were a mirror of his own.

Is it possible, James thought, that we have grown more like? Today he looks to me like my father, damnably like my father.

"None," Byron continued. "No amends can be made, no lives restored, no years relived. It is of no use to me today where I was born, to what woman, or what surname I bear. It is of no use, no matter, no importance. I care not. You do not matter to me, Dunlie. Nothing matters to me, in fact, except . . ."

"Damn you! I'll make you care!" James burst in. "My whole life has been shadowed by you and Orde Barstow before you! You murdered my father and robbed me of clear title to what is rightfully mine! I cannot accept you as a brother. Indeed, I hate you, I hate you passionately with a hatered that has not withered but grown through the years. I have tried to face you in a fair fight before, Byron, and this time I will have it!"

James threw two pistols down on the small table and shoved one toward his twin, as he seized the handle of the other. His hands trembled with emotion.

"Go on! Go ahead and pick it up!" he cried. "I will not wait longer. Before God, let us have an end to this!"

Byron picked up the pistol. Nothing can make me kill him, he thought, even to save my life. He lifted up the pistol and made a motion to hand it back to James.

James gasped. Mistaking the motion, he aimed and fired at his brother's head. His shot went true, through Byron's eye, his brain, and lodged in his skull.

With the other eye still open, still calm, Byron's knees buckled and he fell forward over the table.

James fired again, at the floor of the cell. The hush of the prison exploded into bedlam, and he turned to face the guards.

"He fired at me," James said coolly, "and I had to kill him—in self-defense."

Chapter Twenty-seven

*A Trek to the Mountains—A Funeral
and a Wedding in One Day—
Rosalind Escapes—Col. Brown Has His
Revenge*

A smoky blue haze hung over the low, wooded mountains of eastern North Carolina. It was very early morning. The sky was light, but the sun hid behind the craggy peak to the east of the lush, green-bottomed valley. In the valley, the odd encampment of four hundred women and children still slept, some of them in the few dozen low-sided farm wagons, some in open tents of blankets hung over poles and tree limbs, some on the ground wrapped in furs or lengths of woolen cloth.

A cock, tied by one leg to one of the wagons, crowed. Pittman Stone awoke suddenly. He was one of the score of men in Colonel Elijah Clarke's Georgia Whig brigade who had traveled all the way from Wilkes County, outside Augusta, to guide and protect the flee-ing women and children.

Pittman put out his hand and touched his wife Sally.

"I am awake," she said in a low voice. Instinctively, she looked over at her sleeping children.

"It is time," Pittman said. He glanced at the small tent where Elijah Clarke slept.

These Georgians—driven out of their homes by the savage barbarism of Troy militia and partisans—had nearly reached their goal. They had trekked for hundreds of miles across streams and through virgin forests, and soon, perhaps today, they would reach the small patriot stronghold in the Kings Mountain range, where they hoped to find refuge until the Georgia back-country was safely in patriot hands.

Gradually, each woman waking her neighbor, the entire camp came to life. A tiny baby cried out and its young mother took it to her breast to silence the crying. A small boy, pale and weak with the sweating sickness, began to whimper and his mother took him into her arms. There were some Negro women and children among the others; one strapping black woman, Chloe, had come with Sally and Pittman Stone all the way from Saint Simons Islands, had lived with them in their frontier cabin, and endured the onslaught of random warfare as long as they had.

As silently as possible, without lighting a campfire, taking time only to get water from the creek, the caravan gathered itself up to move on.

Pittman looked at his beloved, red-haired wife and saw clearly the changes in her. He saw lines of exhaustion across her freckled face, tension in every line of her gaunt body. They had endured so much, these patriot women, and now they must endure more. While Pittman had been fighting with Elijah Clarke and John Dooly at Kettle Creek, Whig raiders had attacked his farmstead twice. The first time they had stolen all the food supplies and every article of value—including his mother's violin and the family Bible. The second time they had burned his house and barn to the ground and killed Chloe's husband, Benton, who tried to stop them.

Pittman had returned home to find his wife and family living in a sheep enclosure, with wild grapes, root vegetables, and whortleberries for food. With his younger brother Isaac, also a fiercely patriotic Whig, he had hastily rebuilt a part of the house to shelter them through the winter. But when the men were absent for two days' time, trading for seed corn in Augusta, the Tory raiders had attacked his farm for a third time.

Sally had met them at the door with a rifle. "There weren't but three of them," she told Pittman when he came home. "I handed the baby to Chloe and I shot one of 'em with the deer rifle. Then I picked up your pistol, that you left me in case, and shot the other two before they got over their surprise. God must have guided my aim, husband, 'cause I've never been a fair shot."

But after that, red-headed Sally Stone was a hunted woman. Somehow the story got around to the loyalist militants, and Pittman knew that Sally had to hide. Both sides hanged men—and women—without any pretense of a trial. There was no really safe place in all of up-country Georgia. Control of Augusta had passed back to the Tories and Thomas Brown was back. Colonel Thomas Brown was the lean, sardonic loyalist fugitive from South Carolina who had been brutally treated by the Augusta Sons of Liberty at the beginning of the war. Brown launched a campaign of vengeance, of barbaric guerrilla warfare against the Whig partisans and their families that made all that had already happened look civilized.

Brown was the symbol of Tory villainy; the patriots had villians of their own. One of the most dreaded

among them was the man they called the Rebel Wild
Man, an otherwise nameless frontiersman who dressed
himself in half-tanned skins and whose blue eyes glittered madly in a mane of long and dirty hair, above a
tangled beard. The Wild Man attacked alone, always
choosing isolated Tory households, raping women and
murdering Negroes.

Finally, to get their families out of this no man's
land of cold-blooded murder and midnight raids, Elijah Clarke and the Stones and others of his fighting
men had gathered them together and had led them
into the woods of South Carolina, trekking across that
state, making their way to the mountains for refuge.

For the first days they had traveled without harass-
ment, but now—alerted by Tory sympathizers in South
Carolina, they were being followed—by Indians or Tories or both, invisible snipers who trailed them, hiding
behind trees and rocks, shooting at the horses and the
men on horseback, terrifying the exhausted Georgian
refugees.

"John Clarke has ridden ahead," Pittman told Sally
soon after sunrise. The caravan had started to climb
the rocky, wooded slopes of the next hill. "He looks to
see that the Jasper Pass is still held by friendly forces.
Once we get through that pass, we will be safe."

"And then you will leave us," Sally Stone said with
both fear and sadness in her voice. She and Pittman
walked beside the wagon which carried their children.

"My brave Sally, I should fear more that you will
leave me," Pittman said. "I leave you with Duncan
and Peter and baby Nancy and charge you to tell them
every day that their father is fighting with Colonel Elijah Clarke for the United States of America. And the
day it is safe I will come for you."

"Oh, Pittman, I will tell them! But how I wish that
this war . . ."

Sally stopped, held her breath and looked fearfully into the tall trees. She had heard some odd noises. Her nerves were fine-tuned to danger and her ears as sharp as doe's.

"What is it?"

Noiselessly, a feathered arrow parted the leaves of the beech tree over their head and plunged into the heart of a white-haired woman riding on the wagon.

"Don't stop, keep moving," Pittman commanded Sally. "When you get to the bend, get behind the wagons." She stifled a shriek, seized the buggy whip and forced the old horse pulling the wagon to climb faster. Pittman signalled to his brother, Isaac, and they vanished into the woods.

Isaac, who had been a gay, good-looking, and adventuresome young man when he had left his grandmother's house to join the militia, was a fearless soldier and excellent shot. Pittman motioned him up the slopes, and Isaac climbed as silently as an Indian while his older brother concealed himself behind a boulder.

He had not long to wait. A party of about ten men, not Indians at all but Carolina Tories dressed in hunting clothes, crept up the trail just traveled by the caravan of women. Pittman looked at the men, saw that their leggings were dry, and knew that they must have come on horseback as least as far as the last ford. As he hesitated, the hunter with the bow and arrow dropped out of the beech tree just ahead and he saw that he was at least part Indian and probably Creek.

"Up ahead, many wagons," the Indian told the others in a low voice.

"Go get the horses," one of the Tories told him and he ran down the trail. Pittman watched as the Tories, all armed with rifles, started up the trail on foot.

Sally will have warned the others, Pittman thought, and Isaac will see them coming. Stealthily, he slipped through the underbrush and caught up with the Indian untying the horses. He took careful aim and shot the man through his neck. The Indian fell without crying out. Pittman mounted and rode up the trail, leading two other horses by their reins, yelling and whooping.

"Charge! For'ard!" he yelled, whipping the horse under him till he whinnied in excitement. The path was narrow and steep. Pittman fired his rifle once, regretting the wasted shot. He reloaded.

When he regained the slope where he had hidden before, he saw a buck-skinned Tory running down the hill toward him and shot him like a duck on a pond.

"Charge!" he cried and rounded the bend to see that Isaac and the rest of Clarke's men were meeting the challenge more bravely. Two of the Tories lay wounded, one had run off into the woods and was being pursued by John Clarke; the others fled from his attack, straight into the line of fire.

Bells tolled morning and night on that late fall day in Savannah, still British-occupied, still rife with hunger and disease and even more doleful than before. The morning bells were rung for the funeral service for Catherine Dunlie, as that estimable matriarch had finally breathed her last.

Christ Church was packed with mourners, for in her death Catherine Dunlie—whom the patriots thought a patriot and the loyalists claimed as one of their own—had become a symbol for the old Savannah, the old Georgia. And so she was, in many ways, for she had lived in Georgia for forty-five years when she died. Everyone knew that; it was stated in her obituary in the *Georgia Gazette*, and so was her age at the time of her death, a remarkable seventy-five.

But the truth that lay behind the official dispatch

was more unsavory, just as the Dunlies' family itself
was more complicated and eccentric than was generally known. For when word had reached Catherine
Dunlie that her son James had shot to death her son
Byron Barstow—albeit the official report put it to self-
defense—she had become first hysterical and then uncontrollably disconsolate, and had that night taken a
stiletto with her to bed and slipped it into her own
heart.

Catherine's granddaughter Jenny Stone, who sat on
the aisle in the first pew reserved for the family at the
funeral, had been the one to find Catherine the next
morning. Jenny had found Catherine tight-lipped and
pale, sedate in her lace nightcap and best nightgown,
her soul long since fled as she lay on hand-hemmed
and blood-soaked sheets.

"Here comes Uncle James!" Jenny whispered to her
aunt Cattie, who sat beside her. "How dare he?"

"She is his mother, too," Cattie said, noting with relief that James had taken a seat on the other side of
the center aisle. Jack Barstow sat next to Cattie and
gently took her hand in his. No one noticed.

Heads had turned to see Governor Wright coming
into the Church. Well, of course, Jenny thought, all
the Tories thought Grandmama was a Loyalist. I suppose, in a way, she was . . .

It has been almost twenty years since father
was buried, Cattie thought, and in all that time,
mother has been the head of the family. Now . . .
she looked around. In the pew behind the Dunlies sat
Kate Barstow, Byron's widow, her face completely hidden by a thick black mourning veil. There had been
no funeral service for Kate's husband; Byron's body
had been buried by the British before his death was
announced. Poor Kate, her shoulders shook with sobs—
for herself, her dead husband, or his mother? Byron's

three children sat in a row next to their mother. Perhaps they will all live at Blackwoods one day, Cattie thought. I know mother wanted Roland to have Sea Groves, not James. She wondered if there was anything left of either of the island plantations after the war. Reports had reached them that the British had burned houses and destroyed all the plantations on Saint Simons Island. Those slaves left there had fled, some of them to Florida, some to their own communities in the swamps or on the sea islands, only a few of them reaching Savannah, ever-faithful Mary and Moses Black and their children among them.

Mary and Moses were at home now, in the house on Abercorn Street. Cattie squeezed Jack Barstow's hand. Mary's brother Ira was present in the church. With some other members of Jack's medical team, Ira sat with Abby de Lyon near the rear of the church.

As the organ burst into solemn chords, everyone rose. "I have never been in a church before," Abby confessed to Ira.

"Who was she to us?" Kate Barstow's young son Adam asked in a high, clear voice.

"Hush, dear . . ." Kate Barstow whispered. "She was your grandmother." Whatever happens, they will endure this endless war, she vowed, and then we will leave Savannah and somewhere make a happy life together, the three boys and I. Kate trembled. She was very weak. The tension of not knowing Byron's whereabouts had been almost worse than knowing, now, that he was dead, but since she had heard the news, she had been able neither to eat nor drink. Jenny had insisted that she be here at the funeral, for, as Jenny had said, "for those of us who know how and why my grandmother died, it is as much a memorial service for Byron . . . and you must be present for that, you and his sons."

Kate looked over at James Dunlie, her husband's murderer—for she had no doubt he was that—in the side pew and a wave of revulsion shook her thin body. Under that black veil her pale, blue eyes glittered with hate and her shoulders stiffened. "See," she said in a low voice to the little boys seated beside her, "that is James Dunlie in the bright blue coat. Mark him well and never forget him."

Obediently, the three boys looked at James's back. As if summoned, he turned suddenly and they had a good view of his face: the deep-set eyes, the scattered freckles, the sandy-colored hair. Why, he looks a bit like our father, but fatter, Gibson Barstow, the eldest, thought.

"We brought nothing into this world, and it is certain we can carry nothing out," the lay preacher intoned. "The Lord hath given, and the Lord hath taken away . . ." Savannah had been without a regular minister of the gospel since the last one, a loyalist named Haddon Smith, had fled with his family five years ago. "Blessed be the name of the Lord, Our God, Our Father . . . who art in Heaven . . ."

Praise God, this is nearly over, Cattie thought. She could not be sad, not on this day, not even for the death of her old mother. Mother had certainly lived a full life, she thought—how like her to make her death a drama. She could not die of old age, not she, and she must have her funeral service on the day we had set aside for our wedding.

For Cattie and Jack Barstow had chosen that same day to be married, and despite the funeral in the morning, wed they were, that very night, and it was for them that the bells tolled again.

"I think we have postponed it long enough. To postpone it even one more day would be to provoke the fates," Jack Barstow had said when Cattie had argued to hold the wedding as planned.

"It is very unusual, but in time of war, we are all asked to make sacrifices and to do the unusual," Cattie had explained to Jenny with a slightly defensive air.

"Grandmama would certainly wish you to go ahead," Jenny had said reassuringly, not at all sure she was speaking the truth. But from Jenny's youthful vantage point, the whole idea of Cattie and Jack's marrying was so surprising, so unsettling, that she had been startled out of her usual mode into one of shyness. Could it be, she wondered, that they were really in love? True, she had seen them holding hands and walking about like lovers. Could it be that they would actually go to bed together and do whatever it was men and women did in bed? Really, she couldn't think of it, it made her cheeks go hot.

But Cattie and Jack were very happy. Hands joined, they were married in the Dunlie house on Abercorn Street, the same lay preacher reading the marriage service, and afterward, the few family members toasted them and ate a sweetish coconut cake that Mary had miraculously concocted out of some long-hidden stores.

"To the bride and bridegroom!" Moses Black pronounced.

"Really, this cake is delicious!" Jenny raved.

"It almost tastes like cakes used to taste!" Cattie agreed, taking a second big slice.

Jenny had decorated the table with fall wildflowers, and the few silver pieces they had not sold or hidden looked very festive against snowy white linen.

After the cake was eaten, Jenny discovered a small piece of paper that had been slipped under the silver cake plate. It was addressed to Mistress Catherine Barstow, nee Dunlie. Jenny handed it to Cattie.

"Why, what's this?" Cattie murmured. She opened the paper. It was a note that read:

"All my wishes for your happiness on your wedding day,

Love, Roland. (I am nearby and in good health.)"

Cattie gasped. "Do you know who put it here?" she asked Mary.

"No, ma'am," Mary vowed.

"Do you? Do you?" everyone asked, but no one could tell, for no one knew.

Leaving a few men to guard the isolated mountain fort where the Georgia women and children were hidden, Pittman and Isaac Stone returned with Clarke's forces for a final assault on Augusta. Although Wilkes County was practically the last Whig stronghold in all of the South, Augusta had been retaken by the British in August, 1780, by troops under Colonels Thomas Brown and James Grierson.

Elijah Clarke had about three hundred and fifty men, most of them hardened fighters, and he was joined at Soap Creek by Lt. Col. James McCall, a good Scotsman and Georgian with eighty men under him. Together they advanced on Augusta, forty miles away, and, many of them no better than the Tory partisans they so feared and hated, ransacked fields and storehouses of known Tory sympathizers they encountered on the way.

In truth, many of the once-prosperous Tory farmsteads had nothing left to lose. One of these was the estate that belonged to James Dunlie, the riverside plantation he had called Green Acres, where he had left his wife, Rosalind, to bring up their children and wait out the war.

"The Whig cause is now dead," James had written his wife, in his last letter, dated two months earlier, and sent with a badly needed purse of gold coins. "This war will be over soon, and then, dear wife, you will look on my face again . . ."

Indeed, I shall see it before then, Rosalind vowed. She had been without a husband for nearly two years, and in those years she had hoped and lost hope, suffered awful loneliness and terrible fear, endured the animosity of her neighbors and known the limits of pride, but she had survived, through it all she had survived, managing her meager household and raising her children.

"My husband has sent me some money, and with it I am going to buy a boat and we are all going to Savannah," Rosalind told her maid, Dotty, as soon as the letter had arrived.

"Oh, ma'am, but I am feared to travel on the river," the black woman had moaned.

"Nonsense," Rosalind told her, "you will be as safe there as you are here. But if you won't go, I shall leave you behind. At any rate, I want you to pack all of my clothes and the children's while I am seeing about the boat, and as soon as I return, we will leave . . ."

The war is nearly over, the Whig cause is dead, Rosalind told herself to bolster her spirits as she drove alone into Augusta to buy a boat. It was a clear, sunny fall afternoon, a day that would have been a fine harvest day, if she had had the manpower to plant anything that needed harvesting this year.

It was on such a day that I first saw this country, Rosalind remembered. Ten . . . or was it twelve years ago? She shuddered to think how innocent she had been then. War had seemed an impossibility, life had seemed so exciting . . . and yet so safe. How she had longed to be married, at first to anyone, then to James Dunlie in particular, and how innocent she had been about that, too.

Indeed, I have changed, Rosalind admitted sadly.
She looked down at her sun-browned hands, her faded
cotton dress, the shabby wooden carriage pulled by
one thin, old horse. Then she looked apprehensively
into the bushes at the side of the weedy dirt road. Of
course driving alone was dangerous, patriot ruffians
lurked in every patch of woods, but everything was
dangerous—staying home, going out . . . Whatever
the danger, she intended to get to Savannah.

Augusta, when she arrived, at first seemed a haven
of safety. Red-coated soldiers—some of them a bit dirty
and dishevelled—strolled in the streets, and Rosalind
heard a familiar English drinking song coming from
Oaks's Tavern. But this was not London . . . the
drunken men who rolled out of the tavern were
dressed in scraps of homespun and skins and tumbled
into a fearsome brawl, knives flashing and stinking of
raw liquor.

"Owwwww . . . 'e's put my eye out!" one man
shrieked and Rosalind whipped up her horse. A
stream of brown tobacco juice splashed against her
skirt, and she muttered, "Dirty crackers!" as she drove
past.

As she looked back she saw that the fight had
shaped up between two of them: one spitting out a
broken tooth, the other wiping bloody hands on his
leather breeches. The other men had formed a circle
and were screaming in pleasure at the crude fray.

"Mrs. James Dunlie to see Colonel Brown," Rosalind gasped with relief when she had made her way to
the boarding house where Brown was said to have his
headquarters.

Thomas Brown came out at once, amazed to see
Rosalind. "I had thought you were safe in Savannah,
madam," he said. Brown, whose head had been perma-
nently scarred by the tar-and-feather treatment he had

received at the hands of the Sons of Liberty, wore an odd kerchief under his regimental hat.

"I intend to be, as soon as possible," Rosalind declared, and made arrangements with the Tory colonel for a boat, with two militiamen and a Negro boatman familiar with the waters, to escort her down the river on two days hence.

"God speed you and a safe journey to you," Brown called out as Rosalind drove away.

The sun had already set, and the woods were dark and shadowy as she drove back out to Green Acres. Rosalind was tired and hungry, she had not eaten all the day, and at first she thought she was imagining the presence of a hulking, fur-covered shape ahead of her in the road.

"Get up!" she clicked to her bony horse, but as her small carriage drew closer she saw that it was neither a nightmare nor an animal.

"Stand aside!" she called out, "or I shall run you down!"

But the creature only snarled, and Rosalind knew with a shuddering certainty that it was the abomination that people called the Rebel Wild Man, a maddened creature who attacked loyalist women and slaves.

Pray God, I am done for now, unless I can somehow get past him, Rosalind thought. Her horse shied suddenly, and the rickety carriage trembled on the edge of the roadside ditch.

"What do you want? What do you want from me?" she cried out, terror clipping her words.

The man grabbed the horse's bridle and clung to it; he was so near Rosalind could smell the rank odor of the half-tanned skins he had slung around his upper body. His feet were in moccasins, his legs wrapped in soiled brown leather leggings. His hair, grown wild in a light-brown tangle like so much Spanish moss, was bleached quite blond by the summer sun and out of the uncombed thicket his eyes gleamed a horrible, vacant blue.

"Why you're an Englishman!" Rosalind gasped. "Before God, leave me alone! I have nothing for you. I am only a helpless mother; my children are at home alone and need me! I beg you, let me pass; I have done nothing to harm anyone!"

Rosalind fancied she saw some shadow of comprehension pass over the man's face, and she leaned toward him, "I am a good woman, a good mother, please let me pass, please . . ."

Incredibly, the man loosened his grip on the horse's head.

"Let me pass, let me pass . . ." Rosalind begged "For the sake of my poor children!"

A strange look of sadness crossed the man's face, but Rosalind did not linger to interpret it. Seizing her chance, she jerked fiercely on the bridle and turned the horse back onto the road.

"Get up! Get up!" she called firmly and set off at a wild gallop without looking back.

And two days later, Rosalind Dunlie and her little family left Green Acres and set off on the eighty-mile journey down the river to Savannah.

When Rosalind told the militiamen about her encounter with the Rebel Wild Man, one of them shook his head in astonishment. "You was real lucky, ma'am," he said, "that mad creature isn't known to listen to reason. He's a murderer, ma'am. No sense in frightening you, but that's what he is. Colonel Brown has offered twenty pounds for his scalp and the one who gets it will have done a good turn, ma'am, that's a fact."

Rosalind nodded. She felt a chill of fear whenever

she thought of her close call and knew she would remember those empty blue eyes until the day she died.

Colonel Thomas Brown, who had been shot through
both thighs during the three-day siege, had himself
carried to the ground-floor porch to watch the hangings.

Brown winced in pain as his men lowered him into
a sitting position on a feather mattress. He was glad to
be alive; Cruger had saved him with an eleventh-hour
arrival of reinforcements from Fort Ninety-Six.

"Are you comfortable, sir?" one of Brown's aides
asked.

"Well enough," Brown grunted. It would ease his
pain to see the bastards hang. He was exhausted. He
had not slept since Elijah Clarke had forced them into
the White House, as they called the well-known Indian trading post just outside Augusta where he and
Grierson and their Indian allies had finally taken refuge. Clarke's motley troops had fought fiercely, but
they had been forced to retreat, Brown thought with
satisfaction. At least sixty of them were dead and now
he had the pleasure of dealing with the prisoners.

Brown grinned cruelly. His latest communiqué from
Lord Cornwallis had instructed him to punish all captured rebels with "utmost vigor," and he intended to
do just that. He had thirteen of them lined up—twelve
of them wounded militiamen in tattered uniforms and
the thirteenth—a special prize—that half-human creature from Spirit Creek they called the Rebel Wild
Man.

A roll of drums announced that the first man was
ready to swing. All of Brown's officers had assembled
to witness the hangings, and a score of Indians loitered
on the landing, drinking free rum, ready to watch the
show.

"Are you ready?" called out the lieutenant in charge of the executions.

"On with it!" Brown called out weakly. He had a clear view of the outside staircase, the vaulted porch of the White House, and beyond it, the landing on the Savannah River.

"State your name!" the lieutenant ordered.

The first victim, a young farmboy barely in his teens, sat astride the hanging horse with the noose around his neck. "James Buchanan," he called out in a thin, brave voice.

The end of the rope was tied to the bannister of the outside staircase. The drums rolled again as the horse was led out from under young Buchanan and he dangled, jumping and twitching for a minute or more.

"Cut him down," the lieutenant ordered, and Colonel Brown, in a sudden moment of cruel inspiration, called out, "Give him to the Indians!"

And, as the British watched and cheered, the corrupted Cherokees scalped the boy, cut off his genitals, and tossed his carcass in the river.

"Next, next," the Tory militiamen chanted. The next prisoner to be seated astride the horse was also young and pale-faced from the loss of blood. His right arm hung limply at his side, loosely bound in a dirty homespun bandage.

"Name! State your name!"

The boy raised his head and looked around him, dazed. Was he dreaming this? How could it be that the sun still shone, the river still glittered blue in reflecting the sky above? The drunken, blood-thirsty Indians were like an evil dream of painted devils. How could they be real—they or the ugly, grinning faces of the Whig militia and, at eye's level, on the porch, the satanic Thomas Brown?

"Name, name!"

"Isaac Stone!" he called out with the last of his strength.

Isaac looked down the line of his fellow prisoners, and in the half-minute before the horse stepped forward, he saw the wretched, disheveled, hairy man begin to thrash with astonishing pent-up strength. "Isaac! Isaac! Isaac!" the Wild Man screamed, bursting out of the grasp of the officers who had loosened his wrist irons to lift him onto the horse.

"Grab him!" the lieutenant commanded and two men did, restraining him only as he reached the horse that held Isaac Stone.

Brown sat up and watched curiously.

"Isaac!" the man screamed again, and Isaac Stone looked into the Wild Man's weather-beaten face, saw the tangled blond hair, the unforgettable blue eyes, and knew him.

"Father!" he gasped.

Their eyes met and held as Micah Stone was dragged aside and the drums rolled. As the horse stepped out and Isaac swung by his neck, Micah screamed agonizingly, and he sobbed like a child as he felt himself hoisted astride the hanging horse, but his agonies, too, were short-lived, and his mutilated body soon followed his son's into the river.

When thirteen prisoners had been hung, scalped, cut up and thrown into the river, Colonel Brown fell asleep. The remaining seven were given directly to the Indians to do with as they wished.

Chapter Twenty-eight

Jenny Stone in Captivity—As James
Dunlie Schemes—Roland Is Raided—
And Ira Makes a Dangerous Enemy

It seems the war drags on forever. News of the incredible defeat of Cornwallis at Yorktown last month (October, *anno domini* 1781) gave us all hope of peace, but things continue as usual here in Savannah. As usual means British soldiers quartered in the best houses, not enough food or goods for any of us, and always the risk of raids from Whig partisans. Whenever we get new patients in the hospital, I inquire of them for news of our missing family members, but we have not heard of Pittman or Isaac in over a year."

Jenny sighed and set down her pen to reflect. How much had happened since she had made that entry in her journal-book last winter! "Everything is now changed," she wrote, "or nearly everything."

General Anthony Wayne had entered Georgia early in 1782 and almost immediately loyalists from all over the state swarmed into Savannah for refuge. British defeat was in the air, but the Georgia Tories had become more determined than ever. They had strengthened the defenses of Savannah, assembled their Indians and brought down additional troops from Charleston. Colonel Thomas Brown arrived from Augusta with his men and Indian allies. Daily life had become very difficult for those among Savannah's civilian population who were known patriot sympathizers or had relatives in the Patriot armies.

And then, abruptly one morning in late January, Doctor Jack Barstow had been arrested and taken from his home, first to the British prison ship standing in the harbor and then to the military prison in Charleston.

Jenny's eyes filled with tears when she remembered the day of Doctor Jack's arrest.

"Don't worry, it's a mistake. Doctors are needed. I'll be back by afternoon," he had promised Cattie and Jenny, but he had not come back, and although they had gone to James Dunlie to plead for his release, he had not been released.

It was James Dunlie, though, who had told them that Jack was now in Charleston, and Cattie had traded on James Dunlie's name and Tory credentials to follow him there. She had been gone since March, and Jenny had not heard from her since then.

But the day after Cattie had left, having paid a small fortune, nearly all that was left of her money, for passage on the British mail boat, Jenny had come home from her day's work at the hospital to find that James Dunlie and his family had moved into the house on Abercorn Street.

"It is not safe for you to live here alone," James had told Jenny.

"How delightful to have James's niece living with

us," his wife, Rosalind, had said, in her clipped English accent.

I would have thought that you were coming to live with me, Jenny had thought, and how angry Grandmama would be to see James living in her house, but she had held her tongue, more careful now, now becoming aware of the considerable power her uncle James wielded, how close he was still to Governor Wright, Rosalind's uncle.

And now it is May, [Jenny wrote in her journal] a hot day which promises an early summer. Never before have I been so sad in springtime, but how can I be otherwise when I have lost all my family—except Pittman who is far away—and Roland? Uncle James gave me the news that Isaac had been killed—executed in Augusta for "breaking parole," according to the military report. My poor brother Isaac! He never had a chance to live. I mourn him; I wonder who else does so? Of course, either Pittman or Roland could be killed by now, too; I have only Uncle James's information to go on, and my own fears about him mount daily . . .

Jenny dropped her writing and rose to pace the length of her small bedchamber. The simply-furnished room was without a looking glass, but Jenny, a young woman atypically concerned about her physical appearance, did not miss it. She did not realize, then, that she had changed externally as well as emotionally during the anxious years of war. In fact, she had matured, lost her youthful plumpness and girlish awkwardness and hesitancy.

The Jenny Stone who had emerged was a remarkably beautiful young woman. Very slim, she was still full-breasted and had grown graceful. The noble lines of her face had emerged as the childish rosiness of her cheeks had faded. Her neck and arms were ivory-pale

and slender, her large, clear green eyes set off to enticing splendor by lashes as thick and dark and lustrous
as her curly hair, and most amazingly, she was still almost entirely unaware of her physical charms.

For until now, no man—or woman—had reacted to
Jenny's beauty in a way to make her defensive or self-
conscious. Until now, that is, for Jenny had been made
increasingly aware of her uncle James's distinctly un-
avuncular interest in her. In truth, it was becoming a
problem. James never failed to greet Jenny affection-
ately, kissing her mouth and stroking her hair, even as
his own wife stood by, unkissed, watching with an
emotion that could not be hidden. He watched her
possessively across the dinner table, questioned her
jealously about her day's activities, and Jenny was almost sure, followed her secretly, at a distance, through
the city's streets.

Jenny was made uncomfortable by her uncle's attentions, and equally uncomfortable by her Aunt Rosalind's reactions. Rosalind had grown peevish and cruel.
She, too, treated Jenny physically, pinching her arm
till it was marked with a bruise when Jenny misunder-
stood a request, and slapping her in anger when she
was late getting home.

"You cannot treat me this way; I am not a child,"
Jenny had protested, but Rosalind had retorted,
"Well, you are like an overgrown child, or orphan
without means of your own. And since you are dependent upon our charity, you had better mind your
manners, miss!"

It is only till the war is over, Jenny told herself, determined to keep up her spirits. When the war is
ended, Roland will come home, and Aunt Cattie and
Doctor Jack . . . or perhaps I will take a boat to Augusta and live with Pittman and Sally for a while . . .

Idly, Jenny looked out of her window and saw her

friend Abby de Lyon coming along the path from Abercorn Street.

"Hello, Abby!" she called. "Wait there! I'll be right down!"

Jenny had confided her troubles with aunt and uncle to Abby, still her closest friend and nursing companion, and Abby had smiled wryly. "Get married," she had advised, admittedly expressing her own fond wish, for Abby was in love with Ira Barstow, and knew all the complications of such an unconventional love, and dreaded the consequences, and yet wished it could come true.

"But I could not marry without love," Jenny had protested. "And there is no one I love . . . yet."

Sad, but true, Jenny thought, recollecting the conversation with Abby as she hurried to pin up her dark curls. All the men I meet are sick or dying, and even the healthy soldiers look so weak and tired . . . Dear God, she thought, and then said a little prayer out loud, "Let the war end soon; let Roland and the others come home safely, and I will never ask for anything else till the end of my days!"

"I'm coming, Abby, I'm coming," she called out of the window and took the back staircase down in order to avoid her Aunt Rosalind.

James Dunlie, for reasons infinitely more complicated and desperate than those of his niece, also wished the war over. And, with his more sophisticated intelligence, he understood that the day was not far off. Privately, James believed that British withdrawal was inevitable, if not imminent, although not all the British high command had yet admitted it. The Georgia Whigs grew more confident daily, though still outnumbered and lacking military resources.

Wayne had been camped in Georgia since January,

and there had been little change in the military situation. The Georgia militia was still in the back-country, campaigning with Elijah Clarke against the Cherokees. Wayne had little luck in recruiting additional troops and desertions were increasingly daily.

Of course, as James saw it, there had been no hope since the humiliating defeat at Yorktown. He had realized it immediately and had set about salvaging his own situation as well as he could. At first, James had seriously considered changing sides himself. Many well-known Tories had done it, even as late as '82. But James was so intimately connected with Sir James Wright, as well as being related to him by marriage, that a last-minute change of heart would have been embarrassing. Even so, had it been the only way, he would have done it, damning the embarrassment.

James had long since resolved that he would do anything necessary to attain his goals, and his conscience troubled him not at all. In fact, the suggestion that he had a conscience would have surprised him; he would have raised his eyebrows and declared that a conscience, like a coat of arms, was an unaffordable luxury for a second son, who had been rejected by his family and systematically deprived of what was rightfully his.

Rightfully . . . mine . . . I will have what is rightfully mine, James said to himself as he cantered down the road along the river bluffs that led to Sharon and the American encampment, only five miles from Savannah. Three miles out of town there was another encampment, this one of Creek warriors led by a young Indian named Guristersijo who were allied with the British and kept the American camp under careful surveillance.

James Dunlie rode up to the Indian camp and called for Guristersijo. The young Indian came at once and nodded in recognition of the white man on the big black horse.

"Did you find him?" James Dunlie asked. "The white-haired one I described?"

"Yes," Guristersijo said. Guristersijo, a British ally, first enlisted in defense of his home state, Pennsylvania, had been dispatched on this mission by Alexander McGilvry, the great half-breed Creek leader in Alabama who so detested the Americans.

"You are sure?" James asked.

"I am sure."

"Good. Then tonight, when you attack, take care to get him. I will pay you fifty pounds for his scalp." He handed a paper to the Indian. "Bring it to me at noon. This letter will admit you to the city."

Guristersijo nodded. It was of no interest or importance to him why one white man wanted another killed, nor was it the first time that he had been given a mission of personal vengeance during this long and bloody war.

James Dunlie was pleased as he rode back into Savannah after his meeting with the Indian. Tonight there would be a surprise attack on Mad Anthony Wayne's camp. Whether it was successful or not was of little importance to him, as long as the Indian did his job and brought him the scalp for proof. Whether these American troops were destroyed or not, James suspected it would be the last battle of the Revolution in Georgia.

His thoughts turned to his own personal retreat. Very soon, perhaps within the week, James Dunlie expected to take his wife and children—and his lovely niece Jenny—and board a ship for England. James was both optimistic and sage. This withdrawal, he planned, would not be permanent, only politic. The British retreat from America was likely to be drawn out and agonizing. There would be vulgar patriotic celebrations and looting of Tory properties, and he intended to be well out of the country when they occurred.

James slowed his black horse as he passed the sentries at the city's gates. The guards saluted in recognition. Inside the city, James noticed how battered and shabby it looked after six years of war. Most of the buildings destroyed or pockmarked by British cannonballs during the siege of '79 had not yet been repaired. The churches and the filature had all been used as hospitals. Many of the fine private homes had been looted. The city was already crowded with loyalist refugees and almost six thousand slaves who belonged to loyalists idly loitered about.

I am quite looking forward to resting and enjoying myself in London, James thought. And when I return, Savannah will be waiting for me, Sea Groves will be waiting for me, all the lands that were my father's will be waiting for me. In one year, maybe two, I will return to claim my inheritance, all that is rightfully mine.

James smiled, then he laughed and waved his hat. Several passersby turned to stare. There was something odd in his laugh that attracted attention.

Of course I will return to Georgia, James Dunlie thought. After all, I was born here. I am a Georgian, and I am a Dunlie. That bastard Roland is the only one left who could challenge my claim, and when I sail for England, I will take his scalp with me as a souvenir.

Roland Dunlie paused inside the tent where General Wayne had his headquarters, where he studied his maps, read his reports, ate his meals, and wrote letters to his friends back home in Pennsylvania complaining about the meals, the weather, and the interminable dullness of keeping Savannah bottled up. At thirty-eight, Roland Dunlie was a solid, muscular man who looked younger than his years, except for his prematurely white hair, a striking contrast to his pale blue eyes.

"Disgusting," Wayne whined, pushing aside a nearly empty tin plate of rice and beef and pouring himself another glass of rum. He concentrated on stirring sugar into the amber-colored liquor then finally remembered that Dunlie was still waiting for an answer.

"By your leave, sir, I will ride into the city by a route I know is unguarded, settle my personal business, and be back by dawn." Roland Dunlie watched the general's face by candlelight. Wayne burped and rubbed his stomach.

Roland waited tensely. He had been assigned to General Wayne's staff as a special advisor only after years of service, years of fighting with the Georgia militia under Lachlan McIntosh. He had been in Charleston when that city fell to the British, had been captured, had escaped from a British prison ship, swum to safety and been reassigned to Wayne among five hundred seasoned veterans. Together they had crossed the river from South Carolina into Georgia.

And there they had waited, almost without moving, for months. At first they had been camped at Bethesda, the site of George Whitefield's famous orphanage, but so many of Wayne's men had become ill with fever bred by the Bethesda swamps that they had moved the camp to Sharon, on higher ground.

As soon as he re-entered Georgia, Roland had made attempts to reach his family, but his letters had stirred no response. At first he thought perhaps they had all gone south to Saint Simons Island, but then reports had reached him that his Tory cousin James Dunlie was living in Savannah, and today he had received a very welcome, if unsettling letter from Jenny Stone, addressed to him care of Lachlan McIntosh and forwarded from Virginia.

"I have some urgent family business to attend to," Roland repeated, touching the letter from Jenny. "I pray that you are well and I assure you that I am in health," she had written, "but I am not pleased to say that Uncle James and his family have moved into our house. They say that the war will be over soon and those Dunlies will doubtless repair to England (for you know their sympathies) but, dear Roland, may my fears be groundless, but I fear that if you—or someone—does not appear to aid me, that they will try to make me go with them. Of course, dear Roland, I know not where this will reach you, if at all, and I know that you are very busy . . ."

"Not tonight, Dunlie, not tonight," General Wayne said peevishly, lighting his pipe. "Tonight you must join me at whist. I have arranged for two others, gambling men, with—so I am assured—a considerable purse between them—to join us. No, not another word! I have been looking forward to it all day! You can go tomorrow."

"Sir, I would not ask it, were it not urgent . . ." Roland pleaded. Dealing with General Wayne reminded him more and more of dealing with James Dunlie when they were both boys, except that he had enjoyed more success with his hot-tempered cousin. As children, Roland and James had been closer than brothers, and as Roland recalled it, somewhat shamefacedly, he had manipulated James like a trainer his performing bear. James was older by about two years, and had always been superior in strength, but Roland had always been more shrewd and subtle and had led James a merry race.

As adults, James and Roland had drifted apart, tem-

peramentally opposite, then politically opposed, but
Roland still felt—rightly or wrongly—that he could
manage James, if he needed to. But General Wayne, so
utterly used to self-indulgence, so gloomy and irritable
with the forced idleness, could not be dissuaded from
his game of whist.

"Enough, Dunlie! Get out my cards. You know I am
bored to death by this miserable situation. Do your
duty, sir!"

And Roland had to obey. Lifting the tent flap he
looked out into the darkness. It was a clear, hot June
night. The sky was pitch black and scattered with stars
and a soft wind blew across the camp, stirring the mulberry trees. It was a Georgia night to remind Roland
of hundreds of others: nights he had spent in Savannah or Sea Groves, or just before the war, on the small
Dunlie plantation just outside of Savannah.

Roland thought of his family. He had heard that his
grandmother had died, and he had been amused to
learn that his mother had married Doctor Jack, her
life-long sweetheart. Where were they, he wondered,
that they could not protect Jenny? He frowned, deeply
worried, for Roland was a man with strong family loy-
alties and a strong desire for a family of his own.

"As soon as the war is over," he said to General
Wayne, "I'm going to marry a Georgia-born woman
and settle down to rebuild the plantation where I grew
up . . ."

"Fine, good notion," Wayne said. He smiled con-
tentedly and poured some more rum into his glass.

On that same June night, as the American officers
played cards and drank rum, Indian spies hovered
around the camp, hidden in the tall grass and behind
the trunks of the mulberry trees. The scouts saw that
the camp was poorly guarded. There was a single sen-

try at the rear of the camp and only a handful of sentries at the front, the flank turned toward the British in Savannah.

The spies returned to Guristersijo with the news. Guristersijo had three hundred Creek warriors behind him when he approached the camp. Except for the officers, nearly everyone was asleep. The lone sentry yawned and nodded over his long rifle.

"Kill him," Guristersijo commanded, and the sentry toppled, his throat slit.

Then, with wild war whoops, the Creeks swarmed toward the quiet, unprotected tents.

The Indian war cries were chilling and terrifying. Some of the sleeping Americans woke at once, some of them dreamed that their worst fears were coming true.

"Eeeeowww-ooooooo-ooooo!" the cries shattered the silent blackness.

"God damn! Indians!" General Wayne shouted, rising from his seat, shoving over the card table. Rum splashed on the ground, a candle fell against a side of the tent and set it on fire. "Where's my sword?" Wayne screamed, quick-witted as ever under stress.

With his sword in one hand and his pistol in the other, Wayne burst out of his burning tent. Roland Dunlie was by his side; the other two officers stumbled after them.

General Wayne began to bellow orders. "They're coming from the rear! To arms! To arms! Blow the battle call, bugler!"

Fortunately for the Americans, the Indians had misjudged the distance between the sentry and the main camp. By the time the Creeks reached the first line of tents, the bulk of the soldiers were up and armed. General Wayne mounted his horse to direct the counterattack.

"Charge!" Wayne ordered his men. "Dunlie, take the left flank!"

Roland Dunlie, still on foot, ran to marshal the gunners on the left. As he ran, he saw that one Indian who had made his way through the battle lines, had deliberately turned to follow him. The Indian, proud, dark-eyed, erect, and imperious, painted for war, was obviously a leader of his people.

Roland looked back, his blue eyes narrowed, and he saw, even in the darkness and chaos, that the young chieftain was aiming his pistol at him.

Roland dropped to one knee and took aim at the Indian. Both men pulled the trigger at the same moment and both guns blared.

"Eeeeowww-oooooo-ooooo . . ." the Creeks howled. "Charge!" Wayne shouted as his horse was shot out from under him.

But Guristersijo was silent as he ran toward the fallen Roland Dunlie, his knife in hand, ready to finish the job.

Late the next morning, James Dunlie sat waiting in the airy, ground-floor room in the house on Abercorn Street that had been his father's office and favorite room. James Dunlie was waiting for Guristersijo. It was almost noon, the appointed hour, and he had posted a man at the front gate with instructions to bring the Indian to him at once.

"If any Indian comes," James had ordered. Although the American General Wayne had nearly lost his life, reports were that the colonials had repulsed the Indian attack, even captured one hundred horses from the Creeks. Nevertheless, James had not given up on the savage Guristersijo. It was still possible that he had done his job.

Everything is going splendidly, James thought. Earlier this morning he had informed his family that he had arranged passage for all of them on the British ship *Bethia*. The *Bethia* was taking on cargo already and would sail as soon as ready.

"Pack as quickly as you can," he had instructed Rosalind, "Everything of value that is left in this house." Rosalind had been delighted to hear that they were leaving Savannah, but his niece Jenny had been sulky and bad-tempered, even displayed a stubborn streak that he had not seen in her before.

"Uncle James," she had pleaded, "I do not want to go. Please do not make me go. I have work to do here. I am afraid of a sea voyage. Why should I want to go to England? I have always lived in Georgia!"

"Don't be foolish, Jenny," he had said. "Why, you are a fortunate young woman. This city is ruined by war and even now playing host to the pox. Of course you will come with me—you are my niece and I am your guardian."

And then Jenny had cried, and made her pretty green eyes red, and she had shown an unbecoming bad temper. "I won't go! I won't!" she had screamed, stamping her foot and shaking her fists at him. "You can't make me! I'll take care of myself until Roland or Aunt Cattie . . . Oh!"

"Forget about them," James shouted, slapping Jenny across the face to silence her. "And don't scream at me or I shall whip you till you have something to cry about. There is nothing more to discuss. You will come and you had better get whatever you have ready to sail. There is nowhere you can hide from me that I will not find you and that is the end of it."

But then Jenny had begged to be allowed to say good-bye to her friends at the hospital, and James had agreed to permit her. That young woman needs a good beating, James thought as he saw her flounce down the front path to town. Slapping her had given him a distinct and lingering pleasure. I shall give it to her myself, he resolved.

Contemplating the stimulating prospect, James hummed to himself as he packed some of the books that had been Angus Dunlie's into a leather-covered chest. In a drawer of the desk he used, he came across the packet of letters Roland had sent to Jenny and he had intercepted. ·

"Letters from an impudent bastard," he muttered, as ever prone to violent resentment and jealousy whenever he thought of Roland. Well, Roland would not bother him any longer, would never again come between him and what was rightfully his.

A knock on the door of the office interrupted his thoughts. He lifted his head eagerly. Was it the Indian?

"Come in, the door's open!"

But the man who walked in to James's office was not red but brown. It was Ira Barstow.

"Hello, Mr. Dunlie," Ira said evenly.

James looked startled. "Who the hell are you?"

"I am Ira Barstow. Don't you remember? We have met . . . at Sea Groves. Well, it was some years ago."

"Barstow?" James sneered. Then he laughed. "Are you the son of old Orde and his nigger woman?"

Ira's face was impassive. He ignored the question. "I have come . . . on a delicate matter," he said, "to plead with you on behalf . . ."

"Get to it, my man!" James snapped, annoyed by Ira's cool voice, his refined accent, and above all by his bright blue eyes. How odd, he thought, to see a nigger with blue eyes, and how amusing that this nigger was Orde Barstow's son.

"I will put it bluntly, then," Ira said. "Jenny Stone, who is my friend and co-worker at the hospital, does not wish to go with you to England. I ask you to leave her here, under my protection and that of her good friend Abby de Lyon. Abby's kin live on St. Julian Street. They have a comfortable house and welcome Jenny to it . . ."

"Get out," James said, moving toward Ira. His face was bright red with temper. "Shut up and get out! What you suggest is preposterous. You are preposterous! Your suggestion is god-damn preposterous! Why do you think for a minute that I would allow my niece to shelter with a lot of Jews and niggers? Hah! I cannot believe my ears—or my eyes! Get out, Barstow! If you are here when I find my pistol, I shall shoot you for trespassing . . ."

Gasping with anger, James groped in the top drawer of his desk, and Ira, realizing that he meant it, left at once, stepping out of the door onto the verandah and hurrying away.

He shivered as he took the path back to town. Poor Jenny. Approaching James rationally had been Abby's idea, but Abby had no notion of what James Dunlie was like. Probably Jenny had . . . likely that was why she had sobbed so wretchedly when she had come to them this morning. Ira felt very, very sorry for Jenny Stone and angry and frustrated that he could think of no way to help her.

Had he known what James Dunlie was then planning, he would have been equally concerned about helping himself . . .

Chapter Twenty-nine

A Murder—A Flight—An Escape

The Creek chieftain Guristersijo braced himself as he approached James Dunlie's house. He had suffered a wound in the midnight raid but was determined not to reveal it to the white man. His right arm hung at his side, weak and powerless, for Roland's bullet had pierced his shoulder and chest, but the Indian doctor had removed the bullet, stuffed the wound, and bound it tightly under his buckskin shirt.

In his left hand, Guristersijo carried a leather bag. He entered James Dunlie's office and dropped the bag on Dunlie's desk.

James Dunlie was delighted to see him. "Splendid! Wonderful!" he crowed, "but you are late. I had begun to fear that you had failed me!"

Guristersijo waited. He did not trust Dunlie, and late meant nothing to him. The outcome of the battle had been disastrous for the Creeks; he was disheartened and he was dizzy from loss of blood. He watched the white man carefully.

Dunlie opened the top of the leather bag and saw that it contained a bloody, hairy piece of flesh with what looked like part of a man's brains still attached.

"Errr . . . good job," James Dunlie said. "And now, I suppose you want the money . . ."

"Fifty pounds . . . gold," Guristersijo said loudly.

James Dunlie opened the desk drawer where he kept his pistol and hesitated for a stretch of seconds. It's a shame to have to pay him, he thought.

"Gold," Guristersijo grunted, and Dunlie pulled out a small chamois pouch.

"Here you are," he said regretfully and handed the pouch to Guristersijo.

The Indian took the pouch in his right hand, nodded, and left without speaking. Watching him through the window, James Dunlie noticed that he staggered as he headed down the front walk.

There's something wrong with that Indian, James Dunlie thought. He took his pistol, ran from his office and called to the brawny black man who was walking a horse in the paddock behind the house.

"Africa, ride after that Indian there. The one who's just going out the front gate. When he's a little ways out of town, shoot him and throw the dirty savage's body into the river. And take the chamois pouch away from him before you do. It's mine and I want it back!"

Africa stared at his master, then nodded.

"Hurry up, damn you!"

"Yes, sir," Africa said, mounting the horse with one easy leap and riding after Guristersijo.

In the next few days, loyalist civilians and British militia scrambled to get out of Savannah. Sir Guy Carleton, the new commander of British troops in North

America, had been instructed to withdraw all troops from New York, Charleston, and Savannah. Governor Wright was incensed.

"The fools!" he fumed to James Dunlie, "It is unnecessary! Premature, I tell you! If they would only send us a few more troops we could hold Georgia, I know it!"

"Sir James, you must make arrangements to leave," James Dunlie insisted. "Come with us on the *Bethia*. I have arranged for three cabins."

"Nonsense!" Wright howled. "Why, oh why . . ."

Some loyalists made their way to East Florida, still securely under British rule. Governor Wright requested transportation to Jamaica for many others, including two thousand Negroes. A scourge of smallpox broke out in Savannah. The city was in chaos. Weary soldiers were beginning to return home, finding their farms ruined, their homes desecrated, their families weak and hungry. There was destitution on both sides of the Savannah River: rice paddies and indigo plantations and farmlands had been trampled by marching armies.

Money was worthless and commerce had degenerated into barter. By 1782, paper currency was valued at $16,000 to $1 gold, and to add to the confusion, each state's paper currency was valueless outside the state's boundaries.

After the incident with Ira Barstow, James Dunlie had kept his niece Jenny locked in her room. Jenny wept and fumed. She considered jumping out of her window, but Rosalind spotted her sitting on the sill. James had nailed shut the window and slapped Jenny's arms until she was bruised.

On the night of July 10, James Dunlie received word that the *Bethia* would sail the next morning.

James returned to the house on Abercorn Street, where he had been born, and told his wife, Rosalind.

"Husband, why must we take the girl with us?" Rosalind asked. "She is very naughty and will be of little use to me."

James looked at his red-headed wife, faded now and pale from the years of child-bearing and sacrifice. How ugly she is, he thought.

"I want her," he said, "it is as simple as that. I want her and I shall have her."

And Rosalind, humiliated and sick with jealousy, had no choice but to agree. "We leave tomorrow. I will wake you before dawn," she said to Jenny when she took her a tray of dinner that night.

And so, on the morning of July 11, the Dunlie family rose while it was still dark and made their way to the Strand with the few remaining bags and bundles. James's man Africa carried the two youngest children, and Angus, the eldest, held tightly to his cousin Jenny's hand. Two slave women trailed behind.

Jenny looked around her at the familiar house, the beloved sandy streets and tree-shaded squares of Savannah. She was silent and determined not to give her Uncle James the pleasure of seeing her cry, but when they came in sight of the splendid river bluffs, and she saw the open sky and the calm water of the river, a sob caught in her throat.

Good-bye to the city I love so much, she said to herself in a low voice.

"Cousin Jenny, are you scared to go across the sea in a ship?" twelve-year-old Angus Dunlie asked.

"Of course I'm not," Jenny told him. "I've been in lots of boats on Saint Simons Island. Ships go across the ocean every day . . . and they come back."

That's it, Jenny thought. They can't make me stay. As soon as we're safely in London I'll run away and come back, if I have to sell myself as a bound girl to do so!

James Dunlie, too, was thinking of returning to Georgia. He looked with distaste at the motley crowd already assembled on the wharves, selling fish and loaves of bread and skins and root vegetables, waiting for a job carrying boxes or rowing passengers across the river. Some of them were just camped there, hoping for a bit of excitement. Scum, he thought, they're all scum.

But James's spirits lifted when they had packed themselves into the small rowboat that would take them out to the *Bethia*, anchored in the river. The sky had lightened and gulls crossed and recrossed in the air above their heads. It promised to be a fine, hot day.

Sir James Wright was already aboard the *Bethia*. He and James Dunlie would share a cabin, Rosalind and Jenny would share another, and the children and their nurse, Patty, would take the third.

One by one, they climbed the swinging rope ladder from the little boat to the deck of the ship. Jenny was the last, and she felt her heart sink as she seized the ladder and swung out of the boat.

"Easy, there, miss!" a sailor called down to her.

"Hey, what's the tears for?" another asked, for Jenny's eyes had filled with tears and spilled over.

Well, here I am, she thought as she set foot on deck. The ship rocked placidly in the river's current. The sun rose over Tybee and glittered on the blue water.

"How soon do we sail?" Jenny asked one of the sailors. Most of the passengers stood on deck, enjoying the fresh morning air and their last view of Savannah spread out on the river bluffs.

"We'll weigh anchor as soon as we get the word," the mate replied.

"All aboard?" the ship's captain called from the top deck.

"All aboard," the first mate answered.

Stepping over coiled ropes, Jenny crossed the deck and looked off to the north, toward South Carolina and Hutchinson's Island. And then she saw something that made her stop stock still.

A small piragua was coming toward the *Bethia* from that direction. There were three men in it; one of them was brown-skinned and one of the others looked ever so much like Roland Dunlie, with a rag bandage wrapped around his head.

"Oh! Oh, my word!" Jenny gasped. She ran to the edge of the deck and waved her arms frantically. I must keep quiet, she told herself. Oh, I pray Uncle James doesn't come looking for me just now!

Jenny's heart beat so fast she felt as if she were all heart. Her arms ached with waving and her legs with jumping up to make herself taller. Had they sighted her yet? Yes, they had, they had!

The third figure waved. Jenny squinted. It was a young boy—who was it? She didn't know, and then, suddenly, she made out Kate Barstow's oldest son, Gibson.

Oh, hurry, hurry, please hurry, Jenny thought desperately. Incredibly, none of the other passengers had yet noticed the approaching boat.

"Anchors aweigh!" Jenny heard the first mate sing out.

The sailors started to sing as they pulled on the big rope that hoisted the anchor.

"Heave ho, pull together boys, here we go!" they sang.

Jenny got down on her knees. The piragua was very close now. If I could fly . . . she thought.

And, then, miraculously, the piragua was nearly abreast of the ship, and Roland called out to her.

"Jump! When we get close enough, Jenny, you'll have to jump!"

Jump? Dear God, I am so frightened, she thought. How can I ever do it? She looked down and felt her stomach churn with terror. I can't swim, she thought. Oh, dear, I can't swim a stroke! She closed her eyes and a fearful black dizziness shrouded her brain.

"Jump, Jenny!"

"Stop! Stop at once!"

The two cries rang out simultaneously, one from below and one—in her uncle James's voice—from behind.

That unwelcome voice, shrill with anger, was enough to launch Jenny. Arms spread, she leaped forward off the *Bethia*, easily clearing the gunwales, landing in the river with all her clothes tangled around her, smothering her.

A shot rang out while Jenny was under water, and a ball grazed off the side of the piragua. James Dunlie took aim at Roland and fired again, but the boat spun around and rocked crazily, and the shot lodged harmlessly in the boat's thick log bottom.

"There she is!" Gibson shouted, the first to see Jenny's dark head bobbing up above the water.

Gasping, splashing frantically, fighting the water, Jenny struggled to stay afloat as they rowed toward her. She looked up at the ship and saw her uncle James standing on the deck, aiming his pistol at them again.

"Careful!" she gasped.

Roland threw her a rope and Ira held out one oar. Jenny's hands grasped the oar and clung to it desperately.

"Row! Row!" she cried.

Ira leaned over the side of the piragua and lifted Jenny inside.

"Keep your head down!" Ira ordered her.

The third shot grazed Gibson's left ear.

"I believe," he grinned, "there's only three shots in that pistol. Now let's go!"

Jenny smiled at Gibson and took her place next to Ira to help row the piragua across the river. In less than ten minutes they were sheltered by the reeds and willows on the banks of Hutchinson's Island, and they all looked out to see the little *Bethia* moving slowly down the river to the sea.

And they could see James Dunlie leaning out from the stern deck, but none of them heard him shouting, "God damn you, you bastards! I'll be back! Watch out for me . . ."

Afterword

Later that day, before the *Bethia* had more than cleared the shoals at Tybee, General Wayne's army marched into the city of Savannah. The honor of possessing the city for the United States was given to Colonel James Jackson "in consideration of his severe and fatiguing service in the advance." Crowds cheered to see the Whigs reclaim the town; cannons boomed on the Strand, and the Stars and Stripes flew over the city for the first time since December, 1778.

Roland Dunlie, who had been half-scalped but not killed by Guristersijo, recovered from his wound, but would bear a crooked scar along his hairline until the end of his days. Doctor Jack returned from Charleston, with his beloved wife, Cattie, and called the emergency surgery Ira Barstow had done on Roland's head "brilliant."

Ira himself was not so lucky. In mid-July he was

seized and carried away on the *Celia*, a ship carrying British slaves to Jamaica, never knowing that it was James Dunlie who had falsified the records and arranged for his deportation. Ira was brutally beaten when he demanded his release as a patriot and a free man; none of his friends knew what had happened to him, but as the ship sailed south, Ira, too, vowed to return to Georgia.

Heartbroken, Abby de Lyon left Savannah and went to New York City to live with relatives and try to make a new life for herself. Abby invited her friend Jenny Stone to visit her in New York, but Jenny elected to answer the call of the frontier and traveled upriver, living, at least for a while, with her brother Pittman and his family, who sold their hardscrabble farm and accepted a grant of new acreage in the unspoiled land south and west of Augusta.

Roland Dunlie lived out his dream of rebuilding Sea Groves. He was a man of his times and began experimenting with the new sea island cotton, which thrived in the sandy soil of Saint Simons Island. One of his neighbors was Kate Barstow, who settled at Blackwoods with her three sons.

But what of the Tories? Colonel Thomas Brown left Georgia, first for Nassau, then London where he was convicted of grand forgery and ended his days in disgrace. Governor Wright, safely back in England, wrote a book called *A Concise View of the Situation of the Province of Georgia for Three Years Past*, in which he attempted to explain the Tory defeat and how it could have been prevented.

And James O. Dunlie, miserable in a country of continual fogs and chills where Americans were regarded as peasants and savages, submitted claims to the

Crown for enormous reparations for damages suffered during the war. Thereupon, he set about his campaign to return to Georgia, a rich and powerful man, to take possession of all that he considered his birthright.

"WE ONLY HAVE ONE TEXAS"

People ask if there is really an energy crisis. Look at it this way. World oil consumption is 60 million barrels per day and is growing 5 percent each year. This means the world must find three million barrels of new oil production each day. Three million barrels per day is the amount of oil produced in Texas as its peak was 5 years ago. The problem is that it is not going to be easy to find a Texas-sized new oil supply every year, year after year. In just a few years, it may be impossible to balance demand and supply of oil unless we start conserving oil today. So next time someone asks: "is there really an energy crisis?" Tell them: "yes, we only have one Texas."

ENERGY CONSERVATION - IT'S YOUR CHANCE TO SAVE, AMERICA

Department of Energy, Washington, D.C.